A TOWN SHATTERED.
A HERO BORN.

CLETE SLATER—His fa after the bloody defe rn to a home he har lias, Slate Creed.

DENTON SLA orother, he stayed home durin , inherited the plantation and made a profit . . . by supporting the Union.

COLONEL LUCAS MARKHAM—Commander of the Union garrison at Hallettsville, he ruled the town through force and corruption.

TEXADA BALLARD—Granddaughter of the town's founder, she waited for years for Creed's return . . . and she doesn't mean to let him die.

MALINDA SLATER—Protecting herself and her home, she accepted Colonel Markham's proposal of marriage.

THE DETCHEN TWINS—Their feud with the Slater family refused to die until all the Slaters—especially Creed—died, too.

CREED

CREED

BRYCE HARTE

BERKLEY BOOKS, NEW YORK

CREED

A Berkley Book / published by arrangement with
the author

PRINTING HISTORY
Berkley edition / February 1991

ISBN: 0-425-12562-9

PRINTED IN THE UNITED STATES OF AMERICA

10 9 8 7 6 5 4 3 2 1

The author wishes to express his gratitude to
The Honorable Paul C. Boethel
for the brilliant and entertaining histories that he wrote
about the people of Lavaca County, Texas.
Without them, this book would be without
its river of truth, its sense of history.

To my brother
Gerald
because I love him

AUTHOR'S NOTE:
REAL HISTORY

Although he has woven several fictional characters into a mostly fictional tale, it is the author's desire that those real persons who made the real West—the shopkeepers, the tradesmen, the farmers, the ranchers, the drovers, the women, and the children—should be remembered as the bold and brave souls that they were when they risked all they had, including and especially their lives, to tame the wild land of the American West. With this view in mind, the author has attempted to recreate life in Hallettsville, Texas, in 1865 as it really was, employing as many details as he could that were available to him through extensive historical research—from the name and address of one of the town's seamstresses to the exact location of the town well in the courthouse square.

Every geographical item, meaning every town, river, creek, hill, street name, and so on, existed at the time of the story depicted herein. All of the businesses and their owners named in our story also existed.

Of the characters in our story, some are historical persons, such as Mrs. Margaret Hallet, the founder of Hallettsville, and Mrs. Sophia Campbell, whose name is still a profanity among the descendants of those who toiled as slaves under her lash. Also, most of the characters depicted as veterans of the Confederate States Army did serve their state in the War Between the States.

Several major events mentioned herein are also true to the history of Lavaca County, Texas. Included in these are the raid on John Kelly's store, the raid on the freight wagons on the Victoria road, and the last successful cattle drive from Lavaca County to New Orleans. All of the history of the United States, Texas, Lavaca County, and Hallettsville prior to the time of our story is also true.

FROM THE DICTIONARY

slate [n.] *a compact, fine-grained rock that splits readily into thin and even laminae.*

creed [n.] *any organized system or statement of beliefs, principles, etc.*

THE SLATER CREED
Steadfast in honor and loyalty and justice.

CLETE SLATER
alias
SLATE CREED

A man of many facets; hard when he has to be; empathic at all times; honorable, loyal, just; and in search of the truth to prove his innocence.

PROLOGUE

Return to Texas

Clete Slater was the oldest son of Warren Slater, who was killed by Comanches when Clete was a boy of five, and he was also the grandson of Dougald Slater, the founder of Glengarry Plantation, an eight thousand–acre spread between the Lavaca and Navidad Rivers in south Texas. He had a younger brother, Denton, and a younger sister, Malinda.

When the War Between the States erupted in 1861, old Dougald Slater took aside his two grandsons, both then strapping young men in their teens, and explained to them the Slater way.

"As I've told you on many occasions," said Dougald, "we Slaters belong to the Clan MacDonald, and truer, more loyal Scotsmen have never been born. It was Fergus Slater who gave his life to the treachery of the Campbells at the Battle of Glencoe in 1692, and it was Duncan Slater who stood beside Bonny Prince Charlie when the Redcoats routed the clans at Culloden Moor. Duncan escaped with his chief, then came to America in 1752 to avoid English retribution. Still a hunted man, he took to the mountains of the western Carolinas and finally settled down, taking himself a Cherokee wife. He set up a trading post along the Cherokee Trail and became a family man, raising up two sons, William and John. In time, he cut a plantation out of the forest and became a wealthy planter.

"When word came that the Patriots up North had fought a battle against the British at Bunker Hill, he set his sons down the same as I'm doing with you two now and told them how things were done back in Scotland when the clans rose against the English crown. You see, Duncan was the younger brother to Robert Slater when Bonny Prince Charlie returned to reclaim the throne for his father in 1745. Robert swore his allegiance to the English king, and Duncan joined up with the rebels. They did that because, if the English were victorious, King George would take the lands of the rebels. So as long as one member of the family remained loyal, the king couldn't take their property.

"Well, here it was 1775 and another rebellion against another King George was begun in America. Duncan saw the wisdom of the old way back in Scotland, and he told his sons that one would have to remain loyal to the king and the other should go fight with the rebels. William, my daddy, drew the short straw and joined up with Francis Marion, the Swamp Fox, and fought the British. When the war was over, John moved to Canada with the other Tories, and William inherited the family plantation.

"It looks to me, boys, that we're in another tight like my granddaddy and his kin faced back in 1775. It's hard telling who's going to win this one, the North or the South. No matter. Our first duty is to preserve the birthright of every Slater yet to be born on this plantation just the same as it's the duty of my nephew Stuart back in South Carolina to preserve the birthrights of his branch of the family by having his sons take up different sides in this war. I suspect, if the North wins, President Lincoln will punish the South by taking away the property of every rebel the same as King George did back in Scotland. And if the South wins, this won't be no fit place for any man who remained loyal to the Union.

"So, Clete, you're my heir. This place will be yours one day if you want it, so the choice is yours. I know you're old enough to get into this fight, but you don't have to go to war if you don't want to. It's something you shouldn't decide right now anyway.

"And, Dent, the only way you could take over this plantation is if something should happen to Clete. You're too young to go to war yet, but all the same, you get a say in this, too.

"Well, that's it, boys. One of you has got to side with the North and the other gets to fight for the South. Once you make up your minds, there'll be no changing them later. So I want you both to go off somewhere alone and think this over. Get down on your knees to God Almighty if you have to, but make sure you make a decision you can live with for the rest of your lives, the same as Duncan and Robert did over in Scotland and the same as William and John did back in South Carolina."

Clete and Dent Slater went off together and talked over what their grandfather had told them. Clete, the older at nineteen, wanted to join one of the companies then being recruited in Hallettsville, the seat for Lavaca County, and fight for the South. Dent, having just turned sixteen, could only enlist as a drummer, but that idea held no appeal for him; it was fight or stay home.

The brothers made a pact that no matter which side won the war Glengarry would always be home for the brother on the losing side. Clete went to war.

Already a superb horseman, Clete Slater took his horse, a gray Appaloosa colt, and joined Company F of Terry's Texas Rangers, more properly known as the 8th Texas Cavalry. His unit was assigned to Gen. Sidney Johnston's western branch of the Confederate Army. After their first engagement of the war, the regiment was reorganized and Slater was promoted to corporal because Burr Joiner had been elected third lieutenant of the company. Slater was captured at the Battle of Shiloh, but he later escaped and joined John Hunt Morgan's cavalry, where he learned much about guerrilla warfare. As the war took its toll on Morgan's men, Slater moved up in rank, being elected lieutenant, then captain.

When the Union armies had all but ended the war by late March of '65, Slater decided that the war in the East was lost, so he led a small detachment of fellow Texans westward to join General Edmund Kirby Smith's Trans-Mississippi command, dodging Union patrols at every turn; but before they could reach the Mississippi, General Lee surrendered to Grant at Appomattox.

Hearing the news about Lee and General Johnston's subsequent surrender in North Carolina and General Taylor's surrender in Alabama, Slater and his men rode into New Orleans and gave themselves up. Like many Southerners, they took the oath of allegiance to the Union with their fingers crossed and were given paroles that said they were now loyal citizens of the United States. A decent Union officer explained the terms of Lee's surrender to them. They could keep their side arms and horses but not their rifles and shotguns. After handing over those weapons, Slater headed home, but the other men rode north for Tennessee for what they called "one last raid" in the vicinity of Nashville, meaning they planned to visit some girls they had known when they were fighting in that area.

By May of '65, the Union Army had yet to occupy all of Texas, as General Kirby Smith's trans-Mississippi army, although scattered, was still a force to be reckoned with. A few units along the Rio Grande continued the struggle, and a battle was fought as recently as May 12 and 13 at Palmito Ranch with Texans defeating a small Union detachment. News of the victory was slow to spread across the state, but it made little difference in most areas. The war was lost, and the Yankees were setting up shop in a different town every day.

One of those towns that was occupied early on was Hallettsville, but Clete Slater was unaware of all this when he rode toward Glengarry on that hot, steamy evening.

1

When Dougald Slater built the main house of Glengarry Plantation in 1839, he wisely left as many trees in place as possible, and where there was insufficient shade from the black persimmons, cedar elms, hackberries, and live oaks, he planted southern magnolias imported from Louisiana. As the years passed and the subtropical gales—remnants of the annual hurricane season—destroyed the original foliage, he replaced the lost trees with more magnolias until the two-story white mansion was so surrounded by the gulf giants that only the red brick chimneys, one at each end of the peaked roof, rose above the treetops.

Still more than a mile away from Glengarry, Cletus Slater, the lineal heir to the Georgia-style estate, couldn't yet see his birthplace in the twilight as he approached it on horseback along the road from Columbus to Hallettsville. Even so, he knew it was there. In the distance, yet close. Closer. The white flowers of his grandfather's magnolias were in full bloom, and their sweet perfume wafted gently across the broad valley plain welcoming him. And the idea of finally coming home after three and a half long years at war hastened his heart to beat at a faster clip. He nudged the heels of his scuffed knee-high cavalry boots into the ribs of Nimbus, the silver-gray Appaloosa that had gone to war with him as a colt and was returning a magnificent stallion. He urged the horse into a loping gait. A cranial rush of excitement tingled downward through Slater's ramrod body as he thought of one thing: *Glengarry, home at last!*

Slater's jubilance was short-lived. The ominous echo of a single rifle shot reached out to him from the direction of the main house, and all the instincts of the warrior came to bear in his demeanor.

His gauntleted left hand reined Nimbus to a halt, while his free right reflexively drew the Colt's Navy from the holster strapped to his left front side and held the gun at the ready, upright, beside him. Slater's amber-flecked green eyes scanned the immediate area around him to see only a few longhorns grazing among the scrub oaks and hackberries on each side of the road. His ears, partially covered by thick, curly, strawberry blond hair, strained to pick up every sound in the air but went unrewarded for their effort. He decided that the bullet wasn't meant for him, but even so, he was exposed to a danger that he knew all too well. So he guided his horse toward a thicket of hackberries only a few yards from the road, stopped there, and waited a moment before making another move.

It was a short wait. The heavy clippity-clop of a galloping horse pounded a tattoo on the road coming from Glengarry. Slater squinted into the semidarkness and saw a hatless rider rapidly approaching, a small, ghostly dust cloud rising up behind the fleeing man and beast. He felt Nimbus stiffen beneath him, the stallion poising for the inevitable action that years of combat with his master had trained him to expect at these moments. Slater hunkered down on his mount's neck and continued watching, prepared to defend himself if necessary, preferring not to fight at all if it could be avoided.

The rider was closing fast.

Then there were more hoofbeats, dozens of them. And beyond the solo horseman Slater saw a familiar sight. Yankee cavalry, platoon strength, in heated pursuit. How often during the war had he been the bait in a trap whereby he would lure as many Blue-bellies as possible into a murderous ambush set by his comrades? And how many times had he sat atop Nimbus, just as he was then, waiting with pistol in hand, also just as then, ready to shoot down every Union soldier that rode into the sight of his gun's deadly black eye? Without thinking, he cocked the hammer on the Colt's and started to take aim. Then he remembered. The war was over, the South had lost, and he was supposed to be coming home to civilian life and peace.

The rider, leaning forward with knees bent in the fashion of a race jockey, sped past Slater's position, and he thought he saw something—or someone—familiar. He stared after the rapidly disappearing horse . . . *woman*? It had to be. Her straw-colored pigtails were flowing straight out behind her head. And there was something more about her, something he recognized but couldn't quite remember at the moment. What was it? There was no time for thought. The Yankees were coming.

Nimbus tensed at the reins, ready to leap into the charge he was sure would come. His master restrained him with a tug at the Appaloosa's long black mane. The horse danced nervously in place, not understanding why he shouldn't suddenly burst into a gallop, head low, nostrils flaring as they fought for every breath.

"Easy, Nimbus," said Slater softly into the stallion's ear. "Easy, boy." He stroked the animal's neck for added assurance.

The horse knew the tone, if not the words, and relaxed for a second. Then the Yankee cavalry rumbled by. It was more than the animal could stand. He reared up and turned to race after them, nearly throwing Slater to the ground.

Slater reined up the anxious Appaloosa, while holding his place in the saddle. His broad-brimmed gray hat slipped backward on his head with the sudden movement, but he ignored it, concentrating more on settling Nimbus.

The stallion snorted, but the grumble went unheard by the Blue-bellies. And Slater went unseen by them as well. A relief, of course, but why should he feel it to be so? He scratched the barrel of the Colt's along his rust-colored beard in wonderment as several questions flooded his mind simultaneously.

Who fired the shot? The girl on the horse obviously. But why and at whom? Who was she? What was she doing at Glengarry? And what were those Yankees doing there? Only one way to find out.

Slater eased off the hammer of the revolver and replaced it in its holster, then urged Nimbus back onto the road toward the main house. He reset his hat in place, then kicked the horse into a lope again. No need to go rushing up to the mansion and be mistaken for an unfriendly. He would get there soon enough.

2

The lights of the mansion glowed through the magnolias as Slater turned Nimbus from the road into the tree-lined lane that led up to the front veranda of Glengarry. He slowed the horse to a walk as the crunch of the Appaloosa's feet on the gravel drive reminded him the house was now less than one hundred yards away. The broad evergreen magnolias made the route darker than the actual time of the evening, but not so dark that Slater failed to see two Union soldiers jump suddenly from behind a tree directly into his path, both holding muskets with bayonets pointed straight at him.

"Halt!" shouted one of them, a corporal.

"Who goes there?" questioned the other, a bare-sleeve private.

Slater reined in Nimbus and instinctively reached for his side arm. Then he remembered, the war is over, and he raised the hand high over his head as a sign of peace.

"Name is Slater."

"Slater?" queried the second Yankee.

"That's right. Clete Slater. This is my home."

"You're a liar, mister," said the corporal. "This place belongs to Mr. Denton Slater."

"I'm his brother."

Silence prevailed for a few seconds, then the soldier said, "Advance and be recognized."

Slater nudged Nimbus ahead a dozen paces until he was immediately in front of the guards, where he stopped to let them inspect him.

"You say you're Mr. Slater's brother?" said the same sentry. "Strange, you don't look like him."

Slater had seen a lot of Yankees close up—many of them dead—and, oddly, most all of them looked alike to him. These two were no exception. Both were pale-skinned as if Northerners had an aversion to the sun, and each had a droopy black mustache and blank brown eyes, those features giving them the aspect of angry dimwittedness.

"Hey, he's a Reb," said the first Yankee.

"I can see that!" snapped the corporal. "I ain't blind, you know."

Slater noted the stripes on the second man's sleeve and said, "Corporal, why don't we go up to the house? Any member of my family can identify me."

"We'll just do that, mister," said the corporal, "just as soon as you hand over that horse pistol you're carrying."

There was no use in arguing. Slater obeyed the command, carefully drawing the revolver and presenting it to the soldier.

"Now climb down from there," said the corporal.

Again, Slater followed the order, dismounting slowly. The movement reminded him of how long he'd been in the saddle: every day for the better part of two weeks. He was weary, but he was home—he hoped.

"Follow me, mister," said the corporal. "Tinsley, you keep your piece trained on him. I don't trust no damn Johnny Reb, even if the war is over."

Slater fell in behind the corporal, leading Nimbus by the reins, and the other soldier kept pace three strides to the rear. In a few minutes, they were met at the steps to the low-set veranda by a burly sergeant with a heavy auburn beard.

"What have we here, Riley?" asked the sergeant.

"Caught us a Reb coming up the lane," said the corporal. "He says he's Mr. Slater's brother."

"Is that so? Well, we'll just see about that." The sergeant turned and lumbered up the three steps to the veranda, then to the front door of the mansion. He went inside the house.

Slater looked about him and felt a heartache. This was not the Glengarry he had left in '61. The white paint was cracked and peeling on the house. A family of woodpeckers had moved into the pillar on the southwest corner of the portico. The shutters had become bare wood, those on the upper-story windows hanging by a single hinge or missing altogether. Every shrub around the house needed clipping, and the yard—once such a lush green—needed raking, not just the dried leaves that had fallen from the trees but the horse droppings as well—the Union cavalry had evidently been picketing their horses there for some time. Even the magnolias drooped from neglect. Glengarry had the look of a fancy woman that had gone out for an evening on the town and wound up whoring for a month.

The sergeant returned shortly but not alone. An officer, a young brevet colonel, preceded him through the door. Slater had seen the like before on the field of battle. The look of him—stiff-necked, cold-eyed, thin facial hair grown to give the aspect of maturity and strength of leadership, slight sneer of the lips—all said he was a son of some wealthy businessman, usually a banker, who had bought his son a commission, that the young lieutenant had been promoted beyond his years simply because he was regular Army. Yes, Slater had seen this sort before, and more often than not, he had seen them running . . . away from the fighting.

"This is the man, sir," said the sergeant.

The colonel stood at the top step, fists on hips with elbows crooked, glaring down at Slater. His dark eyes were drawn first to the insignia on Slater's dingy butternut Confederate tunic—tattered braids on his sleeves and three gold bars on a yellow collar signifying cavalry captain.

"Well, Captain," said the brevet colonel disdainfully, "the sergeant tells me that you claim to be the brother of the owner of this house."

Slater snapped to attention and offered a salute to the superior officer, figuring there was no reason to be disrespectful to a guest at Glengarry, even if he was a Yankee. When the courtesy wasn't returned, he lowered his arm slowly.

"I am Captain Cletus Slater, late of the 8th Texas Cavalry, come home to my family, sir," said Slater, fixing his eyes on those of the colonel. He was lying, of course, but he didn't dare tell this Yankee the truth of his last assignment in the Confederate Army. "But I think you're mistaken about the owner of this plantation. My grandfather, Dougald Slater, owns Glengarry."

"Not any more, he doesn't. He died last winter."

The sad news hit Slater hard. He'd loved that old man as much as any human being could love another. A sudden bolt of anguish wracked his heart.

"It's my understanding, Captain," said the colonel, his words barely an echo in Slater's head, "that Mr. Denton Slater, the owner of this house, had a brother once, but he died . . . the day he went off and joined the rebellion against the Union."

When he was a small boy of five and heard the news of his father's death at the hands of a Comanche war chief, Clete Slater had begun to cry. His maternal grandfather, a half-breed Choctaw warrior known as Hawk McConnell, took him aside and told him that he must be brave like his ancestors—the Cherokee, the Choctaw, and the Scots—and not show his emotions, especially to an enemy, for to do so was to admit defeat and subservience like a whipped dog. Quite often through his growing years, Slater had come to appreciate the wisdom of old Hawk's words. And in the war, especially when he was a prisoner after the Battle of Shiloh, his grandfather's teaching had served him well.

Now facing this Bluebelly colonel who was obviously enjoying playing the part of the bearer of discouraging words, Slater again called on that icy will inherent in his bloodlines and refused to give this Yankee bastard the satisfaction of seeing any hurt in his face or his speech.

"If that's so, Colonel," he said evenly, "then I must be mistaken about this place and its master. I hope I haven't inconvenienced you with my folly, and if I have, I offer my apologies, sir."

"No inconvenience at all, Captain," said the colonel. "It's always a pleasure to put a Rebel in his proper place."

Another dig for Slater to ignore. "By your leave, Colonel, I will be on my way then. If you would be so kind as to instruct the corporal here to return my pistol to me?"

"When Lee surrendered to General Grant at Appomattox," said the colonel sternly, "one of the conditions of surrender was that all you Rebs would give up your arms."

"Forgive me, sir," said Slater, "but although I wasn't with General Lee at Appomattox or General Johnston in North Carolina, I was led to understand that the terms of the armistice specifically allowed Confederate officers to keep their side arms."

"That was Virginia, Captain. This is Texas, and here, I make the law . . . for now."

"I see," said Slater. "If that is so, then I shall abide by it. By your leave, sir, I shall be on my way."

The colonel glanced past Slater at Nimbus and said, "Not on that horse, you won't. That animal is obviously too good for a Rebel, so you can just leave it here."

Being spoken to as if he were scum was insult enough for Slater to bear. But to have his horse taken from him was too much. His Scotsman's temper, boiled to the surface for an instant, then subsided at the insistence of the red man within him.

"Sir, it was told to me by a Union officer in New Orleans that General Grant allowed General Lee's officers and men to keep their horses."

The colonel's face flushed with anger as he snapped, "As I

said before, Captain, that was Appomattox. This is Texas, and I'm in command here. Now be off with you before I have you locked up for trespassing on a military post."

"I'll go, Colonel," said Slater evenly, "but I'll ride out of here the same as I rode in."

"Sergeant, arrest this man and—"

"Let him go, Lucas," said a woman from the doorway.

Slater glanced past the Union officer but couldn't see the speaker. He thought the voice was that of his sister, Malinda, but he couldn't be sure. How he longed to see her, grown up now, a lady of twenty-one. She was hardly more than a child when he had left Glengarry. He recalled how she had cried that day, the memory only increasing his longing for their reunion.

The colonel made a half turn, thought better of it, and again faced Slater, wondering if the former Confederate had heard the lady. He couldn't tell by the cold stare in Slater's eyes.

"Cancel that order, Sergeant, and return to your duties."

"Yes, sir," said the sergeant, who turned to the other soldiers. "You heard the colonel, Riley. Get back to your post."

The enlisted men departed, leaving Slater and the officer alone.

"Captain," said the colonel in a lighter tone, "you're a lucky man. I'm feeling rather generous this evening, so I will permit you to keep your horse but not your weapon."

"Fair enough, Colonel," said Slater. "I can get another gun, but a mount like Nimbus is hard to come by."

"Another gun? Captain, ex-Confederates aren't permitted to carry weapons in my jurisdiction."

Slater didn't reply immediately. He turned and climbed into the saddle. Reaching inside his tattered tunic, he felt for the wrinkled piece of yellowed paper, touched it, and was reassured. Then he looked the Yankee square in the eye and said before riding off, "Like you said, Colonel. This is . . . Texas."

3

As Slater rode Nimbus down the lane to the Hallettsville road, his sister, Malinda, joined the Yankee colonel on the veranda. The creaminess of her complexion, blushed cheeks, and ruby lips were enhanced by the fading light. Her long auburn tresses fell over her shoulders, but they weren't enough to keep the cool evening air off the nape of her neck. A shiver spread down her back, but the temperature wasn't totally responsible for the ripple. Her emerald eyes—almost cat's eyes—glistened with tears. She blinked rapidly, wishing to conceal the strong emotional wave that wracked her heart as she watched her brother ride away.

"Thank you, Lucas," she said softly as she stepped up beside the Federal officer.

His name was Markham. Lucas Markham from Pennsylvania. "I thought you said he was dead," said the colonel over his shoulder.

"That's what we thought, Lucas," said Malinda a bit defensively. "We'd heard he was wounded at Shiloh and then captured. When we didn't hear from him after that, we thought sure he was dead."

"Well, he isn't dead," said Markham. "That much is certain." A thought that he considered to be quite amusing crossed his mind, and he threw back his head in laughter. Taking control of himself again, he said, "Won't Dent be surprised when he finds out?" He laughed aloud once more.

That thought hadn't entered into Malinda's mind. Not yet, anyway. Her head drooped as she retreated within herself to consider the possibilities.

Just how would Dent react to Clete's return, she wondered. Not good, probably. There was no telling, though. Who knew Dent any more? He hadn't gone off to fight with Clete, but all the same, the war had changed him, twisting him, almost as soon as Clete was gone. Why, she didn't know. He started by defying their

12

grandfather, who had expressly ordered Dent to stay away from the slaves, especially the women. She couldn't prove it, but Malinda was sure that Dent had been sleeping with one or more of the teenage girls in the slave quarters. Even now, he was down back "visiting" as he called it. Malinda called it something else—drinking and whoring, although she would never utter the latter term, at least not within earshot of polite company.

"Well, how do you think Dent will take the news, my dear?" asked the colonel again, staring hard at Malinda.

"I'm uncertain, Lucas," she said, returning from the reverie that had put a gulf between them. She kept her head lowered.

"Where is he, anyway?" asked Markham, looking around as if he might see the younger Slater. "I'd like to be the one to tell him." He peered back at Malinda, lifted her chin with a gentle hand, then said with a sensitivity that often surprised Malinda, "Or would you prefer to do it, my dear?"

"Yes, I think I should be the one to tell him, Lucas," said Malinda. "But in the morning, if you please. I'm quite tired now, and I think I shall retire, if you don't mind."

Markham turned serious, a touch stern, and said, "No, of course not, my dear." He offered his arm to her. "I'll accompany you to your room."

"That won't be necessary, Lucas. Why don't you return to the parlor and finish your game with Sergeant Wickersham? I'm sure you'll enjoy defeating him again."

"Are you certain that you don't want me to come along, Malinda? It really won't be any trouble."

"Yes, I am certain of it, Lucas. I'll say good night here." She curtsied politely, then moved away toward the door.

"Good night, my dear," said Markham as he watched her enter the house. Then he turned his attention back to the lane leading to the road. So the older brother is back, he thought. What of it? He's a Reb, and that finishes him as far as Glengarry is concerned. Good riddance! Even so, the thought of Clete Slater being around bothered him.

Sergeant Wickersham appeared on the porch. "Was that really their brother, Colonel?" he asked.

"Yes, he's their brother," said Markham with a long sigh of resignation.

"A Reb captain," said Wickersham. "I thought their brother was just another Butternut, not an officer. Guess he was a pretty good soldier to make captain."

"Yes, I suppose so," said Markham absently.

"A man like that could make this place work again," said the sergeant. "Too bad he's a Reb."

Markham hadn't looked at Slater that way, like he was a good man, but he realized that Wickersham was right. Clete Slater was several cuts above his brother Dent. That much was obvious just by looking at him. Wickersham's observation that Slater could make a difference at Glengarry had merit, too, but the colonel had no wish to give him the chance to prove it. Things at Glengarry were just about the way he wanted them to be.

"Do you think he'll come back, sir?" asked Wickersham.

"Probably," said Markham, "and when he does, we'll run him off again. That's an order, Sergeant. I don't want that man on this plantation. Do you understand?"

"Yes, sir."

"Good." Markham turned and went back into the house, his mind now awhirl with thoughts of this Slater who might prove to be a disruption that he could do without. It might be wise to keep a close eye on him, if for no other reason than that he was Reb. Damn! thought Markham. I should have had him followed! Too late for that now. But why bother? He's just another Reb. How much trouble can he be?

Malinda knew all too well how much trouble her older brother could be, but she wasn't about to tell Markham any such thing. Her mind was too confused to know exactly what to do yet. She retired to her room and wept tears of joy and tears of sadness. She was happy that her brother was alive and well and come home, but she was sad that her grandfather hadn't lived to see Clete once more, that old Dougald Slater had died not knowing that his favorite grandson was still alive. She also cried out of shame and self-pity because she had been too weak to run outside when Clete was so close and throw her arms around his neck and hold him to her bosom and welcome him home, his home as well as hers and Dent's. She should have rushed out to him because she and Dent were his family, at least all the family that he had there. Instead she had remained behind the door like a cowed puppy. Oh, what degradation had she brought on the house of Slater! Her only comfort was in the fact that her younger brother was bringing even more shame on their house than she was. Or so she told herself. But that was meager consolation. Realizing this sorrow, she buried her face in her pillow. Morpheus lowered his veil over her eyes, and soon she was asleep, unaware that a sympathetic shoulder was close at hand.

Markham had stood at Malinda's door listening to her weep. His gut instinct was to enter without knocking and rush to her side, if for no other reason than to inquire about what was troubling her. But he had stayed his feet, rationalizing that she was a woman and asking himself, What man really understood women? Certainly not he! His experience with the fairer sex was limited by the restraints of prudish, priggish parents who continually discouraged him from exploring relationships with young ladies his own age, insisting that he wait to indulge himself in female companionship until he had reached a level of maturity where he could rightly choose a lifetime mate with complete objectivity, taking such matters into consideration as her breeding, social standing, and economic circumstance. Thank God that the great rebellion against the Union had called him to duty away from the home hearth! He had sworn to himself so many times during the war, especially when he was in the company of a charming woman, whether she proved to be a porcelain dolly or a pliable doxy. No, he would not enter Malinda's bedroom and make such an inquiry! Rather he should avail himself of the liquor cabinet for a good-night toast to his good fortune to be in this house and his good sense to seize a golden opportunity to achieve financial success without the aid of his distant father.

4

Darkness shrouded the range, but Slater hardly noticed. Not through his tears.

"Never let your enemy see what lies inside you," old Grandfather Hawk McConnell had always told him. "If he cannot see inside you and know what goes on there, he can never hurt you."

"You mean, I should never cry?" asked young Clete.

"No, it is all right to cry," said the old warrior. "Tears are good for the spirit. But never in front of your enemies. A man is just as much a man whether he cries or not."

Slater hadn't let that Yankee colonel see how much he was hurt by the news that Grandfather Dougald was dead, but he still felt the pain of loss, the agony of losing someone that was a part of him, a piece of his heart. Dougald Slater had raised him, had been there after his father was killed by the Comanches, and was still there when his mother remarried and moved off to northern Texas with her new husband. Slater couldn't remember a time when his grandfather wasn't there when he needed him. At least not until he went off to war.

The memory of that day, the last time he saw his grandfather, flooded his mind.

It was late summer, and it was hot and humid. Nobody paid the weather much attention, though, because Louie Strobel was raising a company of Rangers for the 8th Texas Cavalry, and more than three dozen young men from Lavaca County were signing up to fight for the Confederacy. It was a big event, an impromptu holiday, and folks from all parts of the region were riding into Hallettsville to see their young warriors march off to battle.

The Slaters came into town together. Dougald, Dent, and Malinda took the family carriage, a new Studebaker, probably one of the last to be sold south of the Mason-Dixon Line until the war was over. Clete rode Nimbus, then a two-year-old colt. They were dressed in their Sunday best, and Clete wore the new gray uniform that Malinda had made for him. He was proud of his outfit because it made him appear to be much older than his nineteen years, especially when he donned the regulation forage cap that Captain Strobel had handed out to each new enlistee upon their enrollment in their country's service.

As soon as he saw some of his friends gathered near the town well, Clete put the spurs to the Appaloosa and joined them. Together, they yahooed the people in the courthouse square, racing their horses around the block as if they were already chasing those damn Yankees back to where they belonged. Finally, the word was passed that it was time they were leaving. Like all the other recruits did, Clete found his family to say farewell. They were still sitting in the Studebaker.

"Louie says we're going to LaGrange first to round up the rest of the company," he explained to Dougald. "Then we're supposed to go to Houston, where the regiment is forming up. From there, I don't know. Up north, I suppose."

"Most likely," said Dougald. "That's where the fighting is. Virginia right now, but you can bet it won't just be there for long.

Sooner or later, the Yankees will try marching into Tennessee, or they'll try sailing up the Mississippi.''

"Not if Clete and the boys whup them first," said Dent boldly. He was barely sixteen years old, but he was nowhere near being emotionally mature. In looks, he resembled Clete quite closely; it was easy to tell that they were brothers. Dent had hair the same strawberry blond color as Clete's, but his was a little straighter. His eyes were almost as green but without the amber flecks, and he had a few freckles on his cheeks. He was the same height as Clete but not quite as muscular, with a chin and jaw a bit weaker and his nose a little narrower.

Dougald frowned at Dent but said nothing.

"You'll take care of yourself, won't you, Clete?" said Malinda, always the mother hen.

"I'll do the best I can," said Clete with a reassuring smile. "Of course, it won't be easy without you around to pick up after me." Then he looked at Dent and said, "But you'll still have plenty to do just taking care of Grandpa and our baby brother here."

"Who you calling a baby?" demanded Dent in a mock anger that was meant to conceal the real resentment that flared within him. He stood up as if he intended to jump at Clete, but Malinda pulled on his arm, canceling any such notion.

"Sit down, Dent," she said, "and act your age."

With every good-natured intent, Clete joshed, "See what I mean, Malinda? He's still our baby brother."

"I can whup anybody you can whup," sneered Dent.

"Not today, you can't," said Malinda quite sternly. "This is Clete's day. Now you behave or I'll be doing some whupping on you, boy."

Dent knew she meant every word of what she said; Malinda Slater was not one to make idle threats, not even in jest. He sat down like a chastised schoolboy, head lowered, and said, "Sorry, Clete. I forgot."

Clete reached over and tossled Dent's hair lovingly. "You might be my baby brother, but I know you're just as much a man as any of these other fellows here. You know what, little brother? I'd feel a whole lot safer if you were fighting alongside me."

Dent's eyes brightened as he looked up and said, "You really mean that, Clete?"

"I wouldn't have said if I didn't, now would I?"

"That'll be enough of that now," said Dougald. "Dent is staying right here where he belongs. With me and Malinda at Glengarry. You say your good-byes, Cletus Slater, and be gone from here with the other men. Go off and fight this damn fool war and get it over with and get yourself back here where you belong. At Glengarry. With your family."

Clete obeyed his grandfather and said his farewells, and he further obeyed him by fighting that damn fool war and by getting himself back where he belonged. To Glengarry. To his family.

At least, he thought he was returning to his home and his loved ones. Now a Yankee colonel was telling him different, and he wanted to know why.

Slater reined in Nimbus, looked up at the starry night through misty eyes, focused on one particularly bright orb, and asked it, "You saw everything that went on here while I was gone. Care to tell me about it?"

A cool breeze out of the north sent a shiver through him. His shoulders scrunched together in reflex, and he drew in his head almost like a turtle. His view fell on the boundary lane that separated Glengarry from the next farm. That was his answer.

"Come on, Nimbus," he said softly, gently nudging the stallion in the ribs and urging him toward the two-track. "We're going to see Grandpa."

The Slater family cemetery was layed out near the Navidad River almost as early as the foundation for the first cabin on Slater property was built, because that was when the first Slater died in Texas.

One of the first priorities of any new homestead was shelter from the elements. Every single Slater, master and slave alike, joined in the work. Not realizing how weary he was after a full day of chopping logs for the house, Sam Slater, Clete's uncle, swung his double-bladed axe awkwardly at a stump in order to put it to rest. But the blade glanced off its target and ripped through his boot into the top of his foot, giving him a very nasty gash between his big toe and second toe. By the next morning, the wound was badly infected and inflamed, and late the next day he died from the accompanying fever. After some debate, Dougald Slater chose the place to bury his younger son.

"This was going to be Sam's ground," said Dougald as he stood beside the grave. "I was going to give it to him because he wanted to build his own house on this spot. Now it's his for all eternity. Amen."

When Warren Slater's body was brought home, he was layed

to rest with Sam, and thus began the Slater cemetery. Over the next decade and a half, other family members, including some cousins and, against the usual custom of the South, also some slaves, were interred with Sam and Warren, the most recent being the first of the Texas Slaters, Clete's Grandfather Dougald.

A good strong picket fence was placed around Sam's grave to keep the roving cattle from obliterating his final resting place, and gradually, as more graves were added, the fence grew to surround the whole yard. Following an old Indian tradition, Grandfather Hawk McConnell planted a small pine tree near Sam's grave. He did the same for Warren and other members of the clan until a stand of evergreens shaded them from the sun whose warmth they no longer needed.

Slater tied Nimbus to one of his grandfather's pines, then he removed his hat out of respect for the dead, folded it flat, and stuffed it under his bedroll. Turning slowly, he faced the grave-yard, took a deep breath, and washed all those childhood stories about ghosts and bogeymen out of his mind. With careful steps, he wandered through the cemetery in search of Grandpa Dougald's burial plot. He wasn't long finding it because it had the largest marker of all, an obelisk of gray granite standing six feet high and topped with a cross. Carved deep in its base were Dougald's name and birth and death dates. Slater read them, then fell on his knees and began to cry. Not for Dougald, but for himself, releasing all the anguish that he had felt during the recent war and had kept deep within him. He wept for all those young men who had died needlessly; those who had been killed beside him and those that he had killed because they would have killed him first if given the chance. And for all the misery and suffering he had seen—and caused—during the war.

As the pain drained from him and his eyes ran dry of tears, Slater wiped his cheeks and blinked his vision back into focus. Slowly, the words came to him, deep from his heart, and they came out of him in a whisper. "Grandpa, I . . . I love . . . I love you, Grandpa." And the tears burst forth again.

Exhaustion set into Slater. He was finally cried out. He reached inside his collar and removed the red bandanna that he wore around his neck. He wiped his face and blew his nose with the cloth, then stuffed it into an inside pocket of his coat. A heavy sigh rushed from his lungs. He looked up at the same bright star that had attracted his eye earlier.

"Well, you brought me here," he said to the shining light.

"Are you going to tell me what happened while I was away, or do I have to figure it out for myself? I mean, I come home and find my house is full of Yankees who tell me that Glengarry is no longer my home. I suppose I could have demanded to see Dent and Malinda, but I don't think that Yankee colonel was going to let me see them, no matter what I said or did. Most likely, he would have had me locked up someplace if I'd caused a ruckus of some kind. Or maybe he would have had me shot. Hell, I don't know. All I do know is those damn Yankees better get off my property and damn soon before I really lose my temper and cause them a hurt they won't soon forget." He laughed at his foolish display of bravado, then turned serious again. "Dammitall, Star. What's going on around here?"

When the twinkling light failed to answer him, he looked down at his grandfather's grave and said, "Grandpa, I've got a feeling that things ain't been going right around here without you. Of course, I'm not sure that you could make all that much difference with these Yankees being here." He scooped up a handful of dirt and let it sift through his fingers. "I do know you wouldn't let them treat Glengarry the way they have." He dropped the remainder of the soil. "I can't believe Dent and Malinda have let them do this. Something's wrong here, Grandpa, and I mean to find out what it is and then do something about setting things right again. You can mark my words on that, Grandpa, or my name isn't Cletus McConnell Slater."

5

Malinda Slater spent a restless night, refereeing a phantasmal free-for-all between her emotions, her conscience, and her innate pragmatism.

Prior to falling asleep, Malinda had dismissed the shame that she had felt the night before for her lack of action toward her older brother, telling herself that showing any emotion for Clete could drive a wedge between her and her colonel; and that would never do, not now, not with the plans that she had made for them, for Dent, and for Glengarry. She had determined that Clete's return was good on the one hand and bad on the other. She was happy that he was alive and well, but she was also angered that he had come back now instead of sooner—before she had made a commitment to Markham—or later—after it was too late to change any part of her plan.

Upon awaking with the crowing of the cocks before dawn, she came to the conclusion that Clete's presence could only cause trouble, trouble between her and Markham, between her and Dent, and between Dent and Markham. She could already tell that Markham was unhappy about Clete's return, that he felt threatened by it; the tone of his voice during their brief conversation on the veranda the night before had said so. How, she wondered, would Dent react to the news about Clete? There was only one way to find out.

After dressing, Malinda went to Dent's room, but she didn't really expect to find him there. She wasn't disappointed. That meant he had to be down back yet. She took the back stairs down to the kitchen, where she found the two house servants just beginning to prepare breakfast.

When Dougald Slater freed his slaves, all of them remained at Glengarry as unpaid hands and servants, and to reward their loyalty, he allowed each of them an acre of land on which they could grow their own crops, whether they were vegetables to sell in Hallettsville or cotton that could be ginned right there at Glengarry and sold in town, with the funds from the sales going to the workers. When the war ended and the Yankees came, several of the plantation's former slaves struck out on their own, taking their few possessions and their meager sums of money and heading north to Kansas, where they were certain that they would receive better treatment from whites.

The only two servants to stay and work in the mansion were young Hannah, a maid, and old Josephine, the cook. Josephine was born a Slater slave and had come to Texas with the family as a mature woman, while Hannah was only an infant when she became Slater chattel.

Hannah's mother, Dinah, had been a house servant on an east Texas plantation where she gave birth to Hannah and her older brother, Gabriel, and older sister, Sheba, all three of them being the offspring of the master's oldest son. When the son married, his new bride insisted that his nigger whore and her whelps should be sold South. Dougald bought the whole family at the slave market in Houston because he needed another maid for his new mansion and because his grandchildren needed playmates and Dinah's children were approximately the same ages as Clete, Malinda, and Dent.

Soon after coming to Glengarry, Dinah married another Slater slave, and they had their own family. When the presence of Union soldiers guaranteed their freedom and travel seemed relatively safe, Dinah gathered her family about her and declared that they were leaving for Kansas immediately. All but Hannah eagerly agreed to go. All except Dinah tried to dissuade her from staying. Dinah knew Hannah's reason for remaining. She didn't like it, but she understood because she had felt the same about her white lover when she was Hannah's age. "Hannah," she said, "you is a growed-up woman now. You can makes your own decisions. If your heart tell you to stay here, then you stays. But you hear me now, girl. You may thinks everything gonna be all right just 'cause your daddy was a white man and my daddy was a white man, but I knows different. You always gonna be a nigger to white folks, and your chillun gonna be niggers, too, no matter if their daddy is a white man, too. Don't make no difference to white folks that you is three parts white and one part black. To them you might as well be all black. That's the way they sees you, Hannah. I know the census man say we is mulattoes, but that don't make no difference. Like I say before, white folks still say we is just niggers. You just keep that in your mind every time you is laying with him."

Hannah felt certain that her mother was wrong. Dent Slater loved her and had proved his love for her. How, when, and where he had done this was their secret because if Malinda ever found out, God help them both.

Malinda was still unsuspecting that there was anything between Dent and Hannah besides a jug of whiskey and a mutual lust. She had grown up with both of them, and she had loved Hannah almost like a younger sister, that is, she had until Dent started sleeping with Hannah. From that point, she had begun looking at Hannah as just another servant, directing any emotion that she had felt in the past in a different direction.

In the beginning, Malinda tried to dissect her displeasure with Dent and Hannah, and she came up with a few arguments, all of them unpleasant, for feeling the way she did. Fornication was a sin; that was one. The relationship between Dent and Hannah was almost incestuous because of the way they were raised; two. Hannah was a slave at first and now a free servant; three. And last, and the most distasteful of all for Malinda, Hannah was a darky, of a different race because of her African blood, as little as it was. Hannah just wasn't all white, and this made her inferior, never mind that she, Malinda, and Dent were descended from Choctaws and Cherokees as well as Scots and Irishmen, and thus were not all white either. Because of these alleged reasons, Malinda had convinced herself to ignore, even deny, the existence of a relationship between Dent and Hannah, although the coolness in her attitude toward Hannah said quite plainly that she was quite aware of it and that she disapproved.

The truth was deeper than the rationalizations that Malinda had made to justify her resentment of Hannah. She was actually jealous of the servant girl's naturally earthy beauty: amber skin that was unblemished, jet black hair that was soft and silky to the eye as well as to the touch, almond eyes that could be alluring in one instant and filled with motherly love in the next, enticing lips that appeared to be stained with elderberry wine and that begged to be kissed, and a form that was lithe and gently curved and that moved with a grace so sensuous that few men would escape the flames it could fan in their loins. Malinda held the secret desire that men should look upon her in the same manner, if for no other reason than that it would allow her to be particular in her choice of a male companion. Instead, she was forced to take what came her way, such as Lucas Markham had.

Hannah had noticed the change in Malinda's attitude toward her, and she was hurt by it. She chose to return Malinda's cold treatment with equally cold subservience. Her first concern was Dent, and if that meant sacrificing the sisterly love she felt for Malinda, then so be it. But to avoid the possibility of a confrontation of any sort with Malinda, she placed as much distance between them as she could considering the close proximity of their lives at Glengarry.

When Malinda entered the kitchen, Hannah's first thought was to leave the room, and she would have, too, if her arms hadn't been loaded down with firewood for the cookstove. Instead, she turned her back on Malinda.

"Josephine, have you seen my brother this morning?" asked Malinda, ignoring Hannah's presence for the moment.

Josephine glanced sideways at Hannah, who was adding a good-size stick to the fire, then she looked Malinda straight in the eye and said, "No, Miss Malinda, I ain't seen him yet this morning."

"Are you certain of that?" queried Malinda, wishing to avoid speaking to Hannah, if at all possible.

"Yes'm, I's certain," said Josephine.

Malinda heaved a sigh and addressed the other servant. "Hannah," she said evenly, "have you seen my brother this morning?"

Hannah affected her servant's role by turning around and facing her mistress with lowered eyes as she answered the question. "Yes, Miss Malinda."

"Wherever it was you saw him, Hannah," said Malinda, "go and get him for me. I have some important news for him."

"Yes, Miss Malinda," said Hannah. She put the remaining wood in the box beside the stove, brushed the debris from her dress, and hurried out the back door toward her quarters down back, running all the way there.

Dent was still sound asleep in the corner bed when Hannah burst into the little one-room cottage that they shared whenever he desired her, whether wantonly or emotionally, for Hannah filled both exigencies willingly. The noise of her entry and the sudden explosion of daylight through the doorway burning through his eyelids jerked him awake. He sat up reflexively, exposing his naked chest. Squinting in the direction of the sound and light, he demanded angrily, "What the hell's going on?"

"Dent Honey," said Hannah, rushing to his side, "Malinda wants you up to the house right away. She says she's got some important news for you, and you're to come right away." Partly at Dent's request but mostly because she wanted to do it, Hannah worked hard at improving her speech, discarding the slave dialect she had picked up from her family and other slaves since birth and replacing it with the so-called proper English of whites. It had become second nature for her to use the latter in Dent's presence, while falling back on her childhood lingo when others were around.

"Malinda?" queried Dent. Before he could utter another syllable, he realized how much his head hurt. He took it in both hands as if that would help relieve some of the pressure he was feeling from the leftover effects of the previous night's bout with his whiskey. He was wrong; it didn't help. "Goddamn! My head! Shit, Hannah! Get me something for it! The jug! Quick!"

"No, Dent," she said sternly. "Not this early in the morning." She put her arm around his shoulders to assure him.

He pushed her away. "Dammit, Hannah! I said to get my jug, and be quick about it."

"No, Dent," she said even more forcefully. "You can't be going to the house with liquor on your breath this early in the day. I won't have it."

Dent was incredulous; his stare said so. "You won't have it?" he growled. "And who the hell do you think you are?"

"You know perfectly well who I am, Denton Slater." She rose, went to the row of wall hooks where his clothes hung neatly, took them down, then turned back to Dent. She threw the duds on the bed and said, "Get dressed, and get up to the big house right away." She took the latch in her hand and started to close the door behind her, but she stopped and went back to the bedside. She picked up the whiskey jug from the floor and started to leave again. At the doorway, she turned back to Dent once more. "You don't want to keep your sister waiting." She left him alone and returned to the main house.

Dent dressed slowly, painfully, ruefully. He loved Hannah, but sometimes she treated him like a child, which he was at times, and he resented it and loved her all the more for it as well. She was so perplexing and vexing, vivacious and cool, an unsolved mystery, and the more he knew her, the more he wanted to know her. Damn! He loved that woman! That girl! Whichever, he loved her. He would do almost anything for her. Anything except declare his love for her to the world. To her, yes, but to no one else. Not yet, he often told her and occasionally told himself. Their day would come. But not today. Today, Malinda wanted to tell him some important news. What could be so important that he had to be awakened before his alcohol left him? Damn Malinda! Oh, well. Better get up to the house and see what's so goddamned important.

Malinda was waiting for Dent in the parlor. She was sitting at one end of the sofa. She patted the cushion beside her and said, "Come and sit down, Dent. I've got some important news to tell you."

"It better be good, Malinda," said Dent as he sat down.

Malinda took a deep breath, then said what had to be said quickly and bluntly. "Dent, our brother is alive."

Dent wasn't sure that he'd heard her right. He burped a chuckle, then said, "Is this a joke, Malinda?"

She pinpointed her view on his right eye and slowly shook her head. Then to make certain that he understood, she said, "Clete is alive and well, Dent."

Malinda could have told him that Jesus was in the next room and he would have been less shocked. "Clete?" he muttered. "Our brother? Alive?" His eyes couldn't leave Malinda's.

"Yes, it's true, Dent." And quickly she told him about the previous night.

"And you let Lucas send him away?" queried Dent.

"Yes, Dent, I did. It was for the best . . . for all of us. You especially, Dent."

Dent wasn't sure what she meant by that, but he didn't question Malinda about it. After all, she was his older sister, and she had always done what was best for him in the past. Why wouldn't she do so now? No, it was nonsense to question her reasons for sending Clete away. If she wanted him to know, she would tell him. That was all there was to it.

"Clete alive," said Dent softly, still not sure whether to believe it or not.

"Yes, Dent, he's alive," said Malinda to reassure him that he wasn't dreaming. "But for the time being, we should still think of him as being dead."

"But he's alive, Malinda," protested Dent.

"Trust me, Dent. It's for the best. For now."

The tattoo of heavy boots on the hall floor distracted Malinda. Markham was coming. He entered the parlor and said, "Good morning, my dear. Good morning, Dent." Then he realized that he had interrupted them. "Is this a bad time, my dear?"

"No, Lucas," said Dent. "Malinda's already told me about Clete coming home last night."

Markham's face twisted into a feigned quizzical expression as he said, "Clete? Clete who?"

Dent stared back at Markham and said hesitantly, "Clete. My brother, Clete. He came home last night, didn't he?"

"A Reb calling himself Clete Slater showed up here last night," said Markham firmly, "but he isn't your brother, Dent. Your brother is dead. Morally and legally, he's very dead."

"Yes, of course, he is," said Dent uneasily. "If you say so, Lucas."

Dent wasn't sure he understood, but Malinda did. That much he knew by the look on her face. He would sort out the rest later— when he had his jug in one hand and Hannah in the other.

6

Hallettsville's square was filled with people, yet was dead quiet when Slater rode into town the next morning. Men, mostly former Confederates like him, were everywhere—sitting on the edges of the boardwalks with their elbows resting on their knees, resting on the grass beneath the leafy oaks and pecan trees of the courthouse lawn, leaning up against the shady side of the white clapboard county building, standing in knots on street corners—every one of them having the same basic appearance: dirty, unshaven, gaunt, ragged. Once the cream of Texan manhood, now flotsam on a sea of upheaval. It was a grim sight, and Slater felt a gut-wrenching pain in his pride. He needed a drink.

Jess Tate looked up from his spot in front of William Smothers' storehouse on the northwest corner of LaGrange and Third streets and saw Slater ride past. At first, Tate thought he was having another spell, one of those dizzy moments when his belly reached an iron claw up through his throat all the way to his brain and raked his senses, screaming its hunger for just a little food, a morsel of nourishment to sustain his miserable existence for one more hour. He rubbed his red, raw eyes; the lids squeaked like hinges that needed greasing. His vision cleared, and what he was seeing was no lie.

Slater rode up LaGrange past Second Street to old Matthias Lindenberg's saloon, where he reined in Nimbus, dismounted, and tied the Appaloosa to the hitching post in front of the establishment. He climbed onto the board porch and headed for the drinking hole's swinging doors, but he stopped when he heard his name called from behind him.

"Clete Slater, is that you, boy?"

Slater turned around and saw a telegraph pole of a man ambling up the street toward him. The shaggy, dirty face held no familiarity for Slater; its features were that changed from the last time he had seen it. But the gait was certainly recognizable. Only one son-of-a-Texas-buck walked like that: Jess Tate, Slater's oldest childhood friend and chief rival for the affections of the lovely and alluring Miss Lucy May, once the two of them awkwardly entered that stage of life where adolescent males begin to appreciate the difference between giggly girls and wiggly women.

"Jess?"

"Sure enough, it is you," drawled Tate. He wobbled onto the saloon's boardwalk, regained his balance, thrust out his hand in greeting.

Slater looked down at Tate's outstretched hand and felt that just wasn't a suitable way for old friends to greet each other after being apart for as long as they had been separated. He smiled at Tate, then threw his arms around him in a welcoming hug.

The sudden warmth of Slater's greeting surprised Tate, touching his heart and soul so much that tears welled up in his eyes, reddening them even more. It was only natural that he should return the embrace. "Let me look at you, boy," he said, pushing Slater to arm's length. He gave Slater a good going-over, then said, "Boy, I hardly knew you in that squirrel tail wrapped around your jaw. Wouldn't have known you if I hadn't seen old Nimbus there and figured only one good old boy would be riding that stallion around here."

"It's good to see you, Jess," said Slater.

Tate slapped him on the arm jovially and said, "Good to see you, too, Clete. Boy, I thought you were dead these last three years. We all did. We thought for sure that you was killed at Shiloh, but I can see that you wasn't killed at all. What happened to you after Shiloh?"

"Yanks got me."

"Yanks got you? You was captured? Naw! Don't tell me that, boy. I ain't believing it." Tate tugged at the insignia on Slater's collar and added, "You didn't get that in no Yankee prison camp."

"I didn't say the Yanks *held on* to me. I got shut of them soon enough. Joined up with Colonel John Morgan at first and rode with him until he was captured. After that, I was sort of unattached, riding with whoever needed me. In Virginia mostly. I rode with Colonel Mosby's Raiders once."

"You rode with the Gray Ghost?"

"None other," said Slater proudly.

Tate let out a low whistle that said he was impressed.

"What about you?" asked Slater. "What become of you at

Shiloh? Last time I saw you, you were heading south like a swarm of bees was hot on your tail.''

"Boy, you got that right, and them bees was Bluebellies with the sharpest bayonets I ever did see. Hell, boy, I wasn't about to hang around there and find out how they was intending to use them pig stickers. I didn't join up to fight on foot anyway. No how was I going to stand my ground like that fool officer was yelling for us to do.''

"You mean Captain Clemons?"

"Yeah, that's the one. Danged fool was trying to get us all killed. I can still hear him. 'Hold your ground, boys! Rally for the South, boys!' It weren't my ground,' so I did like the rest of the boys and skedaddled on out of there. Last I saw of Captain Clemons, he was standing on top of that rise we was defending. Danged fool was waving that long sword of his and hollering for us to hold our ground.'' He shook his head slowly as he mulled over the memory. Then he said, "Never saw him again after that.''

"I did," said Slater softly, reflecting on the memory. "He stayed there right to the end. It took three Yankee bayonets to bring him down. He took two of them with him though.''

"How come you didn't mount up and ride off with the rest of us, Clete?''

Slater shrugged and said, "Didn't seem right, I guess. I don't know. Maybe it was because I couldn't see leaving Captain Clemons alone there to hold them off by himself. Or maybe it was because Sergeant Dickerson threatened to shoot me himself if I ran. Who knows what makes a man stand his ground in the face of death? I sure don't.''

"Dickerson. I remember him. Did he get it there, too?''

"I don't know for sure. A Yankee ball grazed my skull right after Captain Clemons was killed, and I woke up later with this big ugly Bluebelly staring down at me. He jerked me up by the collar and shoved me into a line of prisoners, and the next day I was on a boat heading north on the Tennessee River. That night, I got free of my chains and slipped over the side and swam to shore. I stole a horse from some farm in Kentucky and headed back to Shiloh.''

"You went back? What on earth for?''

"Some Yankee officer had Nimbus," explained Slater, surprised that Tate had to ask, "and I wanted him back.''

"Well, I can see you got him back, but how'd you do it?''

"That was the easy part. Those Bluebelly sentries were all

asleep, so I just slipped into that Yankee camp in the middle of the night and did a little horse trading.''

A hunger spell suddenly grabbed Tate's innards, causing him to feel faint. He staggered involuntarily, nearly falling forward into Slater.

"You all right, Jess? You look bad, son."

Tate called up all his strength and righted himself. "Ain't had my breakfast yet."

"From the looks of you, I'd say you haven't had your breakfast for a month."

" 'Tain't true. I et breakfast one day last week. I think it was last week anyway. Maybe the week before."

Slater looked his friend straight in the eye and said, "Tell me true, Jess. When was the last time you had a meal?"

"Like I said, last week or the week before."

"Well, come on then. I was just going into Lindenberg's here for a drink. Come with me and I'll buy you some breakfast."

Slater started for the door, but Tate didn't move.

"Hold on, Clete. I can't let you do that."

Slater stopped and turned back to Tate. "Why not?"

"I don't take charity. Not from no one." He eyed Slater purposely and added, "Not even you, Cletus Slater."

"Charity? What on earth are you talking about, Jesse Tate? *I owe you.*"

"You owe me?" queried Tate in total disbelief. "What on earth for? And since when?"

"Don't you recollect?"

Tate shook his head and said, "You better freshen up my memory a mite."

"You'll be embarrassed if I have to do that. Trust me, Jess. I owe you."

"Well, you ain't never lied to me before," said Tate with a shrug. "Leastways, not so that I could prove it. So if you say you owe me, then I guess I'll have to take your word for it." His face turned a bit maniacal as he added, "Let's eat."

The two old friends entered the only true saloon in Hallettsville and stepped up to the bar.

The bartender was casually wiping beer mugs with a blue-and-white checkered towel at the other end of the counter. He put down the last glass and the cloth, wiped his hands on the fresh white apron tied around his bulging waist, and lumbered down to the first patrons of the day. Stopping in front of them, he put his huge hands on the countertop and leaned against it.

"What will it be, boys?" asked the bar dog in a light German accent that rolled R's, turned W's and T's into V's and D's, and hissed a lot of S's. His lips were barely detectable through a thick salt-and-pepper beard.

"Got any food here, Herr Lindenberg?" asked Slater, politely addressing the owner of the establishment with a title from his native tongue.

The barkeeper squinted at them as if he didn't recognize either man; then, as if it didn't matter, he said, "No lunch put out yet, and I let no one eat unless they drink also."

Slater knew this already. A smile crinkled the corners of his eyes as he dug into the coin pocket of his trousers, pulled out a silver dollar, and slapped it down on the bar. "Draw us a couple of beers," he said. "Then see what you can do about getting that lunch out here."

Lindenberg looked quizzically at the pair of former Confederate soldiers, then moved off to fill the order.

"That ain't your last dollar, is it, Clete?" asked Tate.

"No, there's more where that came from," said Slater.

"Well, you best be holding on to what money you got because there ain't no work around here for you to be making more."

"What do you mean, no work around here?"

Lindenberg returned with their brews, then left them again.

"There ain't none, Clete, because there ain't no money around here for no one to pay a body to work for them."

Slater lifted a mug of beer to his lips and drank half the warm beverage in a single breath. He replaced the glass on the bar and wiped the foam from his mouth with a soiled coat sleeve.

Tate did the same, then said, "Believe me, I know. I been trying to get work ever since I come home in March. Ain't none to be had on a regular basis. A body can pick up a dollar now and then loading hides, but there ain't nothing else around here for anyone to do."

"What about the plantations and ranches?" asked Slater.

"Like I done said, Clete. No one's got no money for paying a body to work around here. Not even the plantation and ranch owners."

"I'm finding that hard to believe. Why, I saw all sorts of cattle grazing between here and the Navidad River. The ranchers must have all sorts of work for good men like you."

"Oh, they got the work all right, but like I said before, they ain't got the money to pay no one."

Lindenberg returned with a butter knife and a platter of bread, lard, sliced roast beef, and hard-boiled eggs. He put the food down on the counter in front of Slater and Tate, then picked up the silver dollar and went to get change.

"Times is hard, old friend," said Tate, snatching up a slice of bread in one hand and the butter knife in the other. He smeared the bread with lard, slapped a piece of meat on it, folded it into a half sandwich, then took a big bite out of it. He chewed ravenously for a moment, then washed down the mouthful of food with a swallow of beer.

Slater finished the rest of his drink as Lindenberg returned with the change. He helped himself to the eggs and said, "Give us another round here, Herr Lindenberg."

"How do you come to call me Herr Lindenberg?" asked the saloonkeeper. "Do I know you?"

Slater smiled and said, "Of course, you do, Herr Lindenberg. You used to throw me and Jess out of here a whole lot when we were just kids. Besides that, your son Matt joined up the same time we did back in '61."

The old man gave Slater a hard study, then a hint of recognition crossed his face. "No, you can't be. You must be a ghost. The newspaper said Clete Slater was killed at Shiloh or captured or something."

"Mostly something," said Slater evenly. "Got captured once, wounded once, and nearly got killed a lot."

Lindenberg showed his tobacco-stained teeth in a warm smile that welcomed home the weary warrior, and he thrust an eager hand across the bar and shook Slater's to complete the greeting.

"Look at you," said Lindenberg. "You are no longer a skinny boy. You are a man now. You call me Fritz now, like all the rest." He noted the captain's bars on Slater's collar and added, "You were in much fighting, Clete?"

"More than I care to recollect, Herr Lindenberg."

"Please. Fritz. You call me Fritz."

Slater smiled as an inner glow, brought on by Lindenberg's genuine reception, warmed him. This was more like it, he thought. Then he said, "Sure, Fritz. Say, what happened to Matt? I didn't see much of him or any of the other Lavaca County boys after Shiloh."

"He has not come home yet," said Lindenberg. "We got word

that he was wounded in South Carolina. We have not heard anything since then.''

Slater nodded and said, ''He's probably fine, Fritz. With the Yankees in control now, it's probably taking him forever to get home. South Carolina is a long way from Texas.''

''Too bad we couldn't have whupped those Yankees more often, Clete,'' said Tate. ''Then we wouldn't have none of them around here.''

The mention of Union soldiers suddenly reminded Slater of his encounter with them the night before at Glengarry. He knew there were Yankees occupying most of the South, but they were usually in strategic locales. What they were doing in Lavaca County puzzled him. This part of Texas was far from being of any military importance as far as he could see.

''Yeah, what about that, Fritz?'' asked Slater. ''I noticed a lot of Yankees in the area. How come they're here anyway?''

Lindenberg merely shrugged, pretending innocence. He knew the answer to Slater's question, but he wasn't going to be the one to say it. He left that up to Tate.

''It's got something to do with Hallettsville being halfway between Galveston and San Antone,'' said Tate. Then a thought struck him. ''Say, you been out to your place yet, Clete?''

''It's not mine anymore, I understand, from the way I was told last night by a Yankee colonel.''

''Then you met Colonel Markham?''

''Is that his name? He didn't give it to me when he was throwing me off my own land.''

Tate looked down at the bar as if he knew something that he wished he didn't have to tell Slater.

Slater sensed something was wrong and asked, ''You got something stuck in your craw, Jess?''

''It ain't my place to be telling you this, Clete,'' said Tate slowly as he looked up at Slater and met his gaze eye to eye. ''But you might as well hear it from me as anyone else. I'm your best friend, and a best friend ought to be doing the telling of something like this.'' He swallowed the last of his beer, then slid the mug toward the bartender. ''Why don't you set us up that second round Clete ordered, Mr. Lindenberg, while I give it to him straightaway?''

The old German nodded, took the beer glasses, and moved away toward the tap.

''Give me what straightaway, Jess?'' asked Slater.

"That Yankee colonel was telling you true, Clete. Glengarry ain't yours no more. That was the first place I went to when I come home in March, and your brother threw me off the place no sooner than I stepped foot on it. Treated me like dirt, he did. 'Course, you know there ain't never been no love lost betwixt me and Dent, but he never treated me like I was some sort of trash before. I asked him who the hell he thought he was, and he said he was the owner of Glengarry Plantation and I was to get off his property in a cat's wink or he was going to fill my hide with buckshot. I was looking down the barrels of your granddaddy's shotgun real hard, so I didn't argue none and left. When I got to what was left of my daddy's place and found my mama hoeing weeds in a garden like some darky, I started figuring right off that things wasn't the same around here as when you and me and all the rest rode off to war."

Tate's description of Dent didn't sound like the brother Slater left behind in '61. Dent did have a temper, but he wasn't mean and nasty. But what Tate said about there being no love lost between Dent and him was true. Even so, Dent wouldn't threaten anyone with a shotgun, not without good cause. Not the Denton Slater that Clete Slater knew and loved. Of course, three and a half years had passed since he'd last seen his younger brother, and people do change as time goes by; there was no arguing that. Just the same, Slater found it hard to believe that Dent could have changed that much.

Lindenberg returned with the fresh brews and said, "I thought you were going to tell him straightaway."

"He already knows Glengarry ain't his no more," said Tate rather defensively.

"*Ja!* But you have not told him all of it yet." Lindenberg banged the mugs down on the counter to emphasize his impatience. A little beer sloshed out of each glass, but the barkeeper didn't care; he was making a point.

"I was getting to it, Mr. Lindenberg. I was getting to it. Don't rush me now. This ain't easy to tell, you know."

"Go on, Jess," said Slater softly. "What happened after you got home?"

"Well, like I was saying, I found my mama hoeing weeds in the garden. She was real glad to see me." There was a slight strain in his voice. "Said she hoped I'd come home before she died." He took a draw on the beer before continuing. "She told me my daddy had gone off with the Home Guards and was killed rounding up deserters over by Seguin last year, and with my brother Matt gone off to Colorado back in '59 to dig for gold and me gone off to war, she was left all alone to run the place. Our slaves run off when they heard the Yankees were coming to free them, then a cyclone wrecked the house in November, so she moved into the slave quarters. She was feeling real poorly already by the time I come home, and she up and died three weeks later. But not before she told me all about your brother Dent and what had been happening out to Glengarry." Tate gulped down some more beer, then asked, "Did you know that your granddaddy passed away last winter, Clete?"

"Yes, I know," said Slater softly. "That Yankee colonel told me."

"Well, before he died," said Tate, "he freed all his slaves and then he put it in his will that Glengarry was to go to Dent because he'd remained loyal to the Union. You remember how your granddaddy was, Clete. He was always helping out folks when they needed money. Well, he kept paper on everyone, but he never pressed no one to pay him. Then when your granddaddy was gone, Dent tried to collect all the debts, but folks couldn't come up with the hard cash and Dent wouldn't take no more paper, especially Confederate bank notes. He offered to take their stock or their land or both, but no one would let him do that. So he offered to let the men work for him at Glengarry to pay their debts, and some fellers was hurting enough to do it at first. Then they quit because he was having them work next to the darkies he'd hired to do the same job. No white folks will work out there now.

"Then Markham and his Bluebellies showed up about the time news come that Lee had surrendered. Markham made it known in a hurry that he was the new law around here. Dent went straight to Markham and told him about all the debts owed to him by all us Confederates and now he wanted Markham to collect them for him since he was a loyal Union man and it was Markham's duty to protect Yankee-lovers. Well, them Yankees went right to work and started taking everything Dent said was owed to him. That's what happened to my mama. Dent took all our stock and a piece of land, too. Here he was taking everything from folks and making everyone poor as church mice and he ain't caring one bit about it. Now he owns half the cows and half the land in this county they're grazing on, and he's got them Bluebellies to back him up.

"But that ain't the worst of it, Clete," said Tate, before taking a drink of beer. "The worst part is . . . Markham's going to marry Malinda."

Slater remained calm, showing no reaction to the news at all but thinking about it just the same.

So that was why Markham let Slater go the night before. It made sense to him now. Malinda had been the woman behind the door, and when she told Markham to let him go, he wasn't about to refuse his bride-to-be.

"Everyone around here knowed about Dent's feelings," said Tate, "but no one thought Malinda was a Yankee-lover, too. When word got around, the whole county went to church and prayed for her soul. Imagine, her marrying a Yankee."

"Yeah, imagine that," said Slater. He finished the second beer, then said, "One more, Fritz, then I'd best be going."

"Going?" quizzed Tate. "Out to Glengarry?"

Lindenberg stood still, waiting for Slater's answer.

"No, to a hotel," he said. "I need a place to stay, and I want to take a bath and get a shave." He rubbed his whiskers. "I'm tired of looking like a longhorn in winter." He sniffed the air and added, "And smelling like one in summer."

"If you got enough money for a hotel room and a visit to the barbershop, too," said Tate, "you better not let anyone know about it, Clete. It ain't safe around here for a man with money in his pocket. I know some fellers who'll slit your gizzard for the price of a hot meal."

Slater looked his old friend squarely in the eye and said, "Then maybe you'd better come along with me for protection. Besides, you could use a trip to the barbershop, too."

Lindenberg laughed and said, "You sure got that right, Clete. If there was a fellow who could use a bath, it's Jess here. He does smell like the south end of a northbound horse."

"Why don't you just get the beers, Mr. Lindenberg," said Tate a mite testily, "and mind your own business?"

"Now look here, Jess Tate. If Clete didn't have the price of a beer, I wouldn't even let you in my place."

"Is that so? Well, let me tell you a thing or two, you cabbage-eating old buzzard. If I—"

"Take it easy, Jess," said Slater. "Fritz was just fooling. There's no need to get all riled up."

Tate looked like he was about to turn on his friend as well, but he realized Slater was right. There was no sense in getting angry over a little joke, even if it was on him.

"Yeah, you're right, Clete," said Tate.

"I know I am. So how about those beers, Fritz?"

"Coming right up, Clete." He moved off to draw the brews.

"You had enough to eat, Jess?" asked Slater.

"My gut ain't the size it used to be, Clete. A sandwich and a boiled egg or two is about all I can handle right now."

"Well, we'll just have to get you back to eating regular, that's all."

"Hey, Clete, I done told you already, I don't take charity."

"I know, but how do you feel about working for me?"

"Working for you? Doing what?"

Lindenberg brought the beers, set them down, then picked up the money for them.

"We'll have to give that some thought," said Slater. "But for now, you're working for me, and the first thing we're going to do is get a hotel room, then visit the barbershop."

Then after that, he thought, we'll see what can be done around here to make things right for everyone.

7

High noon was upon Hallettsville when Slater and Tate emerged from Mose Cohen's tonsorial parlor. Both men were clean shaven, had their hair trimmed neatly, and were attired in new duds. Slater wore a light gray linen suit, white ruffled shirt, black silk string tie, and a dark gray stetson. Never a fancy man, Tate had opted for the outfit of a range hand: brown gabardine trousers, tan gabardine shirt, yellow cotton neckerchief, and brown felt plainsman hat with a cowhide band.

It was Slater's opinion that since the war was over he should rid himself of almost every vestige of that great conflict and begin living his new life in a style to which he wanted to become accustomed. To his way of thinking, he had been born a gentleman, and disinheritance or not, he would remain so.

"What do we do now?" asked Tate as they stood on the edge

of the boardwalk in front of the barbershop, casually surveying the town.

Slater glanced skyward. The subtropical sun and high humidity had driven almost every man, woman, and child off the streets of the town to any cool shade that was to be found, whether it was in a house, under a tree, in the shadow of a building, or in Lindenberg's.

"It's just about siesta time, Jess," said Slater, "so let's stroll over to Lindenberg's and have a little bite to eat before heading for the hotel."

"If you say so," said Tate. "You're the boss."

The title seemed foreign to Slater, although it shouldn't have. After all, he'd been raised in such a manner that the only two people who ever told him what to do had been his mother and his grandfather. Even in the Confederate army, he had been quickly promoted to corporal in the first few weeks of his enlistment, then to lieutenant only six months after Shiloh and to captain in less time. He had given more orders than he had ever taken, but he had never thought of himself as the man in charge. It was a concept that would take some getting used to.

A chorus of male laughter broke the noontime quiet as Slater and Tate approached the saloon. They cocked their ears for the next round of mirthful sounds and quickly discerned that it was coming from the alley north of Lindenberg's. The two men exchanged looks that expressed more than spoken words could. Their curiosity piqued, they decided to investigate.

Several dirty, ragged, gaunt men were sitting in the shade along the saloon's north wall. Their attire, what there was of it, marked many of them as Confederate veterans. How proud and boastful they had been when they marched off to war against the Union, thought Slater. Now look at them. They were a pitiful, starving, homeless rabble. What had they done to deserve this plight? Fight for what they thought was right? No, because their Northern counterparts had fought for the same reason. But unlike those boys from the North, they had been on the losing side, and for that alone they suffered. But worse than their condition, these men had degenerated into a mob of savages as witnessed by their choice of entertainment.

In the middle of the alley stood three men: two former masters holding willow switches and threatening a former slave who was cowering between them. Slater recognized all three.

The ex-slave was old Tobias who had been a house servant at

Glengarry when Slater left for the war. He had come to Texas with the Slaters from South Carolina and had served them faithfully until Dougald set him free a year ago.

The white men were the Detchen twins, Harlan and Farley. Slater remembered them from his childhood, when the pair would gang up on anyone who crossed their path. They were mean and sadistic as boys, becoming meaner and more sadistic as they grew older. Both were on the stocky side, a little less than average height, with flaming red hair, freckles, and ocher eyes that strongly resembled those of a feline toying with a mouse just before the delivery of the deathblow. The only way to tell them apart was by a three-inch scar that ran from just below Farley's left ear to the corner of his mouth. Not many people knew how the disfiguring mark had come to be; Slater being one of the few.

Harlan and Farley were orphaned in infancy when their pappy was killed in the Mexican War and their mother died of swamp fever the same year. Their mother's cousin, Sophia Campbell, took them in and raised them as part of her own litter of whelps.

The Campbell plantation was located eight miles east of Hallettsville, opposite Glengarry on the road to Columbus. Because they were fetched up in a family that was financially more fortunate than most, Harlan and Farley were uppity little cusses who abused everything and everyone who got in their way, the same as their Campbell cousins Stewart and Tucker did.

The Detchen twins were Malinda Slater's age, but they were small for their years, shorter than Dent, who was more than a year younger than they were. The two of them jumped Dent on his way home from school one day, neither of them giving a thought to the possibility that the older Slater, who had finished his schooling the previous spring, would seek revenge on them for the dastardly deed. Nor did they count on Clete intervening while they were trying to whip Dent with the same four foot–long piece of horsehair rope that Patrick Nolan, the Campbell's overseer, used on the Campbell slaves. The cord made a nasty torture tool when both ends of it were held in one hand.

The twins had tied Dent to a cottonwood and ripped his shirt off, and Harlan was applying the lash when Clete rode up and dismounted, prepared to rescue his brother. Farley pulled a knife from his boot and told Clete to stand clear or he would go to carving on Dent. Quick thinking, Clete took a step back and fell down intentionally, figuring Farley would attack him. Farley was true to form and made his move. Clete countered by rolling to one side. In another instant, he jerked his right work spur free. Holding it by the heel band and with the shank between the index and middle finger of his right hand, Clete leaped to his feet, placing himself between Dent and Farley. Harlan took a swipe at him with the horsehair rope, but Clete was ready for it, grabbing the lash with his left hand and yanking it away from the Detchen brother. Farley lunged at Clete once more. Clete stepped aside and swung the spur at Farley's face. The star-shaped rowel caught him across his cheek, cutting him deep from his mouth to his ear. Farley screamed, dropped the knife, and fell on his knees, holding his wounded face.

Harlan took one look at his brother and made tracks. Clete put the whip to Farley, and the other Detchen twin was on his way as well. That was the last time the Detchens ever crossed the Slaters.

It was until . . .

Slater stepped into the middle of the lane and caught Harlan's raised hand before he could swing the switch down on the back of old Tobias, who was on his knees, hunched over with his hands covering his head to protect it from the anticipated blow.

"What the hell?" swore Harlan as he was spun around, his face full of hate and anger in the one instant, fear and dread in the next when he recognized the man who stayed his hand.

"You ain't changed a bit, Harlan," said Slater, a bitter fire glazing his eyes as they bore their repulsion for Harlan deep into Detchen's pale orbs. He twisted Harlan's arm downward, forcing the twin to come face-to-face with him. Then, with his forearm, Slater pushed Harlan away from him, causing Detchen to fall backward, landing on his rump in front of Tobias.

"Slater!" muttered Farley, the name filling him with the same two emotions that shivered through his brother. He lowered the willow branch in his hand and took a cautious step backward.

Old Tobias looked first at Harlan, then up at Slater. He couldn't believe what he was seeing. The ways of the plantation, practiced for more than three score years until they were almost instinctive reactions, came to the fore.

"Massuh Clete?" queried the wrinkled, white-haired man in that melodic brand of English spoken by slaves in the presence of whites. "Is that you, Massuh Clete?"

Slater forgot about the Detchens for a second and reached out a hand to help Tobias up. He took the old man by the shoulders and practically lifted him to his feet.

"You all right, Tobias?" asked Slater almost paternally. "Did they hurt you?"

"No-suh, Massuh Clete. They didn't hurt me none. I is just fine." Tobias grinned from ear to ear, showing a nearly toothless smile. "I be fine now. Just fine."

"Good, good, Tobias."

Not every man in the crowd knew Slater before the war, but most had heard of him. Those who had been his friends stepped forward now and welcomed him home with a round of slaps on the back, handshakes, and words of greeting. The rest just stood by and enjoyed the reunion as spectators.

Slater glanced from face to face, recognizing only a few of his boyhood chums behind their dirty, unshaven faces; but before he could acknowledge each of them individually, his attention was drawn back to Tobias and the Detchens as Harlan clambered to his feet and joined his brother.

Almost magically, the crowd parted, forming an aisle from Slater to the Detchens.

Slater scanned the other men, then glared at the brothers, who returned the look eyeball to eyeball, hate for hate. *Bastards!* thought Slater. He'd forgotten about these two. He reckoned that he'd have to deal with them now, but first he turned to the former slave of Glengarry and said, "Tobias, I think you'd best be on your way from here."

Tobias didn't argue. "Yessuh, Massuh Clete. This darky is on his way." And with that, he left.

"You two couldn't beat enough of your own darkies," said Slater, forgetting the new times that were so recently begun, "so now you've taken to beating other folks' slaves?"

"Slaves?" snickered Farley. "You forget that Lincoln freed the slaves two years back?"

Nonplussed, Slater replied, "All the more reason for you two to leave the darkies alone. The law says they're free now, and that gives them the same rights as you and me."

Slater half-expected a few of the men to agree with him and voice their sentiments along with him. But none did.

Seeing that no one was siding with Slater, the Detchens took up the challenge as Farley said, "What is it with you Slaters? First your baby brother becomes a Yankee lover, then your sister starts sleeping with one, and now you turn on your own kind and become a nigger lover.''

Slater was a volcano inside, he was that incensed by Farley's remark about Malinda; but he remained outwardly calm and resolute just as Grandpa Hawk had always told him to be in the face of an enemy. He took deliberate, steady steps in Farley's direction, not saying a word, not yet.

The men held their collective breath in anticipation of what Slater was about to do. Tate moved in behind Slater and picked up the willow switch that Harlan had been using. He stared down at Farley's twin, his eyes telling the Detchen brother to step aside and stay out of the affray that was sure to come in the next few seconds, or else Harlan would have to deal with Slater's second, meaning him, Jess Tate. Harlan took the hint and moved away from Farley.

"When was the last time someone put you in your proper place, Farley?'' asked Slater, moving nearer.

Detchen glanced sideways, looking for his brother, didn't see him, and broke into a cold sweat. He looked back at Slater closing in on him. If only he had a gun, he thought, he'd teach Slater who was the better man. But the only weapon at his command was the willow switch he held in his right hand. He whipped it high over his head, then brought it down hard toward Slater's face.

Slater foresaw the blow and was ready for it. He raised his left arm at an angle in defense. The branch struck it indirectly and slid harmlessly down his sleeve. Simultaneously, Slater lashed out with his right foot, driving it deep into Farley's exposed groin, lifting him a good six inches off the ground with the force of the kick. In another wag of a dog's tail, Slater withdrew his foot and threw a left cross into the side of Farley's head, knocking off Detchen's tattered, greasy plainsman.

Farley reacted as expected. His eyes bulged in surprise and excruciating pain, then his hands reached instantly for his injured genitals as the wind left his lungs. But before he could double up in a fetal position, he crashed into unconsciousness from the power of Slater's fist.

Slater wanted to kick the sonofabitch again but didn't. Instead, he turned toward Harlan.

"Is there something you'd like to say about my sister?'' he asked the other Detchen through gritted teeth.

"Fine, upstanding lady from what I hear,'' said Harlan, pale as the wool on the back of a lost sheep and twice as frightened.

Cold sweat flushed every pore in his body as he swallowed hard, half-expecting Slater to come at him now.

Slater wanted to do just that, go after Harlan, but he never got the chance. The law was about to butt in.

Lavaca County Deputy Sheriff Jim Kindred was from Lyons up on the Fayette County line. He was a little man with a big axe to grind against almost every man who had the good fortune to grow up tall and straight. When Texas voted overwhelmingly for secession in 1861, Kindred was one of the first to raise the Stars and Bars over his place. During the war, he was the enrolling officer for Lavaca County, discharging his duties with all the zeal of a religious convert. Besides encouraging young men to enlist in the Confederate Army, it was Kindred's job to conscript those men between the ages of eighteen and thirty-five who weren't so willing to lay their lives on the line for the South. When the occasional man decided against going off to fight a war he didn't believe in, it was Kindred's additional chore to round up the draft dodger and send him off to battle. To aid him in this pursuit, Kindred had a large contingent of Texas State Troops, Reserve Corps of the Provisional Army of the Confederacy, also known as the Home Guards but more often called the Heel Flies because of their persistence and other characteristics similar to those of that pesky insect. Kindred relished his position and the power it bestowed on him, mostly because he was allowed to legally carry a gun. With the closing of hostilities and the coming of Union forces, he got himself appointed a deputy sheriff.

Kindred heard the ruckus in the alley beside Lindenberg's as he was coming out of Schwartz & Arnold's clothing store on the northwest corner of Second and LaGrange streets. He drew his revolver, a Colt's .36-caliber Navy, and marched straight to the scene, arriving just as Slater was turning his attention toward Harlan Detchen.

"What's going on here?" Kindred demanded to know. "You there," he said, pointing his six-gun at Slater, "did you do that?" He waved the barrel of his weapon in Farley's direction.

"He started it," spoke up Tate, fingering Detchen.

Kindred looked at Tate and said, "Who asked you?"

"Lookey here, Deputy," said Tate, but that was all he got out before Kindred cocked his Colts and aimed it at Tate's nose.

"Like I said, who asked you?" snarled Kindred.

Tate simply put up his hands and backed off.

"He did it, Deputy," said Harlan, wagging a finger at Slater.

"He beat up my brother when he wasn't looking."

"Shut up, Harlan," said Kindred, playing no favorites. "When I want some shit out of you, I'll squeeze some of your brains out of that pimple you call a head." He turned back to Slater. "Now I want an answer from you. Did you do this to Farley?"

Slater merely glared down at the officer of the law, refusing to reply.

Kindred looked around at the crowd, then back at Slater, uncocking his gun as he did. He gave Slater a disarming smile and said, "So you won't talk here, is that it? Well, what say we sashay over to the county jail and see if you're willing to talk with Sheriff Foster?"

"There's no need for that, Deputy," said Slater, putting up his hands in front of him in a conciliatory manner.

Kindred didn't think Slater was being all that friendly with his movements and said so with words and actions. "We're going to the jailhouse, mister," he said as he hit Slater in the jaw with the barrel of the Colt's.

Slater didn't expect the assault. Taking the blow fully, his head snapped to one side. He staggered, then crumpled in a heap.

8

News about Slater's run-in with the Detchens and his subsequent fiasco with Deputy Kindred spread through town like wildfire across the prairie in a high wind. Several dozen people saw Kindred following four men who were carrying Slater's unconscious body to jail, and, of course, their curiosity demanded to know what had happened and who was involved. Questions put to Kindred got them nothing, but one look at Jess Tate brought the whole story out of him.

A crowd gathered around Tate on the courthouse lawn as he related the episode. Among them was Texada Ballard, the one person in Hallettsville who was the most shocked to hear that Clete Slater was still alive.

Texada—so named because she was born in Texas and her maternal grandmother's name was Ada—was often called the menace of the county as a child because she feared nothing on God's green earth—with the exception of her foster grandmother, Margaret Hallet, the grand dame of the county—and chose to prove it at every possible turn by attempting to do everything a boy would do—from riding a half-broken horse to dangling on ropes hanging from the limbs of cottonwoods and swinging out over the Lavaca and dropping into the turbid water that sometimes camouflaged deadly cottonmouths. The trouble was most of the things she did turned out wrong and others suffered for it; like the time she decided to show the boys in town that she could ride one of Crockett Dibrell's new mustangs, and the colt broke through the corral fence and let half the remuda loose. Mrs. Hallet called Texada's behavior "the acts of a precocious child," but most everyone else said she was nothing but a spoiled brat—behind Mrs. Hallet's back, of course.

Like all the others in the audience, Texada hung on every word of Tate's tale. Blond hair in pigtails, a few freckles on her tan cheeks, wearing a man's work shirt, blue jeans, and boots, she was every bit a tomboy, even at nineteen. As soon as she heard that Slater was the man being carried off to jail, she ran across Second Street to her Uncle Coll's store, taking the tall step to the boardwalk in a bound. She burst through the front door and made straight for the rear door, not stopping to tell anyone that her heart was alive again because Slater was alive and back in Hallettsville. There was no time for small talk now. She had to get home as fast as she could and tell her granny. She ran all the way.

Margaret Leatherbury was the youngest child of a prominent Virginia family. In 1808, in spite of her kin's opposition to the union, she married John Hallet, an able-bodied seaman with much promise and dreams aplenty. When her relatives pointed out how much she would be giving up in order to settle down with Hallet on some distant frontier, she replied, "I would rather be the head of a new generation in a new country than the tail end of an old generation in an old state."

The Hallets came to Texas in the 1820s and lived at Goliad, where they owned a trading business before securing a land grant of their own along the Lavaca River. They moved to the Hallet league in 1833, built a log cabin and cattle pens, planted the bois d'arc trees they brought with them, and dug a well. They returned to Goliad early the next year, and Mr. Hallet died a short time later.

With the outbreak of the Texas Revolution, Margaret Hallet's sons, John Jr., and William, joined the fight for independence. Both died in the service of their newly born country.

Margaret and her daughter Mary Jane returned to the Hallet homestead on the Lavaca in 1836 and found that their little cabin had been destroyed by the Mexican army when it marched across the county on its way from victory at the Alamo to defeat at San Jacinto. Mother and daughter rebuilt their home and set up a trading post in it as other folks settled near them. A few years later Collatinus Ballard came to what was being called the Hallet settlement by some and Hidesville by others because of the large buffalo hide stretched on the side of Mrs. Hallet's cabin. In time, Ballard and Mary Jane were married, and he took control of the family trading business, building a bigger log structure on a part of the Hallet land that became the corner of Second and Main streets in Hallettsville.

In 1845, Franklin Ballard, a cousin to Collatinus from back in Culpepper county, Virginia, came to town, having jumped ship at Galveston. During his short stay in Hallettsville, he met and courted Cora Edson, the only daughter of twice-widowed Ada Parks. When he left to fight Comanches along the Nueces River, Ballard didn't know that he had put Cora in a family way. To make matters worse, he was killed in battle before he could return to Hallettsville and do the right thing by Cora.

When word of her condition spread through the community, Cora was shunned by nearly everyone, including her own mother. Ada and her third husband, Albert Parks, couldn't bare the shame of Cora's immorality, so they drove Cora from their home.

Feeling that her son-in-law's relationship to the father of Cora's unborn child made Collatinus somewhat responsible for the welfare of the mother and wanting to show Ada Parks a thing or two about what St. Paul had in mind when he wrote about what it took to be a Christian, Mrs. Hallet took Cora into her home.

The following spring Cora gave birth to a daughter, named her Texada, then died of childbed fever.

Now Mrs. Hallet felt Collatinus was more responsible than ever for the child. At her insistence, he and Mary Jane raised Texada with their own children but never as their own child. To compensate for the stunted love that her daughter and son-in-law had for the orphaned girl, Mrs. Hallet favored Texada over her natural grandchildren. When Texada became a teenager, Mrs. Hallet had her pack her things and move in with her. From that day forward, Mrs. Hallet became more than Texada's granny; they became best friends, sharing their joys, their sorrows, their secrets—mostly Texada's—as friends do.

Mrs. Hallet's house was a good half mile north of the town square, but it made no difference to Texada. Knowing that her granny would be just as happy to hear about Clete as she was put wings on Texada's feet as she ran faster than she ever had in her whole life. She leaped over the picket fence around the yard, stumbled, rolled, and came up running, bounding onto the porch and into the house.

"Granny! Granny!" she shouted at the top of her lungs.

"Texada, is that you?" called out Mrs. Hallet from the kitchen, where she was visiting with her sole servant, an ex-slave named Francie who had been with her since the days of the Republic.

"Lordy, Miz Hallet," said Francie, "that child sure is loud today."

Texada exploded into the room and said with all the excitement of the moment, "Granny! He's alive! He's alive!"

"Goodness gracious, Texada!" said Mrs. Hallet. "What are you going on about?"

"Who's alive, child?" asked Francie.

"Clete!" she gasped.

"Clete?" queried Mrs. Hallet, her memory failing her for the moment. "Clete who?"

Francie remembered. "Clete Slater?" she queried.

Texada sucked in a deep breath and nodded rapidly.

"Cletus Slater?" queried Mrs. Hallet.

"Yes, Granny," said Texada, able to breathe again. "He's alive, and he's in Hallettsville right this minute."

"He is?" asked Mrs. Hallet. "When . . . how . . . ?"

"I don't know for sure, Granny. All I know is he got back this morning, and already he's had trouble from those damn Detchens."

"Texada," said Mrs. Hallet sternly, "you watch your tongue now. There's no need to swear at a time like this."

"That's right, Miss Texada," said Francie. "You mind your granny now."

"Just calm down and tell me all about it, Texada," said Mrs. Hallet. "Where did you hear that Cletus was home?"

Texada sat down at the table and told the two old women

everything that she knew about Slater's homecoming. It wasn't much, but it was wonderful news, just the same.

"And you say he's in jail now?" asked Mrs. Hallet.

"That's right, Granny. I saw them carrying him there." Then it dawned on Texada that Slater might be seriously injured, and fear darkened her face. "Oh, no, Granny," she said excitedly, "he might be hurt bad."

"Now, now, don't you fret, Miss Texada," said Francie. "That puny Jim Kindred got himself a hard time killing a fly with a plank, let alone get hurt to a full-growed man. Mister Clete all right. You can bet on that."

"Francie's right, Texada," said Mrs. Hallet. "I'm sure Cletus is just fine."

"But what if he ain't, Granny? What if he's hurt bad and needs a doctor or something? What then, Granny?"

"Don't you worry about it, Sugar," said Mrs. Hallet. "Francie, you go into town and tell Dr. Bennett to get himself over to the jail and see about Cletus."

"Yes'm, Miz Hallet." Francie got up from the table, removed her apron, hung it neatly on the back door, and left through that exit.

"In the meantime, Texada," said Mrs. Hallet, "I think you should get yourself ready to see Cletus."

"See Clete?" queried Texada.

"That's right, Sugar. You do want to see him, don't you?"

"Oh, yes, Granny, I sure do."

"Then you'd better put on a dress and brush out your hair and maybe put on a sunbonnet." She lifted one of Texada's pigtails, studied it, and added, "Yes, a sunbonnet. Now get to it, girl."

"Yes, Granny."

Texada disappeared in the direction of her room, leaving Mrs. Hallet to ponder this sudden turn of events.

Cletus Slater is home, she thought. This made her very happy. Almost as happy as Texada was. Of course, she wasn't in love with Slater like her foster granddaughter was, but all the same, she was delighted that Slater was back in Lavaca County. If Cletus was anything at all like his grandfather Dougald had been—and he had showed signs of being a real Slater before he went off to war—then he was exactly the patent medicine that the county needed to get well. Of course, she thought, there's no telling what that terrible war has done to him. Maybe I'd better have a look at him myself and see if he's fit for the job.

Mrs. Hallet pushed herself into a standing position, standing quite straight for a woman in her eight decade of life. She walked slowly but with steady steps through the house to Texada's room.

Texada was just slipping into her lady's undergarments when Mrs. Hallet entered the bedroom. She looked up at the old woman, her face filled with chagrin, and said, "Gee, Granny, do I have to put on a dress?"

"What do you think, Texada? Cletus has been gone for almost four years. Do you think he'll want to see a girl who looks like a boy? Or do you think he'll want to see a girl who looks like a lady? You tell me, Texada."

Texada heaved a sigh and said, "A lady, I suppose. All right, Granny, I'll wear the dress."

"I want you to put on some of that perfume that your cousin bought for you last Christmas. Get that boy smell off you for a while."

"Aw, Granny, I hate that stuff."

"Yes, but men like it. Now you do as I say. And no horse riding either. You take the phaeton to town when you go. And if Cletus is all right like I think he is, then you fetch him home for supper, you hear? I want to talk to him."

"Talk to him?" queried Texada. "About what?"

"Never you mind about what. You just do like I told you."

"Yes, ma'am," said Texada as she watched Mrs. Hallet turn and leave the room.

Texada hated dresses, but she wore them—for her granny—to church and other such social functions. She preferred men's clothing. Not that she had any desire to be a man. Far from it. No, she simply liked the comfort of a shirt and blue jeans, and she liked men. Or one man, anyway. Clete Slater. Trouble was, he hardly ever noticed that she was even alive. That was before the war, she told herself as she admired her form in the long mirror. Things will be different now. Now he'll notice me. Sure he will, Texada. What makes you think anything's going to be different now? He's still Clete, and you're still Texada. She studied herself for a moment, and a new thought crossed her mind. Of course, I wasn't a whole woman when Clete went off to war. She took a deep breath and held it as she continued to look at herself, thinking, But now I am a whole woman. Well, at least I'm more woman than I was four years ago. Now if I can only make Clete see me that way . . .

9

A mosquito buzzing in Slater's ear awakened him. His eyes opened, and he looked around, not liking what he saw.

He was lying on his left side on a cot in a Lavaca County jail cell, his clothes saturated with perspiration. The six-by-ten room was hot, stifling; no air moved through the tiny one-foot-square barred window situated high in the outer wall. The portal barely allowed any light to enter the dimly lit space—a single shaft of sunshine forcing its way inside and splashing onto the corridor wall beyond the bars that confined him.

His tongue moved involuntarily. It was dry and stuck to the roof of his mouth. He swallowed hard in a reflexive action and was reminded of how he came to be asleep. His jaw felt as if a mule had kicked him. Instinctively, he reached for his injured part. Touching it was worse, made it hurt all the more.

The mosquito bit him on the back of the neck. He slapped at it, killed it, but got another reminder of how he came to be in this place when the shock of the blow jangled the nerves in his jaw. He winced with the pain, hissing in a breath ever so slowly as if that would ease the agony. It didn't.

Gingerly, Slater sat up on the edge of the cot. For the first time, he noticed the stench: a combination of urine and vomited whiskey and beer. It was bad, but it was nothing compared to the odor of human flesh rotting under a hot sun burning down on a two-day-old battlefield. Such a scene flashed into Slater's mind, sending a shiver through him. He shook it off, wishing, hoping, silently praying never again to smell the mephitis of decaying dead men.

Taking stock of himself, Slater saw that his new clothes were dirty and one sleeve of his coat split from the shoulder seam. He surmised that he'd been dragged unconscious to the jailhouse. The little bastard who hit him would pay for the coat, he thought, and he just might pay for hitting him as well. But before he could do anything about either problem, he had to get out of there. He stood up and felt a tinge of vertigo, but it passed as fast as it had come. He stepped to the door of bars, got his face as close to them as possible, and had a look up and down the hallway.

Nothing out there. Just a few more cells like the one he was in and two doors, one at each end of the corridor. He guessed one led to the sheriff's office and the other went outside, probably to an outhouse in back of the building. Although he'd grown up in Lavaca County and had been to Hallettsville more than a hundred times during his childhood and youth, he'd never had occasion to visit the county lockup, so he couldn't be sure of what was where. He did know that the jail was on Front Street between First and Second on the bluff overlooking the Lavaca River, and he knew that the cell block was on the second floor of the building.

Slater walked to the back wall to have a look out the window. He could see plenty of blue sky but little else. He grabbed the two bars in the portal and pulled himself up for a better view.

The river was closer than he had imagined; only twenty yards or so away. A small barge steamer was docked on the levee. The paleness and apparent stiffness of its tethers said it hadn't left its moorings in quite some time. Across the Lavaca was a pasture with a dozen brown-and-white milch cows and half as many calves of varying sizes grazing contentedly on fresh spring grass. The violet, yellow, and scarlet wildflowers added a touch of color to the bucolic setting.

Satisfied that that was all that he could see from his vantage point, Slater dropped himself down, his boots making a resounding thud on the wooden floor. As he turned to walk back to the door, he heard muffled voices below. He strained to make out what they were saying but couldn't, especially when he was distracted by the creak-creak-creak of someone plodding their way up a set of stairs beyond the door at the north end of the corridor. Positive that someone was coming up to the cell block, he stepped anxiously to the cell door, not knowing exactly what to expect next. He looked down the hallway and heard the rattle of keys followed by the sound of one of their number entering a lock. There was a click, then the door opened.

Light from below silhouetted the bareheaded man in the doorway. The jailer, thought Slater. Or was it that deputy who had thwacked him with his pistol? Slater was right in the first instance; it was the jailer, Bill Thornton. Slater knew him, not so much as an acquaintance but as a man who had been around the county for a long time, since back in the days of the Republic. Thornton was getting up in years, having seen more than half a century of life. His age showed in his walk—slow, deliberate, a bit limpy—brought on by what most older folks called the rheumatiz, especially when they had it.

"You awake back there?" Thornton called out.

When no one else answered, Slater spoke up. "I'm awake, Mr. Thornton, if I'm the one you're asking."

"You're the only one I got, son." He pulled the key from the lock, all the keys jangling as he did, and started down the corridor toward Slater's cell. "Sheriff said to let you go when you woke up, but that Yankee colonel's downstairs wanting to keep you locked up for a while. Don't know why. You don't suppose it's got something to do with your brother now, do you?"

Slater was hesitant to answer anything about his family until he'd had the chance to speak with Malinda and Dent and heard their side of matters concerning them, the Yankees, and Glengarry; so he kept his mouth shut for the time being.

The jailer noticed that Slater was reluctant to respond to his question, so he replied, "No, I reckon you wouldn't know anything about that yet," said Thornton, answering his own question. He reached the door to Slater's cell, found the right key, inserted it in the lock, turned it, and opened the door for Slater. "Got your hat downstairs. Jess Tate brought it in for you. Put in the good word to the sheriff for you, too. That's why the sheriff says to let you go. He don't like them Detchen boys neither." Thornton's leathery face spread wide and showed a mouth with a few teeth missing. "Laughed like hell when he heard what you done to Farley. Wished he'd been there to see it." The jailer chuckled and added, "Me, too."

"What about the deputy that hit me with his pistol?" asked Slater. "Did the sheriff do anything about him?"

"Nope. Says that's up to you. Kindred ain't none too popular around here, even if he is a sheriff's deputy. Sheriff says if you want to swear out a paper on him, it's okay by him."

Slater gave the notion half a penny's thought, then said, "Let me talk to him first. What did you say his name was?"

"Kindred. Jim Kindred. Comes from up to Lyons on the county line. He was the enrolling officer around here during the war. That's why he ain't too popular. He sent a lot of good men off to die, and them what wouldn't go was hounded until they had to leave the country. Whole bunch of them lit out for Mexico last year. Ain't heard much about them since."

"You say that Yankee colonel is downstairs?"

"He was when I come up here. Of course, he could've got tired of waiting for you to come down and left. Only way to find out is to go down and see if he's still there."

Slater walked ahead of Thornton to the doorway leading downstairs. He hesitated at the top of the stairs, then went on down.

Colonel Markham was waiting patiently in the sheriff's chair. The same sergeant that Slater had met the night before stood at parade rest beside the door to the street.

"So, Slater," said Markham as soon as Slater finished descending the staircase, "you couldn't wait to cause trouble around here, could you?"

"I was defending the honor of a lady, Colonel," said Slater in his defense. "Of course, you Yankees wouldn't know much about that now, would you?"

Markham popped into a standing position, glared at Slater, and said, "Your insolent tongue will get you into a lot of trouble, Reb!" He moved around the desk and confronted Slater eye to eye. "Just what lady in these parts has enough honor that it requires defending?"

Slater gave Markham look for look and said evenly yet forcefully, "My sister, sir."

Markham flinched first. His gaze fell on the toes of his boots, then haphazardly darted from object to object within the room—the stairs, the rear door, the hat tree in the corner, the lithograph of Sam Houston on the wall—all in a matter of a flutter of his eyelids.

"Your sister, you say?" he muttered. "What has she got to do with you fighting in the streets?"

Slater looked past Markham at the sergeant, then around at Thornton. The jailer took the hint; besides, he knew the story already and he could eavesdrop through the back door if he wanted to badly enough.

"If you'll excuse me, gents," said Thornton, "I got me some business to attend to out back." With that, he was out the door.

Markham caught on, too. "Wickersham, step outside and make certain our horses are all right."

The sergeant snapped to attention, saluted, then departed as ordered.

A little calmer now, Markham stared hard at Slater and said, "Now what about Malinda?"

"It seems some folks around here think you and Malinda

shouldn't be sleeping under the same roof before the wedding,''
said Slater as delicately as he could.

"Is that what you think?" asked Markham, catching Slater's
drift.

"I haven't been home long enough to form any opinions about
much of anything, Colonel. All I know is you won't let me into
my own house—''

Markham interrupted him, saying almost apologetically, "It
isn't me, Slater. Last night, I was merely carrying out the wishes
of your brother. I am just a guest at Glengarry."

"A guest, Colonel?" paried Slater, feeling he had the upper
hand in their conversation. "A guest doesn't bivouac his troops
on the front lawn. Glengarry looks more like an armed fortress
than a plantation.''

"I felt it was the best place to set up headquarters for this
county. But never mind that. What about these lies about Malinda
and me?''

"Yes, what do you propose to do about them, Colonel?"

Markham started to speak but hesitated. He knew there was
only one correct answer, and he loathed giving it. But he had no
other choice except—

"I don't propose to do anything about them. Anyone who would
think such things about Malinda is obviously beneath my contempt. Therefore, I won't do anything about them except ignore
them.''

"Ignore them?" Slater was beside himself. "You're talking
about my sister, Colonel.''

"Correction, Slater," said Markham, regaining control of their
verbal duel. "Your former sister. When your grandfather died and
left Glengarry to Dent, he also had the foresight to legally disown
you, and Dent and Malinda were wise enough to follow his example.''

This was news Slater hadn't expected at all. He knew Dent
might get the plantation when their grandfather passed on, but he
never thought Grandpa Dougald would disown him. And Dent
and Malinda doing the same? This was too much to believe. He
scowled his defiance at Markham.

"Tell me why I don't believe you, Colonel."

"You don't have to believe me, Slater," said Markham, acting
quite the innocent. "Just go over to the courthouse and check the
records for yourself. I'm sure the county clerk will be more than
happy to supply you with the right documents.''

"I'm not that easily convinced, Colonel. Anybody can write anything on a piece of paper and call it legal. I want to hear it straight from Dent and Malinda."

"As I told you last night, your presence at Glengarry is not desired. You have no rights there, and if I catch you there, I will prosecute you for trespassing. Have I made myself clear on that point, Slater?"

"I hear you, Colonel," said Slater begrudgingly. "I don't have to go out to Glengarry to see Malinda and Dent. Hallettsville is a small place. I'll see them when they come into town."

"I don't think that would be wise, Slater. You could cause a scene that you might later regret."

"Are you forbidding me to speak with Malinda and Dent?"

"I wouldn't think of such a thing," said Markham, his tone mocking and disdainful. "No, Slater, I'm not forbidding you to talk with them. Let's just call it a word to the wise."

"Let me ask you something, Colonel."

"By all means."

"You're planning to marry Malinda, right?"

"That's correct."

"Then what? I mean, are you planning on staying here? Or are you a career officer and you're planning to take Malinda away from here when you're transferred elsewhere?"

"Actually, I hadn't given that much thought. I do like it here, and this is Malinda's home. And outside of Washington or some foreign station, the Army doesn't really offer me as much as I thought it would. Hm-m." He stroked his chin in thought. "You've raised an interesting point, Slater. I'll have to speak with Malinda and see how she feels about the matter." He paused for another thought, then said, "Why, what difference does it make to you, Slater?"

"I was just wondering how long it would be before you Yankees would be going back north, that's all."

"I wouldn't concern myself with that, if I were you, Slater. I'd be more worried about staying on the right side of the law. You've only been back here one day, and already you've spent time in jail. You're lucky Sheriff Foster decided not to accept the complaint of the man you assaulted. If I were him—"

"But you're not him, Colonel," interjected Slater in a tone that said he was just about fed up with Markham for this day.

Markham noted the irritation in Slater's voice but paid it little heed. "No, I'm not, Slater. I'm the military commander for this

county, and that gives me every right to have you arrested for
seditious acts, then lock you up and throw away the key until my
superiors say differently. Do you understand that? I can do it, you
know. But I made a bargain with the local authorities when I first
arrived here. I agreed to leave to them all matters that didn't
involve the commerce of this area and the security of the Union's
interests. Your little affray of this afternoon comes under their
jurisdiction, Slater, but I warn you here and now. Cross the line
into my jurisdiction and I'll hang you if the offense calls for it.
Do you understand me now, Slater?''

"Colonel Markham," said Slater slowly and deliberately, "during our nation's recent difficulty, I had the honor of opposing
some of the bravest men ever to do battle, and I had to kill several
of them in the defense of my country. I also came up against some
of the lowest, meanest snakes ever to put on a soldier's uniform,
and I killed a lot of them, too, because they deserved to die. I
regret having had to take the lives of brave men, but I never
hesitated to shoot down the cowardly sonofabitch who wouldn't
stand his ground and fight."

"Get to the point, Slater. I'm a busy man."

Although aggravated by the interruption, Slater nodded and
said, "You and your men are interlopers here, Colonel. This is
my state, my county. I wouldn't let you Yankees run over me
when we were at war, and I sure as hell don't intend to let you
do it now. Not in Texas." He paused for effect. "Now have I
made myself clear to you, sir?"

Eyeing his adversary keenly, Markham queried, "Are you
threatening me, Slater?"

"No, sir. Just offering a friendly piece of advice. Marry Malinda, if that's what she wants, and settle down right here in Lavaca
County, if that's what you want. But don't you ever try to tell
me how to run my life."

Markham nodded and said, "I see. So now we both know where
the other stands. But just you don't forget who has the power,
Slater, and we'll get along just fine."

"And don't you forget what I said last night, Colonel. You're
in Texas now."

10

Slater's remark about his presence at Glengarry being a source for gossip concerning Malinda's virtue disturbed Colonel Markham deeply. He certainly didn't wish to harm the love of his life in any way, including being the cause for anyone to besmirch Malinda's honor as a lady. If Slater's hinting that such profane rumors were already rife in Hallettsville was true, then he felt that he must do something to correct the situation immediately.

Markham's reason for being in town that day was routine military business. He had brought Malinda along because she wished to do some shopping. They hadn't been in town ten minutes before someone told them about Slater's run-in with the Detchens and the ensuing difficulty with Deputy Kindred that had landed Slater in the county jailhouse.

Markham said nothing about the story until he saw the worry in Malinda's eyes. "Maybe I should go over to the jailhouse and see what this is all about," he said. "You go about your shopping, my dear, and I'll catch up to you later."

They parted company: he to the courthouse to tend to Army matters before going over to the jailhouse to lecture Slater, and she to Collatinus Ballard's store on Second Street, making it her first stop of the day.

After leaving the jailhouse, Markham went about town looking for Malinda. He saw her at the door of Ballard's store, just then bidding farewell to the storekeeper's son. Odd, he thought, that's where she went when I left her. Was she in there all this time? Then noting how friendly she was being to young Coll Ballard, Markham felt a twinge of jealousy, and this devilish emotion spurred him to hurry to her side.

Seeing Markham coming her way, Malinda said a hasty good-bye and stepped into the street to meet the colonel. "I've finished my shopping, Lucas," she said. "Did you see Clete?"

"Yes, I did," said Markham absently as he glanced past Malinda at Coll, who was then disappearing into the store. He made a mental note to talk to this fellow, sound him out a bit, let him know that Malinda was his and that no interloping would be tolerated.

Malinda noticed how Markham's attention was elsewhere and realized that he was looking behind her—probably at Coll—and that he was just a bit more than curious. "How was he?" asked Malinda, trying to draw his concentration back to her.

"What, my dear?" asked Markham, trying to focus on Malinda.

"How was Clete?"

"Oh, yes, him." Disgust colored his words. "He had a bad bruise on his jaw, but he acted just the same as he did last night. If that tells you anything."

It did. Malinda was relieved to learn that her brother was all right, but she was also distressed that Markham was using such a nasty tone, meaning he and Clete hadn't been friendly with each other—again. She wondered if these two aggressive men would ever see eye to eye about anything. She really wished that they would. After all, they were soon to be family.

"Come along, my dear," said Markham, taking Malinda by the arm and leading her toward the carriage. "We should be getting along before it gets dark."

They rode back to the plantation without saying much of anything to each other. He spent the time deep in thought on what he should do about his situation with Malinda, and she centered her thinking on the future of Glengarry, wondering how Clete's return would affect the plans that she had made already. By the time they returned to the mansion, Markham had come to a clear decision on what he should do, while Malinda was more confused than before about the days ahead.

Dent was in the parlor when Markham and Malinda entered the house. He left the room to meet them in the foyer. "Well, Sister, did you see our resurrected brother in town today?" he asked rather sarcastically. He held a glass of whiskey in his hand. From the look and sound of him, Malinda figured it was his first of many for the evening.

"No, I did not," said Malinda rather sternly.

"But I did," said Markham.

"And how is the great warrior today?" asked Dent.

Markham wasn't sure whether Dent's venomous query was being aimed at his brother or at him. Slowly, he said, "He's fine, all things considered."

"All things considered?" queried Dent.

"Considering that horrible man, Jim Kindred, pistol-whipped him," said Malinda as she moved toward the parlor.

Dent was incredulous. "Pistol-whipped him?" He looked at Markham for confirmation of the news.

"That's right," said Markham, following Malinda into the living room.

Dent was morbidly excited about this news. He eagerly traipsed after Markham and demanded, "But why? I mean, why did Kindred pistol-whip Clete? Did Clete insult the little bastard or something?"

"No, nothing like that," said Malinda. She sat on the sofa.

Markham sat down beside her and quickly retold the story that they had heard in town about Clete stopping the Detchens from whipping old Tobias only to have Kindred knock him cold with his revolver and haul Clete off to jail. "I saw him just as he was being released."

"What did he have to say for himself?" asked Dent.

"Nothing much," said Markham, "except that he was concerned about my presence here at Glengarry."

"Did you tell him that it was none of his business what goes on here?" asked Dent bitterly.

"Yes, I did," said Markham, "and he argued the point with me, saying that it was his business as long as his sister was living here."

"You two talked about me?" queried Malinda. She was more than a little surprised and very concerned.

"Yes, we did, my dear." Markham cleared his throat before continuing. "Your brother pointed out that your virtue was in doubt as long as I made Glengarry my headquarters."

"That's ridiculous!" said Dent. He began pacing in front of the fireplace. "You've been a real gentleman the whole time you've been here, Lucas."

"Thank you for that, Dent," said Markham. "That means a lot coming from you."

"Yes, Lucas, you've been a perfect gentleman," said Malinda, "but why are you talking about this now?"

"Because I'm moving into town first thing tomorrow morning," said Markham, getting straight to the point.

"Moving into town?" queried Dent. "Why? Because Clete made some stupid remark about people gossiping?"

"I know why, Dent," said Malinda. "To protect my honor. Isn't that it, Lucas?"

"Yes, my dear, it is. I won't have the woman I'm going to marry made the object of every wagging tongue in the county, and the only way I can protect you is to leave Glengarry until after we're married, Malinda."

Dent stopped his pacing and turned to Markham. "That's nonsense, Lucas," he said. "You're the military commander here. You shouldn't have to worry about what these people think. You're the law, Lucas."

"That's not exactly true, Dent," said Markham. "I should worry about what these people think. In fact, I have to worry about what they think. It's my duty to keep the peace in Lavaca County. My men are here to maintain law and order and to aid the Freedman's Bureau agent. I can't do that without the support and cooperation of the local population, Negro and white."

"All right, that's your duty," said Dent, "but we're talking about your personal life here. That's no one else's business except yours. And Malinda's. Everybody else should butt out."

"That's not the way people are, Dent," said Malinda. "You know as well as I do that people are going to talk, especially about Lucas and me because he's a Northerner and I'm the sister of a Unionist."

"Malinda's right, Dent," said Markham. "People are talking, and that is enough reason for me to move into town. I need their respect as well as their cooperation, and I won't be able to get that if they think something . . . sinful is going on here."

Dent knew Markham was right, but that wasn't what he wanted to hear. His face grew red with anger and his voice went up a notch in volume and pitch. "That's a lot of bullshit," he said, "and you know it, Lucas. You don't give a damn about the people of this county!" He became louder as his vocal cords reached for a higher octave. "Your only concern is for yourself, and to hell with everyone else. To hell with Malinda. To hell with me. All you care about is yourself." His eyes filled with hurt as well as fury as he screamed, "Well, to hell with you, Lucas Markham." He threw his glass of whiskey into the fireplace, smashing it to bits, then stormed out of the room.

Markham looked at Malinda, not knowing what to think, but saying, "What brought that on?"

"I don't know, Lucas." Malinda stood up and thought to follow her brother, to find him and try to reason with him, but she knew it would do no good. He was already feeling the effects of his alcohol, and soon he would be absolutely drunk and beyond any sort of comprehension. Besides that, he was probably headed down back to Hannah.

That was exactly where Dent had gone. To Hannah. The only person that he felt cared enough about him to understand him. She was working in the kitchen, cutting bread, and as he passed through the room, he grabbed her by the arm and said, "Let's go, girl. I need you. I need you now."

Instantly upset by his violent action, Hannah pulled herself free and said, "Not yet, Dent. I've got to serve supper first."

"Let Josephine do it!" snapped Dent. "We're going down back, and we're going now." He reached for her again, but she eluded him. Seeing the fire in her eyes, he realized that this wasn't the way to treat the woman he loved. "Please," he said much softer. "I need you, Hannah."

Hannah weakened. She turned to Josephine, who was pretending not to be watching and listening. "Do you mind, Josephine?" she asked.

Without looking at Hannah, Josephine replied, "Go on, child. Go on and give the massuh his jelly roll and be done with it."

That hurt. Josephine hadn't used the exact words, but she implied them. Her tone said them. Go on and be massuh's nigger whore. Go on and disgrace yourself, your mother, your family, your people. Go on, bitch. Lay down and give massuh what he wants. God, that hurt, but as much as Hannah wanted to reveal her secret to Josephine, she knew she couldn't. Instead of saying anything, she took Dent's hand and led him through the back door and down to her cabin, their cabin, where he would get drunk and tell her everything that he couldn't or wouldn't tell Malinda or Markham.

11

A school teacher once compared Harlan and Farley Detchen with Remus and Romulus, the legendary founders of ancient Rome. Not that he expected great things from the pair. As the instructor put it, "They were a couple of whelps raised by a bitch."

Of course, Sophia Campbell wasn't born that way. She came from a good family, the salt of the earth, the Foleys from Lauderdale County, Alabama. She was the youngest of seven children, and as such, she was spoiled. She had been but a ten-year-old child when the Foleys left their prosperous plantation. Like most children being uprooted for the first time in their lives, she resented leaving her friends and the growing social station at which the older Foleys seemed ill-at-ease, and she further complained about being carried off to the frontier of Texas to cut a new home out of a wilderness that was fraught with life and death danger from savage Indians who carried little girls off with them and made them slaves and squaws for filthy warriors who tortured their women into subservience. She vowed that she would escape the white trash way of living that her father imposed on her as soon as the opportunity to do so presented itself.

Washington Green Lee Foley came to Lavaca County in 1838 with his wife, Sarah, daughter, Sophia, and sons, Mason, Stewart, and James. Two older sons, Arthur and Tucker, had arrived in Texas five years earlier and had served in the Texan army during the Revolution. Arthur was one of those massacred by the Mexican army at Goliad in 1836; and Tucker, long after having avenged Arthur at San Jacinto, was caught, tortured, murdered, and scalped by Comanches along Ponton's Creek in 1840. The youngest brother, James, was a Ranger who was killed and mutilated by Mexicans—his corpse was found with his genitals stuffed in his mouth—while on a "greaser hunt" to Southwest Texas in '39.

Upon Tucker's death, Wash Foley, also known as Ol' Foley, took charge of the 466 acres that Tucker had been granted for his

military service. The old man—he was already sixty years old—
was granted a headright of land for himself in 1841, and he purchased several other parcels of land until he owned an aggregate
of more than twelve thousand acres that, with the labor of several
dozen slaves, he worked into the richest plantation in the county.

In spite of her father's new wealth, Sophia continued to show
her displeasure at being forced to live a life that wasn't much
better than that of their slaves. When Dr. John Campbell came
along in 1843 and offered Sophia the out that she desired so
desperately, she ran off with him to Columbus and got married.
She was then fourteen, and he was thirty-eight.

Having his daughter nearly stolen from him by a man almost
three times her age riled Ol' Foley to the point that he forbade
either of them to set foot on his property ever again. He accused
Campbell of being a fortune hunter and an adventurer who was
hoping to help himself to Foley's money. The old man had completely opposite thoughts. Instead of staying in the county, the
newlyweds moved to Goliad, where Campbell set up a practice
and ran a drugstore.

Although he was a very wealthy man, Foley lived like a miser,
wearing a hat plaited out of corn husks, clothes made of homespun
cotton, and shoes of rawhide fashioned in his own blacksmith
shop. Whenever he went to town, he ate an extra rasher of bacon
for breakfast and carried corn pone to eat until he could return to
his own table to dine on his own produce.

Despite his reputation for frugality, Wash Foley wasn't totally
selfish. In fact, he was downright generous with his older daughter,
Betsy, and her husband, John Woods, a widely known and respected educator in Alabama. When they came to Texas in 1852,
John, Betsy, and their six children settled near Ol' Foley's plantation and John became one of Foley's most trusted advisers. Foley
paid Woods handsomely for his work, and he supplemented his
son-in-law's efforts at being a planter with interest-free loans and
the labor of his own slaves. He even went so far as to gift a family
of slaves to Woods.

However, the old man's philanthropy wasn't directed elsewhere, and this rankled his other children.

Foley's son, Mason, built up his own plantation just north of
his father's, between Mixon Creek and the west bank of the Navidad River. Just south of the old man's place was the land of
another Foley son, Stewart. When Mason died suddenly in 1858
without issue and without a wife, Stewart claimed that his brother

had left an estate of almost ten thousand acres to him, giving Stewart two large tracts that were separated by their father's property.

Ol' Foley didn't mind Stewart's claim to Mason's plantation until Sophia and John Campbell brought their brood of brats to live in Mason's old house. Vowing that Campbell would never own a single square foot of Foley land, the old man filed suit in the county court to gain ownership of Mason's plantation, stating that the gift deed that Stewart claimed as Mason's will was a forgery. Before the issue could be settled, Stewart died and left his property, including his claim to Mason's estate, to their sister, Sophia Campbell.

Upon inheriting Stewart's holdings, Sophia continued the legal fight for Mason's plantation that Stewart had begun. In the meantime, she and John Campbell tried to operate their massive acreage. Neither proved very capable of managing the property, and gradually, it declined in size and quality. The causes for this leprous descent in their fortune were the tax burdens placed on the larger planters by the Confederacy and an inordinate amount of attorney fees. And, of course, John died in 1864, leaving Sophia all alone to handle the plantation.

Besides the court quarrel with her father over Mason's estate, Sophia had a propensity for legal disputes, nearly all of which were brought on by her reprehensible business conduct. She hired overseers to help run her plantations, contracting with them for their services but seldom fulfilling more than the bare essentials of the agreements, which led these men to sue for their just due in court. Sophia also treated storekeepers in much the same manner by running large credit balances, then refusing to pay them until forced to do so by the county sheriff.

As if Sophia couldn't get herself into enough trouble, her foster sons, Harlan and Farley Detchen, were frequently in need of a lawyer to extricate them from their problems, and the man who usually did the extricating was A. P. Bagby, attorney-at-law.

Besides slugging Slater and having him hauled off to jail, Deputy Kindred arrested the Detchens for disturbing the peace and held them in the county jailhouse until Bagby received word that his services were needed again. The lawyer found Judge Lemond and asked him to have the brothers brought before the bench as soon as possible. His honor was amenable to Bagby's request, and he sent word to the sheriff's office to have the Detchens brought before him immediately. Kindred complied to the order posthaste. Bagby recited some legal mumbo jumbo, and Lemond responded by releasing the Detchens with a gentle warning to leave the darkies alone now that the Yankees were running things in Lavaca County.

Harlan and Farley left town that afternoon without even thanking Bagby for getting them off so quickly. They rode home casually and reported to their foster mother, who was sitting in a rocker on the porch of the house that her brother Stewart built. Standing behind her was her natural son, seventeen-year-old Stewart, whom she had named for her late brother.

"I heard you boys got yourselves in some trouble in town again," said Sophia, practically challenging them to deny it.

Farley glared at Stewart but said nothing. Little bastard told on us, he thought.

"Clete Slater is back," said Harlan, ignoring Stewart.

"I see," said Sophia, looking from one brother to the other and back again. "Well, that explains that. What happened? Did he whip your asses for you like he did when you was kids?"

They both blushed and hung their heads. Farley peeked up and said, "He had help this time."

"Since when did Clete Slater need help to whip the two of you?" asked Sophia sarcastically.

"That's right, Ma," said Harlan eagerly. "Jess Tate was with him."

Sophia felt her sensibilities being stretched, and she let them know it, screeching angrily, "Jess Tate? That string bean? He helped Clete Slater whip your asses? You're lying to me! I won't take that from the two of you. Why, I'll whip your asses myself, if I have to, to get the truth out of you."

"It's true, Ma," said Farley, his face full of fear as he backed away from Sophia an inch at a time. "Tate helped him. He did, Ma. I swear."

"Me, too, Ma!" said Harlan, looking just as scared as his twin and also edging away from Sophia.

Sophia looked them over carefully and concluded that they were telling the truth as far as they believed it to be the truth. It made no difference, though. Not now, anyway. She had a bigger reason for being angry with them. "What the hell were you two doing in town in the first place?" she demanded. "I thought I told you this morning that I wanted you to ride down to the river and hunt up some of our stock and drive it back here by sundown. Didn't I tell you two to do that?"

"Well, sure, Ma," said Farley, "but we thought we'd go into town and get a couple of the boys to give us hand."

Sophia leaned forward and said, "Who the hell told you to do that? I know it sure as hell wasn't me. So who was it? Stewart? Tucker? Lizzie?" When they hesitated to answer, she jumped up and screamed, "Answer me! Who told you to go to town and get help?"

"No one, Ma," said Farley, his voice dry and a bit shaky.

Sophia reached out and slapped Harlan across the mouth. This was a trick she'd learned long ago and hadn't used for a few years. Slap the one who ain't looking, and the other one will pay better attention.

"It was Farley's idea," said Harlan, whimpering but not touching his cheek. He knew if he made any kind of move to rub away the pain that Sophia would whack him again.

"And you went along with him, didn't you?" snapped Sophia at Harlan. In the next breath, her other hand struck like a rattler and caught Farley flat on the ear.

"Yeow!" he screamed in pain and fell backward off the porch. He was out of range now, so he rubbed his wounded member and complained, "We don't need those cows from down to the river bottom, Ma. We got plenty right around here we can hunt up and drive into the pens."

Sophia moved down the steps after Farley, who raised his arms in front of him to fend off the blows she delivered while screaming, "That ain't your decision to make, Farley Detchen! I run this plantation, and you do as you're told or you can set your ass down to someone else's table from now on. You hear me, boy? You understand me?" She slugged him as hard as she could in the ribs with the back of her fist.

"Yes, ma'am!" shouted Farley. "Yes, ma'am, I understand! Yes, ma'am, I do! Yes, ma'am!"

"See that you do, boy!" She turned and headed back up the steps toward Harlan.

"I understand, too, Ma," he whined, sure that she was about to lay the same punishment on him. "I do, I swear."

Sophia marched right past him to the door, where she stopped, turned, and glared at Stewart, who was grinning ear to ear at his natural cousins and foster brothers, glad that it was they and not he who were getting a whupping. "What the hell are you so happy about?" she screeched, and without warning, she swung her hand at him, catching him on the back of the head and snapping it forward meanly. "You ain't no better than they are, running off to town with them!" She kicked the back of his left calf, buckling the leg and causing him to lose his balance and drop to one knee. "I ought to take my shotgun to the lot of you and be done with it once and for all!" She gave him a backhand up side the head for good measure, sprawling him on the porch. Satisfied that she'd made her point, she went inside the house and flopped down in her favorite chair to contemplate some of the problems facing her.

On the day the Yankees marched into the county, all of Sophia's slaves ran off, leaving her completely without the labor she needed to run her huge plantation and her household. Sophia and her children hadn't worked a day in their lives, including the time when they lived in Goliad, and suddenly, they had to fend for themselves. Fortunately, they had an abundance of stock roaming wild on the place, so they weren't about to go hungry. Even so, they had crops to get planted and a million other chores to do and no one around to do them. What were they going to do?

Before Sophia could start feeling sorry for herself, Stewart, Harlan, and Farley came into the house, looking sullen and sorry. She gave them half a glance and was reminded that Harlan and Farley had been whipped by Clete Slater that afternoon and that got her to thinking about Slater, about how his return must have been a real surprise for his brother and sister and that Yankee colonel who was over to Glengarry getting all the sugar he wanted from that miss-prissy Malinda Slater. Goddamn them Slaters anyway, she swore to herself. It'd sure serve them right if Clete was to sue his brother for his rightful share of Glengarry and put them in the same fix as me. Goddamn Slaters. Always so high and mighty. Bunch of do-gooders and Yankee-lovers is all they are. Even that Clete. She smiled to herself and thought, I'd sure like to see their pot go to boiling over and burning every one of them. It'd serve them all just right. Her smile widened as another thought struck her. Just maybe I might be able to stir that pot a little for them. Make me a little Slater stew for the whole county to have a good time with. Who knows? Why, sure. Slater stew.

Sophia began to laugh aloud. Just a chuckle at first, then more to cackling until she was guffawing out of control.

Stewart and the twins stopped, stared at Sophia, then looked at each other quizzically, all three wondering what the hell was going on in their mother's mind. Evil, they hoped.

12

A gulf breeze skittered through Hallettsville, cooling down the air considerably and announcing the setting of the sun. That was all right with Slater. He'd had a long and stressful day, and he was dog tired from it. Part of him wanted to go over to Lindenberg's saloon and drink himself into forgetting the worst of things, but the majority of his being told him to stay put in his hotel room bed and get some much needed rest. Majority ruled. He would lie there and recount only those events of the day which had pleased him.

After Markham left Slater at the jailhouse, Jess Tate entered the sheriff's office and Bill Thornton returned from out back.

"You sure told him a thing or two," said Thornton with all the enthusiasm of a spectator at a cockfight. "Made me proud to be a Texan. Can't stand that uppity little Yankee bastard no how. Wish I'd said those things to him."

"What happened, Clete?" asked Tate.

"I'll tell you what happened," said Thornton as if it were his duty to speak for Slater. "He told that Bluebelly colonel just where he stood with folks around here. That's what he did. Told him right good, too."

"Is that right, Clete?" asked Tate with all the excitement of a schoolboy hearing about another boy's first tryst with the girl who has the worst reputation in town.

"Of course, that's right!" snapped Thornton. "I wouldn't say such a thing if it weren't so."

Slater ignored both of them. His attention was elsewhere, being drawn through the window to the street outside, where Colonel Markham was talking to the driver of a phaeton: a young woman with flaxen hair falling to her shoulders, pavonine eyes, and tawny complexion, wearing a simple safflower cotton dress, white gloves, and a straw sunbonnet with plum-colored satin ribbon wrapped around the crown and hanging down over the back rim.

Slater couldn't hear what she was saying to Markham, but from her stolid expression, he knew it wasn't exactly friendly. She looked familiar to him, but he couldn't quite tie a name to her face. There was something else about her; something mysterious, haunting, distant but just over the horizon. He felt as if he should know everything about her and did but couldn't recall it at that particular moment. Her mere appearance intrigued him, making him want to be alone with her just to get to know her.

"Well, what are you planning to do now, Clete?" asked Tate. He looked expectantly at Slater, but when his friend didn't answer him immediately, a frown turned down the corners of his mouth. Then he noticed that Slater wasn't listening to him but was looking outside. His gaze naturally followed Slater's through the window, and a puzzled look furrowed his brow as he said, "What's she doing talking to him?"

"Confounds me, too," said Thornton. "She hated them Yankees more than anyone around here ever since . . . since . . ." He took hold of his chin and looked into thin air as if the answer were written on the ceiling. "Hm-m. Now when was that?"

"Who is she?" asked Slater. He mouthed the words softly, almost as if by accident, unintentionally. His eyes were glassed over; his thoughts racing to his favorite place, an idyllic meadow in a bend of the Navidad, with him and the girl lying on a blanket under a tree whispering words of tenderness so that even the angels couldn't hear them. A flush came to his face as his heart beat to the rhythm of a new drummer. He hadn't felt like this since his school days, when he first saw Lucy May.

"Don't you know who that is?" chortled Tate, sounding a bit like a hound chewing on a haunch of beef.

Slater couldn't reply with more than a slight shake of his head as he refused to take his eyes from her.

Tate smiled like the proverbial Cheshire cat and said, "Do the words, 'Wait'll my granny hears about this!' mean anything to you?"

They did.

Slater was jerked back to reality by the recollections that those words stirred in his mind.

Jess and Clete were two healthy lads just entering their pubescence, and it was a hot day, hotter than usual for mid-July. The waters of the Lavaca looked so cool and inviting; it was as if Jess and Clete had no choice but to strip off every stitch of clothing and jump in the river for a lifesaving swim. They were already shed of their long johns before they discovered they were being watched from the shadowy bushes. After an exchange of knowing winks, they grabbed the spy and in the same motion threw the culprit into the river. They began roaring out their laughter with the first splash, and they kept it up when their victim surfaced and began hollering to beat the band, "Wait'll my granny hears about this! Wait'll my granny hears about this!" Jess was the first to recognize the voice as belonging to Texada Ballard, Hallettsville's definition of mischief who was also the granddaughter of the town's founder and the niece of Collatinus Ballard, the town's most influential citizen. Jess stopped laughing right then, but Clete kept on—for a moment—until he came to the realization that ten-year-old Texada was no longer exercising her lungs. There they were, two thirteen-year-old boys, naked as jaybirds, being gawked at by the town brat.

The memory of the embarrassment of that moment sent a shiver down Slater's spine. A vision of a scrawny little girl with pigtails and freckles dressed in the clothes of a field hand from head to toe stumbled across his brain. He felt another shiver.

Anyone else, he thought, she could have been anyone else, anyone except Texada Ballard. Why did she have to be Texada? Why couldn't she have been Lucy May's little sister Marcella or even Tate's cousin Ruth? Maybe Marcella May wasn't as pretty as Lucy and maybe Ruth Tate was always a bit on the skinny side with slightly bucked teeth, but that was when they were kids. Either one of them could have blossomed into a lovely, desirable woman because both of them had always been beautiful inside, in their hearts. Why did this pretty young thing have to be Texada Ballard?

But just possibly Jess was wrong about the identity of this beautiful girl outside the jailhouse, thought Slater. "Are you sure?" he asked.

"That's Texada all right," said Tate. "Ain't that her, Mr. Thornton?"

"I hate to say it, Clete," said Thornton, "but he's right about that. That girl is none other than Texada Ballard."

Slater looked nervously around the room. "Where's my hat?" he asked. Before Thornton could answer him, he saw it hanging on the hat tree in the corner. He took three giant steps toward it, snatched it from its hook, and donned it as he made his way to the rear door.

"Hold on, son," said Thornton. "I got some other things of

yours here in the desk." He walked over to the sheriff's desk, pulled open a drawer, and started removing a few items. "You'll be wanting your money and this, of course." He held up Slater's parole paper. "You wouldn't want that Yankee colonel catching you without it now, would you?"

Slater stepped quickly back to the desk to retrieve his property, taking a quick glance out the window as he did.

"She's coming in," said Tate.

"Make sure it's all there," said Thornton as he handed Slater a short stack of coins.

"I trust you, Mr. Thornton," said Slater as he pocketed the silver in his trousers and slipped the parole inside his coat. He turned to go a second time but bumped into Tate.

"What's your hurry, Clete?" asked his friend.

"Never mind that now," said Slater. "Let's just get out of here."

He was too late. Texada came through the front door just as he reached for the handle to the rear exit.

"Good afternoon, Mr. Thornton," said Texada to the jailer, although she was looking elsewhere, specifically in Slater's direction. "Why, if it isn't Clete Slater," she said coyly. "Home from the war."

Slater stopped, rolled his eyes heavenward, and heaved a sigh of resignation. Then he turned around, removed his hat, and said sort of sheepishly, "Good afternoon, Texada."

"Texada," said Tate, also doffing his hat.

"This is a pleasant surprise," said Texada, ignoring Tate's greeting. "We'd heard you were killed at Shiloh back in '62."

"I already told him that," said Tate.

Texada ignored Tate again and walked over to Slater. "It's nice to see you back home and in one piece." She whisked a bit of lint from the lapel of his coat with her right hand. "Such a handsome suit, Clete, but it could stand a brushing and a little mending. Why don't you let me take you over to Mrs. Rice's tailoring shop and have her sew that up for you? We can have a nice talk while she's doing the mending."

Slater wasn't sure how to answer her; this Texada—unlike the one he knew before the war—had him confused. She was prettier close up, and her voice was so soft and charming; it was nothing like the spine-tingling screech he remembered from his youth. And she smelled nice, too. What to do?

"Why, thank you for the offer, Texada," said Slater, his pitch

a level higher than normal, "but Jess here already said he'd take
it over to Mrs. Rice for me."

Tate was quick to take a cue. "That's right, Texada, I did. I
said to Clete, 'I'd be—'"

Texada interrupted him by saying, "Is that why you were
headed out the back door when I came in? Why, there's nothing
back there but the outhouse." She moved to Slater's side and slid
her arm around his. "You just come with me, Clete Slater, and
we'll get you all fixed up."

Slater felt powerless, impelled to go with Texada, as if he were
so much chaff in her hurricane. He had his hat on and was walking
toward the door before he realized he was in motion.

"What about me?" asked Tate.

"I'm sorry, Jess," said Texada, "but my carriage only has
room for two."

At the door, Slater turned back to his friend and said, "I'll see
you later, Jess. At the hotel. Wait for me."

"Sure thing, Clete."

Slater opened the door for Texada, then followed her out to the
phaeton. He helped her into the seat; not that she needed any
assistance, but it seemed like the thing to do. Then he climbed
into the seat beside her and took the reins.

"Does Mrs. Rice still live on First Street?" asked Slater.

"Yes, she does," said Texada.

Slater rippled the reins over the chestnut gelding's back, and
the phaeton lurched forward. He guided the carriage around the
corner and up First Street for the three blocks to the Rice house
between Main and LaGrange, where Slater tied the horse to the
hitching post out front before helping Texada from the buggy.

"Thank you, Clete," said Texada. "You are such a gentleman
these days."

Slater stopped and took a hard look at Texada, wondering what
she was implying by that remark. Of course, she was right; he
wasn't always well-mannered, especially when it came to her.

The day Texada saw Clete and Jess in their birthday suits on
the banks of the Lavaca wasn't the first time she met young Slater.
Texada unwillingly attended classes at Alma Institute in Hallettsville along with Malinda Slater, who boarded at the school during
the week and went home for weekends. Delivering Malinda to
school every Monday morning and picking her up every Friday
afternoon was her older brother Clete, who got his schooling closer
to home. The first time Texada saw Clete leaving Malinda off in

front of the Institute she was duly impressed by the manly way he handled a buckboard, although he was only twelve. From that moment forward, she began shadowing him whenever she could, much to Clete's annoyance. When the other boys began teasing him about being the object of Texada's attentions, he decided it was time to do something about her. He enlisted Jess Tate's help, and the two of them began playing mostly harmless pranks on Texada. The most memorable of these—and the one that got him into the most trouble—was when he and Jess set a snare trap with a branch of a cottonwood along the Lavaca, caught her by the ankle, and left her suspended over the river screaming for her granny.

No, Slater hadn't always been so well-mannered toward Texada. Of course, Texada hadn't always been so ladylike with him either.

After the incident with the snare trap, Texada sought revenge on those two louts. She thought on how she would go about getting even with them for the better part of a year before coming up with the perfect scheme. Texada didn't care much for dresses and other girl things, usually attiring herself in her cousin Coll's hand-me-downs when not attending school or church or the formal functions that accompanied those two institutions. But just once she decided to pretty herself up with a dress and other such feminine essentials in the middle of a week, on a day when there was no school and she knew for sure that Clete was coming to town. Just as he would be several years later, young Slater was caught off guard by this metamorphosis in the vivacious Miss Ballard. He unwittingly allowed himself to be led around town by her most of the afternoon, even to the point of taking her to her uncle's drugstore and buying her a penny sweet drink. From there, they wandered down to the levee to watch the slaves unload the river barges. It was here that Texada exacted her price from Clete. As they sat side by side on a rail of the landing boardwalk, she secretly reached behind him and carefully hooked a line that she had previously concealed there to the junction of his suspenders. The next time the loading boom swung out over the river Clete was snatched up from his perch and sent sailing over the water. The unexpected flight put the fear of God in him—for a few seconds—until he saw Texada laughing uncontrollably and pointing at him. He started to swear at her, but the sound of cloth tearing held his tongue. He frantically tried to grab the line but couldn't reach it. His struggle only hastened the dreaded moment when his pants ripped through and he fell, flailing the air all the way, into the river.

Texada had gotten her revenge that day, and the memory of that incident shook Slater as he wondered whether she wasn't up to her old tricks again. He cast a suspicious eye on her as he followed her up the walkway to the little shop at the front of the house. He opened the door, ringing a little bell over it as they entered.

Matronly Mrs. Rice came through a doorway opposite the entrance and welcomed them, although from the quizzical expression on her face, it was plain that she didn't recognize Slater.

"Mrs. Rice, you remember Clete Slater?" said Texada. "He's come back to us from the war."

"Clete Slater," said Mrs. Rice, totally surprised by his identity. "Why, you've become such a man since I last saw you. Now when was that? Before the war, I suspect. My-my, that's been such a long time, hasn't it?"

"Clete had a slight mishap this afternoon, Mrs. Rice," said Texada, getting down to business, "and he tore his coat. Would you have time to mend it right away and possibly give it a good brushing, too?"

"Yes, of course," said Mrs. Rice. She moved behind Slater in order to help him remove the garment. "You just take it off and give it to me, and I'll have it ready for you in a jiffy. You two can have a seat, and I'll be back in just a few minutes." She took the coat, then reached for his hat. "Looks like this could stand a little brushing, too." Then she turned and left them.

Texada sat down on the short sofa and patted the seat beside her. "Come and sit, Clete."

Slater could stand it no longer; he had to find out whether Texada was up to something or not. He remained standing, staring down at her.

"All right, Texada," he said impatiently, "what sort of mischief are you planning here?"

"Why, whatever do you mean?" she asked so innocently as she removed her gloves.

Slater felt a touch of anger boiling within him; it flushed his face. "You know exactly what I mean, Texada Ballard. Just what are you trying to do?"

"Why, get your coat fixed and cleaned, silly."

"Oh, no, you're not. You're up to something, Texada, and I know it."

Texada said nothing in reply. She merely gazed up at Slater, and as she did, the mask over her emotions slowly dissolved, her eyes revealing what was truly in her heart.

The sudden change in her confounded Slater. He flinched, taken aback by her new aspect. His point of focus flitted around the room, anywhere to avoid looking into her eyes and seeing what he feared most. But try as he might to escape the inevitable, he finally surrendered to those twin magnets so beautifully iridescent in their hue.

"Please, Clete," she said, her voice different now, lower, softer, warmer, and more genuine, "come sit beside me."

Something was in her tone—a plea, perhaps—that said he would be the cad if he failed to grant her wish. Still, he was reluctant, hesitant, to comply. With stuttering steps, he moved toward the sofa, keeping a watchful eye out for any sort of trickery. Seeing none, he sat down at a three-quarter angle in order to face her as best as he could.

A smile of inner knowledge sweetened Texada's face as she reached her right hand to Slater's cheek. He leaned away from her touch at first, then let her have her way.

"I think I know what's going through your mind, Clete," she said in that same gentle tone, "but let me assure you that I mean you no ill."

"Then what . . . what are you up to, Texada?"

She withdrew her hand and was pensive for a few seconds before answering. "Clete, would you think me too forward if I were to say that I am the happiest person to live and breathe since I heard that you had come home?"

Slater was more perplexed than ever. "I'm not quite sure I'm following you, Texada."

"Like I said over at the jailhouse, word came that you'd been killed at Shiloh back in '62. Ever since then, I thought you were dead, and now to find out that you aren't, that you're alive and all in one piece . . ." Her voice drifted off, and tears welled up in her eyes, making them shine all the more. "Well, I'm just so happy you're home." And she touched his face again.

Their eyes met.

Her hand felt cool and soothing and warm and gentle—all at the same time. Slater hadn't known a caress like that since he was sick as a child and his mother had placed her hand on his cheek in much the same manner to reassure him that all would be well with him soon. He had accepted his mother's love without question, without doubt. But now, with Texada, from Texada, love? He was a man, not an ailing little boy. Was love her motive? He couldn't tell; he was more confused than ever, and it wracked him inside. On the one hand, there was something urgent, something driving him to return the gesture, to reciprocate the feelings she was stirring within him. On the other, a frantic voice from the deepest recesses of his soul echoed a warning against revealing his heart's desire, telling him to turn away.

He sat motionless.

Texada had thrown the dice, and they had come up—? She couldn't tell through her blurry vision. She started to withdraw her hand, certain she had made a serious mistake, had misread Slater, had failed to convey her feelings correctly, to let him know how she felt for him.

When she broke the connection between them, Slater felt a loss, a great chasm opening between them. It frightened him for just an instant; no longer than it took him to reach up and catch her hand in his. The bond returned. The warmth, the glow, the aura of love enveloped them. Slater couldn't recall ever having felt such joy, such euphoria. He felt himself being drawn toward Texada, toward her lips, toward her—

"There we are," said Mrs. Rice, returning through the same doorway. "All nicely mended and clean as can be."

The moment was lost.

Slater nearly leaped to his feet as if he had to escape detection for some minor infraction of the rules of polite society. He looked nervous, guilty, felt like running but held his ground. He didn't realize at first that he was still holding Texada's hand. Once he did, he pulled on it slightly, bringing her to her feet, then squeezed it ever so gently before releasing it. His view slipped to his feet.

Texada let her fingers trace over the palm of his hand and down his fingers before reluctantly accepting the break. An excitement swept through her. Was it love? His love? Oh, yes, yes, yes! said the thrill coursing through her soul, wishing to be set free to tell the whole world. But she must contain herself. After all, she was a lady. Or at least she had been since early that afternoon when she learned Slater was back.

"How much do I owe you, Mrs. Rice?" asked Slater, digging into the coin pocket of his trousers.

The mention of money seemed to agitate Mrs. Rice. Unsure of how to respond, she said, "A dime?" She held out his coat and hat to him.

"Ten cents is much too small a price for such a job well done," said Slater, the jubilance of the moment gaining the upper hand on his emotions. "I would say this work is worth at least two bits." He dug out a quarter and gave it to the tailor, taking his hat so she could accept the silver.

"Why, that's real generous of you, Clete," said Mrs. Rice. "Thank you so very much." She deposited the coin in an apron pocket, then held the coat for Slater to get into it.

Slater handed his hat to Texada, then slipped into the coat. He took his hat back from Texada, then turned back to Mrs. Rice.

"Thank you, ma'am," said Slater.

"Yes, thank you, Mrs. Rice," said Texada.

"It's so good to see you home again, Clete," said Mrs. Rice. She looked at Texada and added, "I hope we'll be seeing you at Sunday meeting soon."

"Don't you worry none, Mrs. Rice," said Texada. "I'll see that he get's there all right."

"Well, we'd best be going now," said Slater. He took his hat from Texada, then gave Mrs. Rice a nod of a bow before bidding her adieu.

Texada said her farewell, and the two of them left the shop, the doorbell jingling merrily in their wake. With Texada holding onto Slater's arm, they hurried down the walk to the buggy. Forgetting that Texada had once been able to whip any boy her size in a fair fight, Slater helped her into the seat, then jumped in beside her.

"Where to now?" he asked.

"I know where I'd like to go," she said with a slight touch of both disappointment and mischief in her voice, "but I promised Granny I'd bring you home for supper."

Back to reality. Slater knew what she meant. A command performance in front of Hallettsville's most regal lady.

13

It was around the time of Texada's birth that Mrs. Hallet donated land for the town that would bear her family's name and become the county seat. Already, most folks in the area held Mrs. Hallet in high esteem, but with the passing of time and with an increase in the family fortune, due mostly to the efforts of her son-in-law, Collatinus Ballard, legends began to grow around the grand old lady of the Lavaca until it was thought that a visit with her was near to being unattainable, and when an audience was granted it was at her request only. By the time the War Between the States came, Mrs. Hallet was the closest thing to royalty in southern Texas.

It was with this knowledge that Slater accompanied Texada to the Hallet home on the north edge of Hallettsville.

Texada's announcement that she had promised her grandmother that she would bring him home for supper took all the romance out of Slater but not Texada. As he drove the phaeton, she held onto his arm with both hands, as if she were afraid he might fly away at any second. Slater was grateful that she was too caught up in her feelings to talk; he was too concerned about eating at the same table with Mrs. Hallet to take part in any idle conversation.

Young Coll Ballard was a year older than Texada, an inch or so on the tall side, lean, a bit homely, with brown eyes and hair; he was clean and neat at all times, with a touch of sissy in him. Although they were natural cousins, he thought of Texada as a younger sister but treated her like a younger brother.

Coll was sitting on the front porch of the white clapboard house when Slater and Texada drove up. He jumped to his feet, skipped down the three steps to the walkway, then dashed down the path that led to the gate in the whitewashed picket fence. As Slater halted the phaeton at the hitching post, Coll came through the gate to greet them.

"Hey, Clete," said Coll with a big grin, "how are you doing? We heard about what you did to Farley Detchen this afternoon over to Lindenberg's. Wish I'd seen that. Whoo-wee! That must've been something!"

Slater didn't have the same enthusiasm for the incident that Coll had. In an even voice, he said, "How are you doing, Coll?"

"I'm doing okay. But how about you? You okay? We heard you had a run-in with Jim Kindred after you whupped Farley. Heard he pistol-whipped you or something."

Slater felt his jaw; more than a little sting was still in it. "Yeah, you might say that," he said.

"You going after him for it?" asked Coll.

"What kind of fool question is that to ask, Coll Ballard?" demanded Texada, suddenly forgetting she was supposed to be a lady now. "Of course, he's going after Kindred."

Ignoring Texada's reply, Slater said, "No, I'm not going to bother him for it. Not this time anyway."

"You're going to let him get away with it?" queried Texada, surprised by his attitude.

"The man was wearing a badge," said Slater.

"That don't give him the right to go around beating on people," said Texada. "Badge or no badge, he needs putting in his place for what he done to you."

"She's right, Clete," said Coll. "Jim Kindred ain't exactly popular around here. He was the county enrolling officer during the war, you know."

"Enrolling officer?" asked Slater. "What's that?"

Slater and Texada alighted from the buggy, and as the three of them led the horse and carriage around the house to the barn in back, Coll explained about Kindred and his position as county enrolling officer. By the time they reached the house after putting the rig and gelding in their proper places, Slater knew everything he'd ever want to know about Kindred and what went on in Lavaca county while he was off to war.

The trio passed through the kitchen and dining room to the parlor where Mrs. Hallet sat on what some folks called her throne, an old rocking chair upholstered in silver brocade with little blue and red flowers accented by yellow and green stems and leaves. Although she had lived seventy-six years, the great lady hardly looked her age. Her gray-streaked deep-brunette hair was tied in a bun with a green velvet ribbon that matched her full-skirt dress accented with white collar and cuffs. She had eyes the color of black walnuts, and her skin had neither pallor nor a web of wrinkles but possessed the soft, pink aspect of youth. As a sign of her good health and vitality, she still had all of her teeth.

"Welcome to my home, Cletus Slater," said Mrs. Hallet, her voice strong and firm. She held out her right hand to him.

Slater suddenly recalled all the good Southern manners his mother tried to teach him when he was young. Having already removed his hat when they entered the house, he took her hand, bowed from the waist, and brushed the middle and ring fingers with a polite kiss. He straightened up and said, "I am honored to be a guest in your house, Mrs. Hallet." Then he released her hand.

"Well," she said with a pleased smile, "I'm glad to see you haven't forgotten where you come from." She tilted her head to one side and looked him over. "A little taller, a little thinner, a lot older, and"—shifting her view to Texada—"a lot handsomer than before you went off to fight the Yankees."

Slater blushed and said, "Thank you, ma'am. Might I say that you're looking fit as ever?"

"You may," she said. "Even if it isn't true, a lady still likes to hear such things, especially when she's old and broken down."

"You're hardly broken down, Granny," said Texada.

"But I am old. Is that what you're trying to tell me, child?"

"No, ma'am."

"It makes no difference anyway," said Mrs. Hallet. "Getting old is only a fact of life. You come into this world kicking and screaming, and if you're worth your salt, you go out the same way. Am I right, Cletus?"

"I guess so, ma'am," muttered Slater.

"You guess so? Hell's bells, boy—"

"Granny!" interjected Coll, shocked by his grandmother's usage of even such a mild epithet.

"—if you don't know that I'm right," said Mrs. Hallet, ignoring Coll's interruption, "then maybe I misjudged you." She leaned forward, squinted one eye, and bore the other into his soul. "I thought your name was Slater, not Milquetoast."

Slater knew exactly what she meant by that verbal slap at his ego. He stiffened and—grand old lady of the county or not—glared back at her with as good as he got. His lips barely parted as he said, "My name is Slater, Mrs. Hallet."

Texada and Coll drew deep breaths and held them, both knowing how their grandmother reacted whenever someone challenged her authority.

The widow never flinched but said, "Yes, it is, and Slaters don't stand second to no one, do they?"

"No, ma'am, they don't," said Slater as evenly as the surface of a becalmed sea in the eye of a hurricane.

Mrs. Hallet sat back in her chair, and the features of her face relaxed. "Texada, you and Coll go see if supper's ready yet."

"Coll can do it by himself," said Texada, not moving.

"Texada, I said for both of you to do it," said Mrs. Hallet firmly. "Now get to it." She smiled mischievously at Slater. "I want some time alone with this handsome young man."

"But, Granny," pleaded Texada.

"I said to get to it, child." The look in her eyes punctuated the command.

Both grandchildren left the room.

"Sit down, Cletus." She waved a hand at the sofa to her right. "And let's talk."

The tension left Slater for the moment as he said, "Thank you, ma'am," and sat down where she indicated.

"Cletus, when we heard that you'd been killed at Shiloh, it liked to broke my heart. I know it broke your granddaddy's heart and Texada's, too. That girl cried for a week, and Dougald Slater was never the same man again. If only he was alive today to see you come home in one piece! Of course, I don't think he'd be too happy to see what's going on out to Glengarry, what with your sister fixing to marry up with that Yankee colonel and all."

Slater lowered his head at the mention of his grandfather, allowing the remark about Texada's feelings to slip by him for the moment. He nervously played with his hat as Mrs. Hallet continued to speak.

"You know, Cletus, I would have married Dougald if he had only asked me. Of course, he didn't, but we were great friends just the same. Sunday meeting just isn't the same without seeing him across the aisle from me. But I suppose it won't be too much longer before he and I meet again."

Her last statement caught Slater's attention, and he looked up at the lady. He looked her straight in the eye and said, "Are you ailing, Mrs. Hallet?" Then he wondered why he had asked that question. Nothing in her outward appearance suggested she might be in ill health, but something in her tone hinted that she was hiding a secret, a sorrowful secret. His gut told him so.

"You mind your own business, Cletus Slater," she said firmly, wagging a scolding finger at him. "That's between me and the good Lord. I've lived a long and full life, and I've had my share of joy and sorrow. My only complaint might be that the Lord took my sons from me way too soon, but I can't say anything about that now. I'll discuss it with the Lord when I see Him up yonder."

His suspicion was correct, but he wished it wasn't. For as long as he could remember, he'd felt there was something special about this grand lady, something that awed him, something he wanted to emulate. Grandpa Dougald had always held her in high esteem, and that alone put an aura of majesty around her. Now to think that she might be departing this world, soon or not, racked the very marrow of his soul. He wanted to reach out and touch her hand to convey all that he was feeling for her to her, but he couldn't move, fearing that any such display of emotion might be misinterpreted, or worse, rejected.

Mrs. Hallet recognized the empathy in Slater's eyes, and a touch of guilt shivered through her. She reached out, patted his hand, and said, "But never mind all that now. That's not why I wanted to talk to you alone. I told Texada to fetch you home for supper with us because I want to talk about you and the future of Lavaca County. Your future, Cletus. Yours and Texada's."

Slater gasped, swallowed hard, and thought, My God! She's got me married off to the girl already. But he said aloud, "Mine and Texada's, Mrs. Hallet? I'm not sure I follow you, ma'am."

"I think you do, Cletus, but that can wait for now. Just hush up and listen to me now."

"Yes, ma'am."

"As soon as we heard that you were home today," she said, "Texada jumped up and down and danced all around like a calf in spring. It was all that I could do to hold her back and keep her from chasing after you right then and there. Once I got her calmed down and convinced that you wouldn't be wanting to see no girl in long pants and a field hand's shirt, she went to prettying herself up for you." The great lady winked and added, "She didn't do too bad neither, did she?"

Slater said nothing, just blushed, and looked down at his feet again.

"Anyway," said Mrs. Hallet, continuing, "that's when I finally got some time to think about what your coming home could mean to this county, Cletus. Tell me, son, about your plans for the future." When he didn't respond immediately, didn't even look up at her, she grew impatient and said, "Well?"

Slater's head jerked up, and his eyes searched for anything to focus on except her face as he said, "I'm not sure I follow you, ma'am."

A bit exasperated, Mrs. Hallet allowed her posture to slump and her head to loll to one side before saying, "Son, I don't blame you." She patted his hand. "It's your blood. You cross an Indian with a Scot, and you're bound to come up with something a little on the muley side."

Slater felt like a schoolboy again, made to stand in the corner for not giving the obvious answer to a simple question. He stopped fidgeting with his hat and hung his head again.

Mrs. Hallet continued talking. "I suppose just about everyone you've met since coming home has told you about who owns Glengarry now, haven't they?"

That struck a nerve. He looked up, and this time looked her straight in the eye and said, "Yes, ma'am. I've heard the story a time or two today."

"I heard you got it first last night. Personally. From that Yankee, Colonel Markham." She watched him closely for his reaction to this bit of news.

Slater's face became perfectly placid, blank. Flatly, he asked, "How did you hear about that?"

Mrs. Hallet had seen this expression before but on a different face, on Dougald Slater whenever he meant business, whether good or bad. It pleased her to see Clete look this way. It would have pleased Dougald, too.

"Cletus, there's hardly anything that happens in this county that I don't hear about it before too long. You got home to Glengarry just about the time someone took a shot at Colonel Markham from the pecan grove. Isn't that right?"

He didn't answer her, but he thought, How does she know that? Who told her?

She didn't wait for a reply. Smiling, she said, "I know what you're thinking, Cletus, and you can just forget wondering how I learn these things. Let's just say that I have my ways of finding out what's what."

"Yes, ma'am," said Slater, a little impressed.

"Now what about you, Cletus? What are you going to do now that you can't return to Glengarry?"

Slater shrugged his shoulders and said, "I haven't given it much thought yet to tell you the truth, Mrs. Hallet. I suppose I'll try to get me a job somewhere around here."

"A job? Boy, hasn't anyone told you yet? There aren't any jobs around here because no one has any money."

"Yes, ma'am. That's what Jess Tate told me."

"Then you know what a tight fix folks around here are in?"

Slater nodded and said, "Yes, I guess I do."

"And what do you plan to do about it?" asked Mrs. Hallet.

Taken aback, Slater said, "Me?"

"You're the only one in this room besides me, aren't you? Of course, you. Who else?"

"I don't follow you, Mrs. Hallet."

The old woman leaned forward and said, "Cletus, things were hard on a lot of folks around here during the war, and they don't look to get better now that the Yankees are here. There isn't a whole lot of hard cash in these parts, and what little there is is in the hands of Yankees. Someone has got to get that money into the hands of our people, Cletus, and I think the man to do it is you."

"Me?"

Mrs. Hallet reeled back in her chair and said, "There you go with that *me stuff* again. Of course, you. Especially you. You. Cletus Slater. The Slater of Glengarry who's been disinherited. You're the one who's lost the most around here, so you should be the one who most wants to get back what he's lost. Or at least some of it."

"I think I know what you're talking about now," said Slater, "but I haven't got the slightest idea about how you think I should go about getting back what's mine."

Texada came into the room and said, "Excuse me, Granny, but dinner's ready."

14

Slater awakened in the darkness of his hotel room, drenched in sweat, partly from the heat and partly from a dream. He rolled out of bed and stood at the open window to gaze out at sleeping Hallettsville. The eastern horizon was a shade lighter than the rest of the sky. It would be morning soon.

A shiver played havoc on his spine, and his skin went all goose-pimply. The chilling sensation was induced by the kiss of a breeze stealing into the room, then was reinforced when he recalled the haunting vision of his slumber.

With the news of his father's death, Slater's mother took to her sickbed for the longest time, and for a while, it was thought that Mary Slater might be joining her husband in the hereafter. She recovered finally, and life around Glengarry returned to some semblance of normalcy. Good man that he was, Dougald Slater told Mary that she and the children could stay at Glengarry as long as she wanted to make it their home, especially since he had no other direct heirs. Mary accepted his offer without hesitation because she had no other place to go. As time went by, Mary grew lonely and wished for the touch of a good man. She had suitors, to be sure, but none were really to her liking until Howard Loving came along. Loving was a happy man who was at peace with himself and the world around him. He fell in love with Mary the first moment he set eyes on her, but it took him five years to convince her to marry him. That happy day came the year before the war began, and only then because Loving said he was moving north to go into business with his cousin Oliver and would no longer be seeing Mary unless she went with him as his bride. They were wed, then they moved to Weatherford, Texas, without any of Mary's children moving with them—which was their choice, not Loving's or Mary's.

Slater hadn't seen his mother since her wedding day, and from that time, he had had a recurring dream of seeing her again but always under strange conditions. He could never be certain what those conditions were, but each one had the underlying thread of urgency about it.

In this latest dreamscape, he recalled she was serving him dinner in a house he had never seen before. As he was eating, the table turned into a campfire, the chair he was sitting in became his saddle, and the faceless guests were transformed into stable hands who were also sitting on saddles. Even his mother was changed from being herself to a cook beside a covered wagon.

Of course, he knew why he had dreamed this dream. It was brought on by a nervous stomach, the conversation he'd had with Mrs. Hallet after dinner the evening before, and a third event that happened during the night.

Texada was the cause of his gastric disorder. Well, partly anyway. She had clung to him throughout most of the evening just as she had in the phaeton when they were driving out to the Hallet place, and this bothered Slater. When it came to girls, at least those he had known before the war, he had always been the aggressor. This was the natural order of things, or so he had always been told. Texada being so forward was a little on the scary side as far as he was concerned, and he felt it was only proper for him to be aloof, especially when they were alone just before he left to walk back into town. She wanted him to kiss her, but he was having none of that. Not yet anyway. He had too much on his mind then, and he felt he should be the one to decide when and where they shared their first kiss. Without stating his position on kissing her, he simply said good night to Texada on the front porch and started back to town.

Mrs. Hallet fostered another source of his anxiety when she explained her ideas on how he could go about reviving the economy of Hallettsville and Lavaca County. "Cletus," she said, "what's the most plentiful resource we have in these parts?"

Slater thought for a moment, then said, "Cattle."

Mrs. Hallet smiled and said, "That's right, son. We've got more cattle roaming our ranges than we'll ever need for our own sustenance. But the people of the North and the East? Why, they're cattle poor. They don't have the grasslands that we have down here in Texas to raise anywhere near the numbers of cattle they'd like to have up that way."

"Are you suggesting I get up a cattle drive to New Orleans or maybe all the way to Chicago like George and Marcellus Turner did just before the war?"

"That's exactly what I'm saying, Cletus. There's a fortune eating grass out there on the range. All you have to do is drive it up and trail it to market."

Mrs. Hallet made it sound so easy, but Slater knew better. For certain, a lot of beeves were roaming the ranges of Lavaca County, but most of them belonged to someone, even if they were unbranded or didn't have their ears notched. Of course, the law said that an unmarked cow was fair game, but a fellow could get himself shot if he rounded up the wrong stock.

"All by myself?" asked Slater a bit sarcastically.

Mrs. Hallet glared at Slater and said, wagging a finger at him, "Don't you take that tone with me, Cletus Slater. I won't have it. I wouldn't take it from Dougald, and I'm sure as hell not going to take it from you. You hear me, Cletus?"

Slater was ashamed of himself. He knew better. "I'm sorry, Mrs. Hallet," he said.

"That's better," she said. "Now where was I? Oh, yes. As I was about to say, there's plenty of men around here looking for work. All you have to do is hire a few of them and you're all set to get to it."

"Mrs. Hallet, I've seen most of the men you're talking about," said Slater, trying hard not to show any disrespect. "They're hardly in any condition to work the range, and besides that, I don't think any of them own a horse or any trappings for a horse. How am I supposed to pay these men or get them mounts, saddles, bedrolls, and all the other supplies needed for a cowhunt and a drive?"

"Losing the war didn't make poor folks out of everyone, Cletus. I managed to set aside some silver and a little gold. How much do you think you'd need to outfit a good crew for a cowhunt and a drive and then trail a herd to Chicago?"

Slater stroked his chin as he'd seen his grandfather do so many times when he was contemplating a business deal. Then he looked at Mrs. Hallet and said, "Maybe three or four thousand."

Mrs. Hallet was unprepared for his reply, and she looked it as she said, "Three or four thousand? How come so much?"

"If you're going to trail a herd to Chicago," said Slater, "you got to have enough cattle to make the trip worth your while, Mrs. Hallet, and that means buying some stock from some folks."

Mrs. Hallet frowned, then said, "I see. Yes, you shouldn't go off trailing a herd without enough cattle to make the trip worth all the work." She thought for a second before asking, "Maybe you could get folks to let you drive their cattle to market on shares?''

''That's possible but not likely.''

''Why not?''

''Would you bet your last dollar on a risky venture like a cattle drive?''

''That's exactly what I'm doing, Cletus.''

A twinkle of devilment sparkled in Slater's eyes as he said, ''Yes, ma'am, but most folks aren't like you.''

Mrs. Hallet recognized the gleam in Slater's eyes. She'd seen it several times before but then in the eyes of Dougald Slater when he was funning with her. A smile brightened her face as she said, ''I don't think I want to know what you meant by that, Cletus.'' She became pensive for a moment, then asked, ''How much would it take to trail a herd to Missouri?''

Slater smiled and said, ''Almost as much?''

''Hm-m. What about New Orleans? Could you make a drive there for say less than a thousand dollars?''

Still smiling, Slater shook his head, and said, ''No, ma'am, I don't think it could be done.''

Mrs. Hallet's eyes narrowed into a mean squint, then pinpointed a spot on Slater's nose. ''I don't believe you said that, Cletus Slater. I don't believe you'd pass up a challenge like taking a herd of beeves to New Orleans by simply saying you don't think it could be done. What's wrong with you, son? Did the war take the backbone out of you?''

Slater's hackles were up again. He returned Mrs. Hallet's look and said, ''No, ma'am, it didn't. But it didn't addle my brain neither. I'm telling you that any man in his right mind wouldn't try to trail two thousand or a thousand or even five hundred beeves to New Orleans or even to Galveston without getting proper backing first.''

''I think you're just making excuses, Cletus. If I'm willing to risk my last good dollar on such a venture, then I think you should at least give it a try. Or maybe your name is Milquetoast after all.''

That was the last thing Slater needed to hear. Mrs. Hallet had slapped his ego with a verbal glove, then dropped it at his feet. Without thinking, he picked it up and threw it back in her face. ''All right, I'll do it, Mrs. Hallet,'' he said. ''I'll get up a drive for New Orleans, but I want you to keep one thing in mind. I warned you against it.''

"It's my money, Cletus."

"That's right, it is. And when it's all gone and we're only half way to New Orleans, what do I do then?"

Mrs. Hallet smiled and said, "You'll think of something, Cletus. That's what I'm betting on. You. Cletus Slater. I'm betting you can do it, if anyone can. The whole community will be depending on you."

"Mrs. Hallet, you're making me feel like I'm supposed to be some sort of Moses leading his people to the Promised Land."

The grand lady smiled and said, "I hadn't thought of it that way, Cletus, but you're right. You're going to be our Moses. In a way, I mean. You see, we're already in the Promised Land. Only someone's turned off the flow of milk and honey. It's up to you to make it flow again, Cletus."

Just that easy, Mrs. Hallet had heaped the responsibility of saving the financial fortunes of Lavaca County on his shoulders.

After leaving Mrs. Hallet and Texada, Slater returned to his hotel room and tried to get some rest. The weight of that burden had kept him from sleeping very well. Only two hours into the night, he decided to take a walk about town and mull over the task that he'd accepted so reluctantly that evening.

As he left the Planters Hotel, Slater contemplated walking up the street to Lindenberg's, thinking a stiff drink might calm him down and maybe he might find an old friend or two there to talk to. He started off in the direction of the saloon, but as he passed the courthouse, he noticed a clump of Yankee soldiers—five, maybe six, it was hard to distinguish their precise number in the darkness—gathered at the eastern steps to the county building. They were on their knees in a circle, and although he couldn't understand their words clearly, Slater knew they were gambling—probably drinking, too. Taking that possibility into mind and wishing to avoid trouble, he started to cross LaGrange, pointing himself at Henry Reese's leather goods store in the middle of the block.

"Hey, you! Reb!" called one of the soldiers.

Slater tried to ignore him, kept walking.

"You heard me, Reb!" shouted the man. "Just hold on there."

The street and sidewalks were vacant of other pedestrians, so Slater knew there was no avoiding this loudmouth. He halted in the middle of the street, turned, and waited for the Yank to come to him. Not too much to Slater's surprise, more than one of the Federals headed his way, a trio, in fact. Although the light wasn't good, Slater recognized two of the soldiers as the sentry and corporal who had been at Glengarry the night before. Bluebelly bastards! he thought. Now what?

"As I was telling you, Tinsley," said Corporal Riley, slipping into an Irish accent that was slurred by liquor and sounded forced. "it's himself, the lord of the manor, the master of Glengarry. Top o' the evenin', yer lordship." Riley doffed his forage cap and bowed low to Slater.

The others laughed. Long and hard. So did Riley when he straightened up.

A foul air of cheap whiskey surrounded them, insulting Slater's nostrils with its stench. He put on his red man's face, trying to ignore their smell and their words as he stood completely still and waited for them to finish their fun and leave him be. That wasn't to happen too soon, however.

When Slater didn't reply, Riley took offense and said, "Would something be troubling yer lordship? It wouldn't be having anything to do with the fact that yer baby brother is runnin' the roost, now would it, yer lordship?" He broke into laughter again, and so did his friends.

You sonofabitch! thought Slater, but he showed no emotion at all to the Yanks. To them, he was as stoical and as passive as a cigar store Indian.

Noting Slater's calm aspect, Private Tinsley took up the challenge and said, "You ain't pulling his tail strong enough, Riley. Let me have a crack at him."

"Be my guest, Tinsley," said Riley, slapping the private on the back. "Have a go at him, if it pleases you."

"I know what's bothering his lordship," said Tinsley. His face was all twisted up as he tried mockingly to hide the gist to the joke that he was about to make. "It's his lordship's sister that's troubling him, boys. He ain't liking the fact that she's consorting with a good Union man like our Colonel Markham." Then in imitation of Riley's Irish, he added, "Wouldn't that be it, yer lordship?"

Slater hadn't thought of that as a reason for his immediate concern, but since Tinsley had mentioned it, maybe it was. He doubled up his fists and without warning smashed the boorish private squarely in the middle of his hyena face, instantly breaking the Yank's nose and rocking him backward into an unconscious heap on the ground.

Riley and the other private reacted in kind, each swinging wildly at Slater but neither connecting with more than a glancing blow to his shoulders or to his arms, which he used to fend off their attack.

Two of the other three soldiers who had been gambling with Riley and Tinsley came rushing into the affray. One of them plowed into Slater's midsection with his shoulder, driving the Texan backward and to the ground. They rolled in the street until Slater came out on top holding the Yank by his partially buttoned tunic with his left hand while he slugged the man's jaw with his right. Before he could land another punch, Riley and the other two soldiers grabbed Slater and jerked him to his feet.

"Hold him, boys!" said Riley as he backed away and prepared to do his worst on Slater.

The pair held the Texan by his arms, but he offered them no resistance, choosing instead to wait for the opening that he knew would be coming. A long time before this moment Grandpa Dougald had taught him that only cowards gang up on a lone man and cowards were poor battlers, stupid fighters. "They will always give you an opening," he'd said, "that will allow you to give them what they wished that they had the sand to give to you."

As Riley came at him, Slater made his move. He grabbed the two men holding him by their cartridge belts to brace himself, leaned back, kicked his feet high in the air, and stomped Riley in the chest, sending the corporal reeling and gasping desperately for the air that Slater had just driven so violently from his lungs. Coming down, the Texan slammed his heels into the shins of his captors, causing the three of them to collapse in a pile that was joined by the Yankee that had tried to wrestle with Slater before and had lost the first fall. Slater threw off the late arrival, then jumped up to a fighting stance. The first man to get up went down twice as fast, as Slater landed a left then a right to the fool's head, putting him out for the count. The wrestler made another lunge at him, but this time the Texan was ready for him. Like a matador, he neatly sidestepped the oncoming bull, but instead of sticking the beast with a sword, Slater merely slammed his fist into the nape of the man's neck, landing him in the street beside Tinsley and leaving him in the same condition as the private.

Seeing that he was now alone to face Slater, the fifth man turned and ran back toward the courthouse steps, where the last of the gamblers had stayed to watch the proceedings.

Slater couldn't say for sure, but he thought he recognized this last man as the burly bearded sergeant that he had met at Glengarry the night before. The thought of tangling with a man as powerful as Sergeant Wickersham appeared to hold no appeal for the Texan, but he wasn't about to run away from a fight, not with a Yankee, not in his own town, not in Texas, or anywhere else for that matter. He simply stiffened his resolve to give as good as he got or go down trying.

"Get back there and fight like a man!" roared Wickersham at the fleeing soldier.

"But, Sergeant, he's—" Poor fellow never got a chance to finish the sentence.

Wickersham hated cowardice—in any form. He decked the private with a mighty fist, then said, "Chicken shit little bastard!" as he stood over the private that he had just sent to the same dreamland that Tinsley and the other two Yankees were presently visiting. Noting that Riley was all right, although still gasping a bit, he turned his attention to Slater, walking cautiously toward the Texan.

Slater was about as ready for Wickersham as he would ever be. Fists doubled and held high, body in a crouch and angled to the side, eyes filled with determination.

The sergeant stopped a good three paces away from Slater, raised his hands palms out in front of him, and said, "I had enough of fighting you Rebs these last four years, Captain Slater. I don't think I really want any more from you, sir." He lowered his hands, put them on his hips, scanned the area, then clucked. "I don't know how we whipped you Rebs with the likes of these on our side, sir."

Slater was taken completely aback. Could he trust this brawny Yank or not? he wondered. Only one way to find out. He straightened up and moved a step farther away from Wickersham, just for insurance against a sudden assault, one which didn't seem to be coming, much to his delight.

"I guess you can be on your way now, sir," said Wickersham. "I'll see to this bunch myself. Good evening, Captain." He tipped his hat in a half salute.

This is too easy, thought Slater. He had to ask. "I don't understand, Sergeant, uh . . ."

"Wickersham, sir. John Wickersham."

"Why, Sergeant Wickersham?"

"Why, sir?"

"Yes, why?" said Slater. "Why aren't you like them?" He waved a hand in a sweeping motion to indicate the four men lying in the street around them and Corporal Riley who was now sprawled on the courthouse lawn. "Or like that Colonel Markham, for that matter?"

Wickersham shrugged and said, "I don't know, Captain. I can't answer that."

"That's another thing, Sergeant. You keep addressing me with military courtesy. Why? I was a captain in the Confederate army, not the Union's. Why treat me with so much respect?"

The Federal considered the question a moment before answering, saying, "Let's just say that it's not the rank or the uniform, sir. Let's just say that it's time we start putting the war behind us and start looking ahead. I've had a chance to look at this big state of yours, Captain Slater. This Texas of yours. I like it. It's . . . it's . . ." He seemed lost for the right words, but one finally came to him, bringing a smile to his lips. "It's so free, sir, and I think I might want to be a part of that freedom sometime in the future. Does that sound too odd to you, Captain?"

Slater gave it some quick thought and said, "Not at all, Sergeant. Not at all."

As Slater recalled Wickersham's words the next morning while he watched the sun rise, he couldn't help repeating aloud his own parting words if only to the dawn. "No, Sergeant, not at all. In fact, they ring true to me. Texas and freedom. Yes, Texas and freedom."

And giving that last much more consideration, Slater thought, There won't be any freedom for anyone if there's no honest work around here. He let out a laugh at the irony of his next thought. We'll become the slaves ourselves, and that's what we fought four long years to preserve. Wouldn't that be a poke in the eye with a sharp stick?

He turned serious again as the first ray of sunshine peeked over the horizon. He finally realized the gravity of the situation in Lavaca County, in Texas, in the whole South. The saturnine picture that Mrs. Hallet had been trying to paint for him had found animation in his encounter with Corporal Riley and the four privates. Scenes like that one would be repeated over and over again as long as men like those Yanks thought Texans as well as other Southerners were weaklings. Like so many bullies, they would push and push and push some more until someone stood up to them and pushed back. Sure, he had pushed back, but who else would do it? Those ragged shadows of manhood that he had seen in the alley next to Lindenberg's? Not likely. Not unless someone gave them back their spines, their self-respect, and helped them to stand tall again. And who would do that? Him? Mrs. Hallet had said that he was the one to do it. She believed it so much that she was betting her last dollar on him. How much more encouragement did he think he needed?

Lots.

15

Slater decided that it would serve no good purpose to tell anyone— not even his best friend—about his fight with the soldiers the night before. He figured that it would only stir up folks around town against the Yankees, and the last thing that they needed now was to start butting heads with the Federals.

After a breakfast of ham, eggs, toast, fried potatoes, and coffee at the Planters Hotel dining room, Slater and Tate hiked a mile out Fourth Street to Alamo Creek, the unofficial eastern boundary of Hallettsville. A well-worn path led north from the road to a hackberry thicket along the stream. Beyond the protecting brush was a squalid camp of lean-tos and rough little shacks—the new homes for some of the county's dispossessed war veterans.

Slater and Tate stopped at the edge of the camp and looked around. Actually, it didn't appear to be all that much different than most of the army bivouacs Slater had seen or lived in during the last two years of the war. He could have mistaken it for a Confederate post if a few of the obvious accoutrements hadn't been missing from it. For sure, the men were almost all in ragged gray uniforms, but that was where the similarity ended. No muskets stood all in a row in stalks of three; no horses picketed in the clearing; no cannon; no armed guards. Less than that, no battle flags floated on gentle breezes from proud standards in front of officers' tents.

"You say there's about thirty men here?" asked Slater.

"Twenty-nine now," said Tate, "since I moved into the hotel with you." He pointed toward a man lying on his side and propped up on one elbow. "That's Bill Simons over there." His finger aimed at another fellow who was sitting cross-legged beside a cold fire ring. "That's Jake Flewellyn. And over there is Seth Noble. Volney Cook is here, too. Biff Jackson, Bill Harris, Hank Jones, the Reeves boys, Bill Simpson, John Black, Sam Green, Charlie Dunneway, Stan Thigpen, Bert Watson, John Humphrey, Pick Arnold, Jed Andrews, and some boys who signed up later here in Hallettsville and some that never signed up at all."

Slater's head bobbed slightly as he listened to Tate. He'd seen a few of these men in town the day before, but he hadn't gotten a chance to visit with any of them then, thanks to the Detchens and Deputy Kindred. Now he was here to do more than talk about old times. He had business to conduct. "Any of them got horses?" he asked.

"A few," said Tate, "but they're sorrowful-looking animals. No one's had the price of a bucket of oats since we got home."

Slater nodded, then started toward Jake Flewellyn, the first man in Terry's Rangers credited with killing a Yankee. Tate was a half step behind him.

Flewellyn tilted his head up at Slater and Tate as they approached. He bore little resemblance to the gallant soldier charging the Union lines at Bowling Green. His brown eyes, sunken in dark circles, seemed lifeless, empty, without hope. His hollow cheeks and swollen lips were mostly hidden by a shaggy, tobacco-stained, crusty black beard. His tattered old uniform was so dirty that it appeared to be brown instead of gray, and he was so gaunt that the cloth seemed draped over his weary bones.

Slater was speechless at the sight of his former valiant comrade-in-arms.

"Jake, how are you doing today?" asked Tate.

"Fair to middling," drawled Flewellyn, not moving and still looking at Slater. "Thought you were dead, Clete. You must be. I'm seeing me a ghost wearing a burying suit." He shifted his gaze to Tate. "And look at you, Jess. What did you do to yourself? Take a bath in the creek and scrape your face with a sharp rock? And where'd you get them clothes? Go to grave robbing or something?"

Tate felt a sharp pang of embarrassment. His lot had improved tenfold over the other men in the camp in a single day, and it imbued him with the shame of selfishness. "You got no cause to go on like that, Jake," he said, his pride wounded. "I didn't do no hurt to you."

The war had made Flewellyn a sour man, and from the looks

of the others in this camp, he wasn't the only one. "Just standing there all gussied up like that you're doing me a hurt," he said. "Me and all the boys here." He glared back at Slater and added, "Same goes for you, Clete."

Flewellyn's bitter remark pinched a raw nerve in Slater. He winced, knowing the man was right, and it angered him. This wasn't the way that he wanted the conversation to go. He hadn't seen Flewellyn in town the day before, so he figured when they did meet again that there would be lots of smiles, hand shaking, back slapping, and jovial talk. *I guess I was wrong about that,* he thought. "Get up, Jake," said Slater evenly, casting the defy at Flewellyn. "Get up, and fight like a man."

Mostly Welsh with a Scot and a Cherokee hanging from the family tree, Jake Flewellyn was a good four years older than Slater but not bigger or stronger, especially on this day of their lives. Even so, he knew no fear. "Fight?" he queried angrily. "I'll give both of you sons of bitches a fight." He struggled to stand up on his own, throwing off an attempt by Tate to help him. Once erect, he stared Slater straight in the eye with all the defiance of a cornered boar. "You come here to whup me for sport, Clete? You got nothing better to do?" Flewellyn spoke loud enough for half the camp to hear him.

Slater saw movement out of the corner of his eye. Some of the others were stirring, coming closer for a better view or to hear better or to take sides. This concerned Slater on the one hand and gladdened him on the other. He had everybody's attention, at least, which was what he wanted in the first place.

"My granddaddy never kicked a man when he was down," said Slater, "and I'm not about to disgrace his name by doing such a low deed now. I just wanted to see if you still had any gumption left in you, Jake." He knelt down beside the fire ring, picked up a twig, and tossed it inside the circle. Looking back up at Flewellyn, he said, "I don't want to fight you, Jake. I want to ride with you again."

Flewellyn twisted his head to one side and studied Slater for a moment, then said, "What are you up to, Clete? Something tells me you ain't all right in the head, boy. You catch a Minie ball along your scalp like Johnny Humphrey and get your brains addled or something?"

Tate was beginning to wonder the same thing. Slater hadn't told him anything about the previous night's conversations with Mrs. Hallet or the affray with the Yankees. All Tate knew was that Slater had wanted to see the boys at the Alamo Creek camp right away that morning and that he'd asked to be taken to them. Tate had done that, and now this. *What the hell is going on?* he asked himself.

By now, most of the men in camp had gathered in the vicinity of the trio.

Slater smiled and said, "Caught one in the leg once in a fight in the Shenandoah Valley. Stung pretty bad for a few days, then the doc finally dug it out. I don't recollect which hurt the more. Going in or coming out."

"Clete rode with Morgan," said Tate, as if he were mouthing the words of a magic spell.

Flewellyn blinked away the animosity in his eyes and said in a voice that conveyed a mixture of respect and disbelief, "You rode with Morgan?"

"He did," said Tate, "and he got made a captain, too."

"Is that right, Clete?" asked Flewellyn, knowing Tate had a penchant for exaggeration.

Slater lowered his head in modesty and said, "Yeah, it's true. I rode with Mosby once, too, and I was made a captain under Morgan. I wasn't one for long though."

"Makes no matter," said Tate, "does it, Jake? A captain's a captain."

"That's right," said Flewellyn.

"Look, Jake," said Slater, "I came here looking for some men who'd be willing to come ride with me again."

"Ride with you?" asked Flewellyn. "Against the Yankees? Are you loco, Clete?"

"No," said Slater, "not against the Yankees."

Flewellyn smiled and said, "I see. Against them uppity niggers then?"

Slater frowned and said firmly, "No."

"Then who?" asked Tate impatiently and just as perplexed as everybody else was.

Slater stood up and said, "I was thinking about going on a cowhunt, and I was wondering if some of you boys wouldn't want to ride with me. That's all."

"You mean, work for you?" queried Flewellyn.

"Well, yes, I suppose so," stammered Slater.

Tate stared at Slater, not believing what he heard. "You got that kind of money, Clete?"

Slater gave Tate an annoyed side glance, then recollecting Mrs.

Hallet's remark about him and milquetoast, he reiterated his answer to Flewellyn's question but this time with conviction. "Yes, for me. I'm getting up a crowd for a cowhunt and a drive. Then I'm planning to trail a herd to New Orleans. I need good men who know their way around mossy horns. Any of you interested?"

"Sure, I am, Clete," said Tate.

"Hey, how about me?" asked Bill Simons from the edge of the growing crowd. He looked much the same as Flewellyn except with blue eyes and brown hair.

"Yeah, how about me?" asked another.

"Yeah, what about us?" called a third.

"Now hold on," said Slater. "I can't take everyone. I haven't got that kind of money."

"You got some beans and bacon?" asked Simons. "I'll work just to fill my belly."

"Yeah, me, too," said a chorus of others.

"Not me," said Flewellyn.

Slater was elated by the reactions of the majority, but his delight was cut short by Flewellyn's negative reply.

"Why not?" asked Slater.

"I ain't got a horse or chaps or even a rope," said Flewellyn. "How am I going to hunt cows without trappings?"

"He's got a good point there," said Tate. "Most of us either traded or sold nearly everything we ever owned in this world just to buy a little food to stay alive. We got nothing to work with, Clete."

That thought had crossed Slater's mind, and he felt that he had a reasonable solution to the problem.

"You can get trappings in town," said Slater.

"Who's going to pay for the bill?" asked Flewellyn. "You already said you ain't got that kind of money."

"You can buy on credit," said Slater.

That brought a round of laughter from the men. Slater didn't understand why they were amused.

"Credit?" snickered Flewellyn. "Ain't you heard, boy? The Yankees are running things now."

"What Jake's trying to say is," said Tate, "most of the storekeepers won't give out any credit to Confederates because they're afraid Markham will stop doing business with them."

"That makes no sense to me," said Slater. "What's Markham got to do with it?"

"The Yankees are about the only ones around here what got

any hard cash,'' said Flewellyn. ''You catch on now, Clete? Already, Mr. Ballard's closed up one of his businesses, and the Dibrell brothers took in new partners. I suspect John Kelly and the others will be closing up as well, if things don't change soon.''

''That's what I'm getting at, boys,'' said Slater. ''We got to get back on our feet around here, and the best way of doing it is by hunting up as many beeves as we can and then trailing them to market where we can get some good hard cash for them.''

''That's all well and good, Clete,'' said Flewellyn, ''but that don't solve the problem of the moment. How are we going to get trappings and horses to do all this hunting and driving and trailing to market? You ain't said yet.''

Slater thought for a moment as he looked around at the faces of the men about him, then he said, ''Has anyone here asked any of the merchants for credit?''

''Sure, we have,'' said Flewellyn. ''Lots of us, and they turned us down without so much as a thanks-for-asking.''

''That's right, Clete,'' said Tate. ''Most of them have been acting like it was our fault we lost the war and we personally put them in the tight they're in.''

I told Mrs. Hallet this wasn't going to be easy, thought Slater. He looked at Flewellyn and said, ''When was the last time you asked someone for credit?''

''Couple of weeks back,'' said Flewellyn. ''Why?''

''Well, maybe one of them has had a change of heart since then,'' said Slater, ''and maybe we should ask again.''

''Won't do no good,'' said Flewellyn.

''We won't know that unless we try,'' said Slater.

''And what if they say no again?'' asked Flewellyn. ''Then what, Clete? Do we come back here with our tails between our legs? Hell, no, boy! I ain't going. I know what they'll say, and I ain't going in there to beg for what I thought I was fighting for when we was at Shiloh and all them other places. I ain't going, Clete. I ain't humiliating myself no more.''

''Me neither,'' said a few of the others. There were other murmurs of discontent and dissatisfaction with Slater's proposal.

Slater was suddenly struck with an anxiety he didn't want to feel. He was losing them, and he knew it. He had to say something or do something to keep them with him.

''Then if they won't give us credit,'' said Slater firmly and with determination, ''we'll take what we need.''

That quieted everyone except Flewellyn. ''You are addled,

Clete. What are we supposed to do? Ride into town awhooping and ahollering like we was charging Yankees or something? Are we supposed to ransack every store in town or do we just loot half of them before Markham's cavalry shows up to cut us to pieces?''

"No, we don't ride into town at all," said Slater. He snickered and said, "We don't have enough horses for a decent charge." He paused as most of the boys laughed at the jest. "No, sir. We march into town. Peacefully. And we go up to the store that has everything we need, and I talk to the storekeeper. If he won't deal with me, then we'll insist that he deals with all of us."

"How are you going to do that?" asked Flewellyn. "Every storekeeper in town has got himself a double-barrel persuader under his counter. How are you going to deal with that?"

"Who'll lend me a gun?" asked Slater.

Flewellyn pulled a Colt's Navy from the belt inside his coat. "You can take mine," he said, handing it to Slater butt first. "You take it and do what you say you're planning to do. You do that, and I'll follow you to Hell, Clete Slater, if that's what it takes."

16

If Slater learned one thing in the war, it was never tip off the enemy about your plans. With that in mind, he put his strategy before the men.

Marching into the Hallettsville square in a single unit would be tantamount to sending a herald ahead of them to announce their intentions. Therefore, Slater would have the men go into town the same as they had every other day since returning from the war; then they were to drift slowly toward their objective and enter the premises as inconspicuously as possible. After a few of them were inside, Slater would come in and speak with the storekeeper. If all went well, Slater would make an agreement with the man to extend them credit and there would be no trouble. If matters should go contrarily, then Slater and his friends would take what they wanted and credit be damned.

Slater selected John Kelly's establishment on LaGrange Street north of Second as their target because of the large quantity of goods that Kelly had in stock and because it was the only store that wasn't on the square facing the county courthouse. Also, Kelly had been an outspoken Secessionist and had little use for Markham and his troops, making him the most likely merchant to extend credit to former Confederate soldiers, but if he should take exception to Slater and the boys helping themselves to his wares, then it was unlikely Markham would come to his rescue. As for Sheriff Foster, interference from that quarter wasn't probable because the sheriff had gone out of town and had left Deputy Kindred in charge and Kindred was too much of a coward to face a mob without a small army to back him.

Bill Simons and the Reeves brothers, Kent and Clark, were the first group to enter Kelly's store. The only other person in the store was the proprietor himself. John Kelly was a squat man, seemingly without a neck, with a short salt-and-pepper beard and matching hair, and blue eyes that were perpetually bloodshot. He eyed the trio suspiciously, but before he could say or do anything, Slater and Tate walked in.

"Clete Slater," called Kelly cheerfully, "I'd heard that you were back. Ben Schwartz was telling me last night how you bought a new suit from him yesterday and paid cash for it. He said you looked right smart in it, and if the suit he meant is the one you're wearing now, then he wasn't wrong."

"Thank you for that, Mr. Kelly," said Slater a bit uneasily as he walked up to the counter.

"Well, what can I do for you, Clete?" asked Kelly.

Slater glanced sideways at Tate, then past him at Simons, who was looking at spurs. The Reeves brothers were on the other side of the store inspecting men's shirts. Flewellyn, Stan Thigpen, and Pick Arnold entered the store just then. Kelly stretched to see over Slater's shoulder, saw who it was, and frowned.

"Mr. Kelly," said Slater, "I'm getting some of the boys together for a cowhunt and a drive, and then I'm planning to trail a herd to New Orleans. I was hoping to get some credit so I could outfit the boys with some work clothes and food and eating and cooking utensils."

"How many men were you thinking about outfitting, Clete?" asked Kelly as he watched three more of the boys enter the store.

"About thirty or so," said Slater.

"That would be a tall order, Clete," said Kelly. "You'd be running up quite a bill, and I'm not so sure I could carry that kind of a tab for you."

Another trio came through the door, making the total fourteen now.

"Well, I could put down some cash, Mr. Kelly, say a hundred dollars or so."

"I'm afraid that wouldn't be enough, Clete. Why, you're talking about buying six or seven hundred dollars worth of goods. That's a lot of credit to be asking during these times."

"I know, Mr. Kelly, but you know I'm good for it."

"Well, if your grandfather was still alive or if you were the master of Glengarry, then I could go along with you, Clete. But I just can't, considering things as they are. You know how it is, Clete."

Slater's jaw tightened when Kelly mentioned Glengarry. There it is again, he thought. Already, I'm being treated like white trash because I'm not the master of Glengarry or even a part owner of it. This will never do, Cletus Slater. He nodded and said, "I see how it is, Mr. Kelly." He turned in time to see four more men step inside the store. A fiendish thrill took hold of him. "Come on in, boys, and pick out whatever you want. Mr. Kelly just said to help ourselves to anything we want. He's giving us unlimited credit."

"Now hold on, Clete," said Kelly. "That's not what I said at all."

Slater drew Flewellyn's big Colt's from inside his coat, cocked the hammer, spun around, and put the muzzle to Kelly's nose, all in one smooth motion. "Like I said, Mr. Kelly. I'm good for it."

Kelly stared cross-eyed at the barrel of the revolver and said with great agitation, "Yes, of course. Of course, you are, Clete. You boys help yourselves to anything you want. Anything at all."

"Take it easy, Mr. Kelly," said Slater as he lowered the gun. "As long as you don't do anything foolish, you won't be harmed. I promise you that."

Kelly swallowed hard and looked Slater in the eye. "It's a good thing your grandfather isn't alive to see this fine thing happening here."

Slater's teeth clenched, and through them, he growled, "If my grandfather was alive, Mr. Kelly, those damned Yankees wouldn't be out to Glengarry and I wouldn't be here holding a gun on you fixing to blow your fool head off." He raised the Colt's, held it at arm's length, and aimed at Kelly's face. "Mr. Kelly, I don't want to hear another word from you about my grandfather or Glengarry or anything. Do you hear me?"

Kelly's eyes got as white as they could as he backed away from the counter into the shelves behind him. When he could go no farther, he threw up his hands in defeat. "Don't shoot me, Clete," whined Kelly. "Please don't shoot me."

The incredible, immense fear in Kelly's voice shot a barbed dart into Slater's soul. Although outwardly presenting an aspect of utter cruelty, inside Slater was grappling with his conscience, attempting desperately to find an even course here—for everyone—before matters got out of hand. My God! he thought. What am I doing here? The realization that he was only a heartbeat away from murdering a defenseless man shook Slater to the core.

The last group of men entered the store.

Slater lowered the gun slowly and calmly said without taking his eyes from Kelly and without changing his expression, "Be sure to get everything you think you'll need, boys."

"Including guns?" asked Simons.

"Especially guns," said Slater. "Something tells me we'll be needing them before long."

17

Isaac Samusch was a stocky fellow with a black mustache, bald pate, fat cheeks, double chins, and brown eyes, who worried a lot because his bulbous nose was always poking into places where it shouldn't. This was another one of those occasions.

Samusch owned a grocery store on the northeast corner of Second and LaGrange streets. He was looking out his front window when Simons and the Reeves brothers entered Kelly's store. He didn't think too much of it at the time, but when three more former Confederate soldiers went inside Kelly's, then three more, then another three, he became suspicious. He kept watching until all of the men from the Alamo Creek thicket had gone into Kelly's place. When none of them came out right away, curiosity got the best of the grocer.

Lindenberg's Saloon was next door to Samusch's store. Old Fritz was just opening up for the day when Samusch backed into the place.

"Something's going on over to John Kelly's," said Samusch, still looking across the street. "Did you see all those men go in there, Lindenberg?"

"I didn't see anyone go in anywhere, Samusch," said Lindenberg, mildly annoyed. "I have just now come into the barroom. What men are you talking about?"

"Jake Flewellyn, Bill Simons, Kent and Clark Reeves. That bunch from the camp out on Alamo Creek. They all went into Kelly's just a few minutes ago."

"All at the same time?" asked Lindenberg, his curiosity aroused now. He came out from behind the bar, stood beside Samusch, and looked across the street with his neighbor.

"Of course not, *dumpfkopf*!" said Samusch. "They went in three at a time."

Lindenberg's eyebrows jumped up his forehead, and he asked, "Three at a time? Why would they go into a store three at a time?"

"That is what I want to find out," said Samusch. He moved closer to the door. "What do you think they are up to over there? No good maybe?"

"I think you are right, Samusch. They are up to no good, I bet. Why don't you go see?"

Samusch looked at Lindenberg as if he was crazy and said, "And if they are up to no good and I get killed, are you going to look after my Anna and my children?"

Lindenberg glared back at Samusch. "I am too old to go snooping. You should go. If they are up to no good, they could be coming to your place next."

That idea scared the hell out of Samusch. His eyes bugged out so far that white could be seen all around the irises. "I didn't think of that," he said. "Yes, I should go see. But how do I do it?"

"Go out and walk over to Schwartz's shop," said Lindenberg. "Go around the corner for a second, then come back along the side of Schwartz's and peek into Kelly's window."

Samusch pinched his lower lip between the thumb and index

finger of his right hand as he considered Lindenberg's hastily conceived plan. Confident that he understood, he released the flap of flesh and said, "Yes, of course. I see. I will do that." But Samusch didn't move.

"Well, are you going or not?" asked Lindenberg impatiently.

"Yes, I'm going. I'm going." This time he moved.

Just as Lindenberg suggested, Samusch crossed the street to Schwartz & Arnold, Clothiers, on the northwest corner of La-Grange and Second, with its front facing the courthouse across Second. He stepped around the corner, stopped, glanced heavenward as if saying a short prayer, then came back around the corner, hugging the wall. Slowly, he crept toward Kelly's store until he was within a foot of the window. Again, he stopped with his back pressed hard against the wall and glanced heavenward as if praying. Satisfied that he would survive this ordeal, he leaned toward the glass and peeked through it.

Slater was still holding a gun on Kelly. That much Samusch saw for sure. All of the other men were helping themselves to everything in the place: guns, ammunition, knives, ropes, boots, hats, clothing, underwear, blankets for horses as well as people, canned goods, cooking utensils, tinware, carpentry tools, nails, and chains. Some of the boys had already discarded their old ragged uniforms and longjohns and were doing the rest of their shopping in nothing but new union suits, socks, boots, and a hat. Others thought of their bellies first, had opened cans of fruit and meat, and were getting their fill.

Samusch had seen enough. He knew trouble when he saw it. Slater and the boys were robbing Kelly, and he had to tell the law. The grocer slid away from the window certain that he hadn't been seen by anyone inside Kelly's. He wondered what to do next. Inform the law, yes. But how? The sheriff's office was on the other side of town. Run as fast as he could? Isaac Samusch was not a well man. Already, his heart was taking such a pounding from the excitement. Send a boy? No boys in sight. The bell! Yes, the town bell on the courthouse grounds! That would alert everyone, the whole community all at once. Go ring the town bell, Samusch, he thought.

He did. He hurried down the boardwalk to Second Street, waddled across it to the courthouse grounds, then stumbled on to the bell next to the east entrance of the building. Already perspiring heavily, he grabbed the rope and gave it as strong a jerk as he could muster. *Clang-clang! Clang-clang!* The sound reverberated off the walls of the surrounding structures, making it that much more ominous. He pulled hard again. *Clang-clang! Clang-clang!*

Every man doing business that morning on the square came out in the streets to see what was the matter. They were followed outside by the shopkeepers and their helpers. The women —lady shoppers and the wives and daughters of the businessmen— stopped at the doorways because it could be hazardous outside and it was a man's place to stand up to danger.

Samusch continued to ring the bell.

Men came running toward the grocer now, some asking what was the trouble. Was there a fire? Was someone hurt in an accident? What was wrong?

Henry Reese, the bootmaker, was the first to reach Samusch. The thin, little man was still wearing his spectacles down over the end of his nose, and he held his cobbler's hammer in his right hand. His apron jingled softly as the shoe nails in its pockets were jostled about. "Samusch, what's the matter?" asked Reese.

Breathless, Samusch tried to reply. He pointed up the street toward his establishment and blustered out the words. "Thieves! Robbers! At Kelly's store!"

A crowd had gathered around him. Some of them repeated his words in disbelief.

"What's this?" asked Reese.

Samusch caught his breath and said, "Those men! Our soldiers! They are thieves and robbers!"

"Our soldiers?" quizzed Reese. "The Yankees?"

Someone heard that much and immediately came to the wrong conclusion that Union soldiers were robbing Kelly's store. Another man suggested that they get their shotguns and rout the Yankee bastards.

"No!" shouted Samusch, now in better control of himself. "They are not Yankees! They are our boys! Clete Slater is holding a gun on John Kelly. I saw it. And the others. Jake Flewellyn, Pick Arnold, Bill Simons. All of them from the camp on Alamo Creek. They're inside Kelly's taking everything he has."

Silence suddenly draped an invisible shroud over the crowd, paralyzing everyone for the moment.

The folks in the town square weren't the only people to hear the emergency bell.

Jim Kindred and Bill Thornton heard the town bell over at the jailhouse. Thornton followed Kindred to the door but went no farther because his job was to stay in the jailhouse at all times unless it was on fire. It wasn't, so he wasn't going anywhere. Kindred was excited. He grabbed the reins of his horse tied up out front and threw himself into the saddle. It was his theory that a mounted man held more power over people than one on foot. He kicked the steed in the ribs and rode off at a gallop for the courthouse just two blocks away.

Colonel Markham had taken Slater's words to heart. Folks whispering about his relationship with Malinda was reason enough for him to remove himself from Glengarry and establish his headquarters at the courthouse in Hallettsville and move himself into the hotel. Although he hated Rebels, his orders were to *quell* trouble, not cause it.

Markham was leading the first contingent of his 77th Pennsylvania Volunteers into town when Samusch began ringing the town bell. They were just crossing the bridge over Alamo Creek on the road from Columbus when the first peels reached their ears. He halted the troop and listened hard. More ringing. He scanned the horizon for smoke. There was none, ruling out a fire. That meant there was some other emergency, possibly an accident with injured people. If so, then a surgeon would be necessary. He happened to have one available. Seeing an opportunity to gain favor with the locals, Markham ordered his men to move out at double time.

Mrs. Hallet heard the town bell as she sat in the rocker on the front porch of her house. She stopped rocking and scanned the sky for smoke. When she saw that there was none other than the normal few plumes from home cooking fires, she smiled to herself, then masked her feelings when Texada came running from the barn in back.

"Granny, did you hear the bell?" asked Texada.

"I surely did, girl," said the old woman as she pushed herself erect. "You better hitch up the phaeton for me. We've got business to attend to in town."

Deputy Kindred rode up to the crowd on the courthouse grounds and demanded to know why the bell had been rung. Samusch was quick to tell him.

"Is that so?" asked Kindred. "Well, we'll just see about that. I'm deputizing every man here, and we'll just go see what Mr.

Clete Slater and that bunch are up to. Every man raise your right hand and take the oath."

Samusch looked at Reese, who looked at Crockett Dibrell, who looked at his brother Bill, who looked at Abe Schwartz, and so on around the crowd. But not one of them raised his right hand as Kindred had ordered.

"What's the matter with you men?" demanded Kindred. "Didn't you hear what I said? I'm forming a posse to take care of this business before it gets out of hand. Now raise your right hands like you were told."

He got the same response as before.

"Listen here," said Kindred, beginning to sound frustrated. "You let them do this to John Kelly and they'll be coming into your place next, Mr. Schwartz. Or yours, Mr. Dibrell. Or they'll be wanting to live in the hotel free, Mr. Sokol. You men going to just stand by and let all that happen?"

Reese spoke up. "We pay taxes and license fees for you to do this for us, Mr. Kindred. We aren't lawmen."

"And we aren't soldiers either," said Samusch. "Those men in there fought for the Confederacy. They are hardened veterans. What chance would we have against them?"

"Samusch is right," said Crockett Dibrell. "Kelly has enough guns and ammunition in his place to arm two or three companies of men. We'd be fools to go up against a bunch of men armed like that. Especially these men. No, sir. I will not take up arms against those men."

"So that's how it is," said Kindred. He looked over the whole crowd, his head bobbing as he did. "You all remember this day. Get it down good in your memories because the time is going to come when you'll regret your cowardice."

"You have no right to call us cowards, Kindred," said Reese angrily, shaking his fist at the deputy.

"That's right!" said Crockett Dibrell. "Just who do you think you are, Kindred?"

Before the deputy could answer, a small boy came running up LaGrange Street, shouting, "The Yankees is coming! The Yankees is coming!"

"Good!" said Kindred. "Now we'll get some law laid down here." He spurred his horse and rode off to meet the soldiers.

Markham and his men turned the corner from Fourth onto LaGrange and were met half a block up the street by Kindred. The colonel halted the troop in order to inquire of the deputy.

"Mr. Kindred, what seems to be the matter here?" asked Markham, looking past the horseman at the gathering on the courthouse lawn.

"Seems some rabble are robbing Mr. Kelly's store up the way, Colonel," said Kindred after bringing his mount to a stop. He smiled slyly and added, "Clete Slater's leading them."

Markham was surprised on the one hand to hear Slater's name mentioned as being among the troublemakers, and he was delighted on the other to hear that Slater was actually leading a mob. So the Reb brother shows his true colors after all, he thought. "Slater, you say?" he queried for confirmation.

"That's right, Colonel."

"I see," said Markham, nodding. "So what have you done about the situation so far?"

"Nothing yet. I was trying to get up a posse, but none of them yellow-bellied cowards want to fight." He motioned with a thumb over his shoulder. "Seems they don't want to go up against men who once wore the Confederate gray."

"Is that so?"

"Of course, I can't rightly blame them a whole lot," said Kindred. "Most of them were in Terry's Rangers. You heard of them, haven't you, Colonel?"

Markham certainly had. He had also fought at Shiloh, had heard their Rebel yell, and had seen a fellow officer, his best friend, trying to surrender only to be shot down in cold blood.

When Markham didn't respond to his question, Kindred said, "You might have known them as the 8th Texas Cavalry."

No, he hadn't known them as that, but now he did. And now he knew why he hated and feared Clete Slater.

"And you say Clete Slater is leading them?" asked Markham.

"Yes, sir, I did say that for a fact."

"Thank you, Mr. Kindred," said Markham with the slightest of smiles. "You may stand aside now. I'll take charge from here."

18

Jess Tate caught a glimpse of Isaac Samusch peeking through the window of John Kelly's store and immediately whispered in Slater's ear about seeing him. Slater didn't react outwardly. Instead, he saw his plan working much as he had thought it would.

When the town bell rang, the sound startled every man in the store into motionless silence. Many of them exchanged looks, all wondering what would happen next.

"Hurry up and get what you want, boys," said Slater. "It's high time we were moving on. Jess, you keep an eye on what's happening outside."

"Sure thing, Clete," said Tate. He went to the door, opened it, and craned his head out in time to see the merchants across the street come out of their stores and head down LaGrange to the courthouse square. Cautiously, he edged his way along the boardwalk to the corner of Schwartz and Arnold's store to observe the scene at the town bell.

Slater lowered the gun from Kelly's face. "Mr. Kelly, I want you to write up a receipt for all this and sign it."

"How can I do that, Clete?" asked Kelly. "You're taking so much. I'll be a whole week trying to inventory my goods just to see what you took."

"Bought, Mr. Kelly, bought. Like I said before, you're giving us credit for these goods. I promised you'd be paid for everything, and I mean to keep that promise. Now write up a receipt for me. You put my name on it. No one else's. Just mine. You're extending . . . hm-m . . . let's see. How about ten thousand dollars worth of credit? Does that sound like a good number to you, Mr. Kelly?"

Kelly looked around the store and said, "But, Clete, that's nearly my whole stock. How can you do this to me?"

"It isn't you, Mr. Kelly. I'm doing this for these men and for all the people of this town and this county. Folks are hurting real bad, Mr. Kelly. You know that. The only way we're going to get back on our feet around here is to move some of those cattle that have gotten nice and fat out there on range. We need hard cash around here, Mr. Kelly, and I aim to get us some.''

Tate came back inside just then. ''Clete, it looks like the whole town is meeting on the courthouse lawn.''

''Any law there?'' asked Slater.

''Just like you said it would be. Kindred won't come after us without a posse, and none of the businessmen want any part of being deputies. It looks like we're free and clear.''

''Good,'' said Slater. ''But go back and make sure.''

Tate waved a finger in the air and did as he was told.

''Now how about that receipt, Mr. Kelly?'' asked Slater.

Kelly looked around the store again and said, ''No, I can't do it. I won't do it. You're robbing me, and I won't be a party to it even though it might cost me my life.''

Slater started to raise the Colt to Kelly's nose again, but Tate suddenly burst through the door.

''Clete!'' shouted Tate. ''We got us a whole pack of trouble now. It's Markham. He's coming down the street with a whole troop of cavalry right behind him.''

Most of the men, including Slater, rushed to the front of the store.

''You'll pay for this now!'' shouted Kelly. ''Now you'll pay! Just you wait and see!''

Flewellyn put the muzzle of a shotgun to Kelly's temple and said, ''Now why don't you just shut your mouth, storekeeper? Or do I have to shut it for you?''

Kelly had no way of knowing that Flewellyn had no intention of killing him. Like Slater, Flewellyn was just playing the part of a badman in order to get what they needed.

Slater stuck his head out the door and saw Markham deploying his troops, sending some around the block to surround them, while others dismounted and took up positions in Samusch's grocery and Lindenberg's saloon.

''Sonofabitch!'' swore Tate. ''They got us penned down. What are we going to do, Clete?''

Slater stepped back into the store and looked at thirty grim faces. ''Jake, bring Mr. Kelly over here.''

Flewellyn did as he was ordered.

''Stand in the doorway, Mr. Kelly,'' said Slater, ''and don't do anything else. If you try to run, we'll cut you down before you get five feet away. Now I don't want to have to kill you, but I will if I have to.'' Slater didn't believe his own words, but he hoped Kelly would.

Kelly moved into the doorway and stood as still as he could. Slater stepped up behind him and looked out into the street. It was plain to see that Markham knew what he was doing. Slater turned away and faced his men again.

"Jess is right, boys," said Slater. "We got us a whole peck of trouble out there. We got choices though. Three of them, I figure. We can let Mr. Kelly go and fight it out with those Yankees. Or we can surrender now so no one gets hurt. Or we can hold Mr. Kelly hostage and try to bargain our way out of here." He waited a moment before continuing. "I'd rather not fight, but I don't want to surrender either. I can't promise you anything about how we can talk our way out of this, but I got a feeling that's our best choice. What do you think?"

"Let's fight!" said Flewellyn. "We've whupped more Yankees than this before. We can do it again."

"I had my fill of fighting Yankees," said Simons. "I say we talk it over with them first."

Most of the men agreed with Simons. To those that sided with Flewellyn, Slater said, "You boys willing to go along with the majority here?"

Before they could answer, Texada Ballard and Mrs. Hallet came down LaGrange Street in the phaeton. A soldier tried to stop them before they could cross First Street, but Texada put the whip to him in quick fashion and drove on by, finally pulling up in front of Kelly's store.

"Good Lord! What now?" said Tate, peering through the window. "You got to see this, Clete."

Slater looked out the doorway and saw Texada tying up the gelding at the hitching post. Then she went around the horse to help her grandmother down from the buggy.

Markham saw them, too. "Miss Ballard!" he called from Lindenberg's doorway. "Miss Ballard, you and Mrs. Hallet are in danger. There are armed men in Mr. Kelly's store. Please get back into your carriage and go home."

Texada ignored him as she helped Mrs. Hallet from the phaeton. As always when she came to town, Mrs. Hallet was wearing a brightly colored dress—this time a lavender print with white flowers—and she was carrying her famous chatelaine bag. Local legend had it that Mrs. Hallet carried an old flintlock pistol in that bag. Her late husband had given the weapon to her years ago as protection against marauding Indians, and she had kept it close to her at all times as a sort of keepsake and for those times when it came in handy. Some wags related how she only took it out when she was sure to use the gun. One episode had her clubbing a Tonkawa warrior with it, raising a "knowledge knot" on his head because he insisted on helping himself to a keg of whiskey in her storehouse. For her bravery she was made an honorary member of the tribe. Another relation told of the time when a hide buyer had tried to cheat her on a purchase, and after accusing him of the misdeed, she gave him a running start, then assisted him along his way with a blast of birdshot in his hinder parts. Her own family members fed the legend with reports of how she would threaten to open her bag and let the devil out after them if they didn't behave.

"What's that Yankee going on about, Texada?" asked Mrs. Hallet as if she couldn't hear Markham's every word.

"It ain't nothing, Granny," said Texada, also ignoring Markham's command.

"That's what I thought."

The two of them stepped onto the boardwalk and walked up to the entrance of Kelly's store.

"Morning, John Kelly," said Mrs. Hallet. "You're looking a little peaked these days. Something troubling you?"

Kelly didn't answer.

"Well, don't just stand there, man," said Mrs. Hallet. "Move aside so we can go inside. I've got business here."

Kelly didn't know what to do, but Flewellyn did. He jerked the storekeeper back into the store.

"That's better," said Mrs. Hallet. Then she and Texada walked inside. "Where's Cletus Slater?" she demanded.

"Right here, ma'am," said Slater, moving closer to the lady.

"What's the problem here, Cletus?" asked Mrs. Hallet. "Are you boys having so much trouble finding everything you need that you need to get service at gunpoint? And what are all those Yankees doing out there? Texada, I want you to go and find out what all those Yankees are doing out there."

"Sure thing, Granny," said Texada. Before Slater could stop her, she ran out the door, skipped down from the boardwalk, and sprinted across the street toward Lindenberg's.

Mrs. Hallet watched Texada leave, then said, "Cletus, do you think those guns are necessary?"

"Ask Mr. Kelly, Mrs. Hallet," said Slater. "He's the one being stubborn here."

She eyed Kelly, then said, "We'll talk about this later. Right now, I want to keep an eye on Texada." She moved closer to the window for a better look, nudging a few of the men out of her way.

Markham watched Texada burst out of the store, run over to the saloon, then stop short of the front door. "Miss Ballard, didn't you hear me warn you and your grandmother about those men in the store over there?" he asked through the open door.

"I heard you just fine, Colonel Markham," said Texada, standing in the street with her hands in the back pockets of her blue jeans, "but Granny said to pay you no mind. Now she wants to know what you and all these soldiers are doing here."

"Miss Ballard, those men in the store are armed and dangerous," said Markham, "and they're robbing Mr. Kelly's store. Can't you see that?"

"That's not what Granny wants to know, Colonel. She wants to know what you and your soldiers are doing here."

Markham was incredulous. How could this girl not understand what was going on?

"Miss Ballard, I'm here to stop those men from robbing Mr. Kelly's store."

"All right. I'll go tell Granny that." She spun around and ran back across the street and into the store.

"Did you find out what they're doing out there, Texada?" asked Mrs. Hallet.

"Colonel Markham said Clete and these men are robbing Mr. Kelly's store," said Texada, a little out of breath.

"Cletus, is that true?"

"No, it isn't," said Slater.

"Yes, it is, Mrs. Hallet!" spoke up Kelly.

"I thought I told you to keep your mouth shut," said Flewellyn, tightening his grip on Kelly's arm.

"Take it easy on Mr. Kelly, Jake," said Slater. "I think he's figured out what this is all about now."

Flewellyn nodded, relieved that he could back off from his badman act.

"Well, Cletus, which is it?" asked Mrs. Hallet like a stern parent trying to pry the truth from a guilty child. "Are you robbing this place or not? And don't you lie to me. I won't tolerate a liar."

"No, ma'am, we're not robbing anyone," said Slater. "We

came in here to buy some clothes and things, and I told Mr. Kelly I needed him to carry us on his books for a while. Leastways, until we can hunt up some beeves and trail them to market and get back here with some hard cash to pay him with.''

Mrs. Hallet turned on Kelly and said, ''That don't sound like robbing to me, John Kelly. Where do you come off saying these good boys are here robbing you?''

Kelly looked at Flewellyn, who said, ''Don't be rude now, Mr. Kelly. Answer Mrs. Hallet.''

''But, Mrs. Hallet, I can't give Clete that much credit,'' whined Kelly. ''It'll ruin me.''

''No, it won't, John Kelly,'' said Mrs. Hallet. ''It'll ruin you if you don't. Cletus, did you give your word that you'd pay for these goods you boys have picked out?''

''Yes, ma'am, I did.''

''There you go, John Kelly,'' said Mrs. Hallet. ''You've got Cletus's word on it. What more do you need?''

''I need cash, Mrs. Hallet.''

''No, you don't. You've got Cletus's word, and that's as good as gold. I've known Cletus since he was a babe, and I've never known him to lie or go back on his word. His granddaddy raised him to be honest and sincere. You should know that, John Kelly. You dealt enough with Dougald, God rest his soul. Cletus is a true Slater, and that's all the payment you need until he hands you the cash himself. Isn't that so?''

Kelly knew when he was licked. ''Yes, ma'am. I suppose it is so.'' He turned to Slater. ''I suppose you'll still be wanting a receipt for all this, Clete?''

Slater smiled and said, ''Yes, I would, Mr. Kelly. I'll need it to keep the books straight.''

''Hello in the store!'' called Markham from across the street.

''Now who is that?'' asked Mrs. Hallet.

''It's that Yankee colonel, Granny,'' said Texada.

''Oh, yes. Him. Go tell him there isn't anyone in here robbing John Kelly's store, and if he doesn't believe you, tell him I said for him to come over here and see for himself.''

Texada grinned and said, ''Sure thing, Granny.''

Just as she had before, Texada dashed out of the store and across the street to the exact same spot from where she had spoken to Markham the first time.

''Miss Ballard, what's going on in there?'' demanded Markham.

''Nothing, Colonel Markham,'' said Texada, ''and Granny says there ain't no one robbing no one neither. And if you don't believe her, then you're to come and see for yourself.''

Markham was incredulous again. ''Do you take me for a fool, Miss Ballard? I know there is a robbery going on over there, and I intend to stop it. Now you go get your grandmother out of there so I can do my duty.''

''I'm telling you, Colonel, Granny said there ain't no robbery and for you to come see for yourself.''

Markham thought about it for a second, then called out, ''Hello in the store! Clete Slater, I want to talk with you.''

Slater moved toward the door.

''Hold on, Cletus,'' said Mrs. Hallet. ''That's a Yankee out there, and he's not to be trusted.'' She turned to Kelly and said, ''John Kelly, I think you should tell that Yankee everything is just fine and dandy in here and for him to take his soldier boys and go about his business elsewhere.'' When Kelly didn't move right off, she added, ''Get a move on, John Kelly, or would you like to see what I've got in my bag?''

Kelly flinched at the mention of her bag, then said, ''No, ma'am, I wouldn't.''

Instead of Slater coming out, Kelly stepped into the doorway of his store. ''Colonel Markham, this is John Kelly. What Miss Texada says is true. There is no one robbing my store. Everything is just fine over here, so why don't you take your men and go about your business?''

''See? I told you so,'' said Texada snidely. ''Why don't you Yankees just go about your business and leave peaceable folks alone?'' Then she went back to the store.

''Slater, I still want to talk with you!'' shouted Markham.

Slater stepped up behind Kelly in the doorway and answered, ''Come on over here, Colonel,'' answered Slater, ''and we can talk all you like.''

Markham turned to a lieutenant beside him and said, ''It looks like we were misinformed about this incident, Stoiber. So form up the men, and I'll join you at the town square as soon as I've had my say with Slater.''

''Yes, sir,'' said Stoiber, saluting.

Markham holstered his revolver and walked across the street to Kelly's store. He stepped onto the boardwalk and halted.

''Slater, I'd rather talk out here.''

Slater came outside and faced the colonel. ''Something on your mind, Colonel?''

"Listen, Slater. I don't know exactly what you're trying to pull off here, but let me warn you that I won't tolerate any lawlessness out of you or this rabble that I hear is following you now. You step across the line of the law just once, and I'll be waiting there to put you behind bars myself. You're getting off today, but only because you Rebel cowards had an old woman's skirts to hide behind."

"Are you finished, Colonel?"

"I think that about says it all."

"Not quite, Colonel," said Slater as coldly as he could. "The war's over for me, Colonel Markham, and it's over for those men in there as well. We're home now, and you're trespassing here as far as we're concerned. As long as you and your men mind your manners, we'll all get along peacefully."

"Are you threatening me, Slater?"

"No, he's not," said Mrs. Hallet, coming through the doorway, "but I am, Colonel Markham. These boys are tired of fighting. All they want is to be left alone so they can go about earning a living again. That's all they want, and if you don't leave them be, I'll shoot you myself, Colonel Markham." She patted her bag to punctuate her point. "And don't think I won't do it. I may be old, but I can still pull the trigger on a handgun."

Markham had been in Lavaca County long enough to know all about Mrs. Hallet and her chatelaine bag. He was sufficiently impressed with her threat and looked it.

"Like Cletus said, Colonel Markham," continued Mrs. Hallet, "you're trespassing on our land. You mind your manners as guests here, and we'll all get along peacefully."

Markham didn't know what to say except, "Yes, ma'am." He tipped his hat and added, "Good day, Mrs. Hallet." And he left to join his men in the town square.

Mrs. Hallet turned to Slater and said, "Cletus, next time you boys need a little credit here in town you'd better come see me first." She patted his hand, winked, and added, "You hear?"

Slater smiled, tipped his hat, and said, "Yes, ma'am, we sure will do that."

19

Once the other merchants of Hallettsville heard about Mrs. Hallet's intervention, credit was no longer a problem for Slater. Crockett and William Dibrell sold him horses; the Kuehne brothers sold him saddles and other leather goods; and Frank Richarts sold him a wagon. All on credit.

With all the gear and supplies they needed to start ranching, Slater and his newly hired hands from the thicket camp on Alamo Creek moved out to what was left of the Tate farm.

The Tates came to Lavaca County in 1850 and bought a quarter of a headright about six miles east of Hallettsville. Their purchase lay just to the south and west of Glengarry, close enough that the northeast corner of the Tate property touched the southwest corner of the Slater plantation. Most of the ground was flat and covered with a heavy growth of oaks and hackberries. Wild cattle and hogs roamed everywhere on it, but they usually bedded down close to the spring that was the beginning of a feeder for Sandies Creek.

That first year Jedadiah Tate, Jess's father, cleared ten acres, built a cabin for the family and a lean-to for the tame stock, sank a well, and planted a few acres of cotton and a few acres of corn. In 1851, he constructed corn cribs, cotton bins, and cowpens, including one for the three milch cows they kept, and he added a log barn that he replaced in '58 with a real frame structure. Each year after that he cleared and planted another five acres: two in cotton, two in corn, and one in white peas. Twice a year he hunted up a few unmarked cows and hogs, butchered them for meat, and tanned the cowhides himself to make shoes and other leather goods for the family's use. With each passing year, the Tates prospered a little better than the year before. In 1857, they were even able to buy clapboards to weatherboard their cabin and make it into a real house.

All was going fine for the Tates until Matt, the older of the two sons, heard about the gold rush to Colorado and struck out for

Denver, leaving Jedadiah with only two-thirds of his labor force. Then the War Between the States broke out, and Jess enlisted in Terry's Rangers. Jedadiah was himself forced into the Home Guards, and gradually, the Tates began losing the economic ground that they had gained in the previous decade.

When Jedadiah was killed in action against a band of deserters and draft dodgers near Seguin, his wife, Nancy, was left alone to run the place. She was forced to sell all the livestock to pay some debts and meet the heavy taxes placed on the property by the Confederacy just to keep the farm until Jess came back from the war. That spring, shortly after Jess returned, she died, leaving the farm to Jess and Matt, should he ever return to claim his inheritance.

Not having a cent to his name or owning a horse or even a pistol, Jess Tate buried his mother and left the farm. He joined his fellow veterans at the camp on Alamo Creek and tried to eke out an existence until the day he prayed would come along soon, when his brother would return from Colorado with enough money for them to take up farming again. He never expected his prayers would be answered by Clete Slater.

Tate warned Slater that the old place was in fairly bad condition. He wasn't wrong. In the short time since Nancy Tate's demise, wild cattle and hogs had moved into the house and destroyed most of the furniture and other household goods that Tate had left behind when he moved to the thicket camp. The fences and pens were all broken down, and the barn was in need of a new roof. Even the well needed priming.

"First things first," said Slater as he and Tate inspected the house from the front doorway. "Let's get these critters out of here." He pointed at the hogs wallowing in the wreckage they had made. Turning to Tate, he added, "Get some of the boys to help us."

Tate nodded, stepped back on the porch, and called to the other men to aid them in ridding the house of critters, and six men responded.

"Go slow, boys," said Slater, meeting them on the porch. "There might be rattlers or some other kind of snake in here. Better get some long sticks to poke around with."

The men armed themselves and went in through the front door, hollering at the top of their lungs and poking at the debris with their sticks, and the sows, suckers, and boars exited through the rear doorway. No one turned up any snakes.

Slater followed the animals outside, drew the new Colt's .44 that he had purchased from Kelly's store, and shot the biggest boar behind an ear, dropping the beast before it could wander off to the brush. He tried to take aim at another but held back because the first shot had scared the other varmints into running for safety. Turning to the other men, he said, "Let's get a good fire going here and roast this porker right now. Jake, have you got strength enough to gut this hog?"

Flewellyn smiled broadly, whipped a big bowie knife from its sheath inside his right boot, and said, "You just stand back and see how much strength I got to gut that hog." He hurried past Slater to the hog and went right to work bleeding and disemboweling the carcass.

Tate and the other men gathered firewood—mostly broken fence rails, broken boards from the bins and cribs, and sticks from the cowpens—and piled it in the yard. Slater found an old wagon axle and two wheels in the barn. He dragged them over to Flewellyn, who had finished his job. With some help from a few of the others, he mounted the hog on the axle, made a spit of it between the wheels, and placed the porker over the fire that Tate had started.

"We'll eat first," said Slater. "Then we'll go about making this farm fit for people again."

And so it went. They ate, then worked. They ate again, then slept.

The next morning Slater shot another boar, and they started the new day with fresh meat. Then he made the work assignments. He put Flewellyn in charge of the others and told them to work on roofing the barn, cutting rails and posts for a new stable, and remodeling the house. "See if you can't make us bunk beds," he told the boys. "I had enough of sleeping on the ground during the war." He got a lot of amens to that remark, and everybody set to working.

At the same time, Slater and Tate rode from one homestead to the next dealing with the owners on their cattle. Slater couldn't offer them hard cash on the spot, so he made working agreements with them: his outfit would hunt up all the cattle on the place, drive them to the landowner's pens, brand all the unmarked stock, and castrate all the bull calves and yearlings. As payment for their labor, Slater's crowd would be given every tenth steer and every twentieth unbred heifer, and for trailing the owner's herd to market with theirs, they would receive half of the money from the sale of the herd. Slater made deals like this with almost every stockman between the Navidad and Lavaca rivers, from the Gonzalez-Columbus Road on the north to the old Colorado county line on the south.

The only two places that Slater and Tate didn't visit were the Campbell plantation and Glengarry. Slater knew that Sophia Campbell would probably shoot him on sight, and if she didn't, her foster sons just might bushwhack him and Tate. As for Glengarry, Colonel Markham had forbidden him to come near his home. He would obey that order for now because he wasn't sure that Dent and Malinda weren't going along with Markham on his order. Until he learned different, he'd keep his distance. "We don't need their cattle, anyway," he told Tate as they crossed the road that separated the Campbell place from Glengarry on their way back to the Tate ranch. He was only fooling himself with that line, but Tate wasn't about to call him on it. Not yet, anyway.

As they neared home, Tate asked, "What do you plan to call this here ranch, Clete?"

"What am I going to call it?" asked Slater, surprised that Tate should ask him such a question. "It's your place. You name it something."

"Sure, I know I'm the owner, but you're the one putting up the money here. Naming this outfit should be up to you."

Slater's mind was elsewhere and Tate's conversation irritated him. He showed his displeasure when he said, "I don't want to name it, Jess. You do it."

Tate twisted up his face and frowned at his friend. "Are you ducking your responsibility here, Clete?"

"Hell no!" snapped Slater. "I just don't care to do the naming, that's all. You name it something and be done with it."

"Well, I suppose," said Tate as he drifted off in thought, ignoring Slater's ire. Only a few seconds passed before he said, "I think I got it." He reined in his horse and jumped down. "Hold on, Clete, and have a lookey here." He slipped his knife from the sheath in his boot and knelt down on the ground.

Slater pulled up on Nimbus, dismounted, and stood beside Tate, watching him draw in the dirt with his knife.

"The flag of Texas has one star on it, right?" queried Tate.

"Sure. One star," said Slater. "What about it?"

"Well, that's one star," said Tate as he drew a star in the dirt. "One star for Texas." He drew another star with two of its points touching two points of the first one. "And this star is for us. Or this star can be for me and that one for you. Either way, I think we should call our ranch the Double Star Ranch. What do you think of that, Clete?"

"First off," he said, "since when did it become our ranch? This place belongs to you and your brother, Matt. Not me."

"Until Matt comes home," said Tate, standing up, "I'm making you my partner. We'll go thirds in this, if that makes you feel better."

"Thirds?"

"That's right," said Tate, mounting up again. "A third for you. A third for me. A third for Matt. Fair enough?"

"Sounds fair enough to me," said Slater, climbing into the saddle again. "I just hope Matt thinks so when he comes home."

"Well, we'll just cross that bridge when Matt brings it home to us," said Tate. He thrust a hand at Slater and said, "Until then, it's just us, partner."

Slater couldn't stay angry with his oldest and best friend. He shook Tate's hand and thought, At least some things stay the same. Thanks, Lord, for a friend like Jess Tate.

And the Double Star Ranch was born.

20

Although he wouldn't admit it openly, Denton Slater was rankled by his brother's business dealings. It wasn't the fact that he was left out of Clete's plans; no, it was being shown up again—whether intentionally or not—that bothered Dent.

Being raised in the shadow of a brother who was popular with everyone and who always seemed to do the right thing put a lot of pressure on Denton Slater to turn out the same way, especially since he resembled Clete so much. He didn't need to look so much like Clete; it was tough enough already just being a scion of one of Lavaca County's leading families. If he'd been given a nickel for every time he heard someone say, "Why can't you be more like your brother?" or "You have a family name to be proud of," he would have had enough money to leave Lavaca County and make his own fortune elsewhere.

But that wasn't how it was. Dent's older brother went off to war in 1861 after most of the summer work was done, leaving him at home with an elderly grandfather and a sister who had decided that she was the lady of the house the day after their mother had wed her second husband and moved away with him. The comparisons to his brother had been bad enough to endure when Clete was at home, but they became worse and more frequent after he was gone, especially after Clete was reported killed at Shiloh. That put the specter of a dead hero hanging over Dent.

As the war worsened for the Confederacy, his grandfather's health began to fail, placing the responsibilities of the master of Glengarry on Dent. His youth and inexperience worked against him, and he made mistakes, such as planting the corn too early and losing much of the crop to a late frost; if he'd only noted that the horses and cattle hadn't shed their winter coats yet, he would have realized that one more cold spell was likely to occur. The demands of running the plantation grew and grew, leaving Dent with less and less time to spend socializing with his friends, even when the party was at Glengarry. The pressures became too great for him, so to relieve some of the stress, he took to the jug—and Hannah.

Dent changed with each passing season, but only Hannah noticed the difference. She knew about the seed of resentment that was planted in Dent on the day when Clete rode off with Jess Tate and the others to join Terry's Rangers. Everyone patted Clete on the back and told him what a glorious thing it was that he was doing, while all they could say to Dent was something about how it was too bad he couldn't go, too. Then when news came of Clete's alleged death at Shiloh, the seed sprouted because some people were saying Dent should enlist and avenge his brother's death; but, of course, he couldn't go. It was his duty to stay home; being the sole male heir now, he had to perpetuate the family name. And when his grandfather died, Dent's growing resentment toward Clete came out into the open with the filing of Dougald Slater's will. In one part of the document, Dougald praised Clete for giving his life for Texas, but in the next paragraph, he bequeathed Glengarry to Dent for remaining loyal to the Union.

Inheriting Glengarry as he did almost led to Dent's undoing. Until the contents of Dougald's will became widely known through the spread of gossip, no one had suspected Dent of having Union sympathies. Nor did anyone except Dent, Aaron Miller, and Jim

Kindred, the county enrolling officer, know that Dougald had made
a deal with Kindred to hire Miller to go in Dent's place when he
was drafted into the Confederate army shortly after his nineteenth
birthday; and that fact wouldn't have gotten out if not for Miller.
He deserted and joined up with other deserters and draft dodgers
holed up in Somer's Thicket, then he got caught and told everyone
about being "that Yankee-loving Dent Slater's replacement" in
order to save his neck from a lynching. Miller's declaration reinforced all the rumors surrounding Dougald's will, turning the
Home Guards—who were about to string up Miller—into a mob
bent on doing the same to the master of Glengarry. Dent's savior
was Sheriff Joe Loe, who convinced the mob that if they hanged
one Yankee sympathizer, then they had better hang them all because any survivors would tell the Union Army—when it came,
and it was sure to come—about the lynchings, and there was no
telling how those Yankees might react to such unpleasantness.

Dent never felt very secure after that incident until Colonel
Markham arrived with the first contingent of Federals and declared
Lavaca County as captured territory subject to his authority. As
soon as he heard that Union cavalry were coming up the road from
Matagorda Bay, Dent rode out to introduce himself to the commander of the troop, hoping to endear himself as a loyal Unionist.
During the ride into Hallettsville, Dent invited Markham to come
out to Glengarry and make it his headquarters. The colonel took
one look at the town and accepted the invitation with the hope
that the plantation would prove to be more to his liking.

At first sight of Glengarry, Markham wasn't impressed, and he
began wondering if he hadn't made a mistake. Then he saw Malinda standing on the veranda, and suddenly, he saw himself as
the knight-errant riding up to a castle in a distant land to rescue
the lovely damsel in distress. Malinda—with her emerald eyes,
auburn hair, creamy complexion, blushed cheeks, and ruby lips—
was attired in a dark green flowing dress with a low lace collar
that revealed every bit of her slender neck. He was smitten with
her at first sight. No, he had not made a mistake in coming to
Glengarry. He and his men would stay.

Over the next few weeks, Markham assisted Dent in collecting
many of the debts owed to Dougald Slater's estate simply by
sending a detachment of soldiers with Dent as he called on the
debtors. The cavalrymen never made any threats in Dent's behalf.
They didn't have to. Dent did it for them, telling the delinquent
payer if they didn't settle up with him at that very moment that

the Yankees would take everything they owned and throw them off their property or, worse, jail them. Dent never failed to collect, sometimes in cash but more often in services or stock.

While Dent was away foreclosing, Markham remained at Glengarry most of the time romancing Malinda, and she was receptive to his advances. He was fairly handsome, charming, educated, well mannered, and cultured. She would have to travel far to find another potential husband with as many attributes. Even so, something was missing; there was no chemistry between them. This would come, she felt, with the consummation of their marriage. Until then, it was unimportant.

All seemed to be going as well as expected for Dent, Malinda, and Markham. The two men had become close friends as Markham unknowingly became the authority figure that Dent needed in his life. Malinda had found a satisfactory mate, and Markham had fallen in love.

Then Clete came home, and once again Dent felt the pressure of his brother's shadow. Damn him! Dent would swear during his nightly stupors. Why couldn't he stay dead? Why did he have to come home?

Hannah would try to reason with him and convince him that he shouldn't feel that way about Clete. "He's your brother," she would say. "Your own flesh and blood. You should love him, not hate him. Hate like that will eat you alive, Dent Honey."

"I don't care," he'd snap back. "I hate him."

Hannah would then take him to bed and try to get his mind off his brother. If nothing else, lovemaking would let him fall asleep easily, and for that much, Hannah was grateful. She would then pray that something would happen to remake Dent into the man that she always imagined he would become, a man of kindness, a man of feelings, a man who would appreciate the gentler side of life and who would work to make his world a more beautiful place for everybody. That man was inside Dent; she knew he was there. She'd seen him on more than one occasion. If she could only set him free!

21

In the days following the incident at John Kelly's store, Markham heard about Clete's plans for a cowhunt and drive and took the news to Dent and Malinda at Glengarry. It was early afternoon when he arrived. Dent and Malinda received him in the parlor. They exchanged pleasantries, then got down to the purpose of Markham's visit. Markham stood by the fireplace, and Malinda sat on the sofa that faced the doors to the foyer and allowed her a view through the front windows, while Dent sat in his overstuffed chair between the fireplace and the side window.

"Word has it," said Markham, "that Mrs. Hallet is backing Clete in this venture."

"Who gives a damn?" complained Dent. He twisted uncomfortably in his chair and took a swallow of corn whiskey from a drinking glass. "She hasn't got any money." He glanced at Malinda on the sofa. "Not enough to back a cattle drive, anyway."

"With all the merchants giving him credit, Clete doesn't need cash," said Markham. "And from what I'm hearing about the deals he's making with every stockman, farmer, and planter between the rivers, he won't have to spend a dime. All he has to do is round up everybody's cows and drive them to market."

"Not everybody's cows," said Malinda, reminding Markham that Clete hadn't been to Glengarry to transact any business.

"That's right, dear sister," said Dent bitterly. "Not everybody's cows. He won't come here and try to make a deal with me, his own brother."

"And why should he?" asked Malinda. "Have you made any effort to approach him?" She waited for an answer, but when Dent didn't offer one, she continued speaking. "No, of course not."

Markham joined Malinda on the sofa. "You don't need Clete," he said. "You have all the men you need to have your own cattle drive."

Dent laughed and said, "You mean those darkies? Hell's bells, Lucas! Those darkies don't know enough about cowhunting and cattle drives and branding to do a job like that. And they sure as hell don't know anything about trailing a herd to market. Most of them have never even been out of the county. How do you think they'd do trying to find a place in New Orleans? All they know is planting, weeding, and picking. Tell them to round up a few bales of cotton and you'll do just fine. But tell them to go near a bunch of moss horns? Hell, you might as well tell them to take a running jump off a cliff."

Malinda glanced through a front window at an approaching carriage and said, "Good Lord! It's Sophia Campbell and those loathsome Detchen brothers coming up the drive." She stood, prompting Markham to do the same. "I do not wish to be in the same room with that woman, Lucas."

"Why not?" asked Markham.

"There's not enough time now to tell you about Sophia Campbell, Lucas," said Malinda. "Please excuse me. I'll be in my room until she leaves." And Malinda marched from the parlor.

"Never mind her," said Dent. "Sophia Campbell isn't very popular with anyone in the county. Neither are Harlan and Farley." He paused, then reflected, "I wish I'd seen that fight they had with Clete. Both those bastards should be whipped regular."

Markham moved over to the front windows, looked out, and saw a bony stick of a woman, who appeared to be about forty, wearing a homespun brown dress and straw sun hat, pulling up her buggy in front of the house with Harlan and Farley Detchen riding up behind her. Sophia stepped down from the conveyance carrying an umbrella and tied up the chestnut mare at the hitching post. Harlan and Farley Detchen dismounted and tied their horses to the same hitching post. They followed Sophia up the steps to the door, which she rapped soundly with the handle of the umbrella.

Hannah answered the door.

"Where's your master, girl?" asked Sophia as she came through the door.

Hannah stood back with lowered eyes, not out of fear but out of hatred and repugnance. There wasn't an ex-slave in the county who didn't hate the Campbells and Detchens and with good reason. Slaves on the Campbell plantation were frequently beaten to work harder, and two of them were murdered by Sophia's overseers. Afraid that her slaves would find out how bad they had it and would run off, she forbade them to fraternize with slaves from surrounding farms and ranches. Although the war was over and the abuses of slavery were supposed to have ended with it, the Campbells and Detchens continued to mistreat Negroes.

"Speak up, girl," said Harlan as he entered.

Raising her head proudly and looking Sophia straight in the eyes, Hannah said, "Mr. Slater is in the parlor."

Sophia and her foster sons were offended by Hannah's attitude. How dare she look at a white person squarely! Sophia raised her hand to slap Hannah's impudent face, but something stayed the blow. Fear? Respect? Certainly not conscience; Sophia had none.

"Go on and hit her, Ma," said Harlan.

"You want me to hit her, Ma?" asked Farley, eager to do it.

Hannah ignored both Detchens, continuing to glare at Sophia, hoping she was making the woman feel all the hate and disgust every former slave in Lavaca County held for her.

Sophia didn't know why she'd held back; she just did, and it shook her deeply. It hurt. The pain was something akin to being told that you're a dinosaur and you're about to become extinct.

Farley stepped forward to slap Hannah, but Sophia, her eyes locked on Hannah's, grabbed his hand. "No," she said. "Leave her be."

"But, Ma—" protested Farley.

"I said to leave her be!" snapped Sophia in a warning growl. She blinked.

Hannah had won. Pouring salt on Sophia's wound, she pointed to the doorway to the parlor and said, "Right through there, Miz Campbell."

"Uppity nigger," muttered Sophia, then without further ado, she marched into the parlor, only to stop abruptly when she saw Markham.

Harlan and Farley were stunned by Sophia's behavior. They had never known her to back down from anyone, least of all a Negro. They didn't understand, and their confusion frightened them. They exchanged looks, then followed Sophia into the parlor, flanking her just inside the doorway.

Hannah remained in the foyer, knowing that she would be needed soon. Glengarry had guests. Despicable guests, but guests all the same. And as such, they would be extended the hospitality of the plantation. That was the Slater way.

"Well, Miz Campbell," said Denton, not rising from his over-stuffed easy chair between the fireplace and the side window, "to what do I owe the pleasure of your company?''

"Denton Slater, you're drunk," said Sophia, "and the day is only half-over."

"I'm not drunk, ma'am, but I intend to be before the day is over."

Sophia turned to Markham standing before the front window and stared at him.

Markham suddenly realized that he had been a spectator to this point but should have been a participant. In a reflex, he came to attention, gave Sophia a half bow from the waist, then straightened to address her.

"Madam, I don't believe we've been properly introduced," said Markham. "I am Colonel Lucas—"

"I know who you are, Yankee. You're the one who's been sparking Malinda. Going to marry her, I hear. Might as well. No one around here wants her now. Not since she's been de—"

She stopped herself from saying, "Not since she's been deflowered by a Yankee." Of course, it was only rumored that Malinda and the colonel had known each other in the Biblical sense, but even Sophia, as rude as she was, knew there were limits to crude conversation. Had she completed the sentence, she would have offended Markham so greatly that were she a man he might have drawn his Colt's revolver and shot her on the spot. Woman or not, he might have been offended enough to do it anyway.

Sophia cleared her throat and said, feigning a friendly smile, "I meant to say, Colonel Markham, that no man around here would dare show any romantic attentions toward dear Malinda now that she is betrothed to a northern gentleman such as yourself."

Markham unclenched his jaws and said, "I believe I am addressing the renowned Mrs. Sophia Campbell, am I not?"

"Yes, you are," said Sophia, not sure how to take this man.

"Mrs. Campbell, I am pleased to make your acquaintance," said Markham. Then he bowed again.

"Well, you've got good manners," said Sophia. "Especially for a Yankee, er, I mean, a northern gentleman."

Dent laughed and said, "Hell, Miz Campbell, Lucas won't take offense for you calling him a Yankee. There's folks calling him a lot worse, I hear."

"Denton Slater," said Sophia, turning on him like a maiden aunt, "you should be ashamed of yourself. Drinking in the middle

of the day when there's work to be done. Why, your granddaddy
would—''

''My granddaddy's dead,'' said Dent, cutting her short, ''and
I'd appreciate it if you'd leave him rest in peace.'' He looked past
Sophia at Harlan and Farley. ''State your business, Miz Campbell,
then take your two dogs out of here.''

Farley took offense and said, ''You ain't got no call to talk to
my mama that way.''

''Never mind, Farley,'' said Sophia, half-turning to speak to
her adopted son. ''Dent's right. We didn't come here to socialize.
We came here to conduct a little business.'' She turned back to
her host. ''Denton, are you aware of what your brother is up to?''

''My brother's dead,'' said Dent.

''Dent, there's no reason to talk like that,'' said Markham
evenly. ''We all know Clete is alive, and we all know what he's
been doing since he came back to Lavaca County. So why not
behave yourself and act like the master of Glengarry?''

If the same lecture had come from any other quarter, Dent would
have rebutted it with juvenile sarcasm or adolescent miscreance.
Instead, he accepted the scolding with maturity because he felt
Markham was genuinely concerned about him.

Suddenly sobered, Dent put his glass down on the end table
and pushed himself erect. He turned to Sophia and said, ''Excuse
me, Miz Campbell. Won't you please sit down? Could I offer you
a cool drink?''

Sophia went to the davenport facing the fireplace and sat down.
''Thank you, Denton. A cool drink would be nice.'' She glanced
over her shoulder at Farley and Harlan, who had taken positions
behind the sofa. ''Something for the boys, too.''

''Hannah!'' shouted Dent.

Playing her role as the servant, Hannah stepped into the doorway
of the parlor and said, ''Yes, Mr. Dent?''

''Hannah, bring our guests some cider,'' said Dent.

''Right away, Mr. Dent,'' said Hannah. Then she curtsied and
left for the kitchen.

''Lucas,'' said Dent, ''why don't you sit, too?''

Markham sat in the chair that had become his over the past
several weeks, and Dent also seated himself.

''Now what brings you to Glengarry, Miz Campbell?'' asked
Dent. ''You said something about business.''

''Yes, business,'' said Sophia slowly, still a bit unnerved by
Hannah's attitude. ''As you know, Clete and that bunch of no-

goods he hired are hunting up cows for just about everyone in this part of the county except you and me. That sort of puts you and me in the same pea pod. Well, I don't like it. It ain't that I object to sharing the same place as you, Denton Slater. It's being left out when there's money to be made. Trouble is, I don't have all that many cows on my range, so I wouldn't stand to make a whole lot even if I was one of the honored. Now you're in the same boat as me, Denton, but you're at the other end of it. You got plenty of cows roaming around Glengarry, but you don't have anyone to hunt them up for you.''

''What makes you think I want to hunt up my cattle, Miz Campbell? This is a cotton plantation, not *el rancho ganado*.''

''I know you, Denton Slater,'' said Sophia. ''You're a Scotsman, the same as I am. You want to make money any way you can as long as it's legal. Am I right or not?''

''What's your proposition, Miz Campbell?'' asked Dent impatiently.

''My sons, them that can, and a few other lads are willing to hunt up your cows with mine, brand your calves for you, and drive your older stock to market for you, and all I'm asking is for you to let them put my brand on half the unmarked stock found on your range. That's the deal Clete is giving folks. I should think you'd want no less.''

Before Dent could answer, Hannah came into the room carrying a pewter tray that had five crystal tumblers and a pitcher of cider on it. She served everyone, then left.

''Odd that you should come here at this particular time with your proposition, Mrs. Campbell,'' said Markham, dangling the bait in front of the hungry fish.

''How's that, Colonel Markham?'' asked Sophia.

''Dent and I were discussing hunting up cattle and driving them to market just before you arrived.''

''My, that is interesting, Colonel,'' said Sophia, practically licking her lips with anticipation. ''And did you come to any conclusion?''

''Only that darkies don't like cattle,'' said Dent dryly.

''Well, we were discussing the possible use of the coloreds,'' said Markham.

''You don't want to use niggers, Colonel,'' said Sophia as if she'd just caught scent of a pack of skunks. ''They're all lazy and useless unless you keep the whip apopping over their heads all the time.''

"And how often on their backs, Miz Campbell?" queried Dent.

Irately, she replied, "Whenever it's necessary to make them work proper."

Changing the subject, Markham said, "You mentioned your sons, Mrs. Campbell. How many do you have?"

"Five, including my adopted sons, Harlan and Farley here. My Stewart is big enough to help on a drive. Tucker and Mason are only youngsters."

"You and Mr. Campbell are quite fortunate, Mrs. Campbell," said Markham.

"I am a widow, Colonel." Then rather proudly, she added, "My late husband, Dr. John Campbell, passed away during the war."

"My condolences, madam," said Markham.

"Thank you, Colonel," said Sophia. "But back to the discussion of cowhunts and cattle drives."

"Miz Campbell, I don't think I'd be interested in having your boys rounding up my cattle," said Dent.

Sophia glared at Dent for a moment before saying, "Is that your final word on the matter, Denton?"

"Mrs. Campbell, excuse me for interrupting," said Markham, "but would you please allow me a minute alone with Dent?"

"Why, certainly, Colonel," said Sophia.

"Dent, could we go to the kitchen?" asked Markham.

"You're wasting your breath, Lucas," said Dent.

"Let's discuss it in the kitchen," said Markham, rising from his chair.

"All right, if you insist," said Dent, also getting up.

The two men left the parlor, walked through the foyer, then down a short hall to the kitchen, bypassing the dining room.

Hannah was busy at the sink when they entered. She stopped working and looked at them.

Seeing Hannah there bothered Markham. "Get rid of the girl," he said to Dent.

"Why?" asked Dent.

"I'd rather talk to you alone," said Markham.

"It's all right to talk in front of Hannah," said Dent. "She's—"

Markham held up a hand to interrupt Dent and said, "Get rid of her."

Dent shrugged and said, "All right, Lucas, I'll tell her to leave." He turned to Hannah and simply said, "Would you mind leaving us, Hannah?"

Hannah didn't like Markham, but she loved Dent. "I'll be down back if you need me," she said. Then she stepped out the back door.

Satisfied that Hannah was out of earshot, Markham returned to the reason for them to be in the kitchen. "Now look, Dent," he said, "I don't see what your objection is to Mrs. Campbell's proposition."

"It isn't her, Lucas. It's Harlan and Farley. Clete—" He stopped himself from finishing the story, and instead, he said, "I've never gotten along with those boys. Nobody has. They're two of the meanest bastards in the county."

"Did they take part in the Rebellion?" asked Markham.

"They were Heel Flies."

"Heel Flies?" queried Markham.

"Home Guards, Lucas. That didn't do anything to help their popularity. A lot of folks around here liked the idea of leaving the Union, but they didn't want to fight for the Confederacy. Harlan and Farley joined the Home Guards almost as soon as Jim Kindred got his appointment as enrolling officer. That kept them from being conscripted by Kindred."

"Then they wouldn't be friends with anyone in your brother's crowd, I take it," asked Markham.

"Hardly. Most of them wouldn't walk across the street to spit on either Harlan or Farley."

Markham nodded, became pensive for a moment, then said, "How do you think your brother and his friends are going to feel if you and Mrs. Campbell join together to compete with them for the stray cattle roaming the range? Don't you think that it will stick in their craw just a bit?"

Dent thought about it for a few seconds, and a smile came over his face. Sophia's proposition had appeal after all.

"You know, Lucas, you just might have something there. It would be nice to show up my big brother, even if just this once. All right, I'll make a deal with Miz Campbell but on my terms."

Markham frowned and said, "Such as?"

"Such as we divide the maverick stock a bit differently. She gets every sixth unmarked cow and no more. After all, there may be several hundred unbranded and unmarked cows roaming around out there. At the going rate of twenty dollars a head, I'd be a fool to let her have half of them."

Markham's face showed his pleasure as he patted Dent on the shoulder and said, "Let's go strike the bargain with the lady."

Dent stopped and said, "Don't ever underestimate Sophia Campbell, Lucas. That woman in the parlor is no more a lady than a black widow spider is."

Markham laughed at the comparison but felt strangely uncomfortable as he did.

22

Word about the alliance between Dent Slater and Sophia Campbell spread around Lavaca County in no time at all, giving more than one wag the chance to repeat the old adage about bad news traveling fast. Their working agreement became the number one topic of conversation throughout the countryside and in the towns, too. All the stockmen and farmers who had lined up with Clete wondered how he would take the news, while those folks not in agriculture perked up at the possibility that there might be some excitement in the near future because sooner or later the two outfits were bound to collide.

Slater was bothered by the arrangement between his brother and the Detchens more than he cared to admit. Not having spoken with Dent since returning home, he was having a hard time believing everything he was hearing about his sibling. He kept asking himself how Dent could have changed so much in such a short time, and each time he did he would realize that four years of war was an eternity to some people. It had been to him.

Slater would consider himself, how he was a different man now, wiser, better educated in the ways of the world and the rules of life and death. He had killed men—in the heat of battle, to be sure, but they were dead by his hand just the same. That fact alone made a significant difference in him.

Before his company's first fight, he hadn't given the idea of killing another human being much thought, but after seeing Jake Flewellyn shoot down a Union soldier in the skirmish near Bowling Green and seeing Willie Beall die just seconds later, killing other men took up a lot of his thinking time. He reasoned that he was a small part of an army that was fighting for the freedom of its country and that the men on the other side of the war were bent on killing him and his friends; therefore, he had to kill them first. Coming to this conclusion made killing easier, impersonal, a matter of course. He refused to consider that the men he killed were anything like him or his friends, that they could talk and think like them, that they had families and friends of their own. To think of these things would drive him mad; he would not let them prey on his sanity, so he swept such thoughts from his mind. The war had hardened him this way.

Slater knew that much about himself. So why shouldn't the war have had some drastic effect on Dent as well? But, he asked himself, could the change in Dent be so great that he would sidle up to Sophia Campbell and the Detchens? Evidently so.

This thought plagued Slater as he, Tate, Flewellyn, and the rest turned their energies toward hunting up every cow, calf, bull, and steer they could find in an area of the county that covered almost a hundred square miles. They started by working Tate's land, bringing in only a few dozen head with his family brand on their hides but corralling twice that number in calves and mavericks.

Slater divided his men into four crowds, each consisting of a boss and six hands. Flewellyn headed up one group, Simons another, Tate a third, and Pick Arnold took the fourth. Two men remained at Tate's place, where they tended to the chores of the ranch. Each day the Double Star outfit would rise at first daylight, then move out after breakfast, each crowd going off to work a different place. They would be in the saddle almost the entire day, taking only a short respite for lunch; then as the sun began to sink, the cowhunters would drive the day's gather to the stockman's or farmer's pens. As soon as they satisfied themselves that they had corralled every head of stock on the place, they would commence branding and separating the herd into three groups: those that belonged to owner of the land and would be returning to the range, those that belonged to the owner and would be going to market, and those that were their payment for doing the work.

The first week went by rather routinely for Slater and his men as they worked the four farms directly south of Glengarry, but that time was past before Dent and Sophia joined forces.

During the second week, things were different. The Double Star crews had moved to the four small ranches just west of Glengarry. Each day Slater rode from one place to the next, helping out when he was needed and talking with the owners when he wasn't. The first three days passed without incident, but the fourth didn't.

Slater was working with Jess Tate's crowd on Joe Kaylor's six hundred forty acres bordered on the east by Glengarry, on the north by the Hallettsville-Columbus road, on the west by Tom Ware's place, and on the south by Eldon Seals's headright. They had been at it most of the morning and were due to break for a bite to eat and a short siesta, but they had one more hackberry patch to punch out first.

"Clete, you take the right flank," said Tate, giving the orders because it was his crew, "and I'll take the left. The rest of you space yourselves out between us. On my signal, Clete and me will start moving along the outside of the thicket. When we've gone ten yards or so, the next man in from each of us should start ahead. When they've gone ten yards, the next man in from each of them should go. And when they've gone ten yards, the last two men should move. Everyone understand?" They all nodded that they did. "All right, let's get set then."

Tate and Slater rode off for the edges of the thicket, while the other six men spread out as Tate had instructed them to do. As soon as he saw that everyone was stationed right, Tate raised his right hand, then motioned for Slater to move ahead. The two of them nudged their mounts in the ribs and started forward. At the proper intervals, the other six men in the crew went into motion. Tate's plan worked according to design until they were halfway through the brushy area. Just then, they heard the shouts and whistles of other men in front of them, obviously cowhunters like them, driving the cattle toward them from the opposite end of the thicket. As soon as they realized this, the Double Star crowd halted.

Slater recognized the man nearest to him as Harlan Detchen. Damn! he swore to himself. He had worried that this might happen; his men meeting up with the Detchens and their boys out on the range, followed by the inevitable argument over whose cattle they were rounding up. Well, he knew it would happen sooner or later. Might as well be now, when he was along, as when he was somewhere else. Maybe with him there the matter could be settled amicably. He could only hope.

"Hold up there, Detchen!" called Slater.

Harlan hadn't seen any of the Double Star crowd yet, so the sound of Slater's voice caught him off his guard. He reined up and scanned the brush. A few seconds passed before he finally spotted Slater at the edge of the thicket just twenty yards ahead of him.

"Well, as I live and breathe," said Harlan, "if it isn't Clete Slater. Fancy running into you out here on the range." He turned to his right and yelled, "Hey, Farley! Guess who I just run into!"

A few seconds later a cow and her calf bolted from the thicket to Harlan's right, immediately followed by Farley Detchen. He looked for his brother, found him, and replied, "What are you going on about, Harlan?"

Harlan pointed toward Slater and said, "Take a look over there, Farley. It's Clete Slater out here all by his lonesome."

Farley's gaze traced an invisible line from Harlan's finger to Slater. "I believe you're right, Harlan. It is Clete Slater. What are you doing out here, Slater? This is Glengarry land."

"You out here cowboying?" asked Harlan. "That ain't legal, you know? Is it, Farley?"

"Nope, it ain't," said Farley.

"Your mother sent me to fetch you boys home," said Slater, ignoring their insinuation that he was stealing cows from Glengarry. "It seems she starts to hurting around the middle whenever you two stretch out her apron strings this far."

"Ain't you the funny one though," said Farley. "Ain't he funny, Harlan? Makes you want to laugh right out loud. Well, ha-ha, Slater." Farley pulled a double-barreled shotgun from a saddle scabbard and commenced loading it.

Harlan saw what Farley was doing and followed his twin's example.

"You boys ought to put those away before you hurt yourselves," said Slater quite calmly. He pushed back his hat, then leaned forward on his saddle horn.

Tate and two other Double Star riders had heard the conversation between Slater and the Detchens. Quietly, they came out of the thicket, already armed with Henry rifles and prepared to fight. "Or before we do," said Tate.

Farley and Harlan made a quick count; four against two. A few seconds later the odds were six against two, then eight against two. They wondered what became of their own men, the ones who were driving the thicket with them.

"McElroy, where are you?" called Farley. There was no answer. "Stewart?" No reply. "Merritt?" No reply.

"Seems to me," said Slater, "you boys have been left to fend for yourselves."

"I'm gonna kick that Stewart's ass when I catch up to him," said Harlan under his breath.

Nervously, Farley said, "Now look here, Slater. You're on Glengarry land, and that means you're rustling Glengarry cattle. You leave now, and we won't say anything to the law about it."

"I think you're a little mixed up, Farley," said Slater. "This isn't Glengarry land. You forget that I was born and raised here. I know every inch of the plantation, and I know this isn't part of Glengarry. You're the ones trespassing here. This is Joe Kaylor's land, and we're gathering in his stock for him. If there's any rustling going on here, it's being done by you boys. So I'll tell you what I'll do. You boys throw down your shotguns and hightail it out of here, and I won't tell the law about it." He chuckled and added, "Hell, I won't even tell your mama about it."

"I ain't giving up my gun, Slater," said Harlan.

Tate raised his rifle to his shoulder and drew a bead on Harlan's forehead. "I got him in my sights, Clete. Just say the word and I'll put one just under the brim of his hat."

"You hear that, Harlan?" asked Slater. "At Shiloh, I saw Jess pick off a Yankee officer who was a lot farther away than you are now, and Jess wasn't even using a brand new Henry then." Not taking his eyes off Harlan, Slater leaned toward Tate and asked, "What was that you were using then, Jess? Was that a Sharps carbine or a Plainsman rifle?"

"Sharps rifle," said Tate. "It just looks like a carbine when I hold one."

Harlan began to sweat copiously.

Farley threw down his weapon and said, "Best do like he says, Harlan. Mama won't like it if I let you get yourself killed. Go ahead and drop it. You can always get another."

Harlan took his brother's advice and dropped the shotgun.

"Now ride on back to Glengarry, boys," said Slater. He pointed eastward. "It's over there . . . about a hundred yards on the other side of that ravine."

"Come on, Harlan," said Farley, "let's ride."

Slater watched the Detchens leave the area, then turned to Tate and said, "Go pick up those shotguns, Jess. We'll take them into Hallettsville and hand them over to Sheriff Foster. He can give them back to those two varmints if he wants." He continued to stare after the Detchens, wondering when they'd meet up again and what would happen then. A little voice inside him said the time would be soon and the results would be none too pleasant.

23

The Detchens bypassed Glengarry and rode straight home to the Campbell plantation and their foster mother. They told Sophia what had happened out on the range; at least, they told their version of the episode: Slater and his whole gang had jumped them from the bushes, disarmed them, and took the cattle they had already rounded up. Sophia believed every word of it until her natural son, Stewart, came in with a slightly different tale.

"We'll get you for that," said Harlan.

"You won't be getting anyone!" snapped Sophia. She slapped Farley's mouth for Harlan's transgression. "You ain't got no one to blame but yourselves for this. You ought to be ashamed of yourselves for letting Clete Slater get the best of you again. You ought to be thinking of ways to get done with him once and for all. Of course, that might be too much to expect from the two of you. I guess I'll have to do the thinking for you . . . as usual."

Slowly, she paced the sparsely furnished parlor, one hand on a hip and the other stroking her chin, the wooden heels of her shoes beating a steady, funereal tattoo on the bare hardwood floor.

"Why can't we get that Yankee colonel to do something about Slater?" asked Farley. "He's the law now, ain't he? Couldn't we tell him Slater rustled those cows from us and get Slater arrested?"

"He ain't that kind of law," said Sophia. "He's here to keep the peace, to keep us Confederates from rising up again. That's all the law he is. Rustling is still the sheriff's business, and you two ain't exactly on the good side of Sheriff Foster. No, we got to think of some other way to get rid of Clete Slater." She frowned and added, "But I suppose reporting a rustling to the sheriff is about all we can do right now. I guess it's worth a try. Get the mare hitched up to my buggy and let's be getting over to Glengarry to tell Dent what happened, and this time tell it like it really was."

As Sophia and the boys were leaving the house, Jim Kindred rode up on a katty horse. He tipped his hat to Sophia and bid her a good afternoon but didn't dismount.

Sophia returned the salutation curtly from the top step of the porch, then said, "What brings you out this way, Deputy?"

"Just making rounds of the county," said Kindred. He paused as if he expected her to make some remark. When she didn't, he said, "I heard your boys was starting a roundup and had hired some of the men who spent the war at Somer's Thicket."

"So what if they have," said Sophia. "The war's over. Those men ain't wanted no more."

"Yes, ma'am, I know. I just thought I'd stop by and tell them that myself. I was just doing my duty during the war, and now that it's over and I'm a deputy sheriff, I want them to know that I ain't got no cause to roust them now. They're free men now and don't have to worry about me as long as they stay on the right side of the law."

Sophia's mouth twisted to the left side of her face as she studied Kindred. He was a snake. Everybody knew that, and everybody knew you couldn't trust a snake to do anything except sink its fangs into your leg and poison you. Sophia looked away, unsure of what to make of Kindred, uncertain of whether he was up to something or not. "Well, they're all out driving in some stock," she said.

"No, they're not, Mama," said Stewart. "They came in with me, and they were penning up the stock when I come up to the house."

Sophia frowned at Stewart and said, "Thank you, son."

"Mama, Harlan and me can show Deputy Kindred where the pens are," said Farley.

Again, Sophia frowned. Farley was a bit too eager to cooperate with Kindred. What was that snake up to? she wondered. No telling right now, and she had more important business to conduct at Glengarry. "Well, I suppose you can do that," she said. "Stewart, you come with me."

"Aw, Mama, I want to stay with Farley and Harlan."

Sophia rapped his forehead with her knuckles and said, "Don't give me no grief, Stewart. You're going to Glengarry with me, and that's final."

"Yes, ma'am," said Steward dejectedly.

"As soon as you get those cows penned up," said Sophia to Harlan and Farley, "you get yourselves back out on that range and get more of them hunted up and drove back here before sundown. You hear me?"

"Yes, ma'am," said the twins simultaneously.

With that, she climbed into her buggy, put the whip to the mare's hide, and was off to Glengarry with Stewart riding close behind her.

"I thought she'd never leave," said Kindred. "Now where are those cowpens, boys?"

The Detchens mounted their horses and led Kindred around the house and former slave quarters past the barn and cotton sheds to the cowpens. Four hands leaned against the corral fence, which was made of hackberry tree trunks. They were watching another fellow inside the pen as he cut out a single calf and roped it. Two more men waited to wrestle the little heifer to the ground so a fourth man could brand it and a fifth could notch its ear. Kindred and the Detchens rode up to the onlookers and dismounted.

"You boys knock off for a minute," called Farley to the men inside the corral, "and come out here. Kindred's got something he wants to say to all of you."

All the hands hesitated and eyed each other, suspicious of Kindred's intentions.

"It's all right, boys," said Harlan. "He ain't here to arrest no one."

Even with Harlan's reassurance, the men moved slowly, caution still being the watchword. In a minute, they were gathered together in a half circle, facing Kindred and the Detchens, who flanked the deputy.

"Now I know what you boys must be thinking," said Kindred. "I'm the dirty dog that hounded you all through the war and now I'm here to give you more of the same. That's it, ain't it?"

None of the men spoke. They simply glared at Kindred.

"I know that's right," said Kindred, continuing. "And I don't blame you none. But you got to remember that I was just doing my duty to the Confederacy. I had to hunt you boys like I did. That don't mean I liked doing it."

"That's bull," said Deke Merritt dryly. Merritt was a doe-eyed, skinny little man with a wispish mustache that looked more like straw than hair.

"You enjoyed every minute of it, Kindred," said Bob Moore, a broad-shouldered fellow with an iron jaw, evil frown, and dark eyes that had all the meanness of a diamondback rattler that had bitten its own tongue. "We heard about you and all your bragging about how if you couldn't make us serve in the army then you'd make us all wish we was in Hell."

"Liquor talk," said Kindred. "You boys was so good at running and hiding and staying hid that I got so frustrated that I'd get all liquored up and go to bragging to hide my shame that I couldn't catch none of you."

"I heard that," said Jasper Jones, a lean, lanky sort with bright blue eyes that betrayed a gentler nature within him.

The other men snickered in agreement. This was language they understood.

Kindred chuckled along with them to make points in his favor. Once they'd had their laugh, he said, "I'd like to make it up to you boys now."

That quieted them and pricked the interest of most but not all of them.

"How are you going to do that?" asked Merritt. "I had to hide out in that thicket for over two years because of you. How are you going to make up two years of my life to me?"

Kindred bowed his head and said, "You got a good point there, Deke. I can't do that. I can't give back the time you lost hiding in the thicket. All I can do is make this time now a little better for you."

"And how are you going to do that?" asked Moore.

"You boys ain't got a whole lot," said Kindred like a politician starting a speech, "and that's partly my fault. But you can get some of what all you deserve if you want."

"Get to it, Kindred," said Merritt impatiently.

"All right, I will," said Kindred. Since his political tone hadn't worked he switched over to sounding like a hellfire and brimstone preacher at a Sunday evening revival meeting. "I'm sure you all heard about how Clete Slater and that bunch of his from the camp on Alamo Creek helped themselves to anything they wanted from John Kelly's store and how that Yankee colonel and Sheriff Foster let them get away with it."

"So what about it?" asked Merritt, more impatiently than ever.

"Well, I was thinking you boys didn't get your fair share of the goods they took," said Kindred.

"What are you saying, Kindred?" demanded Moore. "Are you suggesting we go ask Slater for a cut?"

"No, absolutely not," said Kindred. "I'm saying you boys ought to help yourselves to some nice, new, store-bought clothes and the like the same as they did."

"Oh, sure, we should," said Jones. "We should just ride into Hallettsville and walk into any old store and start helping ourselves to whatever we want. Is that what you're telling us to do here, Kindred?''

"We ain't crazy enough to do that, Kindred,'' said Merritt. "Ain't none of us sparking Mrs. Hallet's granddaughter.''

"Who'd want to?'' sneered Moore.

"Yeah,'' said Jones, "a fellow might go to milking that little heifer in the dark and find out he's got hold of a bull's parts instead.''

The other men laughed and jostled each other at the reference to Texada's femininity.

"That's a good one, Jasper,'' said Harlan.

Kindred joined their mirth but only halfheartedly. The conversation was getting out of his control. He didn't like it, but he knew it would do him no good to show his displeasure.

"Well, that's not exactly what I had in mind,'' said Kindred slowly. "Actually, I was thinking we might help ourselves to some goods before they reached town.''

"What are you talking about, Kindred?'' asked Farley.

"I know what he's saying,'' said Merritt. "You're talking about robbing some freighter, aren't you?''

"That's it exactly,'' said Kindred. "But not just any freighter. I'm talking about Teddy Johnson.''

"Teddy Johnson?'' queried Moore. "Hell, he's been robbed twice already. What's he got left to take?''

"I'll tell you what he's got,'' said Kindred, again full of enthusiasm. "He's got a whole load of goods he picked up down to Port Lavaca just this morning, and he's heading for Hallettsville right this minute with them. He'll be camping on the road at Gareitis Creek tonight, and tomorrow night he'll be camping on Little Brushy Creek. All we got to do is slip into his camp after dark, get the drop on him and his drivers, and then we just help ourselves to some fine new duds and maybe a new shotgun or a rifle. He ain't got no armed guards, and him and his drivers won't offer no resistance at all. Leastways, they didn't the other two times he was robbed.''

"Sounds too easy to me,'' said Moore. "I don't like it.''

"Hold on there, Bob,'' said Merritt. "Maybe Kindred's got something here.''

"Yeah,'' said Moore. "A ticket to jail.''

"Maybe not,'' said Farley.

"This ain't your affair, Farley,'' said Moore. "You Detchens got all you need.''

"No, we ain't," said Farley. "And even if we did, there's no reason why we shouldn't help you boys out."

"That's right," said Harlan.

"Besides," said Farley, "I got an idea on how we can make sure we get away with it clean."

"Now how are we going to get away with it when Kindred here is the law?" asked Moore.

"Yeah, what about that, Kindred?" asked Merritt. "How come you're really wanting to do this? You tired of working for the law?"

"I'm tired of being poor as a church mouse, same as you fellows," said Kindred. "That's all there is to it. I'd do it all by myself except one man can't do it alone. It'll take a dozen good men to do the job right, and that's why I come to you fellows. I knew Farley and Harlan could go for something like this, and I figured you men would, too."

The men studied Kindred for the truth. None of them felt he could be trusted, but here he was offering them a chance to take part in a simple robbery. It sounded too good to be true.

"What are you worrying about?" asked Farley, breaking the silence of the moment. "Like I was going to say, I got a surefire idea on how we can get away with it clean."

"How's that, Farley?" asked Kindred.

"We put the blame on Clete Slater and his bunch," said Farley proudly.

"Now how are we going to do that?" asked Merritt.

"Simple," said Farley. "We get us some army uniforms and wear them while we're robbing Johnson's wagons. Johnson and his men will think we're all ex-soldiers, and the only ex-soldiers around here are Clete Slater and his bunch."

"Good idea, Farley," said Moore, "except for one thing."

"What's that?" asked Farley.

"Where do we get the army uniforms?"

Farley stiffened because he had no answer for Moore's question. Kindred did. He smiled and said, "We get them from the jailhouse in Hallettsville."

"We do what?" asked Merritt.

"We get them from the jailhouse in Hallettsville," said Kindred. "When Slater and his boys raided Kelly's store, they shed their uniforms right then and there. Kelly gathered them all up and dumped them on Sheriff Foster's desk as a way of telling him that he was none too happy about the law enforcement around here. The sheriff had Bill Thornton get them washed to get the lice and dirt out of them. Then he told him to put them in the storeroom just in case someone might want them again some day. Now wasn't that thoughtful of the sheriff?''

"I still don't feel right about this," said Moore.

"Well, you can feel that way if you want, Bob," said Merritt, "but I'm going to do the one thing Kindred and no else could make me do for four years."

"What's that, Deke?" asked Moore.

"I'm going to put on an army uniform," said Merritt.

Moore still didn't like the plan, but he went along with it because all the others did and he didn't want to be left out.

24

Colonel Markham arrived at Glengarry only minutes after Sophia Campbell and her son Stewart had. He didn't recognize her rig out front, but there was no mistaking her voice when he heard it inside the house.

"We have to do something about your brother," Sophia was saying as Markham entered the parlor. She looked up at him standing in the doorway and was startled. His sudden appearance caused Sophia to blanch and suck in a short breath before she said ever so sweetly, "Why, Colonel Markham, I didn't know you were here."

Markham smiled, pleased with himself for having such an effect on this notorious woman. "I wasn't, Mrs. Campbell. I arrived just now." He walked over to Sophia, who was sitting on the davenport, and gave her a half bow. "How are you this fine day, Mrs. Campbell?"

"I'm fine, thank you, sir," said Sophia.

Markham looked at Stewart standing where Harlan and Farley had stood when they were there and said, "Is this young man your son, Mrs. Campbell?"

"Why, yes, he is, Colonel. This is Stewart, my oldest boy.

Stewart, say hello to Colonel Markham.''

Stewart frowned at his mother, then nodded curtly at Markham.

Markham returned the greeting in kind, then looked over at Dent sitting in his favorite chair and said, ''Dent, how are you this afternoon?''

''I'm still sober,'' said Dent, ''if that's what you're asking, Lucas.''

Markham ignored Dent's remark, turned to Sophia, and said, ''As I was coming in, did I overhear you say something has to be done about Clete?''

''That's what she was saying,'' said Dent. ''Seems Clete and his boys caught Farley and Harlan rounding up some of Joe Kaylor's cows and made them stop it.''

''Who is Joe Kaylor?'' asked Markham after sitting down in his usual place.

''He owns a headright just west of here,'' said Dent. ''Seems Clete and his boys are working Kaylor's place this week.''

''I thought it was all right to round up cattle on the open range,'' said Markham.

''On the open range, yes, but not on your neighbor's property,'' said Dent. ''If you cross over the line and start rounding up cattle without your neighbor's permission, he could take offense, and then you could have a problem.''

''But not if you're rounding up your own cows that have strayed onto your neighbor's land,'' said Sophia.

Markham looked perplexed and said so. ''I don't understand, Mrs. Campbell.''

''It's like this, Colonel,'' said Sophia. ''If some of your cows stray onto your neighbor's land, then you have the right to go after them without his permission, and if you take home a few unbranded cows doing it, then so be it. Your neighbor can't do nothing about it.''

''But that's not exactly how it's done, Lucas,'' said Dent. ''Sure, it's all right to go after your own cattle on your neighbor's land, but it isn't done that way. You work your own land, and if you come across any cattle belonging to your neighbor, you drive them back to his land. And your neighbor does the same if he comes across any of your cattle on his land.''

''I think I understand now,'' said Markham. ''Then you just can't ride out on the range and start rounding up just any unmarked cattle. Is that it?''

''On the open range, yes,'' said Dent, ''but around here, nearly every acre of ground belongs to someone. There isn't a whole lot of public land left in these parts.''

"I see," said Markham.

"We're getting away from the point here," said Sophia impatiently. "Our problem is Clete. Him and his boys are gathering up cows we could be putting our brand to."

"But they're doing it legally, you said," said Markham.

"Legal ain't got nothing to with it, Colonel," said Sophia. "They're cutting into our profits taking in all those critters we could be rounding up. We need to get Clete and his boys off the range, so Harlan and Farley can have a clear field at getting all the unbranded stock."

"What about these people Clete's made contracts with?" asked Markham. "Won't they object to your sons rounding up cattle on their land?"

"Let them," said Sophia. "By the time they can get the sheriff out to their property, the boys will be long gone with the cattle."

"But what if someone starts shooting at them?" asked Markham. "I mean, there is that possibility, isn't there?"

"They shoot back," said Sophia matter-of-factly.

"Like they did today, Miz Campbell?" queried Dent.

Sophia glared at Dent for a second, then remembered that Markham was there. She sweetened her face and said, "There wasn't any shooting today, Dent. Clete and his boys simply got the drop on Harlan and Farley. That's all there was to it."

"And they took away their shotguns," said Stewart with a snicker.

"Hush up, Stewart!" snapped Sophia. Then to Dent and Markham, she said, "So what are we going to do about Clete and his cowboys?"

Markham smiled to himself with a devilish thought, then said, "Well, I can get them off the range for a few days, but after that—"

Sophia interrupted. "You can? How?" she asked eagerly.

"President Johnson has issued an amnesty proclamation," said Markham. "I just received a copy of it along with some orders on how to handle it. It's very complicated, but one thing in my orders is very clear. All former Confederate soldiers are to be rounded up immediately so they can take an oath of allegiance to the Union." He smiled broadly, wickedly. "All the order says is they have to take the oath. It doesn't say anything about when I have to administer it."

Sophia liked the idea. An evil grin spread her thin lips, and she said, "Sounds good enough to me." Then her more usual frown returned as she said, "Well, what are you sitting here for, Colonel? Do your duty and get those boys behind bars immediately."

Markham wanted to laugh at the urgency in Sophia's voice but thought better of it when he saw the set of her jaw. Quite incredulous, he leaned toward her and said, "You're serious, aren't you?"

"You're damn right, I'm serious," said Sophia with all the righteous determination of a Campbellite preacher on a hot Sunday morning. "The sooner you get Clete and his cowboys off the range, the sooner Harlan and Farley can get their men to rounding up those unbranded critters for us."

Markham studied Sophia's countenance, and as he did, Dent's words about her being as much a lady as a black widow spider echoed in his brain.

25

The sun was down, and the evening air was just beginning to cool to a more comfortable level. Slater and the Double Star hands had put in another long day. None of them felt like getting their feathers ruffled as they started to drift toward the supper table of their outdoor dining hall.

Of course, Texada Ballard didn't know how tired they were and didn't really care whether they wanted to be bothered or not. She had news for them, and nothing was going to stop her from delivering it. The pounding hooves of Texada's horse were heard coming down the lane to the rebuilt Tate ranch, drawing the attention of every man on the place. They looked in the direction of the sound to see her riding lickety-split toward them and wondered what in tarnation her hurry was.

Slater saw her coming and experienced a flashback that sent a creepy chill through him. He'd seen this apparition before—hatless rider . . . leaning forward with knees bent in the fashion of a race jockey . . . straw-colored pigtails flying straight out behind her head—only she wasn't riding *toward* him then, but *past* him on the road to Glengarry. He hadn't recognized her as Texada Ballard that previous eve, but this time he knew it was her for certain.

Texada reined in her mount so hard that it nearly sat down on its haunches to catch its breath. The bald-faced bay was in such a lather that it almost appeared to be rabid. Texada wasn't in much better condition.

"Clete!" she yelled as she leaped down from the saddle, her momentum carrying her to him.

"Whoa, Texada!" said Slater, catching her by the arms with his strong hands. "What's the hurry, girl?"

"Clete, you have to hide!" she exclaimed. "All of you have to hide."

"Hide?" asked Slater. "Why?"

"It's Markham," she explained. "He's going to arrest all of you."

"Arrest us?" asked Tate, suddenly agitated.

"Arrest us for what?" asked Slater more calmly. "What are you talking about, Texada?"

"Markham got some kind of order today," said Texada, "that says he has to arrest all former Confederate soldiers."

"How do you know this?" asked Slater, concerned but not panicky as she was and the men were getting to be.

"A darky at the courthouse overheard two Yankee officers talking about it," said Texada, "and pretty soon, it was all over town. The Yankees are supposed to arrest all the men who served in the Confederate army, navy, or government and lock them up. If any of them try to resist, they're supposed to be shot. Clete, you've got to hide."

By this time, all the men had gathered around Slater and Texada and had heard at least a part of what she had said. Slater scanned their faces and saw a mixture of reactions, ranging from fear to hatred, and he realized that he had better act fast or lose control of them.

"Have the Yankees put up any bulletins yet?" asked Slater.

"Bulletins?" queried Texada, not understanding the term.

"Notices," said Slater. "Have they put up any notices of their plan to arrest everyone?"

"Why, no," said Texada. "Why should they?"

"She's right, Clete," said Flewellyn. "Why would the Yankees announce their plans to the whole world like that?''

"Because that's the way they do things," said Slater. "The Yankees always print up some sort of notice whenever they plan to do something like this, and then they put it up in plain sight so everyone can read it. It's just their way of doing things."

"Well, they haven't done anything like that yet," said Texada in a less excited tone now.

"And you say a darky overheard two Yankee officers talking about it at the courthouse?" asked Slater.

"That's right," said Texada.

"And what's everybody else in town doing about the news?" he asked. "Are they all getting their guns to fight the Yankees again?"

"Well, no," said Texada slowly. "Not exactly."

"Then exactly what are they doing? Are they all riding around the countryside like you, yelling, 'The Yankees are coming! The Yankees are coming!' like they were Paul Revere on his midnight ride?"

Texada stared into Slater's eyes and caught a glimpse of mirth. She didn't like it, not now anyway.

"Cletus Slater, are you making fun of me?" she asked, suspicious of his purpose.

"Yes, darling, I am," he said in perfect honesty as she wrenched herself free of his gentle hold.

"Well, that's a fine thank you," she said, nearly spitting the words at him. "Here, I ride out here as fast as I can, nearly break my neck doing it, just to warn the man I love that he's in danger, and this is the thanks I get?"

"Love?" giggled Tate. "Did you hear that?"

"I heard it," said Simons, all set to guffaw at the next joke that was bound to come.

"I thought I saw scratches on the boy the other night when he came back from town," said Flewellyn, "and I thought a wildcat had jumped him."

"One did," said Tate, starting the men to laughing and slapping their knees.

"If that's going to be your attitude, Cletus Slater," said Texada, ignoring the ribald insinuations and just getting into a real tirade, "then I'll be damned if I'll ever do it again. Go ahead and let the Yankees shoot you down like a dog and see if I care." She kicked dirt on his boots and said, "Get used to it, Clete, because you're going to have dirt piled six feet over you if you don't—''

Slater stopped her, saying, "Texada, I'm sorry I made fun of you." He waited for her to reply, but when she didn't speak right away, he said, "But don't you think you should have thought this out a little before coming all the way out here? I mean, think about it. A darky overhears two Yankee officers in the courthouse talking about arresting us. That much alone should have made you doubt the truth to it."

Texada knew he was right, but she was angry and wanted to stay that way for a while. It was unfair of him to be so calm and so logical about it. But Slater had always been like that, even tempered for the most part, since they were children. It was part of why she loved him so, because he seemed so strong and mature when he didn't get excited the way she did.

"But how do you know it isn't true, Clete?" She pouted. "It could be, and then what?"

"Yeah, Clete," said Tate, suddenly serious again, "what about that? Supposing what she says is true, then what?"

Several men repeated Tate's sentiments, although in different words, all at once, causing Slater to raise his voice to quiet them.

"Boys, let's cross that bridge when we get to it," he said. "I'll ride back into town with Texada and stay over at the hotel. Tomorrow, I'll go straight to the courthouse and see Markham personally and find out what this is all about. If Texada is right, I'll be going to jail tomorrow morning. If she's wrong, I'll be back here for lunch."

26

The shortest route between the Tate ranch and Hallettsville followed the surveyor's trail along the western boundary of Glengarry Plantation to the Columbus-Hallettsville road and from there westward to town, a total distance of seven miles, give or take a rod or two. In daylight with dry weather conditions, the average horseman could make the ride in an hour without difficulty. After dark was another matter completely.

Slater and Texada had less than a quarter of a new moon to brighten their path as they let their horses walk toward the road to Hallettsville. Texada insisted that they ride close enough together to hold hands, and Slater agreed to the romantic notion, although he felt a little strange doing it with a girl who was wearing long pants. They waited until they were certain that they were out of earshot of the ranch before beginning any conversations.

"Texada," said Slater, finally, "the night I came home I went straight to Glengarry, but before I got there, I heard a rifle shot coming from the direction of the house. At first, I thought someone was shooting at me, so I hid in a hackberry thicket. In a minute, a rider came along with a troop of Yankee cavalry in pursuit. I didn't know who the rider was that night, but I do now."

"So what if it was me?" said Texada.

"Who were you shooting at?"

"Markham, that's who."

"All right. Why were you shooting at him?"

"Because . . ." She stopped herself from telling the truth right off, thought about it for a second, then told him anyway. "Because he was a Yankee and the Yankees had killed you. Or at least, I thought they had killed you."

Slater smiled and said, "They might yet, if what you said back at the ranch is true."

"It's not a joking matter, Cletus Slater," said Texada, sounding a bit like her grandmother.

"All right, no jokes," he said. "So how come you missed?"

"Mosquito bit me just as I pulled the trigger on Uncle Coll's Sharps, and I jerked it a little. Before I could set myself for another shot at him, there were Yankees all over the place. I thought about taking a shot at any one of them, but then I heard someone yell that he'd seen a rifle flash in the apple orchard. I figured it was high time I was making tracks out of there."

"You shot at him from the apple orchard?"

"That's right."

"But you were heading toward Columbus when you passed me on the road. What were you thinking of, girl?"

"I had my escape figured out before I ever pulled the trigger. I rode back through the orchard to the road and crossed it to the bushes on the other side. I circled the bushes and came out opposite the peach orchard and got back on the road. I figured that would throw them off long enough for me to get a good head start on them."

"Well, you certainly had a big lead on them when you rode past me," said Slater. "When did they give up the chase?"

"They kept it up all the way to the Navidad. That's where I lost them. In the river bottoms. I crossed over the bridge, then up to the flat on the other side. I went a bit farther down the road before turning off and riding north along the river until I got to the mouth of Mixon Creek. I crossed back over the river there and followed the creek until I was on Ol' Foley's plantation. Then I stopped to rest Pixie there. The only thing I heard was some Yankees way off behind me, cussing up a storm because they'd lost me."

As he listened to Texada tell her story, a wave of emotion rolled gently over Slater. It was a warm feeling, sort of like the ethereality a body gets when its in a sleeping state but the mind is still alert and aware and able to enjoy this natural physicality. It perplexed him, threw his sensibilities into a pandemonious tempest that simultaneously frightened him and pleased him. A kaleidoscope of images burst into his mind, for an instant shooting him backward in time to all the battles in which he had been a participant; the cannons, the rockets, the bombs—all exploding in rapid succession.

Slater regained control of his senses—to some extent, anyway. He still had that wonderful corporeal feeling, but now he understood it, understood what it was, understood why he had it.

Texada had aroused this feeling in Slater. She had touched his soul with her own. She had cared so much for him when she thought him to be dead at the hands of Yankees that she had attempted to avenge his death at the risk of losing her own life. And now that he was alive and she thought he might be in jeopardy again, she had ridden to warn him of the danger.

This is love, he thought. She said it, and she showed it.

Slater reined in Nimbus, forcing Texada to do the same with Pixie. He squeezed her hand and said, "Texada, you amaze me sometimes. I thought that first day back when I saw you in a dress that you'd changed."

A worried frown crinkled Texada's face, and her eyes began to droop. "I'm trying to be a lady, Clete. Honest, I am. I'm not sure that I like it all that much, but I am trying."

A boyish giddiness suddenly gripped Slater's senses, and the world about them vanished. He couldn't help himself as he leaned over and kissed her lips. Just once, but with feeling, a taste of passion.

"What was that for?" she asked.

A glow of a smile curled the corners of his mouth as he admitted to himself what he was feeling. Love, he thought. I love her, too. He said, "You don't have to do anything just because you think it will please me, Texada. I love you just the way you are." He couldn't have said anything else that would have surprised and delighted her more.

"Oh, Clete!" said Texada, losing control of her emotions and her good sense. She dropped the reins and his hand, then reached out with both arms to embrace Slater. Pixie was spooked by the sudden freedom from restraint. Texada had just gotten one hand hold on Slater's neck when the horse lurched ahead. It was just enough movement to pull Texada from the saddle, causing Pixie to lurch again, breaking Texada's hold on Slater. She fell between her man and her horse. *Oof!*

"Texada!" Slater jumped down immediately and was by her side in an instant. "Texada, are you all right?"

The girl rolled over and threw her arms around Slater's neck. In the next heartbeat, she was kissing him—hard, deep, passionately, with parted lips and darting tongue meeting his. He was her man at last and—

"Clete?" called a woman. "Clete? Is that you up ahead?"

The voice was familiar to Slater. He knew that much, but a name wouldn't attach itself to the sound.

Texada moved away from Slater and said softly with surprise, "Malinda?"

"Malinda?" said Slater, just as surprised. He stood up, pulling Texada erect beside him, her arms still around his neck. "Malinda?" he called back. "Where are you?"

"In the road ahead of you," said his sister as she came toward them in the darkness.

Still holding the reins to Nimbus, Slater had the sense to grab Pixie's reins before she bolted again. The mare snorted and pranced about a bit but didn't fight to be free.

"What's she doing out here?" grumbled Texada.

"Malinda, is it really you?" asked Slater as a shadowy figure came into view.

Malinda drew back on her horse's reins and halted the animal. "Yes, it's me, Clete," she said, her tone happy and excited. She slid down from the sidesaddle.

Slater freed himself of Texada's hold and held out the reins to Nimbus and Pixie to her as if she were a servant. "Hold these for me, Texada."

She took them reluctantly and watched as brother and sister were reunited. Slater hugged Malinda and kissed her cheek.

"Oh, Clete," gasped Malinda, returning his show of emotion, "I'm so glad you're safe. All this time we thought you were dead."

Slater stood back from her and said, "Yes, I know. Texada told me all about it."

"Texada?" queried Malinda. "Texada Ballard?"

"Right here, Malinda," said Texada with a touch of impudence.

Malinda stared into the dark and said, "Well, I'll be." Then she looked at Slater and said, "You and Texada Ballard?" A little laugh slipped through her lips as her eyes rolled heavenward. "I'm ready to go, Lord. I've seen it all now."

"He won't have to come for you, Yankee lover," hissed Texada. "One more word out of you, and I'll send you up there myself."

"That's exactly the sort of thing one would expect from a creature like you," said Malinda.

"Creature? Who you calling a creature?" Texada released the reins to Nimbus and Pixie and started marching toward Malinda and her brother.

Slater was dumfounded. What was happening here? His sister and his sweetheart were acting like a couple of felines about to tear each other to furry little pieces.

Malinda let go of Slater and started toward Texada, saying, "You, you little—"

Time to step in, thought Slater, as he interrupted and intercepted Malinda. "Whoa! Girls! What's going on here?" He pulled Malinda back and placed himself between the two women. "What's all the fuss about?"

Texada didn't stop, kept on coming. "What were you about to call me, you Yankee lov—"

Slater held Malinda off with one hand and reached to do the same to Texada with the other, managing to put it in her face in time to keep her from uttering a name she wouldn't want anyone calling her. A bitten finger was his reward. "Ouch!"

"Get out of my way, Clete!" commanded Malinda as she fought to get by him.

"Let me at her, Clete!" said Texada at the same time.

Slater got an arm in front of Malinda and pushed her back,

then he caught Texada by a pigtail and held on as if she were a vicious wildcat.

"Ow!" cried Texada. "That hurts, Clete!"

"Let me give it a pull, Clete!" said Malinda. "I'll show her some pain she'll never forget."

"What's going on here?" demanded Slater. "Malinda, what's wrong with you?"

"It isn't me, Clete," said Malinda. "It's her, that little hellion you're—"

"That's enough of that, Malinda!" said Slater, beginning to lose his temper. "I don't want to hear you call her anything like that again!"

"That's telling her, Clete," said Texada.

"And the same goes for you, Texada!" said Slater, growing equally impatient with her. "Look, I don't know what it is between you two, but I want it to stop here and now. You hear me?" When they didn't answer him immediately, he grabbed Malinda by an arm, shook her, and pulled Texada's hair as he had done when he was a schoolboy. "You hear me?"

"Yes, Clete," said Malinda.

"All right, all right!" said Texada. "Just let go of my hair."

Slater released Texada's pigtail and said, "Now tell me what this is all about. You two used to be friends. Or at least, I thought you were friends. If you weren't, you sure fooled everybody. Especially me."

Neither one of them would speak. Instead, they turned away from each other.

Slater nodded his head and said, "All right, have it your way. We won't talk about the past. Let's talk about tonight. What were you doing out here, Malinda? So far from the house?"

"I was coming to see you," she said.

"To spy on you more than likely, Clete," said Texada, "for that Yankee colonel of hers."

"Hush up, Texada!" snapped Slater, grabbing Texada by an arm.

"I came to warn you, Clete," said Malinda.

"Yeah, I'll bet," sneered Texada.

"Texada, one more word out of you," said Slater, "and I'm going to . . . I'm . . . Never mind what I'm liable to do, Texada. Just hush your mouth and let me talk with Malinda. Would you mind doing that for me? Just once?"

"Oh, all right," said Texada. "But let go of my arm."

Slater let her go and watched her walk over to Nimbus and Pixie to pick up their reins. Then he turned back to Malinda. "Now what was that you were saying?" he asked her.

"I said I was coming to warn you."

"Warn me about what?"

"Lucas . . . Colonel Markham to you, I guess. He's going to arrest you and all your friends tomorrow."

"See, I told you so," said Texada.

"Texada, please!" snapped Slater angrily. "I'm just about at the end of my patience with you." He had to be in love with her, he thought; she'd gotten so far under his skin that he'd lost his temper.

"Clete, it isn't all that bad," said Malinda. "Lucas only wants to get you all off the range for a while."

"Why would he want to do that?"

"It's that woman, Sophia Campbell. Dent made a deal with her to have her boys gather in Glengarry cattle—"

"I know about that, Malinda. It was all over the county the day after they made the contract. But I didn't know your, uh, colonel . . . I didn't know he was involved in it, too."

"Yes, he is my colonel, Clete." Malinda glared in Texada's direction, then said, "I'm sure you know all about that by now."

"That's right, I do," said Slater. "Jess Tate told me about it the first day I was back. But what's this about Markham being part of the business between Dent and Miz Campbell?"

Malinda was hesitant, reluctant to tell Slater the real truth, the whole truth, but she knew she must. The wounds could never begin to heal if she didn't.

"Clete, I don't know for sure how to tell you this," said Malinda, "but I'll try my best. It's Dent. He's different now. He's not the same as he was when you went away to the war. He started changing right then, the day you left. Grandpa was partly to blame. He kept comparing him to you and yelling at him when he made mistakes around the plantation. I could see Dent was beginning to hate you, Clete. It wasn't anything you'd done. It was just that he wasn't as good at things as you were, and he wanted so bad to be like you. He only got worse when they told us you'd been killed at Shiloh. Grandpa only made things harder on him after that. Then Grandpa died last winter, and Dent was like a lost puppy. Did they tell you there was talk of lynching him?"

"No, I hadn't heard that," said Slater.

"Well, fortunately, the sheriff stopped it," said Malinda.

"Then Lucas and his soldiers came, and Dent took to Lucas right from the start. It was like he'd found . . . a friend. And Lucas has treated him like a little brother. Now Dent doesn't do anything without talking to Lucas first, and Lucas does everything he can to help out."

"Even going so far as to arrest me and my men?" asked Slater, his voice tinged with sarcasm.

"Yes, even going that far," said Malinda. "Lucas and Dent have talked about forming some sort of business arrangement after he and I are married. So it's only natural that he should involve himself in the affairs of Glengarry now."

"And the first thing he does is make an alliance with Sophia Campbell and those two adopted snakes of hers. Doesn't he know about Sophia Campbell?"

"I tried to warn him, Clete," said Malinda, "but he simply wouldn't pay me any heed."

"Well, never mind that now," said Slater. "When does he plan to arrest us?"

"Yeah, what about that, Malinda?" demanded Texada.

"That's not what's important, Clete," said Malinda, ignoring Texada and speaking directly to Slater. "He doesn't have the right to arrest you. It seems President Johnson has offered amnesty to most of the men who ever served in the Confederate army or navy. All they have to do is take an oath of allegiance to the Union and all is forgiven. Lucas is planning on holding you all in jail for a few days so that the Detchen boys can get the best of the wild stock into their pens."

Slater laughed and said, "I see what he's up to." He patted his breast pocket and said, "I don't think I have anything to worry about."

27

After attending services the next morning at the Methodist church with Texada and Mrs. Hallet, Slater excused himself and walked across the intersection of Second and Main streets to the town well on the northwest corner of the courthouse grounds. He dropped the bucket down the shaft, drew it up again, then took the dipper and helped himself to a cool drink of water. As he drank, he saw, out of the corner of his eye, a soldier approaching him. He finished drinking and replaced the dipper on its hook, then faced Sergeant Wickersham, who came to attention to address him.

"Good morning, Sergeant," said Slater. "Fine day, don't you think?"

"Yes, sir, it is," said Wickersham with respect. "Mr. Slater, sir, Colonel Markham sends his compliments and requests your presence in his office immediately, sir."

"Immediately?"

"Yes, sir."

"Must be important."

Wickersham turned aside and said, "After you, sir."

"Sergeant," said Slater. He tipped his hat in lieu of a salute, then stepped past Wickersham toward the courthouse.

Wickersham fell in step behind Slater, and the two of them entered the county building by its west entrance. The sergeant told Slater that Markham's office was on the second floor, so they went upstairs to the room that had been the judge's chambers. Wickersham knocked twice on the door, then a voice within bid him to enter. He opened the door and let Slater go inside first.

Markham was sitting in a pine armchair behind a large oak desk, a few papers, pen, and inkwell in front of him. He looked up at his visitors.

Wickersham saluted and said, "Mr. Slater, sir."

"Thank you, Wickersham," said Markham, returning the courtesy. "That will be all."

Wickersham departed.

Slater waited to be acknowledged before moving or saying anything.

"Sit down, Slater," said Markham, motioning to a chair at the corner of the desk.

"Thank you, Colonel," said Slater, and he seated himself.

Markham sat back in his chair, elbows resting on its arms, hands folded in front of him, looking quite smug, very pleased with himself, like the chess player who is positive that he has lured his opponent into checkmate. He said, "Slater, I'll come straight to the point. You're under arrest."

Slater smiled back at his host and replied, "No, Colonel, I'm not."

Markham sat up a little straighter in surprise and said, "What's that you say?"

"I said I'm not under arrest."

Markham's temperature began to rise. "You're being insolent, Slater, and I won't tolerate it."

Slater crossed his legs, leaned back, and said casually, "And you're abusing your authority, Colonel, and I won't tolerate that."

Markham jumped to his feet and pointed a finger at Slater. "I'm having you locked up, Slater."

"On what charge?"

"I don't need any charges to throw you in jail, Slater."

"Let me remind you, Colonel, that this is Texas. Down here, we don't cotton to people trying to deprive us of our rights as free men. You put me or any man in jail without proper charges, and you'll find yourself in more trouble than a one-legged man in a butt-kicking free-for-all."

"Are you threatening me, Slater?" hissed Markham.

Slater shook his head and said, "Colonel, I don't have to threaten you." He reached inside his coat and pulled out a wrinkled, yellowed piece of paper. He dropped it on the desk and said, "Go ahead and read that, Colonel, and then you'll know what I'm talking about."

Markham picked up the paper, stared at it for a second, then said, "What's this?"

"It's my pardon, Colonel," said Slate. "It's my pardon and a little more. Go ahead and read it. And when you're finished, we'll talk."

Markham reluctantly unfolded the document and read it with even more reluctance.

In no uncertain terms, it stated that Captain Cletus Slater, 8th Texas Cavalry, Confederate Army, had surrendered himself to the commanding general of federal forces in New Orleans on May 5, 1865, and had taken the oath of allegiance to the Union as prescribed by President Lincoln's amnesty proclamation of March 26, 1864, and was granted a pardon for taking part in the Rebellion. It further stated that Slater had served his country, meaning the United States, by bringing in various units of rebellious soldiers for the purpose of ending hostilities between North and South. As a reward for his assistance in these matters, no Union officer or soldier was to harm or molest Slater in any way without a written order from the signer of this document or an officer or member of government of higher rank. The order was signed by E.R.S. Canby, Major General, United States Army.

"This means nothing," sneered Markham.

"Yes, it does, Colonel," said Slater firmly, "and you know it does. I know my rights here, Colonel. I am once again a citizen of the United States, and I am entitled to every legal benefit of that citizenship. In simpler terms, Colonel, you can't arrest me without bringing charges and without clearing it with General Canby first. But that's just the legal end of it. The other part is this. If you lock me up without bringing charges, the local citizenry is liable to take offense at such action and do something you wouldn't like at all."

"Like attack my men?" asked Markham.

"Oh, better than that, Colonel. They're liable to go over your head to Canby, and from what I understand, the general doesn't like his officers countermanding his orders."

Markham knew this to be true. Slater had him checked but not checkmated.

"This pardon is only good for you," said Markham. "It doesn't apply to anyone else, especially those men you have working for you."

"Colonel, will you stop this nonsense? I know what you're up to, and it won't work."

"How do you know what my plans are?"

"This is not a big town, Colonel," said Slater. "You sneeze at one end of it, and someone says bless you at the other. The same goes for the county. Just about everybody knows everybody else's business. Or at least, thinks they do. The point is I know you're supposed to advise all ex-Confederates to come in and take the same oath I took in New Orleans. You can't arrest them unless they refuse to come in voluntarily. But once they've taken it, they're free again. Am I right or not?''

"All right, so what if you are right?''

"Colonel, I also know that Sophia Campbell put you up to this because we chased her boys off Joe Kaylor's ranch yesterday.''

"I did receive such a complaint from Mrs. Campbell," said Markham. "It was her contention that your men used force to take some cattle that they had rounded up.''

"I wouldn't quite put it that way, but she's right. We did take the cattle that her boys were driving.''

"Then you admit to rustling?''

"We kept the unbranded critters and the stock that had Kaylor's brand on them," said Slater, "but we drove the Glengarry stock back over the line. We didn't rustle anything. But that's old news, Colonel. Let's get down to facts here. I've got it figured that you've got your sights set on getting a piece of Glengarry when you marry Malinda, so—''

Markham jumped in, saying, "I have no such intentions, Slater. Is that another rumor you've heard?''

Slater leaned forward and pointed a finger at Markham, saying, "Colonel, right now I don't care if you do get *a piece* of Glengarry or *all of it*. My concern now is to get those mossy horns rounded up and trailed to market so the people around here can get some hard cash in their pockets again. I can do it *with . . . or without . . . your help*." He paused for effect. "I'd prefer we worked together on it just to make things easier all around, but that's up to you.''

Markham studied Slater's face, saw no deception in it, and said, "All right, Slater, I'll listen to your proposition.''

Slater smiled and said, "Good enough, Colonel. Here it is.''

After making Markham realize that they could accomplish more by working together instead of against each other, Slater led Markham and a patrol of cavalry out to the Tate ranch, where the colonel administered the oath of allegiance to the men and Markham's clerk gave each man a written pardon.

It was twilight when Markham rode off for Glengarry to explain Slater's plan to Dent and Malinda. Slater felt his brother and sister would be easily convinced to join forces in the cowhunt and drive, but he knew Markham would be hard-pressed to persuade Sophia Campbell it was a good idea.

28

When Teddy Johnson roared into Hallettsville on Monday afternoon with what was left of his freight, he headed straight for the county sheriff's office to report the robbery of his wagon train. The sheriff wasn't in, but his full-time deputy was.

"Good afternoon, Mr. Johnson," said Kindred nervously when Johnson entered the office. The deputy was sitting in the sheriff's chair.

"No, it ain't," said Johnson with more than a touch of anger in his voice. "I've been robbed."

Bill Thornton, the jailer, was also there, sitting at his little table in the corner, dozing until now. This was his kind of news. He perked up and said, "Robbed?"

"You heard me," said Johnson, a squat man with bandy legs, round head, dirty face, pug nose, little lips, squinty blue eyes, and no eyebrows to speak of.

"When did it happen?" asked Thornton eagerly.

"I'll ask the questions around here," said Kindred, annoyed by Thornton's interjection. "All right, now when did you say you were robbed, Mr. Johnson?"

"I didn't say, but it was last night. We were camped for the night on this side of Little Brushy Creek when they came sneaking into camp around midnight or so."

"How many of them were there?" asked Kindred.

"It was hard to count them in the dark," said Johnson, "but they had to have been at least twenty men. Maybe more. Like I said, I couldn't count them all in the dark."

"Was there any shooting?" asked Thornton.

"Hey, old man," snarled Kindred, turning on the jailer, "I said I'd ask the questions." He aimed a finger at Thornton. "Now you stay out of this, you hear?" He turned back to Johnson and asked the same question that Thornton had asked.

"No, not a shot was fired," said Johnson. "I said they came

sneaking into camp, didn't I? By the time we knew they were there, they had the drop on us. I woke up with the black eye of a big old Colt's .44 staring me in the face.''

"Got any idea who did it?" asked Kindred cautiously.

"Soldiers, that's who did it," said Johnson.

"Yankees?" queried Thornton, who was about to bust a gut with excitement.

"No!" snapped Johnson. "They were our boys!"

"Our boys?" asked Thornton with raised eyebrows. "How do you know that?"

"Thornton, I told you to butt out!" growled Kindred.

"They were wearing Confederate uniforms," said Johnson.

Kindred cleared his throat and asked, "Did you know any of them?"

"Couldn't tell who they were," said Johnson. "They were all wearing neckerchiefs over their faces. I did hear one of them call another Slater, and he called one Tate."

"Tate and Slater, you say?" queried Thornton, his face all pinched together as if he'd just sucked on a lemon wedge laced with alum. "I don't believe that."

"You better believe it, old man," said Kindred, suddenly relaxed. "They robbed John Kelly's store, didn't they? Why wouldn't they do the same to Mr. Johnson here?"

"I still don't believe it," said Thornton, turning away in disgust.

"Do you know them?" asked Johnson.

"Sure, we know them," said Kindred with an evil smile, "and I know exactly where to find them, too." He was pensive for a moment before saying, "But first, I'll need a posse. How about you, Mr. Johnson? Would you care to come along and help get back some of your goods?"

"You bet I would," said Johnson. "And I'll bring my drivers and guards, too."

Thornton didn't like the look on Kindred's face when he left the jailhouse with Johnson. He was too well acquainted with the deputy not to recognize evil in the man's eyes when he saw it. Kindred was up to no good, and he had to be stopped before some innocent person wound up dead.

Everyone in Hallettsville knew that Slater had a good friend in Mrs. Hallet and that he was sparking her granddaughter. If someone wanted to make certain that a message was delivered to Slater, all that was required was to tell Texada or one of the other Ballards, and out of love for Slater or fear of Mrs. Hallet it would reach him in no time at all.

Thornton left the jailhouse right after Kindred and Johnson and walked over to Collatinus Ballard's business establishment on the square, where he found young Coll Ballard and Texada minding the general store.

"Good afternoon, Mr. Thornton," said Coll. "Is there something I can do for you?"

"It ain't me that's needing help," said Thornton, his voice full of agitation. "It's Clete Slater who needs helping right now."

"Clete?" queried Texada at the mention of his name. "Is something wrong with Clete?"

"Not yet, there ain't," said Thornton, "but there could be before long. Teddy Johnson was just in the jailhouse claiming he was robbed last night by Clete and Jess Tate and them."

"That can't be," said Texada.

"That's what I said," said Thornton, "but Kindred's got it set in his mind that Clete and his boys are responsible for the holdup, so he's getting a posse together to go after them."

"Well, Clete can handle that," said Coll.

"I ain't so sure about that, sonny," said Thornton. "Kindred is a mean one who shoots first and asks questions later. He's liable to start some trouble with Clete, and before you know it, all Hell is going to break loose."

"Well, what do you think should be done?" asked Texada.

"I'm thinking someone ought to find Clete and tell him what's afoot," said Thornton.

"You're right," said Texada. "And that's exactly what I'm going to do. Coll, you tell Granny where I'm going."

"Where are you going?" asked Coll.

Texada thought about it for a second, then said, "I'm going to warn Clete about Kindred and the posse."

And with that Texada was out the door and into the phaeton. She wasn't positive about which ranch Slater would be working that Monday, but she knew it had to be one belonging to Joe Kaylor, Eldon Seals, or Tom Ware. She cracked the whip over the mare's head and started through the square toward Fourth Street and the road out of town. Then the thought struck her that she might have to take a shortcut or two and that meant taking trails that weren't exactly suitable for a buggy. At Third and LaGrange streets, she turned around and headed home to change clothes and get her horse.

Mrs. Hallet questioned her granddaughter about the hurry, and

Texada explained while she slipped out of her button-top shoes and dress and into her boots, a brown shirt, and a pair of faded dungarees. There wasn't enough time to braid her hair. Mrs. Hallet told Texada not to spare the whip but to race with the wind to find Slater and warn him about Kindred and the posse.

Texada saddled Pixie as fast as humanly possible, mounted up, and headed back down LaGrange to the town square. She passed by the courthouse with the bay running at a full gallop, causing several people, including a knot of Yankee soldiers, to express their displeasure over her recklessness. Ignoring their gestures and curses, she sped down to Fourth Street and turned eastward on the Columbus road. Less than a mile out of town, she saw Colonel Markham and Malinda in a surrey coming down the road toward her. She thought of stopping to tell them about Kindred and the posse but changed her mind because she didn't trust Markham. She passed them without slowing down.

In another minute, Texada overtook Teddy Johnson and his teamsters in one of Johnson's freight wagons. The men were all holding rifles or shotguns upright in the rear of the wagon. Kindred wasn't with them. Texada thought that was odd, but then she began adding up what she knew about the deputy and figured out that he had probably ridden ahead to the Campbell Plantation to recruit the Detchens and their hired hands for the posse. A quick glance at the road told her that someone had ridden it at a gallop just minutes earlier and was going in the same direction as she was. This is good, she thought. I'm not too late.

At the Kaylor ranch, Texada explained the emergency to Joe Kaylor, and he told her that the Double Star crews had finished working his place, as well as the ranches of Eldon Seals and Tom Ware, the Saturday before. To the best of his knowledge, Slater's men were rounding up cattle on the spreads along the Lavaca River, those belonging to Lou Whitehead, Joe Tucker, and J. B. Stacy. She thanked him, then headed south on the surveyor trail that led to the Tate ranch.

The Reeves brothers were at the Tate place, taking their turns at cooking, cleaning, and doing the chores. Texada told them about Kindred and the posse, and they told her that Slater had mentioned he might work the Tucker ranch this day with Jake Flewellyn's crew. She cautioned them to get ready for Kindred and his men, then raced off down the Petersburg road toward the Tucker ranch.

29

When Markham and Malinda arrived in Hallettsville, Sergeant Wickersham met them in front of the county courthouse. They exchanged the usual formal greetings, then Markham asked Wickersham if anything of note had happened in the town during his absence of the last twenty-four hours.

"Nothing much, sir," said Wickersham, "although there is some excitement about a robbery."

"A robbery?" asked Markham.

"Yes, sir," said Wickersham. "It seems a train of freight wagons was held up last night somewhere south of town on the road to Victoria, sir. The owner of the wagons claims, uh—" He stopped in midsentence and eyed Malinda.

"Claims what, Wickersham?" queried Markham impatiently. Then he noticed the sergeant was looking at Malinda and said, "Speak up, man. If this concerns Miss Slater, then she has a right to hear it, too."

"Yes, sir," said Wickersham. He cleared his throat, swallowed hard, and looked at the ground like a schoolboy caught with a piece of chalk in his hand and an unflattering caricature of the teacher on the blackboard. "Well, sir, the owner claims Mr. Slater and his group of ex-Confederates robbed him, sir."

Mr. Slater? queried Markham in his head. The respect that Wickersham was showing this Reb disturbed him. He made a mental note to discuss this attitude with the sergeant at a later time.

Malinda's brow twisted and bunched up over the bridge of her nose as she said, "Mr. Slater? Do you mean my brother Clete?"

"Yes, ma'am," said Wickersham almost with shame.

"I find that hard to believe, Sergeant," said Malinda.

"Yes, ma'am, I know," said Wickersham, looking up at Malinda. "I don't believe it myself, but I have to report what I heard."

Malinda's immediate thought was to defend her brother. She

knew he couldn't steal anything, never mind what happened at John Kelly's store. That wasn't a robbery; he was only obtaining those things on credit. "Just how far south of town did this robbery happen, Sergeant?" asked Malinda.

"Someone said it happened just this side of Little Brushy Creek, ma'am, wherever that is."

"And you say the robbery took place last night?" she asked.

"Yes, ma'am. Word has it that it happened around midnight."

"What else do you know about it?" asked Markham.

"Well, no one was hurt, sir," said Wickersham. "There wasn't any shooting."

"That's good," said Markham.

"There's one other thing, sir," said the sergeant.

"Yes, what is it, Wickersham?" asked Markham.

"Deputy Sheriff Kindred has gotten up a party of citizens," said Wickersham, "and they're presently on their way to arrest Mr. Slater and his men, sir."

Markham and Malinda exchanged looks as both wondered if that explained why Texada had passed them in such a hurry only minutes earlier, why they had met a wagon filled with armed men just before that, and why Kindred had raced by them only a few minutes prior to that. Markham turned away first. "That will be all, Wickersham," said the colonel.

Wickersham displayed proper military courtesy, then removed himself from their vicinity.

"Malinda, I know what you're thinking," said Markham, "but I can't interfere with Kindred. Not at this point anyway."

"But you know Clete and his men couldn't have been involved in that robbery," she argued. "Little Brushy Creek is over twenty miles from here. It would have taken them at least four hours to ride down there, and you were with them until almost dark last night. There is no way on earth that they could have ridden down there by midnight." She paused then added, "Not without riding at a full gallop all the way. And I know for a fact that Clete would never ride that fast in the dark unless he was absolutely positive that he knew every inch of the way. No, Lucas. My brother couldn't have been involved in that robbery."

Markham looked frustrated as he said, "But, my dear, I can't interfere with the civilian authorities in a matter that falls under their jurisdiction."

"Is it that you can't, Lucas . . . or that you won't?" she demanded, her tone accusing him of insincerity. When Markham hesitated to answer, she said, "Lucas, it's your duty to preserve the peace around here, to protect innocent people from mob actions and the like. I know enough about Jim Kindred to think that he might do something foolish, and I know that Clete and his men are all hotheaded enough to be just as foolish. You saw the look on Kindred's face when he passed us on the road, and you also saw all those men in the wagon with their rifles and shotguns. You put all that together, Lucas, and someone is sure to get hurt or even killed."

"All right," said Markham, almost whining, "what do you want from me?"

"I want you to take some of your men out to the Tate ranch and prevent any blood from being shed needlessly," said Malinda.

"But I told you I can't interfere in civilian matters."

"Yes, I know, you said that. But you can keep the peace in this county, can't you?"

"Yes, I suppose I can," said Markham with a heavy sigh. "All right, I'll go." He looked about for Wickersham, saw him standing near the town well, and called out to him. "Sergeant, assemble the troops!"

30

The sun was a big orange on the horizon when Slater and the Double Star hands called it quits for the day. Slater had chosen to ride with Tate's group again on Monday as they worked Lou Whitehead's spread south of Hallettsville. They had had a good day rounding up Whitehead's cattle, and Slater was beginning to feel a little smug about everything as they started back to the Tate ranch.

The shortest route between the Whitehead place and Tate's was the surveyor trail along the property lines. Riding two abreast with Slater and Tate in the lead, the cowhunters were taking this way home and were almost to the Petersburg road when Nimbus began to act a little skittishly. The stallion broke stride, shook his head, and snorted, giving Slater good cause for concern. After four years of war, the Appaloosa had developed a keen sense for trouble. Slater reined in his horse and raised his right hand simultaneously to halt the men behind him.

"What's up, Clete?" asked Tate softly as he stared at the road ahead.

"Nimbus is telling me something's not right," said Slater.

"Nimbus?" queried Tate. "I always knew he was a great horse, but I didn't know he could talk, too. And he did it without even moving his lips."

"Don't make fun, Jess," said Slater. "I've learned to trust him, and he's never let me down." He reached for his rifle and said, "I think we got trouble coming our way."

Clusters of hackberries and live oaks flanked the trail ahead, and even more foliage surrounded the junction with another path and the Petersburg road. A good spot for an ambush, thought Slater. I know I'd pick it, if I was looking to waylay somebody.

Kindred looked on the location the same as Slater did; it was a good place for doing a little bushwhacking. The deputy and his posse, consisting of Teddy Johnson and his teamsters and the Detchens and their cowboys, were hiding in the brush with their guns at the ready. Kindred saw the Double Star men stop on the trail, then watched as Slater drew his Henry from its scabbard. The latter movement prompted him to action.

"Hold it right there, Slater!" yelled Kindred. "This is Deputy Sheriff Jim Kindred talking. You're all under arrest."

Slater continued to pull the rifle from its sheathing as he hollered back, "What's the charge, Mr. Kindred?"

"Robbing Teddy Johnson's freight wagons!"

"You got the wrong men, Mr. Kindred!" Then softer, Slater said, "I don't like this at all, Jess. Tell the boys to start dropping back."

"No, we ain't!" yelled Farley Detchen.

"Throw down your weapons and come along peaceable!" shouted Kindred. "There's no need for any shooting here!"

"Something tells me we'd never make it to the jail," said Tate as he reached for his rifle.

Bang! The first shot was fired, coming from the bushes at the junction. More bullets followed, several dozens of them as the entire posse opened fire.

Slater and his men, all of them combat veterans, remained calm and cool. They split into two groups, each man going to the side of the trail closest to him. As soon as they were under some sort of cover, they drew their weapons and dismounted, letting their horses run free. With lead zinging over their heads, breaking off branches and riddling leaves, they hunkered down as close to the ground as they could get and started looking for something or someone to shoot.

"Hold your fire," said Slater, the instincts of leadership taking hold of him, "until we know what we're up against here."

Slater looked through the fading twilight toward the junction, which was now shrouded with gun smoke. The Double Star men had the advantage of having the setting sun at their backs, making them hard to see, while the bushwhackers were easy to pick out by the flashes from their guns. Slater counted them coming from at least twenty different spots.

"Jess? Can you hear me, son?" called Slater in a little louder than normal voice.

"Perfectly, Clete."

"I want everyone to spread out," said Slater. "They don't know where we are in here. Stay low. Shoot at their gun flashes, then move to another spot. Pass that on."

Every man heard him, then did as ordered. In the next few seconds, Slater and his men were at war again.

31

Texada met Jake Flewellyn and his crew just outside of Petersburg as they were starting back to the Tate ranch after a long day that was about to get longer. They quickly exchanged information, then departed, each going a different way: Texada north for the Whitehead ranch and Flewellyn and the boys east to their own place.

Texada missed Pick Arnold and his group of cowhunters but found Bill Simons and his crowd on the Stacy ranch. She told them about Kindred and the posse, and Simons said that they had seen Slater with Tate's crew heading home fifteen or twenty minutes earlier and that they should just about then be getting to the Petersburg road. Texada sensed that there was no time to waste and prompted Simons to stop work and follow after Slater.

Flewellyn and his men were almost to the junction when they heard the first shots being fired by the posse. They halted and took cover, then slowly worked their way toward the source of the shooting.

When they heard the gunfire begin, the Reeves brothers left off fixing supper for the Double Star hands, saddled up their horses, and rode out to the Petersburg road to find out what was happening.

Pick Arnold and his crew had worked the Duffner spread that day and had chosen the way to go home that brought them to the junction from the north. When they heard the shooting ahead of them, they proceeded cautiously.

Texada rode with Simons and his bunch along the same trail that Slater and Tate's crew had taken. They were only a half mile away when the battle started.

In the next two minutes, these four groups joined the action, making contact with each other or with Slater's contingent as they did. When Slater learned that all of the Double Star men were now with him, he had them encircle the posse's position and wait for his command to commence firing. In the meantime, Texada found him.

"Oh, Clete!" she said, throwing herself on him as he lay on the ground avoiding the posse's bullets. She hugged and kissed him anxiously as she said, "Thank the Lord, you're all right."

Slater rolled her off him and pinned her to the ground. "What the hell are you doing here, girl?" he demanded angrily. "Those men are shooting real bullets at us! Are you crazy?"

Shocked by his reaction, Texada could only say, "Aren't you glad to see me, Clete darling?"

With the wind blown completely from his masculine sails, Slater shook his bowed head in frustration and said, "Yes, darling, I am. Now will you stay down and keep out of the way so I'll be glad to see you tomorrow, too?"

She smiled at him and said, "I knew you loved me."

"Yes, I love you," he said, "but stay down." Then raising up a bit, he put a hand to his mouth and shouted, "Kindred! We need to talk!"

Slater could hear Kindred telling his men to hold their fire, then the deputy yelled back, "You ready to surrender, Slater?"

"I was just about to ask you the same thing!" shouted Slater. "We have you surrounded!"

"The hell, you say!" yelled Kindred.

"Take a good look around, Kindred! I'm about to have my men fire a volley at you! Take a good look at where all the shots come from! Ready, boys?"

More than half of them responded that they were, but before Slater could give the order to fire, Kindred piped up.

"Hold on, Slater! There's no need for any more shooting! We can talk this out, can't we?"

"Hold your fire, boys!" Slater ordered his men. "Sure, we can talk, Kindred! You and your boys throw out your weapons, then come out on the road with your hands up, and we can talk all you want! But not until then!" There was no immediate response from Kindred. "I'm going to give you a minute to think it over, then if you don't come out like I said, we start shooting!"

"Go to Hell, Slater!" yelled Farley Detchen. Then he fired at Slater.

"Let her rip, boys!" commanded Slater.

The Double Star hands opened fire with all they had, but they didn't get to shoot more than a few rounds before the familiar sound of a bugle reached their ears.

"It's those damned Yankees!" shouted Flewellyn. "Come on, boys! We're going to get another chance to whup them Bluebellies again!"

"Hold on, boys!" shouted Slater. "Hold your fire! Don't any of you shoot at those Yankees!"

"But, Clete!" protested Tate. "They're Yankees!"

"The war's over, Jess!" shouted Slater. "You heard me, boys! Don't shoot the Yankees or there will be Hell to pay! I promise you that!"

The bugling grew louder, and the sound of a hundred or more horses' hooves came rumbling down the surveyor's trail that ran north and south along the western boundary of Glengarry. Just as the military unit reached the junction, Colonel Markham halted it in a cloud of dust and gun smoke. The officer scanned the area and quickly surmised that he was in the middle of the fray.

"Deputy Sheriff Kindred?" called Markham. "Are you here?"

"Yes, sir, I am!"

"Clete Slater? Are you here?"

"Yes, Colonel, I am!"

"In the name of the Union of the United States of America, I order all of you to lay down weapons and cease this disturbance immediately!"

"Now hold on, Colonel!" yelled Kindred from his place of concealment. "I came out here to arrest Slater and his boys for robbing Mr. Johnson's freight wagons last night down on the Little Brushy. I—"

Markham cut him off. "I know perfectly well what you are doing here, Mr. Kindred! I'm here to inform you that you are pursuing the wrong men. I can personally vouch for their whereabouts last night at the time of the robbery, and that is all the reason you need to withdraw."

Kindred started to protest. "But, Colonel—"

"Enough, Mr. Kindred!" shouted Markham as angrily as he could get. "Put up your weapons and disperse! Or I will place you and every man with you under military arrest and take you back to Hallettsville in chains! Have I made myself perfectly clear, sir?"

"Colonel, my name is Teddy Johnson! My boys and I are coming out! We don't want no argument with you Yankees!"

"We're coming out, too!" yelled Kindred.

"Mr. Slater?" shouted the colonel. "What are your intentions, sir?"

Slater stood up and shouted, "We've had a long day, Colonel! We'd just like to go back to the ranch and have a little supper before we turn in for the night! You and your men are welcome to join us, if you like!"

"Thank you, sir!" shouted Markham. "I believe we'll accept that invitation!"

No one except Clark Reeves heard Kent Reeves say, "Aw, hell, Clete! There won't be any seconds on dessert tonight!"

And only Kent heard Clark moan, "Sonofabitch! That means I got to wash twice as many dishes!"

32

Colonel Markham approached Sophia Campbell with the idea of a merger between her outfit and the Double Star, and she rejected him outright, saying that her boys would never ride for Clete Slater. Markham reminded her that never was a long time and that the nearest market for Texas cattle was a long way off over the horizon. Before leaving, he told her that she might want to reconsider Slater's offer to take her hands and cattle with him when he started to New Orleans.

The next day Markham rode out to the Sheldon plantation to relate Sophia's stance to Slater.

"She's a stubborn woman," said Markham as he sat atop his horse talking with Slater.

Slater was also in the saddle. He removed his hat and wiped the sweat from his brow with his forearm, then said, "Stubborn is being kind, Colonel. Sophia Campbell is as wicked as they come. She'll lie with every breath she takes if that's what it takes to get her what she wants." He replaced his hat.

"I take it you don't like the woman," said Markham.

"It's not a matter of not liking her," said Slater, "as much as it's a matter of understanding her. Has anyone ever told you how she got such a big plantation?"

"I've heard a tale or two," said Markham.

"Did you know that she ran off and married Dr. Campbell when she was only fourteen and he was thirty-eight?"

Markham smiled at the suggestion that the doctor had robbed the Foley cradle and said, "Yes, I heard that part of it. And I've heard how she and her father have been feuding ever since then."

"Wash Foley is a good man, Colonel," said Slater. "You should get to know him. My granddaddy always said he was a straightforward, honest man who expected a good day's work out of his slaves and treated them good for giving him that good day's work six days a week. Like a lot of the older planters, he gave his slaves the Sabbath as a day of rest and for learning about the Lord. He even let his field hands off for holidays like Christmas and the Fourth of July. When I was over bargaining with him for his cattle, I noticed how most of his former slaves were still living on the place. Does that tell you anything about how he treated them when they were his chattel?''

"I suppose it does speak well of him," said Markham, "but he was still a slaveholder.''

"So was just about everybody in these parts who had fields to be worked," said Slater. "You've got to understand how it was around here, Colonel. This isn't the North. This is Texas, and Texas isn't even like the rest of the South. Did you know we didn't even have overseers for our slaves until a few years before the war? Most of the folks who settled Texas before the Revolution didn't have slaves to begin with, and when they got some, they handled them personally, almost like they were their own children. That's the way the older folks still treat the Negroes. Like children. It's the younger landowners like Sophia Campbell who have mistreated their slaves. Most of the people in these parts aren't the monsters those Abolitionists made them out to be, Colonel.''

"Are you saying slavery is a proper way of life, Slater?''

"No, sir, I'm not. Slavery is not right. It's never been right. Not here. Not anywhere in America. Not anywhere in history. Not even in the Bible, although it does say something stupid about it being all right for God's chosen people to have slaves. I never could understand how smart people could believe that hogwash and still call themselves Christians. I guess they figured that if a preacher said slavery was all right with the Lord then they didn't have to carry it on their consciences that slavery is wrong.

"I've been around Negroes all my life. I know them for what they are, Colonel. They're people . . . just like you and me, and it isn't right to put chains on people and force them to break their backs for you in your fields." He studied Markham for a second before asking, "Colonel, have you got any Indian blood in you?''

Markham was caught off guard and blustered, "No, no, I haven't. Why do you ask?''

"Because I have," said Slater. "There's Choctaw on one side and Cherokee on the other. Up in the Indian Territory, I hear they call them the Civilized Tribes. Does the fact that there's Indian blood running in my family's veins disturb you any?''

Again, Markham was abashed, didn't know what to say exactly. He looked away from Slater, his eyes darting from the sky to the ground to the horizon and finally back to Slater. He cleared his throat and said, "I've never given it any thought, to be perfectly honest about it. From the looks of you," he said, embarrassed, and shifted his gaze away, "and Malinda and Dent, too, I would never have guessed that you had Indians in your ancestry."

"Well, it's true, Colonel. The first Slater to come to America, my great-great-grandfather, married a Cherokee woman because there weren't enough white women to go around. My great-grand-father then married a woman who was half-Cherokee and half-Scot, the same as he was. My grandfather did the same thing, and my father married my mother, who is half-Choctaw. In fact, my other grandfather, Hawk McConnell, has lived like an Indian all of his life. As far as I know, he's still alive up in the Choctaw Nation right now.

"Now I'd be willing to bet, Colonel, that you can trace your ancestry all the way back to England on both sides of your family, and there isn't a redskin or even a Scot among them. And you think that makes you better than us, don't you?"

Markham flushed with shame and anger at the same time. His first reaction was to agree with Slater; yes, he did feel superior to him because all his ancestors were white and English. But he chose to lie, not only to Slater but also to himself. "No, of course not," he said.

"You aren't being honest, Colonel," said Slater in a matter-of-fact way, "but it's all right. You see, I understand you, too, the same as I understand Sophia Campbell. Sophia thinks she's better than all of us. Better because she's white and so is everybody in her ancestry. She also thinks that everybody should give her whatever she wants, and she thinks like that because she's white." Slater let out a quick laugh before saying, "She looks down on us because we're part Indian, and she's always hated us because we always had more than she did."

"If that's so," said Markham, "then why was she willing to form a partnership with Dent?"

"Because Dent has something she wants," said Slater.

"You mean his cattle?"

"Yes, his cattle," said Slater, "and because he's so young and inexperienced in business matters. I'm sure she thought she could take advantage of him in some way or another."

"But I'm the one who convinced Dent to make the deal with her," said Markham.

"Don't take offense, Colonel, but that's exactly my point. You may not be as young as Dent is, but you're just as green as he is when it comes to things like this.''

Markham knew Slater was right, but he would never admit it to him. Pretending to ignore Slater's last remark, he said, "So what do you suggest we do about the situation?"

"It's not my problem, Colonel," said Slater. "I've got enough men to handle the cattle we've gathered in. The question is this: Do the Detchens have enough men to trail their cattle to market? I don't think they do, and I know for a fact that there isn't another man in the county who is so desperate that he'll work for them. We're nearly done driving in a herd, Colonel, and I'm planning to start trailing them for New Orleans before the end of the month.''

"New Orleans?" queried Markham. "I thought you would be going north to Missouri.''

"We might get a better price in Missouri," said Slater, "but New Orleans is closer and safer. It's only half the distance, and we won't have to deal with the Indians or worry about border bandits in Missouri. It'll take us about forty days to reach New Orleans, weather permitting, of course. And we can get back here with the money in less than two weeks. Then folks around here can start getting back on their feet.''

"That's all well and good for the people you're contracted with, Slater," said Markham, "but what about Glengarry?"

With a touch of bitterness, Slater said, "Glengarry is no longer mine to worry about, Colonel. You and Dent made your bed with Sophia Campbell. I guess now you'll have to sleep in it.''

"Slater, you've got no call to take that attitude.''

"I haven't? Colonel, I'm being friendly with you because you're going to marry my sister. If not for that, I would extend to you all the same courtesy that you've given me since I returned home last month.'' Slater felt his temper reaching for the boiling point. He aimed a finger at Markham and said, "You and your men are unwelcome in these parts, Colonel, because you continue to drag on the war.''

Markham took offense and said, "We drag on the war? You have your nerve saying that when you Confederates still raid our supply trains, attack our men when they are alone and vulnerable, and you still mistreat your coloreds. Maybe not here in Lavaca County, but elsewhere in the South.''

"No, sir!" said Slater, exploding and jabbing his gloved finger at Markham to accentuate his words. "You are wrong there! If your supply trains are being raided like you say, then it's probably because you have everything and we have nothing and you are taking away what little we do have and you are giving us nothing in return. If your claim that your men are being murdered by ex-Confederates is true, then that's probably because you people continue to wage war on us with your abuse of us and our women, treating us like a conquered foe instead of trying to heal the wounds of our nation. And we *do not mistreat* our coloreds as you call them because they are no longer ours. They are yours now, and your people have given some of them the idea that *they are now our masters*. They are not our masters, Colonel. Not even with your Yankee bayonets to back them up are they our masters. The law says they are our equals now. I say it's about time that came to be because the Negroes are people just the same as we are and as people they deserve to be treated fairly and honestly just the same as any other people.

"But let me tell you this, Colonel Lucas Markham. I will not let you . . . or any man . . . lord himself over me, and I can safely say that there isn't a man in the South . . . or the North, for that matter . . . who doesn't feel the same about that as I do. If you Yankees continue to insist on treating us like your conquered enemy, then we will have no choice but to resist you with whatever means become necessary for the moment."

"You're treading on treasonous ground, Slater!" retorted Markham angrily. "I could have you thrown in jail for talking like that."

"You could," said Slater sardonically, "but you won't."

"And why won't I do it?"

"For several reasons, Colonel. One, you need me to get Dent's cattle to market because you know as well as I do that the Detchens can't do it. Two, you're afraid of what people around here will do if you do throw me in jail. I understand someone took a shot at you already. And three, you're afraid General Canby won't like it."

"You think you're pretty high and mighty, don't you, Slater?" sneered Markham.

"No, Colonel, I don't. I'm no better than you or any other man, but I do know where and how I stand. That's more than I can say for you. Now if you don't mind, Colonel, I've got a job to finish." With that, he spurred Nimbus and rode away.

As Markham watched Slater go, he gritted his teeth and said aloud, although no one else could hear him, "And I also have a job to finish, Slater."

33

Markham was still fuming over his conversation with Slater when he rode up to Glengarry mansion. Malinda met him at the bottom of the steps to the veranda and immediately remarked about the scowl on his face.

"It's that brother of yours, my dear," said Markham. He turned aside, and Malinda took his arm. They started to stroll down the lane. "He never ceases to irritate me. He is obstinate, audacious, and obnoxious. I know you don't like to hear this sort of talk, Malinda, but I must have my say or I will . . . or I will burst."

"Yes, Lucas, I know."

"I should have done something about him that first night, but now it's too late to rid myself of him."

"Lucas, what happened?" asked Malinda, trying to soothe him.

"I went out to the Sheldon Plantation to talk to him about Sophia Campbell," said Markham, "and he so much as told me that it wasn't his problem and to leave him alone. He also said that you are the only reason that he is being civil with me. I mean, because we are to be married. Then he had the audacity to tell me that all the problems of the South are the fault of the Union. Can you imagine that, my dear? I tell you, I have the most difficult time of it believing that you and he spring from the same well."

Malinda knew better than to defend her brother to her fiancé, so she chose to take a different tack with Markham. "What seems to be the problem with Miz Campbell?" she asked.

"She says her boys won't work with your brother," answered Markham, although he would have preferred to continue ranting about Slater.

"They won't work with him . . . or for him?"

"For him, I guess." Markham stopped, forcing Malinda to do the same. He took her hands in his and said, "Malinda, am I missing something here? I can't understand this business between your family and Sophia Campbell. Slater—I mean, Clete. Clete said she was a wicked woman, but I haven't seen any wickedness in her. She may be a little on the temperamental side and a bit crude at times, but I simply can't see anything else in her that I could call unvirtuous."

Malinda clucked her tongue, then said to him as if he were a naive little boy, "Lucas, you are the innocent, aren't you?" She smiled and shook her head in gentle reproval. "I guess you won't see Miz Campbell and those awful sons of hers for what they really are until they've crossed you and it's too late to do anything about it." She leaned forward, rising on tiptoe as she did, and kissed Markham on the cheek.

"What was that for?" he asked, surprised by the buss.

"If I have to tell you why I kiss you, Lucas, then what's the point in kissing you?"

Markham blushed. He loved Malinda more than anything. There was nothing he wouldn't do for her. He remained silent, just looking into her eyes, worshipping her as his own personal goddess.

A moment passed.

Feeling that Markham was too abashed to speak, Malinda said, "Lucas, I should think a compromise is in order if Miz Campbell wants to get her cattle as well as ours to market this year."

This was not the line of thought coursing through Markham's brain. Hesitantly, he asked, "Did you have something in mind, my dear?"

They broke their hand holding, and she took his arm again as they resumed walking.

"Suppose Dent was to ramrod the cattle drive," said Malinda. "I would think Miz Campbell would be receptive to such a proposition."

"Mrs. Campbell, yes," said Markham, "but what about Clete? Do you think he'll be receptive to taking orders from his younger brother?"

Malinda took a turn at frowning. She felt that she knew her brothers all too well. The fiery tempers of a long line of Highlander warriors was fused in their blood with the iron wills of the women of the proud Choctaw and Cherokee nations, making them two of the stubbornest young men in all Creation. Clete would not relish the idea of being subservient to Dent, and Dent would be opposed to working with Clete on any terms. They would have to be deceived into thinking that they would be cooperating to spite the other.

"Lucas, you will have to speak with Dent first and convince him that this will be his chance to prove his right to be master of Glengarry. Then you will have to go to Miz Campbell and tell her that Dent will ramrod the trail outfit and that her boys will only have to take orders from him. Then you will have to go to Clete and tell him that Miz Campbell has insisted that Dent ride with her sons on the drive to market."

"What good will that do?" asked Markham.

"Clete knows that Miz Campbell has always had her eye set on owning Glengarry," said Malinda. "She's wanted to be mistress of Glengarry ever since she was a young girl. My mother told me how Miz Campbell . . ." She fell silent, feeling that discretion for the past of others should dictate her words.

"How she what?" prompted Markham.

"Lucas, there are some things that are better left unrepeated," she said.

"But how am I to convince Clete to accept Dent as the trail boss if I don't know the whole story?"

"Lucas, this is hard to tell because the subject is a delicate one," said Malinda, stopping and turning to Markham, her eyes pleading with him not to press the matter. She saw instantly that he was adamant on the point and resigned herself to divulging the story. "My mother told me all about what Miz Campbell was like when she was a young girl." She smiled at a remembrance and went on. "My daddy was a handsome man, and all the girls in the county were in love with him, including my mother and Sophia Foley. And rascal that he was at times—at least, that's how my mother told it to me—he was known to take advantage of a girl's innocent feelings. Well, it seems that Sophia threw herself at my daddy when she was only fourteen, then she went about telling folks that she had . . . that he had gotten her in a family way. My daddy denied it, of course, and to prove it, he married my mother. Sophia swore that she would get her revenge on him one day, and then she ran off with Dr. Campbell. My mother said that most folks believe that Dr. Campbell was the one who got Sophia in a family way, and she only tried to blame my daddy because she wanted to be the mistress of Glengarry. Even Sophia's parents believed it was Dr. Campbell who was the father, because they refused to have any truck with him from that time on.''

"So you think Clete will think that Mrs. Campbell has some evil plan for Dent and that he will go along with Dent being the trail boss just to stop her?''

"Yes, that's exactly what I think," said Malinda.

Markham was very surprised at how Malinda's mind seemed to work in such a crafty way. He tilted his head to one side, smiled, then said, "Well, I suppose anything is worth a try.''

34

Markham was amazed at how well Malinda had predicted the outcome of her little scheme.

Dent's ego was properly stroked by Markham, and he agreed readily to ramrod the trail crew.

Sophia Campbell was not only satisfied that Dent would be in charge; she was almost insistent that he hold the reins of leadership, partly because she knew it would stick in Slater's craw but mostly because she had plans of her own that would work better with Dent calling the shots.

Slater opposed the idea at first. He didn't need Dent and the Campbell hands to help the Double Star drovers trail their herd to New Orleans. Still, he wanted to help Dent. Even so, he had his reservations about his younger brother being the boss, because of Dent's age and inexperience, but he gave in to Markham with one very important provision: only Dent and the Detchens could come along from the Campbell crew; the others had to remain behind.

Sophia argued against Slater's amendment to the plan, but Markham convinced her it was the only way she would get her cattle to market.

The trail drive to New Orleans was to begin in late June. Slater and the Double Star men had gathered in close to a thousand head of cattle, but only two-thirds of their number would be trailed to market. The Detchens and their crew had managed to corral a little over four hundred head, and like the Double Star outfit, they left some of them behind for seed. Altogether, the trail herd would have nine hundred head trekking the five hundred miles between Hallettsville and the Crescent City. Slater estimated that they would need five to six weeks to make the trip.

Slater announced that he would join his herd with Dent's at Glengarry early in the morning on the last Monday of the month. It was a newsworthy occasion because their drive was to be the first from Lavaca County since early in the war. Nearly everybody in the region was talking about it. Several folks, including and especially Mrs. Hallet, planned to turn out to witness the reunion of the two brothers.

When the day of the big event arrived, only a small group of Hallettsville townspeople rode out to Glengarry to watch. Colonel Markham was there, of course, with a small detachment of troopers—just in case everything didn't go exactly as designed. Dent waited at the entrance to Glengarry, sitting atop his horse, a dapple gray gelding. Markham and Malinda stood to one side of him, and the Detchens and Sophia Campbell were on the other, they on their mounts and she in her buggy.

Coming up the road from Hallettsville was a great procession led by Texada Ballard driving her grandmother in their phaeton. Slater was right behind them on Nimbus, and following him was the camp wagon, being driven by Jess Tate. Bawling, belligerent cattle being pushed along by determined drovers brought up the rear. Texada and Mrs. Hallet drove up to Dent and stopped, then Slater came up alongside them. No one spoke at first, but several looks were exchanged between all the principals.

Although neither of them would openly reveal his feelings, Clete and Dent were experiencing the same emotion. Both of them wanted to jump down from their horses, embrace his brother, and say all the good things that were pent up in their hearts. But they didn't do that. Neither one was willing to make the first move. Malinda and Mrs. Hallet had them pegged perfectly: cross a Scot with an Indian and you're bound to get something very mule-headed.

Finally, the great lady herself broke the silence. "Cletus, you go over there and shake hands with your brother," said Mrs. Hallet. When Slater hesitated, she reiterated her command. "Go on now. He's your blood kin, and the two of you shouldn't be fussing and feuding with each other. You hear me, Cletus?"

"Yes, ma'am," said Slater without taking his eyes off Dent.

He dismounted and walked over to Dent just as Mrs. Hallet had told him to do, going her one better by removing his hat.

"Denton Slater," said Mrs. Hallet, "you've got no right to sit up there like the lord of a castle and look down on your brother like that. Get down from there and shake your brother's hand. Lord Almighty, you haven't seen him in nearly four years. Isn't there at least an ounce of love for him left in you?"

There was more than an ounce. Dent knew it, but he wouldn't admit it, not even to himself. Even so, he felt compelled to follow Mrs. Hallet's order. He climbed down from his saddle, faced Clete eye to eye, and removed his hat.

Neither brother moved another inch.

"Don't just stand there looking like a pair of sick puppies," said Mrs. Hallet. "Do something or I'll tell your grandfather the second I see him up yonder, and he'll come back down here and whip the tar out of both of you for the way you're behaving yourselves right now."

"We better do what she says, Dent," said Slater, softly, slowly, "or Grandpa will come back and whip us both."

Tears welled up in Dent's eyes. His right hand reached out tentatively, shaking ever so slightly.

Slater saw his brother's hand, grabbed it with his own right, and pulled Dent to him.

Dent neither resisted nor returned the embrace, as he allowed Slater to hold him close.

"I'm happy to see you, Dent," whispered Slater.

"It's good to see you, too, Clete," said Dent, his words stilted, awkward, but only a tiny bit hollow on the ear. "I'm glad you weren't killed like we thought all this time."

Slater broke the contact between them, stepped back, and said, "So am I, Dent. It's good to be home."

"Now that's more like it," said Mrs. Hallet.

Malinda came forward and embraced Slater as if they hadn't seen each other in years. "Welcome home, Clete," she said sincerely.

In keeping with the charade of this, their second, reunion, Slater returned her affection and said, "I'm so happy to see you, too, little sister."

Tears broke through the dams of her eyes and rushed down her cheeks. She kissed Slater first on one cheek, then on his lips. "I only wish Grandpa knew you'd survived. It would have made his last days so much easier for him."

"He knows," said Slater. "He knows."

"All right, enough of this dillydallying," said Sophia Campbell. "There's cattle to be drove to market. You boys quit all this mush-mouth stuff and get them moving."

"You hush your mouth, Sophia Campbell!" snapped Mrs. Hallet. "Just because there isn't a loving bone in your body doesn't mean other folks are just as mean and miserable as you are. You let these young people have their time or so help me I'll take this whip to you." She reached over Texada for the buggy whip, got it, and shook it at Sophia. "You hear me, Sophia Campbell?"

Sophia knew what was politically and socially prudent for the moment. "Yes, ma'am," she said with all the humility she could muster.

Slater backed away from Malinda and looked at Dent. "You're the boss here, Dent. Just say the word, and we'll move them out."

Dent wasn't insensitive to the others around him. There were good-byes to be said now. He replaced his hat and went to Markham first.

"So long, Lucas," said Dent, shaking Markham's hand. "I wish you were coming with us."

"So do I, Dent," said Markham, "but I have my duties here. We'll see you home again in seven or eight weeks anyway."

"Yes, that's right," said Dent. He went to Malinda, gave her a cursory hug, and said, "Take good care of Glengarry while I'm gone, Malinda."

"I will," she said.

Dent remounted his horse and wanted to give the command to start the herd moving east, but he waited while Clete made his farewells.

Like his brother, Slater approached Markham first. "Thank you, Colonel," he said. "I know you're the one responsible for all this, and I won't forget you for it."

Markham looked at him sternly and said, "I didn't do it for you, you know."

"Makes no difference, Colonel. You still did it, and I'm obliged to you for it."

To Malinda, he said, "We just come together again, and now we have to part. It hardly seems fair."

"There will be more time when you return," she said. Then, as she took Markham's hand, she added, "Won't there, Lucas?"

"Yes, I suppose so," said Markham with little enthusiasm.

Slater left them and went to Mrs. Hallet and Texada.

"Now, Cletus, don't you go getting all soft on me now," said Mrs. Hallet. "You're the man for this job, so you be on your way without any pitiful partings."

Slater smiled at the grand lady of the county and said, "Yes, ma'am. I'll be seeing you in eight weeks or so."

Then his eyes turned to Texada, and his heart sank. She was wearing a light blue dress printed with yellow daffodils and adorned with white cuffs and collar. Her hair was brushed out, hanging down to her shoulders, half-curled at the ends. She was lovelier at this moment than at any other time that he could recall, and he loved her more than ever before. During the drive, he would miss her, would dream of her, and would make her his every thought of every waking moment.

Slater took Texada's hand in his and said, "It won't be all that long that I'll be gone, Texada."

"Oh, yes, it will, Clete darling," she said, and in the next instant she threw her arms around his neck and planted her lips on his. She made their kiss long and hard, her tongue darting into his mouth and turning up his temperature. Before he could regain his composure, she backed away and said, "Now when you get to New Orleans, I want you to remember that and think about how fast you want to get home to some more just like it or even better."

"Texada Ballard!" snapped Mrs. Hallet. "I ought to take this whip to you for just thinking such sinful things let alone saying them. You let go of that man and let him be on his way."

Texada partially ignored her grandmother and said to Slater, "You best remember what I said, Clete darling." Then feeling her grandmother's eyes boring into her back, she said, "Now git! Before I decide to do something more foolish!"

Slater said softly, "I love you, Texada," then turned away.

Texada sat back in the buggy, turned her face from him, and said beneath her breath, "I love you, too, Clete Slater."

Seeing the sadness in her granddaughter's eyes, Mrs. Hallet leaned close to her and whispered, "Never mind what I just said, girl. If I was your age, I'd have done the same thing. Maybe more." She looked past Texada at Slater. "He sort of reminds me of Captain Hallet when I first saw him back in Virginia. I'm old, Texada, but I'm not feebleminded. Not yet, I'm not. And I do have my memories. I made them when I was young, and now it's your turn to do the same. Don't let a minute pass without making one. You hear me, child?"

"Yes, ma'am," said Texada a second before hugging the woman who had given her more love than a mother ever could.

Dent rode out to the front of the herd as Slater remounted Nimbus. The younger brother raised his hand and his voice, giving the command, "Let's move 'em out!"

The Double Star drovers hesitated a second, then went into action as they saw Slater remount Nimbus and fall into position behind Dent. They pointed the leaders down the road to Columbus and started the herd moving. No one, especially Slater, looked back.

35

Dent and the Detchens—although the twins put up a fuss about it—agreed to use the Double Star trail brand on their stock, and thus, have the outfit be known by the same name.

Their first day on the trail was the toughest for the Double Star drovers. They spent it making the cattle understand that they had to keep moving, that there would be no stopping until the trail boss allowed them to stop, which would only be for a drink in a cool stream or for the noon meal; otherwise, they kept walking forward until the end of the day, when they were bedded down for the night.

Slater used the pause for lunch to speak to Dent about dividing the crew into two groups for riding night guard on the herd. "You might want to do that now," said Slater, "while all the boys are gathered around here." He felt a little awkward, making the suggestion. Although he had accepted the idea that Dent would ramrod the drive, he knew for a fact that his men would still look to him as their leader.

Dent was also feeling a bit out of step with the notion that he was in charge of all these men who were all older and much more experienced than he. At the same time, he could see that Clete would be behind him, supporting him all the way, and this bolstered his confidence. "Yes, I should do that now," he said to his brother. He called the men together and assigned Slater to take charge of one watch group and Jake Flewellyn the other; they could choose who they wanted working with them.

"That ain't right," said Farley. "I should be in charge of a crew. We're partners in this, too."

Dent glared at Farley, then glanced at Clete as if to ask him what to do. When he saw his brother looking at his feet, he realized that he was on his own here. "You got a point there, Farley," he said reluctantly. "Anybody got any objections to Farley bossing one crew?" He scanned the faces around him and noted that most of them were looking at Clete, who still had his focus on his boots. Not hearing any arguments against Farley, Dent said, "All right then. Farley will take one crew and Clete the other. Let's eat up now and get these cows moving again."

The idea crossed Slater's mind that he should volunteer to ride with the Detchens and let Flewellyn take charge of the second group. That way, he could keep an eye on the twins and not worry about them giving his men any trouble, as they were sure to do, knowing them as he did. Maybe that's not such a good thing to do, he thought. It's Dent's duty to make decisions, right or wrong, risky or not. If I start questioning Dent's authority now, the other men will do it, too. No, Clete, keep still.

At dusk, Slater's crew took the first watch of the night. Slater divided the men into two groups. Then he sent a man from the first bunch around the herd clockwise, while he ordered a drover from the other half to ride in the opposite direction. He waited a minute or so, then repeated the orders, sending a second rider each way. He continued doing this until everyone was circling the herd. By the time each one of them had made one complete circuit, he realized that they didn't need all of them to do the job. Slater told every other man to return to camp and get some sleep, that they would be awakened in a few hours to take their own turn.

The night passed peacefully.

With first light of the new day, Farley Detchen rousted Jess Tate from his bed beneath the camp wagon and grumbled something about getting their breakfast pretty damn quick. In a few minutes, the whole crew was awake and moving about the camp.

The second day was much like the first. The drovers pushed the cattle to keep moving ahead at a good pace until they came to Columbus, the seat of adjacent Colorado County, where they spent the rest of the day ferrying the herd across the Colorado River. The men were so busy that they had little time for socializing, and when they did have the time, they were too tired for even the politest of conversations.

No one regretted this circumstance more than Slater. He had hoped to use some of the time getting reacquainted with Dent, maybe finding out what was stuck in his craw. Of course, he knew that he couldn't force himself on Dent; that would only widen the gap between them. Maybe it was better this way, grabbing little moments to be friendly, taking advantage of the few opportunities that came up occasionally during the day to show Dent that he cared about him. That's probably best, he thought. Just go slow, Clete. He'll come around.

Houston was their goal for the second leg of the journey. They reached the northern outskirts of that town on Saturday afternoon, their sixth day out, and Dent was faced with his second important decision.

Dent was in the saddle on a knoll overlooking an expanse of grass where the drovers had brought the herd to feed and bed down for the night. He was alone until the Detchens rode up to him.

"Hey, Dent," said Farley, "since it's Saturday night and none of us have seen a woman or a jug of whiskey since before we left home, how about us riding into Houston for a little snort and maybe find us a friendly gal or two?"

The idea of a drink sounded fairly good to Dent. He had sworn off the bottle during the daylight hours when work demanded that he keep a clear head, but he still put away half a pint each night before stretching himself out on his bedroll. He gave Farley's request a quick thought, then agreed to it.

Farley and Harlan yahooed down the hill to the rest of the crew, spreading the word that they could all go into town that evening.

When Slater heard the news, he was beside himself but kept his temper under control as usual. He spurred Nimbus into a gallop and raced up the rise to Dent. "Did you approve that?" he asked as soon as he reined in his mount.

"Approve what?" asked Dent.

Slater jerked a thumb over his shoulder and said, "That! Farley and Harlan riding around telling all the boys they can go into Houston tonight."

"Sure, I did. What's wrong with that?"

Slater was aghast at Dent's naïveté. "What's wrong with that? Who in the hell's going to watch the herd while they're all off getting themselves tanked up and who knows what else?"

A sheepish aspect distorted Dent's features, and he stared at the ground like a schoolboy standing in front of the teacher after being caught in the act of throwing a spitball across the classroom in retaliation for being hit by the opening toss from another kid. Then he looked up at his brother and said, "I wasn't thinking about the whole bunch of us going into town, Clete. I thought Farley was only asking for him and Harlan, not the whole outfit."

"Well, they're riding around telling everybody you said they could all go into town."

"Well, I'll just set them straight on that," said Dent. "Farley and Harlan will be the only ones going."

"How can you let them go and not let anybody else go? That won't exactly set well with the boys."

"All right, you tell Farley and Harlan I changed my mind and I said they couldn't go."

Slater heaved a sigh and said, "I think it would sound a lot better if you told them. After all, you're the boss of this outfit, and you've got a right to change your mind if you want."

"That's right, I do," said Dent. "Come on. Let's find those two and get this straightened out right now."

Dent spurred his horse and raced down the hill with Slater close behind. They found the Detchens at the camp wagon with several other cowboys, bragging about what they were going to do in Houston if they found a willing woman.

"I wouldn't count on that none," said Dent as he and his brother walked up to them. "I've changed my mind, boys. No one's going into Houston tonight. We got a herd to watch over until we get it to New Orleans. There will be plenty of time to hurrah then. Besides, how many of you got more than a dime in your pocket right now? Not more than two or three of you, I'll bet."

"But you said, Dent," whined Harlan.

"And now I'm saying different," said Dent. "No one goes into Houston tonight. Tomorrow, with it being Sunday and all, maybe some of you might like to go to preaching in town. We can make time for that. But there won't be any carousing tonight."

"Sure, you can say that," said Farley with a bit of a sneer. "You got your liquor every night."

Without thinking, Dent flattened his hand and gave the back of it to Farley's mouth. Detchen's head snapped back, rocking him on his heels. He stumbled against the side of the wagon, grabbing for anything to steady himself as a taste of blood from a split lip soured his mouth. His hand grasped the handle of a big iron skillet. He pulled it from its hook, and raising the frying pan over his head with both hands, he charged at Dent, the madness of a rabid dog snarling through his teeth.

Again, Dent reacted without thinking. He lowered his shoulder and lunged at Farley, driving the joint deep into Detchen's solar plexus.

Detchen was totally surprised by the counterattack. His eyes bulged, the wind gushed from his lungs, he doubled up, his arms came forward, and his hands involuntarily released the blackened weapon he meant to use on Dent's skull—all this on impact from Dent's shoulder. He was driven backward against the wagon, his own head banging hard on a second skillet.

Dent straightened up and backed off a step. He made fists and prepared to let them fly at Farley's face, but then he saw Detchen slump to the ground, stunned and completely without air in his chest.

Instinctively, Detchen grabbed his gut as if to force his diaphragm into emergency action to restore his breath. He gasped frantically but couldn't get the life-giving gas into his body. His eyes were wide with that panic that comes when life is threatened seriously. His skin reddened, then instantly turned ashen as he fought to breathe.

Fear crinkled up Harlan's face as he watched his brother fight to live. "Farley!" he cried, then fell on his knees beside his twin. With hate in his eyes, he looked up at Dent and said, "You've killed him!"

"No, he hasn't," said Slater as he edged past Dent to Farley. He bent over and grabbed Farley's belt at the buckle. In another move, he slid Farley into a supine position, then lifted him up by the belt, bowing Farley's back and coaxing his shocked diaphragm to function again.

With the pain in his gut gone now, Farley was able to relax enough to get the bellows in his chest going again. He gulped air in wheezes for a few seconds, then took deep breaths to restore the oxygen to his body. As soon as the color returned to his cheeks, Slater dropped him on his back.

"If I was you, Farley," said Slater, bending over Detchen and shaking a scolding finger at him, "the next time I went to blowing off at the mouth like that I'd be sure I had me some air to spare first." He straightened up, turned, and walked away. As he passed Dent, he said quietly, "You handled that real good, boss."

Dent wasn't sure how to take the remark, and Slater wasn't too certain on how he meant it. Neither commented on it, however.

The second week passed without further incident, but that was not to say that Farley had forgotten or forgiven the comeuppance he had received from Dent. He brooded about it but said nothing to anyone except his twin, who acted as if he had also taken a beating from the trail boss. Together, they talked about what they would like to do to Dent and Clete Slater, but they held their tongues when someone came near them. They were able to keep their plotting secret until the night the trail outfit camped before the Sabine River, the border between Texas and Louisiana.

From the start of the drive, Jess Tate had the assignment of trail cook, which meant he drove the camp wagon out ahead of the herd, usually reaching the day's destination a few hours before the rest of the outfit so he could make camp, start a fire, and get supper cooking so it would be ready for the drovers when they finally caught up with him. At the Sabine, Tate went down to the river and looked for one of those sweetwater springs that bubble up along the banks of many rivers. It was his opinion that coffee made with river water tasted about as good as horse piss. His daily routine often called for him to make three or four trips for water, especially if the spring was a bit hard to reach, like the one on the Sabine was.

It was close to sundown, and the drovers were busy settling down the herd for the night. Tate was making his fourth trip to fetch water. As he bent over to dip the pail, he heard voices on the bluff above him. He looked up to see who was talking, but a bush obstructed his view. Then he recognized the voices as those of Harlan and Farley Detchen and decided to eavesdrop on them.

"I've been itching all week to get here," said Farley.

"Me, too," said Harlan.

"Tomorrow we get the herd across the river, and tomorrow night I get me a couple of Slaters."

"Now hold on, Farley. You only get to kill one of them. I get the other one."

"What cause have you got to say that, little brother?" Farley aimed a finger at the scar on his cheek and said, "I got this from Clete," then he pointed out the scab on his mouth, "and I got this from Dent. You got any marks on you from either one of the Slaters?"

"Well, no, I don't," said Harlan, "but it don't seem right that you should get to kill both of them."

"I know you hate them, too, Harlan, but I got the most reason for killing them. Even so, I'm not a selfish man. I'll let you hold them while I cut their throats. How'd that be?''

"It wouldn't be the same as me slicing one of them up," whined Harlan. "The least you can do is to let me carve up Dent a little before you go to cutting his throat."

Farley shook his head and said, "Yeah, I guess I can do that. All right, you can carve on Dent a little, then I'll finish him off. How's that?"

Harlan grinned as wide as he could and said, "Sounds real fine to me, big brother."

When they started to turn their horses back toward camp, a lunker of a bass leaped out of the water near the spring, making a loud splash on the water and startling Tate. The bucket he had been holding slipped from his hands and rolled the few feet down the embankment to the river. It was just enough noise to attract the Detchens' attention.

"Hold on, Harlan," whispered Farley. "Someone's down there."

Harlan whispered back, "You think they heard?"

"Of course, they heard, you ninny!" snapped Farley in a low growl. "Come on. We got to get them so they won't tell."

They jumped down from the saddle, drew their knives, and started down the bank.

Tate had remained where he was, hoping they hadn't heard the bucket rattle on the ground. He listened closely for any sound, especially the pounding of horses' hooves moving away from the river. He didn't hear them. Instead, a twig breaking underfoot reached his ears.

Lord Almighty! he thought. They're coming down here!

No sooner had Tate realized his predicament, than the Detchens were on him. Farley grabbed him around the neck from behind, while Harlan slashed at him from the front, cutting a deep gash in Tate's right hand. Tate tried to cry out, but Farley prevented him doing it by jerking his left forearm against Tate's Adam's apple, effectively crushing the wind out of it.

Tate fought back, kicking Harlan in the shin and elbowing Farley in the stomach. The Detchens had never known a bony string bean like Tate to be so strong. Harlan lashed out at him again, his blade this time catching Tate across his left forearm, blood gushing from the severed veins. Angered by the jab to his sore belly, Farley stuck Tate in the back, the point of the knife sliding easily between two ribs and going deep into his body. The wound was too much for Tate; his eyelids spread like clams' shells when dropped into boiling water, his tongue shot out of his mouth, his whole body went rigid. Harlan came in for the kill, driving his knife into Tate just below his heart, twisting it back and forth before withdrawing it.

Tate died in the next instant, and his body became a heavy load for Farley. Detchen released his hold on the corpse, his knife coming free as it crumpled to the ground and rolled into the river. Harlan pushed the lifeless form into the current, and they watched it float downstream for a minute before it disappeared below the surface.

Harlan started to wipe the blood on his knife on his sleeve, but Farley stopped him, saying, "No, wash it off. And wash your hands, too. We can't let anyone suspect we did this."

With his eyes cold and blank, Harlan mumbled, "Yeah, sure, Farley. Wash my hands."

They cleaned up, then looked around to see if anyone else was near. Satisfied that no one was, they mounted up and rode back to camp.

As they came in, the Detchens eyeballed everyone for suspicious looks before dismounting. When no one gave them so much as a blink, they felt secure and climbed down. They tied up their horses on the picket line, then helped themselves to cups of coffee. No words passed between them or anyone else for some minutes. They had murdered, and it was beginning to look as if they had gotten away with it.

36

The sun was well down below the horizon and the light from the campfire was beginning to cast deep shadows all around when Slater rode into camp. He tied Nimbus to the camp wagon, then headed straight for the coffeepot, the same as everyone else did when they planned to sit a spell. After pouring himself a cup, he squatted down away from the fire and blew on the surface of the black brew to cool it. As he did, he glanced around at the faces of the men. They were all tired, and the sight of them was almost depressing. He looked for Jess Tate to put some cheer into him, but the cook was nowhere to be seen.

"Where's Jess?" asked Slater.

Bill Simons spoke up, saying, "I saw him heading off for the river about an hour ago. He had a couple of pails with him, so I guess he was going to fetch some water."

"An hour ago, you said?" queried Slater.

"About that. Maybe longer. I ain't so sure. It was well before sundown, I know that much."

"That would make it at least an hour," said Jake Flewellyn. "I saw him go, too. He had those two big buckets and a couple of canteens hanging from his shoulders. Yep, it was a good hour ago he went off."

"Yeah, that's right," said Simons. "He was carrying canteens over his shoulders."

"Well, someone better go look for him," said Slater.

Dent rode up about that time and said, "Go look for who?"

"Jess went for water about an hour go," said Slater, "and no one has seen him since."

"Did he take a fishing pole along?" asked Dent. "You know how he likes to fish. Maybe he thought the bass were biting and wanted to catch a bunch of lunkers for supper."

"I don't think so," said Flewellyn. "He's got beans boiling and beef ready for cooking on the fire."

"No, I don't think he went fishing," said Slater. "Bill and Jake said he was carrying buckets and canteens when he went off. I think someone ought to go look for him."

"I guess you're right," said Dent.

Farley and Harlan listened to the conversation as if they weren't hearing a word that was said, but they heard it all, especially the part about the canteens. They had seen the buckets but hadn't noticed any other water receptacles. Where had they been? Did they get blood on them? As Farley thought about it, he broke out in a cold sweat. Harlan began sweating only because his twin was.

Suddenly, Farley jumped up and said, "I'll go."

Dent and Slater peered at Farley with suspicious eyes. Why would Farley volunteer for anything? He saw their looks and answered their unspoken question.

"And when I find him, I'll let him know what's what," said Detchen angrily. "Running off when there's supper to be cooked and cowhands to be fed. Come on, Harlan. Let's go find that mangy sonofabitch and kick his hind end all the way back to camp.''

Harlan wasn't the quickest mind in any part of Texas, but he managed to catch Farley's drift in this case. "Let's find him, and kick his butt all the way back to camp,'' he said.

"Never mind, you two," said Dent. "You two haven't done a lick of work all day. You aren't riding off now and skipping out on more work. You just sit tight, while Clete goes looking for Jess. Jake, you want to go along with him?''

Flewellyn finished loading his mouth with a wad of tobacco, then said, "Sure, I'll go.''

"All right, Clete?" asked Dent.

"We'll be back in no time at all,'' said Clete. He poured his coffee back into the pot. No sense in letting it go to waste.

"In the meantime," said Dent, "Farley and Harlan can get matters smoothed out a bit here by getting supper ready for everybody. How about it, boys? Think you can rustle up the grub for us?''

Farley looked at Harlan before answering, then said, "I suppose we can if we have to.''

"You have to," said Dent.

Slater and Flewellyn mounted up and rode down to the river. It was only a short distance of a few hundred yards, but there was no telling how far up or down the stream Tate had gone. With the light fading rapidly now, they split up and went in opposite directions, riding along the low bluff looking for Tate. Each of them called out Tate's name as they rode along, but neither received a response. After covering a quarter mile each way, they turned around and returned to the spot where they had separated.

"See anything?" asked Slater.

Flewellyn turned his head to the side and spit a stream of tobacco juice on the ground. "Nary a thing," he said. "How about you?''

"Nothing here neither," said Slater. "Where do you suppose he could have gone?''

"I'm thinking that's the wrong question to be asking, Clete. Don't you think we ought to be wondering if something might have happened to Jess?''

Slater hated to admit it, but Flewellyn was right. This was totally uncharacteristic of Tate. There wasn't a more responsible man in the crew than Jess Tate. When there was work to be done, he was there to do it, even if it wasn't his job. Flewellyn was right. Something had happened to Tate. But what?

"I think you're right, Jake. He might have slipped and fallen into the river and got carried downstream a ways. The current is pretty strong here, isn't it?"

"Don't ask me," said Flewellyn. He spit again, then added, "This is my first time here since we rode off back in '61."

"Damn!" swore Slater suddenly out of frustration. "It's too dark to see without lanterns. Go back and get some of the boys and whatever lanterns we've got with us and bring them back here. We're going to look for Jess if it takes all night."

Flewellyn rode off to camp, while Slater dismounted and tied Nimbus to an evergreen sapling. He peered out at the Sabine, straining his eyes to see something, some sign of his friend in the enveloping darkness. He cocked an ear, hoping to hear something besides the nocturnal symphony being played by the crickets and frogs and owls and other creatures of the night. He heard voices coming from the camp. He heard cows lowing softly beyond the wagon, where they were bedded down along a creek that emptied into the river. Dammit, Jess! he thought. Where the hell are you? If you've gone and done yourself a hurt, I'll kick your skinny butt all the way to New Orleans and back home again. The feigned anger was suddenly overwhelmed by a great sense of loss gouging his guts. He tried to deny the morbid sensation but couldn't. It gripped him hard, and he hated it. Fortunately, there wasn't time to dwell on it.

Flewellyn returned in a few minutes, accompanied by Bill Simons, Pick Arnold, and the Reeves brothers, each carrying a lantern or a hastily made torch. They dismounted and approached Slater. "Here you go, Clete," said Flewellyn as he handed a lantern to Slater.

Slater took the light, then he noticed that Flewellyn was armed with a side arm. "What's that for?" he asked.

"Snakes," said Flewellyn. He spit tobacco juice and added, "Here. I brung yours, too." He handed the six-gun and holster to Slater.

"Yeah, right," said Slater, taking the weapon. He set the lantern on the ground, then strapped the holster belt around his waist, positioning the Colt's on his left side. "All right, Jake, let's you and me go down to the riverbank and have a look around. We'll split up when we get down there. You go upriver, Jake, and I'll go down. Bill, you and Pick follow along with me up here. Kent, you and Clark follow Jake from up here. Look for any sign of Jess and holler out if you find something." He picked up his lantern and led Flewellyn down the steep embankment to the river's edge. "All right, let's find something now."

"Sure thing, Clete."

They separated and began the search anew.

Slater didn't want to admit it, but he was getting anxious. Dammit, Jess, he thought, where are you? He edged his way along the bank, hoping for the best and fearing the worst. He held the lantern at shoulder height out in front of him as he kept his eyes focused on the ground. His concentration was so intense that he didn't notice the canteens hanging from a branch of a small cottonwood until his head bumped them, startling him. What the hell? He drew back, thinking he was being attacked by a snake, and instinctively, he reached for the revolver at his waist, whipped it out, cocked the hammer, and pointed it in the direction of whatever it was that had touched him. Then he realized that it hadn't been a snake striking at him. Canteens? he wondered. "Jake!" he called out. "Come on. I found something." He replaced his six-gun and took a closer look at the canteens.

Simons and Arnold, who were searching the bluff above him, leaned over the edge to have a look at Slater. "What did you find?" asked Simons.

"Canteens," said Slater. "Find a way down here, and . . ." He thought better of that idea. "No, wait. Stay up there and look around. Look carefully."

"Look for what?" asked Simons.

"Footprints," said Slater. "Any sign of Jess having been there. You know, Bill."

"Got it, Clete," said Simons. He and Arnold began to search the ground very carefully. They were soon joined by the Reeves brothers.

"Found some canteens, did you, Clete?" asked Flewellyn, rejoining Slater.

Slater raised his lantern for Flewellyn to see the canteens hanging from the cottonwood. "Do those look like they belong to our outfit?" he asked.

Flewellyn squinted in the yellow light and said, "I'd say so, Clete."

"Let's look around here some more," said Slater. "Here, hold my lantern so I can get a better look-see down here." He handed the light to Flewellyn, then stooped closer to the water's edge. "See here?" He pointed to a scrape in the muddy embankment. "Looks to me like someone slid into the water here."

"It looks that way to me, too," said Flewellyn. He spit into the water and asked, "You reckon it was Jess?"

"Seems to add up to that, doesn't it?" said Slater.

"He don't swim none too well, does he, Clete?"

That was a question I could have done without, thought Slater. Flewellyn was right, though. Tate was a poor swimmer. If he fell into the river, chances weren't good that he'd swum to safety. That was a possibility that Slater didn't want to face just yet. He stood up and called out to the men above, "Find anything up there?"

"Nothing, Clete!" shouted Simons back down to him. "Just some hoofprints. From your horses, I reckon, when you and Jake were looking before."

"Keep looking," said Slater. He turned back to Flewellyn and said, "What do you think, Jake? You think Jess slipped into the water here and . . . drowned?"

"I don't know that he drowned, Clete," said Flewellyn, noting the concern in Slater's voice. "He wasn't that poor a swimmer." He spit a big gob of tobacco juice into the river, forced a smile, and added, "You know how shit floats."

Despite the anguish he was enduring, Slater couldn't keep from laughing at the jest. "Yeah, I guess you've got a point there, Jake," he said. "I suppose he could have fallen in and floated downstream a ways. Who knows? He could have floated all the way to the gulf by now."

"Sure, he could've," said Flewellyn. "He could be sitting on the bank somewhere downstream right this minute waiting for someone to come fetch him back here."

"Do you really think so, Jake?"

"Sure, why not? It's a cinch that he ain't around here." He spit again, then added, "He's probably just fine, and we'll find him first thing in the morning. I'd bet on that, Clete, so we might as well head on back to camp and get us a good night's sleep. How about it? We'll find him in the morning."

Slater realized that Flewellyn was only trying to help him maintain a positive outlook. He was grateful for friends like Flewellyn, especially at a time like this. "Yeah, I suppose you're right, Jake. Let's go back to camp. I'll come back down here in the morning for another look around, then I'll ride downriver until I find him."

Getting a good night's sleep was easier said than done for Slater. He was so restless that he rode three shifts of night guard and would have ridden a fourth if he hadn't finally fallen asleep in the saddle. He managed to get in a few hours of sleep before first light shone in the east the next morning.

As soon as he was awake again, Slater saddled up Nimbus and rode down to the spring where Tate had most likely fallen into the river. He carefully inspected the area around the spring and noted two very distinct signs that something was amiss here. First, a branch had been broken off a small tree twenty feet below the spring, and second, part of the embankment appeared to have been washed, as if someone had poured several buckets of water on the spot in order to wash away something. Blood? he thought. Whatever it had been, Slater felt certain that his friend had met with foul play and was now either hurt or dead. Whichever, he intended to find Tate or find his body. He headed back to camp.

Dent was the only man in camp awake. He greeted Slater by the fire, handing him a cup of hot coffee. "You're up earlier than usual, aren't you?" he said.

Slater took the coffee and said, "Jess still hasn't come back, Dent. I want to take a few of the boys and go look for him as soon as we've had breakfast."

Dent noticed that some of the men were beginning to stir. "Let's go over yonder and talk," he said, nodding toward a spot near the horse remuda. He led the way, and Slater followed reluctantly. "I know how you feel, Clete," said Dent as soon as he stopped, "but I can't let you take any of the men and go off looking for Jess now. We've got to get these cattle across the river today, and you know that takes every hand to do that. I know Jess was your close friend, but—"

Slater jumped in, saying, "What do you mean 'was'? He still is my close friend."

Very calmly, Dent resumed speaking. "I started to say, we have to think of the herd before we think about the welfare of any one man. Now I know Jess *is* your close friend, but the herd comes first. If Jess is alive, he'll get back here. If he isn't, then it won't make any difference."

"But what if he's just hurt bad and can't get back here on his own?" demanded Slater. "What about that, Dent?"

The younger Slater mulled over the question for a moment, then said, "Same difference, Clete. The welfare of the herd comes first."

Slater knew Dent was right, but he still didn't want to give up searching for Tate. For the first time in a long time, he let his emotions get the best of his judgment. "I'm going to look for

Jess, and that's all there is to it, Dent," he said angrily. "You can just get the cattle across the river without me."

Dent glared at his brother, challenging him with his eyes as he said, "Are you aiming to take over this outfit, Clete?"

"No, I'm not. I'm quitting."

"Quitting?"

"That's right. I'm going to look for Jess."

"What about your men?"

"They aren't my men, Dent. They're yours. You're the boss of this outfit."

Dent sneered and said, "That's so much bullshit and you know it, Clete. Those men follow you, not me."

"That's where you're wrong, Dent."

A lifetime of jealousy took control of Dent. Fire colored his face as he shouted, "The hell, you say! I've seen how they look at you every time I give them an order. They look to you to see if it's okay or not before they do it. Just who the hell do you think you're trying to fool, Clete? They were your men before we started this drive, and they're still your men."

Slater had more arguments for his brother, but he knew that nothing that he could say now would convince Dent that he was wrong. So he calmly and simply said, "If you think it'll help, Dent, I'll tell them to stay with you. You're right about the herd coming first. Those men need the money that's waiting for them in New Orleans, and so do you and all those folks back home. You can get the herd to New Orleans without me, Dent."

A wave of fear swept over Dent. Up till now, he'd had his big brother to back him in any emergency, and he'd felt secure with that knowledge. Now Slater was leaving him to fend for himself just like their grandfather had died and left him to run Glengarry on his own. Panic drained the flames from his complexion. "Look," he said anxiously, "you don't have to quit. You can go look for Jess if you have to—"

"I have to," interjected Slater firmly.

Dent stared at his older brother and realized that nothing that he could say would change Clete's mind. "All right, then do it," he said coolly. "You go and look for him. If you find him alive, then bring him back with you. But if you don't find him and you decide to give up looking for him, then you can catch up with us. And if he's . . ." He broke off deliberately, figuring that his brother might not wish to face that worst of all possibilities just yet.

"If he's dead?" asked Slater, finishing the sentence for Dent.

"Is that what you were going to say?"

"Since you asked, yes, it was," said Dent. "If he's dead, then bury him and catch up with us as soon as you can. All right? Dead or alive, you catch up with us as soon as you find out what's happened to Jess."

Slater was impressed. Dent was more of a man than he had previously thought. Grandpa Dougald had done a good job with him after all. "All right, Dent," said Slater, extending his hand. "I'll be back as soon as I find out what's happened to Jess."

Dent shook it and said, "You better eat something before you go, and maybe you should take a little something with you, too." Then another thought struck him, and he said, "You'd better take an extra horse, too. For Jess. No sense in making Nimbus carry both of you once you find him."

"Yeah, right," said Slater with a wisp of a smile. He thanked Dent, then left right after eating and speaking to his men.

37

Evening was fast approaching, and Slater was dog tired. This had not been one of his best days, and it held little promise of getting better as he sat at the ferry landing on the west bank of the Sabine.

After leaving the cow camp early that morning, Slater rode south along the Sabine, sticking as close to the Texas bank as he could. His eyes constantly searched the farmlands to his right and the river's edge to his left. More than half the day passed before he found Jess Tate's body tangled in a dead tree half-submerged in the river.

As soon as he ascertained that it was Tate's remains, Slater took a rope and carefully worked his way down the embankment, then out into the water along the tree trunk, using it to keep himself from being swept away in the surprisingly strong current. When he reached the body, he tied the rope around the torso, then returned to the bank, where he began pulling the body to dry ground. He struggled with it for the better part of an hour but finally succeeded.

Before dragging the corpse up the slope to the plain, Slater examined it, finding all four knife wounds easily and noticing the severe bruise on the neck. He correctly concluded how Tate had died, then swore he would avenge his friend's death.

Slater wrapped the body in his blanket, secured it with the rope, then draped it over the back of the horse that Dent had let him bring along for Tate to ride back to camp. Now it was carrying his corpse. The sadness of the moment caught up with Slater, and he wept.

Wiping away his tears and renewing his resolve to avenge Tate's murder, he mounted Nimbus and rode for the nearest town, Orange, where he found an undertaker and a sheriff. He sold the extra horse, then used the money to pay the undertaker to take care of Tate's body and to have it shipped back to Hallettsville for burial. Then he told the sheriff everything he knew about Tate's death. The sheriff didn't have a bit of trouble with Slater's story and let him go his way, which happened to be east, toward the ferry landing on the Sabine.

Now Slater sat on a bench, waiting for the ferry to return from the Louisiana side of the river. He looked up in time to see the flatboat land and disgorge its cargo, a wide assortment of freight wagons, carriages, buggies, horses, mules, and people. As soon as these were gone, the ferry took on a new load that consisted of one man and his horse.

During the crossing, Slater questioned the ferryman about Dent and the trail herd.

"We got them across by noon," said the ferryman. "Best day of ferrying that I've had in long time. You a friend of theirs?"

"My brother is bossing the outfit," said Slater.

"Sure has been a lot of you cattle drovers crossing the last couple of days," said the ferryman.

"Is that right?" asked Slater, his interest piqued a bit more. "You mean you hauled another herd across recently?"

"No cattle. Just horses and men. They looked like drovers though. They were all dressed in the same style as your bunch was today, and they had all the same trappings with them, including a wagon like yours, only it wasn't loaded the same as yours. I sneaked a little peek inside it. It had some provisions in it but not like your wagon had. Funny thing was, these men seemed more like they was going off to war instead of going to herd some cattle."

"Is that right?" queried Slater. "And how many men were in this outfit?"

"Twenty-five, if I recollect rightly. I hope they're not up to trouble with the Yankees. I'd hate to get myself in a bother with those Bluebellies."

"I know what you mean," said Slater. Then he became pensive as he thought over the information the ferryman had given him.

Twenty-five men who looked like drovers but didn't have any cattle and who seemed more like they were going off to war than to herd cattle. What did that mean? Were they heavily armed? Did they talk about fighting? Both?

"You didn't happen to talk to any of them, did you?" asked Slater suddenly.

"Talk to who?" queried the surprised ferryman.

"The men you took across a few days back who looked like drovers," said Slater. "Did you talk to any of them?"

The ferryman scratched his head and said, "I don't rightly recollect if I did or not. But I do recall hearing them talking about a meeting place over in Louisiana. 'Tain't far from here. It's a little place called Choupique. It's about halfway between here and Lake Charles."

"I know the place," said Slater. He recalled that he had spent a night there on his way home that spring. Choupique wasn't much more than an inn, a store, a few houses, and some barns and sheds. Again, he wondered about these so-called drovers who had crossed into Louisiana only a few days before. Why would they be having a meeting in a place like Choupique? "Did they say anything about why they were going to a meeting there?" asked Slater.

"Did I say meeting?"

"Yes, you did."

The ferryman laughed and said, "Well, that's one on me. I meant to say waiting. They said it was a waiting place. I just sort of figured they were planning on waiting there for a herd of cattle."

That's it! thought Slater. They aren't drovers! They're cowboys! Rustlers! And they went to Choupique to wait for a herd! My herd! They're planning on rustling my herd!

Slater had no time to lose. As soon as the flatboat tied up on the Louisiana side and the ferryman dropped its loading gate, he jumped into the saddle, put the spurs to Nimbus, and sped off at a full gallop. Following the herd's trail was no trouble for him, even in the twilight. He raced onward, knowing Dent and the boys couldn't have gotten more than eight or nine miles down the road. Eight or nine miles? Wasn't that just about how far it was to Choupique? No, it was farther. Choupique was a good fifteen to twenty miles away from the Sabine. Then he noticed how the trail began angling toward the northeast, toward—*toward where?* He saw a sign. Vinton. Where was that? How far was it? Were Dent and the boys going there instead of Choupique? Good for Dent, if they were!

The first mile seemed like an eternity to Slater, but in reality, Nimbus covered the distance in a little less than two minutes. The second mile was a bit longer, and the third longer yet. The Appaloosa tired in the fourth, but he showed his breeding in the fifth when he caught his second wind. Slater leaned forward like a jockey, talking into the stallion's ears, encouraging him, coaxing him to run with all his heart. The big stud responded to the sound of his master's voice and gave it his all until another sound, a familiar noise, came at them from the darkness ahead.

Gunfire! Lots of it! Dead ahead!

Slater realized that he was too late to warn Dent and the boys about the rustlers, but maybe he wasn't too late to join them in saving the herd. He reined up Nimbus to a slower gait, enough for him to reach into his saddle bags and take out the two Colt's .44s that he had bought at John Kelly's store. Disregarding the holsters, he stuck one inside his belt, then held the other at the ready as he charged ahead.

38

Because of Jess Tate's disappearance the evening before, Dent assigned the Detchens to be the outfit's cooks for the remainder of the drive. They complained about it openly, but their gripes gained them nothing except more disdain from the other men.

The Detchens and the camp wagon were the first to be ferried over to Louisiana. The twins departed immediately, ostensibly to find a place to set up the night camp that the rest of the outfit would be eager to see at the end of the day.

After spending the morning crossing the Sabine and the afternoon driving a petulant herd, Dent and the Double Star drovers bedded down the cattle for the night, then he and most of the crew began drifting toward the wagon that they thought was their camp. As they came closer to it, Flewellyn noticed that there was no campfire, no picket line set up for the horses, just a wagon that didn't appear to be all that familiar after a second look.

"Something don't look right here, Dent," said Flewellyn.

Dent squinted into the dusk and said, "Yeah, I see what you mean. Where are the Detchens? And why haven't they got supper cooking already?"

His answer came in the form of a gunshot zinging over his head. The first one was followed by a regular fusillade from the wagon. None of the drovers was sure about who was doing the shooting, but they weren't about to sit there like wooden targets until they found out. All but Dent sought cover behind the live oaks and hackberries on each side of the road. Dent failed to move because he had gone rigid with fear. Seeing Dent's condition, Flewellyn rode back, grabbed the reins out of Dent's hand, and led him to safety.

"We're being ambushed, Dent," said Flewellyn as soon as they were safe behind a giant live oak. He looked at Dent and saw how his eyes were glassy with fright. There was only one thing to do. Flewellyn spit a short stream of tobacco juice, then slapped Dent's face, not once but twice. Dent reacted by making fists and preparing to pummel Flewellyn for striking him, but Flewellyn grabbed him in a bear hug, saying, "Hold on, boy. You got no right to act that way. I've seen bigger and better men than you get scared worse than you just did the first time they was in a fight. Now you got to get hold of yourself and tell us what you want us to do. You're the boss here, Dent."

Boss? thought Dent. Me? Clete said—

"Dent," interjected Flewellyn, shaking the younger Slater, "what do you want us to do?"

Dent relaxed and said, "You're right, Jake. Let me go so I can think a bit."

Flewellyn released Dent, and both men hunkered down behind the tree.

Dent scanned the shadows for the rest of the Double Star men. Some of them were returning the gunfire with handguns, but most were doing the same as Dent and Flewellyn: keeping low.

Flewellyn peeked around the trunk to see if he could make out who was shooting at them. When he couldn't see any more than he could the evening Slater and some of the boys were ambushed by Jim Kindred and his posse, a notion suddenly struck him. "Dent, I think I know who that might be out there," he said excitedly. "It's Kindred and that bunch he had with him the night he tried bushwhacking Clete and Jess on the Petersburg road."

"What's that?" asked Dent, disbelieving him.

"I tell you it's them," said Flewellyn, "and I'll bet the Detchens have thrown in with them. They were with Kindred's posse back on that night. I'll bet Kindred's come to rustle the herd."

Dent stuck his head around the oak and said absently, "I'll be damned! I do believe you're right, Jake." At that very second, a bullet grazed the side of his neck. He screamed with pain, grabbed at the wound, and fell back behind the tree. Blood oozed between his fingers, and he was more frightened than ever because he was certain he was dying.

Flewellyn pulled Dent's hand away to look at the injury. "It ain't much," he said. "I've seen a lot worse." He took off his bandanna, folded it quickly, then applied it to the bloody spot. "Hold that there until I can get yours tied around it." And just as fast, he loosened Dent's neckerchief and retied it around his neck but only tight enough to slow the bleeding. "Now hold that down real good and you'll be all right, Dent. I guarantee it."

With Dent taken care of for the moment, Flewellyn turned his attention to the fight. He looked around and saw that more of the drovers were returning fire on the wagon. This was good. He wondered what Slater would do if he were there, then he recalled the fight on the Petersburg road.

"Spread out!" he yelled to the other men. "Some of you try to get around behind them! Stay low and keep shooting! It looks like the Detchens have thrown in with them!"

That was about all the incentive any of them needed to open up with everything they had, but before they could, they found themselves outflanked. Kindred and his gang had learned from their first experience with the Double Star outfit. Besides the men in the wagon, two more groups—one to each side of the road—formed a semicircle in front of the Double Star crew.

Seeing that they were outmaneuvered for the moment, Flewellyn called for the drovers to fall back toward the herd. He helped Dent to his feet and led him and their horses deeper into the woods. They took up a new position behind a fallen log, and Flewellyn began firing at the powder flashes that were coming closer with every passing second.

"You've got to save the herd," said Dent. "Don't let them take the herd."

"Don't worry none about that right now, Dent," said Flewellyn. "We got to save ourselves before we can start thinking about the cattle."

Pick Arnold's crew had been left with the herd to stand the first watch of the night. When they heard the first shots being fired, Arnold wasn't certain what they should do, whether to leave the herd and see who was shooting at who and why, or simply hunker down and wait. He chose to wait but told his men to take cover and to get their weapons ready just in case.

As soon as he spoke those orders, Clark Reeves noticed a lone rider coming toward them on the road from the Sabine. "It looks like Clete," said Reeves.

"It sure does," said his brother.

Arnold was grateful that he would soon be relieved of command. "Boy, am I glad to see you," he said when Slater reined in Nimbus.

"Anyone shooting at you boys?" asked Slater.

"No, not yet," said Arnold.

"Good! Take cover and get ready for action. There's a gang of cowboys up there planning to rustle the herd. Where's camp?"

"Right down that road through those woods," said Arnold.

"Clark, come with me just in case one of our boys forgot what I look like," said Slater. "Don't let them take the herd, Pick. The folks back home are depending on it."

"Give them hell, Clete!" said Arnold as Slater and Reeves rode away.

A minute later the two reinforcements rode up behind the rest of the Double Star men. They dismounted and took cover. While Slater surveyed the scene and summed up the situation, Reeves let it be known that the older Slater was back. Once the word was spread Slater ordered them to fall back to the herd as fast as they could. Everyone mounted up, including Dent and Flewellyn, and rode back through the woods to where Arnold had set up a defense line.

"Everyone gather around!" shouted Slater.

"Clete!" said Dent hoarsely. "Am I glad to see you!"

Slater saw the bandage on his brother's neck and asked anxiously, "Are you hit bad?"

"Just a little nick on the side of the neck," said Flewellyn. "He'll be all right."

"Good, good. Just stay here, Dent, with Pick and his crew. The rest of you reload as fast as you can." He scanned the faces around him and noticed that not everyone was there. "Where are the Detchens?"

"With Kindred and his bunch of rustlers," said Flewellyn.

"Kindred? Is that who's out there?" asked Slater.

"Has to be," said Flewellyn. "Who else would be such a damn fool to try and take our herd?"

"It only figures," said Slater. "The Detchens and Kindred. That fits. All right, so be it." He mulled over the situation for a moment. Kindred and the Detchens! Cowards! Bullies who run at the first sign of a real fight! Bushwhackers without the sand to stand up and go toe to toe. Sons of bitches who will run when their bluff is called. "All right, if that's who it is, then they're nothing but a bunch of yellowbellies who'll run if we charge them."

"Charge them?" queried Flewellyn with a flash of excitement.

"That's right," said Slater. "This is war, boys, and there lies the enemy. What say we give 'em hell?"

"Let's do it!" shouted Flewellyn, and a chorus of similar approvals followed his.

"All right, we'll come at them from three sides," said Slater. "Jake, you take your crew and come at them from the right. Pick, you take the left. Stay spread out and charge on my command." He looked at his brother and realized that Dent had never been in a fight before. "Dent, since you're wounded already, I think you'd better sit this one out. Stay here and guard the herd in case any of them get through us."

Dent appeared to be relieved by his brother's command. "Sure, Clete," he said. "I'll guard the herd with my life."

"Let's hope it doesn't come down to that," said Slater. "Just keep an eye out, all right?"

"Sure, Clete."

Slater turned to see if everyone was in position yet. They were. "All right, boys," he shouted. "Let's give 'em hell!" He pointed his Colt's forward and yelled, "*Charge!*"

With rifles and pistols in hand, the Double Star drovers kicked their mounts in the ribs and raced off at a gallop through the woods, every man screaming his best Rebel yell. In a few seconds, they burst into the clearing in front of Kindred's gang, who had come out of their hiding places to pursue Slater's men.

The outlaws couldn't believe the ferocity of the drovers. Their first reaction was to run, but not all of them got the chance as the former Confederate cavalrymen shot down a quarter of their number with the first volley. Those that could run ran for their lives.

The air was filled with gun smoke and the sounds of gunfire, men shouting, men dying, and the pounding of horses' hooves. It was a rout as the rustlers soon gave up the fight.

"Don't let any of them get away!" yelled Slater. "Take as many of them alive as possible so we can turn them over to the law!"

"Hell, let's just shoot the bastards and be done with them!" shouted Flewellyn.

"Take prisoners!" shouted Slater angrily.

More men heeded Flewellyn than Slater, but there was no slaughter because most of Kindred's men, including Kindred, vanished into the woods. Those who couldn't run now were dead.

The fight was over as fast as it had begun.

39

Slater's first concern after the fight was the well-being of his brother and his men—in that order. He told Flewellyn to make a casualty count and find out where their camp wagon was, then he rode back to the herd to see Dent.

Dent was sitting down, his back against a tree, when Slater returned. He didn't look good; his color was bad, pale.

"How are you feeling, Dent?" asked Slater.

"I've felt better, Clete. Right now, I'm feeling a little puny. You know, like a sick puppy."

Slater knelt down beside his brother and said, "I'd better take a look at that wound." He loosened the neckerchief wrapped around Dent's neck, then peeled back the makeshift bandage. Both cloths were heavy with blood. The wound was still bleeding, but that wasn't the worst of it. Slater wiped away as much blood as he could in order to determine the extent of the injury, and that was when he saw that Dent's carotid artery had been nicked badly and that it was bleeding in spurts. Oh, God, no! he thought. Then he hoped that his fear hadn't shown on his face. "We'd better get you to a doctor," he said as calmly as he could.

Dent saw the look in his brother's eyes, and it scared him. He lurched forward, clutched Slater's arm, and said anxiously, "Is it that bad, Clete? Tell me true. Is it that bad?" His voice was filled with the same fright with which he would often awaken when he'd had a childhood nightmare.

And like those times when they were youngsters sharing the same bed, Slater soothed his brother's fears. He patted Dent's hand and said, "No, it's not bad. It's just a nick. It's just that it's best that a doctor look at it as soon as possible. That's all. You'll be fine."

Slater was lying. He'd seen men bleed to death before. It didn't take long. A few minutes sometimes. An hour or two at others. He could only guess at how long Dent had to live.

Dent relaxed and leaned back against the tree again.

"Now you just sit there and take it easy," said Slater, "while I put a clean bandage on you." He removed his own bandanna, folded it, and applied it to the wound. "Hold that in place, Little Breeches, while I tie it up again."

"Little Breeches?" queried Dent. "No one's called me that for years." He thought about it for a second, then added, "Well, at least not since Grandpa Hawk went away. God, I miss him, Clete."

"Me, too," said Slater.

"Did you get all the rustlers?" asked Dent.

"We got most of them," said Slater as he finished tying up Flewellyn's neckerchief around Dent's neck. "Jake is making a count right now."

Some of the men gathered around the two brothers, but none of them spoke. Being war veterans, they knew when a man was dying, and they knew how to show him the proper respect. This was a different case, however. To them, Dent Slater wasn't much more than a boy, and he was their good friend's brother. They were hardened to death on the battlefield; it was a part of war. But this? They weren't sure how to take it.

"Did you find Jess?" asked Dent.

"Yes, I did," said Slater evenly.

Dent swallowed hard and said, "Is he all right?"

Slater started to answer truthfully, but he couldn't. Not now, he couldn't. "Yes, he's fine. He got lost in the dark and wandered around most of the time until I found him this morning. I took him into Orange for a hot meal. I left him there. I told him to catch up to us tomorrow. I came on because the ferryman told me about a bunch of Texas cowboys coming this way a few days back. That's how I figured you boys were in trouble."

"We sure were," said Dent. "I'm glad you're back, Clete. Did you find the Detchens?"

"Not yet. Like I said, Jake is making a head count now." Slater looked up at Pick Arnold. "Go see what's keeping Jake, will you, Pick?"

"Sure thing, Clete," said Arnold, glad to be excused.

"Clete, I'm feeling mighty weak," said Dent. "Are you sure I'm going to be all right?"

"I'm as sure as the sun's going to come up in the east tomorrow morning," lied Slater.

Dent didn't believe him, but he stubbornly refused to let on that he knew his brother was lying to him, saying, "Clete, I didn't want Glengarry. Not without you."

"I know," said Slater. Suddenly, he realized that Dent knew he was dying, and he felt an indescribable pain in his chest as his heart was rended desolate with grief. He strained mentally to hold back the tears welling up in his eyes but failed.

A faraway gaze came over Dent's eyes as he looked past Slater to a place the living can't see until their time to go there has come. He said, "Clete, I'm starting to feel a little light between the ears. Is that how it's supposed to be?"

"It's all right, Little Breeches," said Slater.

"I'm so tired, Clete, but I want you to know that I didn't want Glengarry without you. I didn't."

All Slater could say was, "I know."

Dent smiled wanly at Slater but only for a second before he said, "Tell Hannah I'll be waiting for her up yonder. Tell her for me, Clete. She's got to know. I love her, Clete. Hannah's my—" Before he could finish, his eyes rolled up, then became glazed. His eyelids fell into a half-closed position, and his lungs wheezed a death sigh.

Oh, God, no! No! Please, God, no!

Slater felt no shame or embarrassment as he took Dent in his arms and wept uncontrollably.

●　　　●　　　●

Flewellyn's casualty count had eleven rustlers dead, one wounded and caught, and one unhurt and caught. Among the Double Star drovers, four had minor wounds and two were dead, including Dent.

Slater told Simons to take some men and bury all the dead outlaws after the two captives identified each corpse. Dent and Stan Grey, the Double Star hand who was killed, were to be taken back to the undertaker in Orange and shipped home for burial. As soon as those orders were finished, Slater had Flewellyn bring the prisoners to him for questioning. The outlaws had their hands tied behind them and were bareheaded.

"Who led you?" Slater asked the first cowboy, who was wounded in his left thigh. When the culprit didn't answer right off, Slater said, "Hang him." He turned to the second man and repeated the question. "Who led you?"

"Jim Kindred," said the first outlaw as soon as two drovers grabbed him by the arms and started to lead him away.

"That's right," said the second anxiously. "It was Kindred, Mr. Slater. Jim Kindred."

"All right, hold up, boys," said Slater to his men. Then to the prisoners, he said, "Now tell me about Harlan and Farley Detchen. Were they in on it, too?"

"They sure were, Mr. Slater," said the first man nervously.

"That's right," said the second. "Kindred led us to this place, and we met the Detchens here and set up the ambush."

"You going to let us go since we talked, Mr. Slater?" asked the first rustler. He smiled, hoping that it would help get a positive answer.

"What are your names?" asked Slater. His face showed as much emotion as the black mask of a headsman.

"What do you want to know that for?" asked the same man.

"I need them for the sign," said Slater.

"What sign?"

"The sign I'm going to put on you after I hang you," said Slater evenly.

"But we talked, Mr. Slater," cried the second rustler. "We talked. We told you what you wanted to know."

"That's right, we did," said the first.

Slater smiled and said, "That's right. You did talk, but you see, boys, that makes no difference to my brother over there. He's dead, and all the talking you sonsabitches do won't make him breathe again. He'll still be dead, boys. He'll still be dead." He turned to Flewellyn and said, "Hang them, Jake."

Both rustlers fell on their knees and began pleading for their lives to be spared.

"It ain't right to hang us after we talked," said the first, crying. "It ain't right!"

"I didn't shoot anyone," whined the second. "I don't deserve to die. Please don't hang me, Mr. Slater. Please don't hang me!"

"Hang them, Jake!" shouted Slater as all the anger in him exploded. He pointed and yelled again, "Hang them from that big oak over there next to the road so every man coming into Texas can see what we do with rustlers! Hang them slow! Don't put them on horses and let them drop! Pull them up slow . . . an inch at a time! You hear me, Jake! Hang them . . . now!" Then he turned away.

"Don't hang me!"

"Shut up, you yellow-bellied bastards!" said Arnold as he dropped a loop around the first man's neck.

Flewellyn did the same to the second cowboy.

With a little help from the other drovers, Flewellyn and Arnold dragged the rustlers kicking and gagging to the oak tree that Slater had indicated, threw their ropes over the strongest limb, and pulled them up—an inch at a time—until their feet were off the ground; then they tied the ropes to the tree trunk and walked away, leaving the outlaws jerking violently in midair as they slowly strangled to death.

40

Slater gave four letters to Mr. Hatton, the undertaker in Orange, to deliver for him in Hallettsville. "This one is to my sister, Miss Malinda Slater," he said. "This one is to Colonel Lucas Markham, the military commander for Lavaca County. Please deliver the one to Colonel Markham first. I'd prefer that you give the letter to my sister personally, but Markham might insist that he do it. If he does, then let him have it. But these two letters . . . these two you must deliver personally to Mrs. Margaret Hallet. One is for her, and the other is for her granddaughter, Miss Texada Ballard. I don't want anybody else to see these two letters, Mr. Hatton. I don't even want Texada to see the letter to Mrs. Hallet. Understand?" When Hatton indicated that he did, Slater continued, saying, "And don't tell anybody about what happened over in Louisiana. The men who are responsible for my brother's death might be back in Lavaca County when you get there. I don't want them to know that we know who they are. At least not until I can get back to Lavaca County and do something about them myself."

Hatton understood completely and agreed to follow Slater's instructions. He embalmed the bodies of Denton Slater, Jess Tate, and Stan Grey that very morning, placed them in coffins, loaded them into his hearse, and started the long trip to Hallettsville that afternoon. Five days later he drove his funeral wagon into the town square and was soon surrounded by several dozen curious people, in whose number were Sergeant Wickersham, Isaac Samusch, John Kelly, Fritz Lindenberg, young Coll Ballard, and Texada, all of whom were talking about the hearse.

Hatton was a tall, thin man with a pallor that gave him a complexion not unlike his stock in trade. He was appropriately attired in black, including a stovepipe hat. "Sergeant," he said, his deep, rich voice flowing down from the seat of his funeral wagon like that of a good gospel preacher coaxing a sinner to the front of the

216

congregation to bare his soul to their delight. "I have a letter for a Colonel Lucas Markham. Could you direct me to him, please?"

"Colonel Markham?" queried Wickersham.

"Yes, Sergeant," said Hatton with a benevolent smile.

"Certainly, sir," said Wickersham. "Just a minute. I'll send a man for him." He turned and saw Private Tinsley standing nearby. "Tinsley, go fetch the colonel down here right now. Tell him this man has a letter for him."

"Sure, Sarge," said Tinsley. He ran off for the courthouse to inform Markham.

"I see that you have three coffins in your hearse, sir," said Wickersham as more people crowded around them. "That's a bit unusual, isn't it?"

"Yes, it is, Sergeant," said Hatton, showing patience with the soldier.

When the undertaker didn't offer any more information, Wickersham pried a little harder. "Are they to be buried near here?" he asked.

"I don't know for sure," said Hatton. "I'm just delivering them here to Hallettsville to your colonel."

"To Colonel Markham?" asked Wickersham, quite surprised by Hatton's statement. "Have you got dead soldiers in those coffins, sir?"

"No," said Hatton.

Frustrated, Wickersham came to the point. "Then who have you got in there?" he demanded.

Hatton glared at the sergeant and said, "Three young men of this county, sir, and that is all you need know until I speak with your colonel."

At Hatton's pronouncement that the deceased were from Lavaca County, a buzz of excitement raced through the crowd that was growing bigger by the minute. Speculation as to the identities of the dead men was on everyone's lips until Markham made an appearance on the courthouse steps.

Surveying the throng in the square, Markham placed his hands on his hips and demanded, "What's going on here, Sergeant?"

"Sir, this man says he has a letter for you," said Wickersham.

Hatton climbed down from the hearse and made his way through the onlookers to the bottom of the steps. "Are you Colonel Lucas Markham, sir?" he asked.

"Who are you?" asked Markham.

"I am Mr. John Hatton, sir, of Orange County. I am an undertaker, and I have a letter for Colonel Lucas Markham. Are you he, sir?"

"Yes, I am," said Markham. "Where's the letter?"

Hatton reached inside his coat and pulled out two envelopes. He read the names on them, then replaced one in his coat pocket. "This one is yours," he said, handing it up to Markham.

"Who's the other letter for?" asked Markham as he accepted his missive.

"A lady, sir," said Hatton, implying that it was none of Markham's business who the lady was.

"Hm-m." Markham was unsure of what to think of Hatton's reply, so he held off pursuing that line of thought until he had read the letter in his hand. "Who's it from?" he asked as he opened the envelope.

Hatton didn't bother to answer Markham as the colonel read:

Dear Colonel,

We were ambushed by rustlers in Louisiana. We don't know who they were, but they killed my brother Dent and Stan Grey, another one of our men. Although we have not found their bodies yet, the Detchens may have been killed by the outlaws as well. Also, Jess Tate was murdered near the Sabine River the night before the ambush, but we don't know who killed him.

I have sent a letter to Malinda by the bearer of this letter to you. I ask that you tell my sister the sad news of our brother's death before she reads that letter.

I do not expect to be back in Hallettsville for some weeks yet, so I can't be there to bury Dent, Jess, and Stan. Would you please take care of this sad business for me? I will stand good for any expense that you may incur.

We are continuing on to New Orleans with the herd.

With kind regards,
Clete Slater

The color drained slowly from Markham's face as he read Slater's letter. Not satisfied that the words were real, he read the message a second time before crumpling it in his hand. He stumbled down the steps and staggered over to the hearse. He peered through the glass at the three coffins within. "Dent?" he whispered.

Hatton followed Markham to the funeral wagon. He patted the

colonel on the shoulder, trying to comfort him, and said, "My sincerest condolences, sir. I understand that the one young man was the brother of your betrothed."

"Denton Slater?" gasped Samusch, who was standing near and overheard Hatton's statement.

"Slater?" repeated Kelly. "Clete Slater?"

"It's Clete Slater in there?" asked Lindenberg. Then turning to those behind him, he said, "It's Clete Slater!"

The surname was soon on everyone's lips, including Texada's, who shrieked, "Not Clete! Oh, God, not Clete!" She broke through the crowd to confront Hatton, grabbing his coat and screaming in his face, "Not Clete! You didn't bring Clete home in one of those boxes! You bastard! Not Clete!" She began beating on him.

Wickersham restrained Texada, taking her arms in his massive hands. "No, Miss Ballard," he said, "it's not him. It's his brother, Denton." He shook her a little. "It's Denton Slater, Miss Ballard. Not Clete."

Texada wasn't sure she heard him right. "What?" she asked with tears streaming down her cheeks. "Denton? Dent? It's not Clete?"

"No, Miss," said Hatton, straightening his coat. "The deceased are Mr. Denton Slater, Mr. Jesse Tate, and Mr. Stanley Grey." He said the names loud enough for most people around them to hear him clearly.

A new flood of tears spewed from Texada's eyes as she looked at Wickersham, her face a mixture of joy and sorrow. On the one hand, she was relieved that Clete wasn't in one of the coffins, while on the other, she was sad that Dent and Jess Tate were in two of them. She began to cry and leaned on Wickersham for support and comfort, which the sergeant supplied as best as he could, considering he was quite conscious of the people around them.

"Thank you, Mr. Hatton," said Markham, regaining control of his emotions. "I believe you have a letter for Miss Malinda Slater in your possession. Miss Slater and I are to be married, sir. I will deliver that letter for you."

"If you insist, Colonel," said Hatton. He handed over the letter to Markham. "Where would you like me to take the bodies for burial, sir?"

"This is rather sudden, Mr. Hatton," said Markham. He turned to Wickersham, who was still comforting Texada. "Sergeant, would you attend to this business for now? I mean, see that Mr. Hatton is . . .'' He wasn't sure what he meant.

Seeing his colonel's predicament, Wickersham said, ''By your leave, sir, I'll take care of Mr. Hatton for now and see that Mr. Slater's coffin is handled properly. And the others, too, sir.''

''Thank you, Sergeant,'' said Markham. ''Would you get my horse, please? I'll be riding out to Glengarry to break this news to Miss Slater personally.'' He returned to the courthouse to be alone with his grief for the moment.

''Yes, sir.''

Texada had her feelings under control again. Sniffling and wiping her eyes with the back of her hand, she backed away from Wickersham and said, ''Thank you, Sergeant.''

''Yes, ma'am,'' said Wickersham. He tipped his hat to her, then turned to Hatton. ''I think we'd best take your hearse to the livery for now, sir. Come along and I'll show you the way.''

Hatton returned to the seat of the funeral wagon, and Wickersham climbed up beside him. ''Go around the corner, Mr. Hatton,'' said the sergeant. ''Then down the block to Dibrell's Livery and Stables on Fourth Street.'' Hatton snapped the reins, and they were gone before anyone in the crowd realized that no one had explained how Denton Slater, Jess Tate, and Stan Grey came to be dead.

''What happened to those boys?'' asked Samusch, always the curious one. ''How did they die?''

These questions were suddenly being uttered by several people at once, but only Texada did anything about finding any answers. She ran into the courthouse and up to Markham's office. She burst inside to find him sitting at his desk with his face buried in his hands.

Markham looked up at her and said, ''What are you doing in here, Miss Ballard?''

''Colonel, what was in that letter?'' she demanded to know.

All the belligerence went out of him as he realized that she had been just as upset as he was, although for the wrong reason. Even so, he figured that she had a right to know. ''Here,'' he said, sliding the crumpled letter across the desk to her. ''Read it for yourself.''

Texada picked up the letter and read it. She was greatly relieved to learn that Clete was all right or at least he was when he wrote the letter. Then she remembered all the people in the square.

"Colonel, folks want to know what happened to those men," she said. "Is it all right for me to read them this letter from Clete?"

"Yes, go ahead, Miss Ballard," said Markham. He stood up, walked over to the hat tree, took down his hat, and put it on. "If you'll excuse me, I have to leave now. I have to tell Malinda the sad news."

Texada didn't envy him that chore. She followed him outside, where several people demanded to know what had happened to the three dead men. Seeing how the crowd beleaguered Markham, she came to his rescue, waving the letter over her head and yelling, "I've got the letter here, everybody!" That drew their attention away from Markham immediately.

While Texada was reading the letter aloud, Markham slipped away, got to his horse, and rode off for Glengarry.

41

Markham barely noticed the landscape as he rode along the Columbus-Hallettsville road toward Glengarry. Grief numbed his senses and clouded his thinking. He was truly fond of Dent, having much the same feeling as a tutor would have for a prize pupil. No. Greater than that. His emotional level stretched beyond friendship to border on the love that brothers would share. In fact, he felt so deeply for Dent that he was actually jealous of Clete for being Dent's natural brother. He hadn't realized this before now, and now it was too late. Dent was dead, and Markham felt that he had been robbed, that he'd been cheated by Clete Slater, who had taken Dent away to be killed. Damn you, Slater! he thought.

Before Markham's anger could mutate into hate, his mind was forced to focus on the road. Coming toward him was Sophia Campbell in her buggy. He edged his horse to the side of the road to allow her room to pass, but she didn't drive by him. Instead, she stopped and called out his name, and he reined in his horse, halting beside the carriage.

"Something ailing you, Colonel?" asked Sophia, peering at

him with a most quizzical expression.

For the first time since reading Slater's letter, Markham became cognizant of the part concerning the Detchen brothers. He had been so disturbed by the loss of Dent that he hadn't given them a second thought. Now he had to think about them. "Mrs. Campbell," he said slowly, "I'm afraid that I have some bad news . . . for you."

"Bad news for me?" asked Sophia cautiously. She cocked her head and squinted at him. "What are you talking about, Colonel?"

"I received a letter today from Clete Slater," he said. "There was an ambush in Louisiana." He choked on the thoughts racing through his brain.

Sophia studied Markham carefully, unsure of what he wanted to say next. "An ambush in Louisiana?" she prompted.

"That's right, Mrs. Campbell," said Markham. "Dent Slater and two other men on the cattle drive were killed, and your sons, Harlan and Farley . . ." He paused, uncertain of how he should tell her.

"Yes, go on," said Sophia slowly, treading lightly here. "What about Harlan and Farley?"

"I'm afraid that they're missing, Mrs. Campbell."

Sophia tilted her head even more to the side and asked, "Missing? What do you mean, 'missing'?"

"That's all I know, Mrs. Campbell. Slater wrote that there was an ambush in Louisiana, and Dent and the other two men were killed and your sons were missing. He suspected that they might have been killed by the bushwhackers."

"Clete Slater wrote that?" she asked quickly.

"Yes, ma'am," said Markham. "I'm terribly sorry to be the bearer of such bad news, Mrs. Campbell."

"It's all right, Colonel," she said slowly. Then as if she'd just remembered something important, she said, "Thank you, Colonel. I'll be running along now. I know you . . . well, you're going out to Glengarry to tell Malinda about it now, ain't you?"

"Yes, I am," said Markham.

"Give her my condolences, Colonel. Thank you again for telling me about Harlan and Farley. I've got to get home now and tell the rest of my family about this. Good-bye, Colonel." She snapped the whip over the mule's ears, turned the buggy around, and drove away for home at a rapid clip.

Markham followed Sophia down the road but continued on past the entrance to her plantation to the lane that led up to Glengarry mansion. He halted his horse at the gateway and took a long look at the house in the early evening light. This was such a happy home just a short time ago, he thought. Now that door will be draped in black. Poor Malinda!

He rode up the driveway, dismounted, tied his horse to the hitching post, then trudged up the veranda steps. Hannah met him at the door. She let him in, took his hat, then watched him as he went into the parlor. He didn't say anything to her; no "Hello, Hannah," no "How are you, Hannah?" Markham was earlier than usual, too. Better get Miss Malinda right now, she thought, sensing something was wrong. She hung Markham's hat on the rack in the foyer, then hurried off to inform Malinda that Markham had arrived already.

Malinda was in the library, reading *David Copperfield*. When Hannah entered, she closed the book over one hand and asked, "What is it, Hannah?"

"Colonel Markham is here already, Miss Malinda," said Hannah, "and he don't look none too happy about something. I think you better come see him right now, Miss Malinda."

Malinda placed a bookmark on the page she had been reading, set the book on the coffee table, then rose gracefully. "Where is he, Hannah?" she asked.

"He went into the parlor."

Malinda swept down the hall to the parlor unaware that Hannah was following her at a distance. She went into the sitting room and closed the doors behind her. This didn't stop Hannah from listening through them.

"Good afternoon, Lucas," said Malinda rather perfunctorily.

Markham was standing at the window that looked out at the front yard. He turned at the sound of Malinda's voice and hurried across the room to meet her, holding his hands out to her, his face twisted in pain, his eyes red and puffy.

The first thought to enter Malinda's mind was that he was either drunk or hungover. Neither one was acceptable, but she said nothing to him about it. Not yet, anyway, not until she was sure of which it was. She took his hands and discreetly tried to smell his breath when he leaned forward to kiss her cheek. Hm-m, no whiskey odor, she thought as he leaned away again.

"My darling," he said, "I have tragic news. Come, sit down with me." He practically pulled her toward the sofa with him, where she sat down and he knelt at her knees. "Malinda dearest, I received a letter today," he said slowly. "From your brother."

"From Clete?" she queried, wondering what bad news he could impart to Markham.

"Yes," said Markham, surprised that she had said Clete's name and not Dent's.

"Has something happened to the herd?" she asked.

"Worse," he said softly, swallowing hard. "Malinda dearest, it's Dent. He's been . . . killed . . . by bushwhackers."

Malinda was disbelieving at first, then when she was certain that Markham had said that Dent was dead, had been killed by outlaws, she rose and asked for confirmation. "Dent is dead?"

Hannah hadn't heard what Markham had said just prior to this, but Malinda's question was loud enough for her. "Dent? Dead?" she whispered into her hand. Oh, Lordy, no! she prayed silently. She pressed her ear to the door again hoping that she had heard wrong.

Markham stood up and took Malinda into his arms, wishing to comfort her. "Yes, dearest," he said softly, hoping to make the news less painful for her.

"How did it happen?" asked Malinda simply, matter-of-factly, as if she were inquiring about a broken vase or the like.

The apparent apathy in Malinda's tone caught Markham off guard, and it disappointed him greatly. Am I more distressed by this than she? he asked himself. "The letter gave no details," he said cautiously. "It just stated that they had been attacked by bushwhackers and that Dent and two other men had been killed."

Hannah heard him perfectly this time. She screamed in agony and fell on her knees weeping violently.

"Good Lord! What was that?" exclaimed Markham, looking toward the closed parlor doors.

"Hannah," said Malinda, breaking away from Markham and rushing to the doorway. She threw open the doors to find Hannah face down on the floor, pounding the surface with her fists and wailing in torment. Malinda bent down to the servant girl. "What is it, Hannah?" she asked, puzzled by this outburst.

Hannah lifted her head up at Malinda, her eyes wet and pleading. "It ain't true, Miss Malinda," she cried. "Tell me it ain't true. Tell me he ain't dead. Tell me, Miss Malinda. Tell me my Dent ain't dead."

It had never occurred to Malinda that Hannah had real feelings of affection for her brother. To her, Hannah was only a house servant and her brother's colored whore. Nothing more, nothing less. To think of Hannah as a person with emotions? Not before now.

And now Malinda felt shame for herself because she was feeling nothing for Dent, while Hannah loved Dent so much that she couldn't hold back her tears over losing him. Of course, she suppressed the guilt by displacing it, turning it to anger and hate that was aimed at Hannah for making her feel the shame in the first place. "Your Dent?" she screamed, grabbing Hannah's arms and jerking her into a sitting position. "How dare you!" She slapped Hannah and continued screaming, "Your Dent? How dare you think of him that way!" She drew back her hand again, but Markham caught it, stopping her from striking Hannah a second time.

"Malinda!" he snapped. "What's gotten into you?"

That thought entered Malinda's mind, too. What had gotten into her? She glared up at Markham and saw the disbelief, confusion, and pain in his eyes. A questioning dart pierced her soul. Why am I behaving like this? she asked herself. She looked down at Hannah, cowering on the floor. Oh, God! What have I done? "Oh, Hannah," she said. "I'm so sorry. I'm so sorry." She reached out to the younger woman, but Hannah shrank away from her. "Oh, Hannah, I'm so sorry. Please forgive me. I didn't know. I didn't know that you loved him so much."

Hannah allowed Malinda to pick her up and embrace her, to offer her comfort. She wept copiously on Malinda's shoulder.

As he watched the two women interact, a host of new thoughts about them deluged Markham's brain. No longer would he consider Hannah to be a mudsill, as most whites considered coloreds to be. He would see through the pigment of her skin and beyond her ancestry and think of her as the complete, caring, feeling person that she was. As for Malinda, he now saw her as a woman instead of the mere girl that he had thought her to be. Yes, a woman with a will, with an iron nerve, a woman in control of herself, a woman that he now respected as an equal, maybe even as a superior. Whichever, he felt a greater devotion to her than ever before. No more would he not take her seriously.

42

For the first time in two days, Sophia Campbell had something to be happy about. She whipped her mule all the way from the road as she rushed home to share her joy with her family and guests.

Stewart was the first Campbell offspring to hear the buggy rattling up the drive. He looked up in time to see his mother pass between the two oaks on either side of the lane. "Mama's coming," he announced to his brothers and sisters who were sitting on the front porch with him.

"And she's sure in a hell of a hurry, too," said Tucker.

"Come on, Tucker," said Stewart, coming to his feet and stretching. "We'd better go meet her or she'll be madder than a nest of hornets rolling down a hill."

The two boys met their mother at the hitching post, where Tucker tied up the mule and Stewart helped Sophia from the buggy.

"Go fetch Farley and Harlan, Tucker," said Sophia. "And tell that damn deputy to get his ass up to the house as well. I got news for them."

"Yes'm," said Tucker, and he ran off to the row of little shacks behind the main house.

"Good news, Mama?" queried Stewart as he followed Sophia to the porch.

"Too early to say," said Sophia, "but it's better than no news at all."

In a few minutes, Tucker returned with Farley and Harlan and Jim Kindred following close behind him.

Sophia sat in her rocker on the front porch like a queen on her throne. As soon as her foster sons and Kindred came before her, she came straight to the point. "You boys really did it now," she said. "You got any idea what you did over there in Louisiana, Mr. Kindred? Besides botch the job you were sent to do, I mean. Do you know what you did?"

A quizzical look came over Kindred's face as he said, "I ain't sure I follow you, Miz Campbell.''

"You don't follow me, you say," said Sophia. "How about you two? Do you follow me, Farley? How about you, Harlan? Do you understand any of this?"

Both Detchens were out of Sophia's reach, but even so, they leaned away as they shook their heads.

"I didn't think so," said Sophia. She stood up and moved closer to the three men. "Well, let me tell you what you did. I just came from seeing that Yankee colonel out on the road. He told me what you boys did. You killed Dent Slater. That's what you did."

Harlan and Farley looked at each other. Both of them were filled with surprise and delight. They turned back to Sophia, moving closer to her, and Farley said, "We did?"

Sophia lost her temper and slapped Harlan up side the head. "Yes, you did, you damn fools!" she snapped. Then she slapped Farley for good measure. "You couldn't just kill Jess Tate. You had to go and kill a Slater. The wrong Slater! If you'd killed Clete, we wouldn't have a damn thing to worry about. But no! You stupid asses kill Dent! Now Clete won't rest until he finds out who killed his brother. Fortunately for you, he doesn't know you did it."

"He don't?" queried Kindred.

"Don't tell me how you got so lucky," said Sophia, "but that Colonel Markham said he got a letter from Clete saying that they were bushwhacked over in Louisiana, but he didn't know who'd done it." She pointed at the twins. "Hell, he even thinks you two are dead. He thinks you were killed by the bushwhackers. Now ain't that something?"

Kindred stared in disbelief at Harlan and Farley. The old bitch is right, he thought. They are two of the luckiest bastards in the world. Then it struck him. Hell, so am I.

"I swear," said Sophia, "the two of you would fall into a bucket of horseshit and come out smelling like bluebonnets."

Farley got up the courage to speak first. "You mean to tell us that Slater don't know we were in on the ambush? Is that it, Ma?"

"Damn, you're quick," said Sophia. "That's exactly what I'm telling you. Slater thinks the bushwhackers killed you and Harlan, and he don't even know that Kindred here was there."

Farley turned to his brother and said, "Do you hear that, Harlan? We don't have to hide no more."

Before either brother could celebrate, Sophia slapped Farley up side the head and said, "That ain't what it means at all, you stupid

ass. Clete Slater is smarter than that. If he comes home and finds
out you two have been here all the time, he'll put two and two
together and figure out you're the ones who killed Jess Tate and
that you might have had something to do with that botched rustling
job. You two are staying right here until I say you can leave this
place. You're going to keep low, just like you been doing, until
I say it's okay for you to show yourselves again. You hear me?''
She slapped Harlan for emphasis.

"Yes, ma'am," said Farley for the both of them.

"As for you, Mr. Kindred," said Sophia, "I suggest that you
get yourself back into Hallettsville as soon as possible and play
dumb. Damn dumb. Act like you don't know that anything has
happened to the Slaters and their drive. And the same goes for
everybody who was with you. I'll tell our hands how to act, but
you tell those others that were with you to keep their mouths shut
about all this. Tell them that they don't know nothing about nothing
when it comes to this business. You hear me, Mr. Kindred?''

He heard her all right, but she wasn't making that much good
sense to him. "Miz Campbell, aren't you forgetting something
here?" he asked.

"Such as?" queried Sophia.

"Such as the fact that we left more than a few dead men behind
us in Louisiana," said Kindred.

"That's right, Ma," said Farley.

Sophia gave him the back of her hand for his insolence, then
said, "And you think that Clete might have figured out that some
of those boys had been working here before the drive was started,
is that it, Mr. Kindred?"

"Something like that, ma'am," said Kindred. "I'm thinking
he might figure out who the rest of us were and come gunning
for us when he gets back here."

"He's got to get back here first, Mr. Kindred," said Sophia.
"So until he does, I wouldn't worry too much about him. I'd be
worried about the folks in town and that Yankee colonel, if I was
you. There's already talk that you might have had something to
do with the raid on Teddy Johnson's wagons. How long have you
been gone now? Two weeks? Folks are wondering where you've
been. Pretty soon they'll start adding things up and figure out that
you had something to do with all this raiding business. I'd get
back to Hallettsville pretty damn soon, Mr. Kindred, and I'd stick
pretty close to that jailhouse for a while until things calm down

around here again. That's what I'd do, if I was you. I'd do it because you ain't welcome here any more, Mr. Kindred." She gave him a cold eye to accentuate her point.

Kindred could take a hint. He was gone within the hour.

43

Slater had drawn a map of Hallettsville for Mr. Hatton, and on it, he indicated Mrs. Hallet's house on the north side of town. "Wait until dark before you go out there," he instructed the undertaker. "There's a lot of curious folks in Hallettsville, and I don't want any of them knowing what you're up to."

Again, Hatton followed Slater's instructions perfectly. He slipped out of his hotel room and down the back stairs right after sundown, pretending to go for an evening walk. He headed up Front Street past the jailhouse to First Street, where he crossed over to Main and continued on to Mrs. Hallet's house. It was quite dark when he walked through the front gate and up to the porch, where Mrs. Hallet sat quietly in her rocker.

"Good evening, sir," she said when Hatton stepped onto the first step.

Hatton hadn't seen her sitting in the shadows. The sound of her voice startled him. He backed up a pace, then said, "Hello?"

"Come ahead, sir," said Mrs. Hallet. "It's quite all right. I am Mrs. Margaret Hallet. I've been expecting you."

"Expecting me?" queried Hatton.

"Yes, of course. Ever since I heard that you'd given a letter to Colonel Markham this afternoon, I figured you'd be coming out here sooner or later. You've got a letter for me, I'll bet. And maybe one for my granddaughter, too."

Hatton retraced his steps to the porch and said, "Why, yes, I do have a letter for you, Mrs. Hallet. And one for your grand-daughter, too. But how did you know that I would have letters for you?"

"I know Cletus Slater, sir. He wouldn't send someone back

here without sending a letter to Texada, and considering all that's happened, I figured he wouldn't send a letter to Colonel Markham without sending one to me, too.''

Texada heard the voices on the porch. ''Granny, who are you talking to out there?'' she called out.

''A gentleman caller, dear,'' said Mrs. Hallet. ''I believe he has something for you.''

''Mrs. Hallet,'' said Hatton in a lowered voice, ''I'm not supposed to let Miss Ballard know about your letter.''

''That's all right,'' she whispered back. ''You just give Texada her letter first and hold on to mine until she goes back into the house to read hers.''

''Yes, ma'am,'' said Hatton.

Texada stood in the doorway, framed by the light from the living room. ''Evening,'' she said stiffly.

''Good evening, Miss Ballard,'' said Hatton.

Texada stared at Hatton's shadowy face and asked, ''Do we know you, sir?'' Then she recognized him. ''Oh, sure,'' she said. ''You're that undertaker fellow from Orange, aren't you?''

''Yes, ma'am,'' said Hatton. He removed his hat. ''Mr. John Hatton at your service.''

''Not at my service, I hope,'' said Texada. ''Not yet, anyway.''

''Mr. Hatton has a letter for you, Texada,'' said Mrs. Hallet. ''It's from Clete.''

''A letter from Clete?'' exclaimed Texada.

''That's right,'' said Hatton. He reached inside his coat and pulled out two envelopes. He tilted them in the light so he could read the names on them. ''This one is yours,'' he said, handing it to Texada.

She snatched the envelope from him, tore it open, then stood in the doorway trying to read it in the dim light.

''Texada, take that letter inside the house to read it,'' said Mrs. Hallet. ''You'll ruin your eyes trying to read it out here.''

The girl obeyed without thinking.

Hatton waited a moment, then gave Mrs. Hallet her letter from Slater.

''Thank you, Mr. Hatton,'' said Mrs. Hallet. She stood up and stuck the letter into an apron pocket. ''Won't you come in, Mr. Hatton? We've got some nice cool lemonade, if you'd care for some.''

''Thank you, Mrs. Hallet, but I'll have to say no. I should be getting back to my hotel as soon as possible.''

"Yes, of course," said Mrs. Hallet. "Well, thank you again, sir. And thank you for bringing those boys home to be buried. It's not right to be planted in dirt that isn't yours."

"No, ma'am," said Hatton. He replaced his hat. "Well, good night, Mrs. Hallet."

"Good night, Mr. Hatton."

The undertaker left, and Mrs. Hallet went into the house, where Texada was reading her letter for the second time already. "Well, read it to me, girl," said Mrs. Hallet.

"Oh, Granny, sure." She blushed, then asked, "Gee, Granny, do I have to read it to you? It's kind of personal, if you know what I mean."

Mrs. Hallet laughed and said, "I'm not that old, Texada. I haven't forgotten how it was to be young. Not yet, anyway. Just tell me what it says about those poor dead boys and what happened to them on the drive."

"Well, it's pretty much what he said in that letter to Colonel Markham," said Texada. "Some rustlers jumped them in Louisiana, and Dent and Stan Grey were killed. He says Jess Tate was killed the night before they crossed the Sabine, but he doesn't know who did it. That's about it, Granny. The rest is personal stuff."

"Did he say that he loves you?" asked Mrs. Hallet.

Texada blushed again and said, "I told you it was personal, Granny, but, yes, he did say that he loved me. Now if you don't mind, I think I'll be going to my room."

"I'm kind of tuckered out, too," said Mrs. Hallet. "I think I'll turn in, too. Good night, Texada."

"Good night, Granny."

Mrs. Hallet went to her room, closed the door behind her, then turned up the flame in the lamp beside her bed. She picked up the spectacles that she kept on the nightstand for reading her Bible every night before going to sleep. She donned the glasses and read Slater's letter:

Dear Mrs. Hallet,

Something tells me this letter is not going to be a surprise to you. I think you will start adding things up and figure out that I could not write to Colonel Markham without writing to you, too. Am I right? I believe I am.

As you know by now, my brother Dent, Jess Tate, and Stan Grey have been killed by badmen and I have had their bodies sent back to Hallettsville for burying. I have not written the complete truth in the letters I sent to Colonel Markham, my sister Malinda, and Texada. I fear that if they know the truth that they will spread it around Lavaca County and the badmen that killed my brother and my best friend will hear of it and will go to ground somewhere. I know that I can trust you to keep this quiet and that you will want to help me bring those badmen to justice when I return to Lavaca County.

First off, I do not know it for certain, but I think the Detchen brothers killed Jess Tate the night before the herd was put across the Sabine. I do know for certain that they threw in with the cowboys who attacked our drovers and killed Dent and Stan Grey. Those badmen were led by Jim Kindred. I know this because we captured two of them and they told us Kindred and the Detchens were in it together. Then I hung them.

We will continue to drive the herd to New Orleans. I expect to get there within the month. We will come home as fast as we can after that, but I will send Texada a letter telling her that we will not be home for some time later.

I do not want Kindred and the Detchens to know that I am wise to them. I want to come home and make them pay for the killings they did here. I do not know exactly how I will do that, but I will do it. I have taken an oath to avenge my brother and my friends, and you know what that means to a Slater.

My only request of you is this. Would you please do what you can to keep Kindred and the Detchens in sight for me until I can get home again? I know this is a difficult request, but I figure that you will come up with a way of doing it. Maybe you could talk to Sheriff Foster or something like that, and he could make sure that Kindred and the Detchens are still around when I get home. Whatever you can do will be greatly appreciated.

I just wanted you to know the truth about all this sorry business and that everything else is all right for now. I look forward to seeing you again.

> With kindest regards,
> Cletus

· · ·

Mrs. Hallet replaced the letter in its envelope, then picked up her Bible. She thumbed through it until she found the scripture that she wanted. It was in The Epistle of Paul to the Romans. She read it to herself. "Repay no one evil for evil, but take thought for what is noble in the sight of all. Beloved, never avenge thyselves, but give place to the wrath of God; for it is written, 'Vengeance is mine, I will repay, sayeth the Lord.' No, 'if thine enemy be hungry, feed him; if he thirsteth, give him drink; for by so doing ye shall reap burning coals upon his head.' Be not overcome by evil, but overcometh evil with good."

"Oh, Cletus," she said softly, "what have you done?"

44

Almost as an afterthought, Markham gave Malinda the letter from Slater. He waited until Malinda returned from helping Josephine take Hannah down back to the house where Dent had spent so many nights. "I didn't read it," said Markham as he handed the envelope to her.

Malinda read it then, and she read it again after Markham left for town shortly before midnight. She hoped that a second reading might stir some emotion within her, but it didn't.

Never before in her life had Malinda known loneliness. Not when her father was killed. Not when her mother remarried and moved away to northern Texas. Not when Clete left for the war. Not when her grandfather died. Not until now. But not because Dent was gone forever. But because she felt nothing for him, no sense of loss, no pain. And she was reminded of this lack of feeling for her brother by Hannah's constant wailing that went on well into the night and echoed up to her from the former slave quarters behind the mansion.

Malinda did feel sorry for Hannah, though. She really loved Dent, she told herself several times during the evening. It must be wonderful to love someone like that. With all your heart and soul. She sighed and felt a little sorry for herself because she thought herself incapable of real love. She didn't love Markham. This much she knew, but it made no difference to her. He would make a suitable husband for her, an adequate father of her children, and a good master of Glengarry, now that it was hers.

But poor Hannah! Suffering like that. Something has to be done for her. An idea struck her.

Malinda took the letter from Clete and went down back to share it with Hannah. She entered the little one-room house to find Josephine sitting on the edge of the bed, trying to comfort Hannah, who had her face buried in a pillow and was crying softly now.

"I can't get her to stop, Miss Malinda," said Josephine.

"It's all right, Josephine," said Malinda. "You go on now. Go back to your house. I'll take care of her now."

Josephine hesitated. She looked down at Hannah, stroked the girl's hair, then slowly stood up. "Okay, Miss Malinda," she said sternly. "I'll be going, but if you needs me, you just hollers now. You understand, chil'?"

Malinda had become unaccustomed to being mammied by Josephine, but hearing the old woman call her "chil'" again was comforting. To show her gratitude for the support, she hugged Josephine and said, "Thank you, Mammy Joe."

"Don't be thanking me, Miss Malinda," said Josephine. "You's the one staying up all night. Not me." And with that, she was gone.

Hannah continued to cry into her pillow, ignoring the changing of the guard.

Malinda sat down on the edge of the bed in the exact spot that Josephine had just vacated. She stroked Hannah's arm tenderly and said, "Hannah, it's Malinda. I came down here to read this letter to you. It's from my brother Clete. He mentions you in it." When the servant made no sign that she was listening to her, Malinda squeezed Hannah's shoulder and added, "I can't say that I understand the pain you're going through now, Hannah, because I'm not feeling the same thing. To tell you something like that would be dishonest, and I can't do that. We've known each other too long to be dishonest with each other now. I hope you're listening to what I'm saying, Hannah. It's important to me and . . . to Dent that you hear what I'm going to read to you now."

Hannah rolled over and looked up at Malinda. Her eyes were red and raw. She sniffed, then wiped her cheeks with the back of her hand. "Important to Dent?" she queried.

"Yes, Hannah. Just listen and you'll know what I mean."
Malinda held up the letter and began to read it aloud:

Dear Malinda,

By now you know that our baby brother has been killed
by rustlers in Louisiana. He took a bullet in the neck that cut
the big blood vessel that goes up in the head. It was not much
of a wound except for this. There was little that we could do
to help him as the blood slowly drained out of him. He died
peacefully.

We took his body back to Orange where I found an undertaker to take it back to Hallettsville. I wrote to your colonel
and asked him to see to it that Dent gets a proper funeral. I
know he will honor my request. I wish I could be there with
you, but I have my duty to get the herd to market in New
Orleans. I hope you understand.

Over these last days of his life, Dent and I had the chance
to be brothers once more. We talked a bit about Glengarry.
He said that he never wanted it without me. I never doubted
that for a minute, not even before this happened. While we
were talking, I came to realize that I hardly knew Dent. He
was so changed from the boy that I knew as my brother when
I left for the war, but never mind all that. I was beginning
to like him and respect him as a man. He quit drinking after
a few days on the drive as an example to the men. I know
it was hard on him in the beginning, but he stuck it out. He
did not even ask for a drink after he figured out he was dying.

Like I already wrote, I hardly knew Dent. That is, I hardly
knew anything about him. I write this because of the last few
minutes of his life and the things he said then.

He was propped up against a tree, and we were talking. He
said he did not want Glengarry without me, and I said
that I understood what he meant by that. Then he said something that I do not understand because I did not know Dent
as well as I wish that I had known him. His final words were
about a girl named Hannah. I do not know who this Hannah
is, but she must have meant a powerful lot to Dent because
of how he said her name. If you know this Hannah, I think
it would only be right if you would read this letter to her and
let her know that Dent's last mortal thoughts were about her.
I hope I am recollecting this correctly as his last words were
these. "Tell Hannah I will be waiting for her up yonder. I

love her.'' I think he was about to say that Hannah was his sweetheart, but the Lord took him before he could finish what he wanted to say.

As I wrote already, I do not know who this Hannah is, but I would like to meet her when I return from New Orleans. I think Dent would want me to visit with her for him.

Well, that is all that I have to write for now. I am all right and in good health. I will finish driving the herd to New Orleans, and then I will be home.

Your loving brother,
Clete

Hannah was staring at the letter in Malinda's hand as if it were a precious jewel that had hypnotized her.

"Would you like to keep this letter, Hannah?" asked Malinda.

Without shifting her view, Hannah said, "Yes, Miss Malinda." She reached out for it, and Malinda handed it to her. "Thank you, Miss Malinda." She held the letter against her breast and curled up again, but no tears came from her eyes.

"Are you all right now?" asked Malinda.

Hannah smiled. It was a real smile. Natural, not forced. She stared into the distance and said, "I'm just fine now, Miss Malinda. I'm just fine now." In her mind, she added, I am now that I know my Dent will be waiting for me up yonder when my time comes. She rubbed her belly. It's okay, though. I still got part of him down here.

Malinda patted Hannah's arm and said, "You get some sleep now. We'll talk about this some more in the morning." She stood up and left Hannah alone.

When morning came, Hannah was gone. So was a horse from the stable. Malinda figured that Hannah had ridden off during the night, probably to Kansas, where her people had moved. Just as well, thought Malinda. She would have been worthless around here now.

45

As much as Slater had wanted to accompany his brother's body back to Hallettsville and see that he was buried proper, he knew that getting the herd to New Orleans was the greater and more important task to be done. He and the Double Star drovers completed the drive in less than four weeks to the Crescent City, where they sold the cattle to the first buyer that they met who would pay them fourteen dollars a head for their eight hundred sixty-three beeves. It wasn't as much as they could have gotten, but Slater was in no mood to haggle. He had more important matters on his mind.

Instead of riding all the way back to Hallettsville, Slater and the Double Star hands bought passage on the *Gulf Queen* for Port Lavaca. From there, they boarded the recently rebuilt San Antonio & Mexican Gulf Railroad to Victoria, then made the remaining seventy miles to home on horseback. They were back a week sooner than Slater had originally projected.

Slater wanted to keep their return a secret, so he made certain that they arrived in Lavaca County after dark. At the ford on Little Brushy Creek, he had Flewellyn lead the rest of the men to the Tate ranch, while he slipped into Hallettsville to see Texada because he missed her and because he wanted to find out about the Detchens and the rest of Kindred's gang.

The lights were all out at Mrs. Hallet's house when Slater sneaked up to Texada's bedroom window. It was partly open for much needed ventilation on such sweltering August nights in Texas, but he didn't push it up the rest of the way and go inside. Instead, he tapped lightly on the glass, waited, then tapped again until he heard Texada stirring within her room.

"Texada!" he whispered as loudly as he could without reaching a normal voice level.

"Clete?" she whispered back. "Is that you, darling? Or am I only dreaming about you again?"

"Yes, it's really me," he said eagerly, his heart jumping in his chest.

The white voile curtains parted, and Texada appeared before him in a long, gray nightshirt that wasn't tied up in front. She opened the window wide, then nearly leaped out at Slater as she threw her arms around his neck and kissed him rapidly and repeatedly on his lips, cheeks, chin, and even his forehead. "Oh, Clete darling!" she cried between kisses. "I've missed you so much. I love you, I love you. Don't ever go away from me again." She backed off for a second, her face as serious as it had ever been in her whole life. "Promise me, Clete darling, that you'll never go away again. Please promise me that."

Slater wanted to grant her request, but he knew he couldn't. There was no way he could make such a promise, not with what he had vowed to do. Even so, he said, "Texada, you'll always be with me wherever I go." He touched his chest and said, "Right here. You'll always be right here. No matter where I go or what I do, you'll always be right here in my heart."

"I don't understand, Clete," she said. "Are you going away again? You can't go away again. You just got back. You can't leave me again."

Slater saw the panic in her eyes and knew he had to reassure her that he wasn't planning to leave her again. Not yet anyway. "Texada, I'm not going anywhere," he said. "I'm here with you now, and that's all that counts."

She wrapped her arms around his neck again and whispered into his ear, "Yes, Clete darling, that's all that counts."

He pulled her through the window and held her close for the moment. Then he said, "Texada, we have to talk."

"Yes, I know," she said. Then with all the sadness one person can feel for another, she added, "Grandma and I felt terrible sorrow when Jess and Dent's bodies came home and we read your letter telling us what had happened. Oh, Clete, your brother and your best friend! I wished I could have been there to comfort you when you needed someone."

"If you only knew how much I wanted you with me right then," said Slater. "I've never felt so alone in all my life, Texada. There aren't any words to describe the pain." Tears coursed his cheeks and fell on Texada's bare shoulder. "Dent and I were just getting to know each other again. I felt sure we were going to be all right once the drive was over. We were going to be brothers again." He fell to weeping, the anguish in him was so great. "God, how

I wish it had been me and not him!''

Texada cried along with him until his eyes were out of salt, but even then, she continued to hold him tightly, cradling his face between her neck and shoulder. They had never before been so close as they were at this moment.

Slater blinked away the last drop from his eyes, sniffed, and straightened up. His head lolled backward as he sought out the stars. Focusing on one particularly bright orb, he said, ''My Grandfather Hawk told me when my father was killed that when a warrior dies a new star appears in the sky. I wonder if that one is Jess's or Dent's.''

Texada gazed upward and said, ''Probably Dent's. It looks about the same color as his eyes.''

''Yeah, you're right,'' said Slater. ''And that one must be Jess's. It sort of looks like it's laughing and happy the way Jess always was.''

''That's right,'' said Texada, although she wasn't sure which star he meant. ''Just like Jess.''

Slater heaved one great sigh, then another. ''I saw a lot of men die during the war, and even when they were good friends, it never felt like this.'' The air hissed through his teeth as he took a deep breath in an effort to regain control of his emotions. ''I don't ever want to go through this again, Texada.''

''I know, Clete darling, I know.''

His chest heaved once more, then he said, ''We've got to talk about the bastards who did it, Texada.'' He looked her straight in the eyes and said, ''Have the Detchens or that sonofabitch Kindred shown their faces around here yet?''

''Kindred and the Detchens?'' Fear and surprise put shadows in her face. ''You never mentioned Kindred in your letter to me or the one you sent Colonel Markham, and you said you thought the outlaws had killed the Detchens as well.''

''I know,'' said Slater. ''I had to do that to make them feel safe until I got back here. I didn't want them to know that I'm on to them.''

''You mean that they killed Dent and Jess?''

''I don't know for sure that they killed Jess, but I do know that Kindred led the cowboys who jumped us in Louisiana and that the Detchens had thrown in with them. We shot it out with them and killed a bunch of them. We caught a couple of them, and I hung them.''

Disbelief colored Texada's voice when she asked, "You hung them?"

"Not before they talked and told us about Kindred and the Detchens being in it together." He saw the look on Texada's face and said, "They were part of the bunch that killed Dent. They deserved to be hung." When she made no reply, he asked, "So what about the Detchens and Kindred? Have they shown up around here yet?"

Texada swallowed hard and said, "Kindred and some of the men who worked for the Detchens have been around town the last few days, but I haven't seen hide nor hair of the Detchens. They could be hiding out to the Campbell Plantation and no one in Hallettsville would ever know a thing about it. There ain't a soul around here who wants to go near Sophia Campbell or the Detchens."

"Well, I do," said Slater. "I want to face them both and hear them tell me that they didn't kill Jess or that they weren't part of the ambush that killed Dent."

"Well, you can find Kindred at the jailhouse almost any time of day or night. He's been staying real close over there ever since he showed up the other day. There's a rumor going around that he and that gang of his are the ones who robbed Teddy Johnson's freight wagons."

"I wouldn't doubt it," said Slater. He became pensive.

"What are you planning to do, Clete?"

"I want to see Kindred hang, but he hasn't done anything here in Texas to get himself strung up legally. Even the Detchens are safe from a Lavaca County hangman. They killed Jess over to Orange, and the sheriff there doesn't give an owl's hoot about who did it. As far as he's concerned, it wasn't none of his affair."

"That's no way to be," said Texada in sympathetic anger.

"No, it's not, so I have to do this my way. Texada, I want you to spread the word around town that you got a letter from me that says I won't be home until next week at the earliest. That'll get Kindred off his guard, and it might get the Detchens to come out of their hole for a bit. If they do, the boys and I will be waiting for them out at the Tate ranch. But whatever you do, Texada, don't let anyone besides your grandmother know that we're back."

"What about Malinda? She's awfully worried about you."

"No, don't tell Malinda. She'd let it slip to Markham, and if I know him right, he'll tell Sophia Campbell and there goes my little surprise for Harlan and Farley. Now promise me you won't tell anyone, Texada."

She looked him straight in the eye and said, "I promise." Of course, she had her fingers crossed.

46

Major Phineas Stephens was an infantry officer, working out of the provost marshal's office in New Orleans. Like Colonel Markham, he was regular army. His home state was Michigan, and he proudly called himself a Republican. His appearance was generally similar to Markham's, too: thin-haired reddish mustache that had pretensions of manliness, pale complexion, gray eyes, brown hair, narrow lips, weak chin made all the weaker by the growth on his upper lip, skinny neck and body, blank look in the eyes like European royalty had when passing among the peasants. He rode into Hallettsville and went straight to the courthouse, where Sergeant Wickersham greeted him on the steps.

"Good morning, sir," said Wickersham, standing rigid in a saluting posture.

Stephens returned the courtesy and said, "Sergeant, take me to Colonel Markham's office at once."

"Yes, sir." Wickersham held the door and said, "It's right up those stairs, sir."

Stephens nodded and entered the building. A minute later he was standing at attention in front of the commanding officer's desk, introducing himself to Markham.

"Sit down, Major Stephens," said Markham, gesturing toward a straight-back chair at one corner of his desk. Once Stephens was seated, Markham asked, "What brings you to Hallettsville, Major?"

Stephens reached inside his blouse, pulled out an official envelope, and placed it on the desk for Markham. Then he said, "Colonel Markham, that is a warrant for the arrest of a Clete Slater, formerly a captain in the Confederate army."

Markham was aghast. His hands trembled as he opened the envelope and removed the warrant.

Stephens noticed Markham's reaction and said, "Do you know this man, Colonel?"

"Yes, I am acquainted with him," said Markham with a touch of nervousness in his voice. "What are the charges against Slater?"

"He led a raid against an Army supply train after he was pardoned by General Canby."

"*After* he was pardoned?"

"That's correct, sir," said Stephens. "The raid took place near Natchez, Mississippi, on May 8. Slater and a band of Texans attacked a supply train, killed all but three of the teamsters and soldiers, and made off with fourteen thousand dollars in gold and silver coins and greenbacks."

"How do you know Slater led the raid?" asked Markham.

"We have testimony from three of the men who were with him," said Stephens. "We captured them near Nashville, Tennessee, when one of them foolishly let a local official see a money pouch that had been taken from the supply train. Upon questioning, he refused to cooperate, but the local commander discovered where he was staying in the area and captured two more men who had taken part in the raid. The commander sent them to us in New Orleans, and they were found guilty at their trial. They were sentenced to hang, but General Canby agreed to pardon them if they would name every man who took part in the raid. When he learned that this Slater had led the attack, the general became furious because he had personally pardoned Slater and now Slater had betrayed the general's trust. So General Canby decided to pardon all the rest of the Texans, but this Slater would have to hang for his crime. As far as General Canby is concerned, Slater has already been tried and convicted. As soon as he is captured, Slater will be given a quick trial, which I will conduct, and then we will hang him like the general wants us to do."

The idea of hanging Slater didn't disturb Markham all that much. In fact, he was almost nonchalant about it as he said, "You're that positive that Slater is guilty, Major?"

"Absolutely. I have a sheath full of depositions that I will enter into the record of his trial as proof that he led the raid."

"But what about a defense for Slater? Suppose he denies the charge and can prove it. Then what?"

"General Canby says Slater is guilty, Colonel Markham. That's all the proof I need to find this Rebel guilty of treason and then hang him.''

Markham wasn't sure that he liked the idea of going through the pretense of a trial, then hanging Slater in Hallettsville. Sending him back to New Orleans would be a much better way of dealing with Slater. In that vein, he said, ''You just missed your chance to capture Slater in New Orleans, Major Stephens, although he's probably not there now.''

Stephens leaned forward in surprise and said, ''In New Orleans? What do you mean, Colonel?''

''Slater left here about six weeks ago with a herd of cattle for the New Orleans market. From what I've heard, he should have gotten there a few days ago, but he's probably left by now and is on his way home.''

Stephens thought for a second, then said, ''Now that you mention cattle, I do recall passing a herd near a place called Lake Charles. That very next day I saw two bodies hanging from a tree beside the road. One had a sign on him that said something to the effect that all Northerners, thieves, and killers should stay out of Texas or they could expect the same. You don't suppose this Slater was responsible for that, too?''

''That sounds like him,'' said Markham as he began forgetting that he was soon to marry Slater's sister and began remembering the hatred that he'd held for Rebels since early in the war. ''Slater is a very dangerous man by himself. He's even more dangerous when he's at the head of that gang of cowboys who work for him. Earlier this summer he resisted arrest by a deputy sheriff and his posse, and he probably would have killed every one of those lawmen if I hadn't intervened.''

''So you've already had trouble with him?'' queried Stephens.

''Nothing serious besides that incident. For the most part, he's been peaceful.'' Then Markham remembered the affair at John Kelly's store. ''No, wait. There was another time. Right after he came home he led his gang into a store here in town and they helped themselves to anything they wanted. I called it robbery, but the storekeeper said he was selling them everything on credit. Of course, he said that with Slater holding a gun in his back.''

Markham didn't realize it, but he was being caught in a trap steeled by hate, fear, and distrust. In his heart, he knew that Slater hadn't done anything so terrible as he was telling Stephens, but he also knew that Stephens was a direct line to Canby and other higher-ups. For too long, he had straddled the fence between his love for Malinda and his duty to the military. Now it was time for him to jump down on the northern side of the Mason-Dixon Line.

"Colonel, when do you think Slater will be coming back here?" asked Stephens.

"I should think that he'll be back within the week. You say you passed a herd of cattle on your way here?"

"Yes, about four weeks ago."

Markham thought for a minute, then said, "Then I'd say he won't be coming back for another four or five days. Until he does return and the opportunity to take him alive comes about, I suggest we keep this," he held up the warrant, "between the two of us. I won't even tell any of my officers. As far as your presence here, Major, I suggest you tell anyone who asks that you're here on an inspection tour to see how things are going since we recovered Texas for the Union."

"Yes, of course, Colonel. I suppose there is a real need for secrecy with all these Rebel ears around."

Major, you only know the half of it, thought Markham.

47

Dent's death did upset Malinda sufficiently to make her melancholy with concern for her other brother. This rankled Markham somewhat, and he thought to get her mind off her worry and sorrow by suggesting that she go into town and do some shopping. She approved of the idea.

Malinda chose the same day as Major Stephens's arrival to follow Markham's suggestion, so she had the orderly Markham had left at her disposal drive her into Hallettsville. She wore her mourning dress and bonnet as she shopped her way around the town square. One of her stops was at the Ballard store, where Texada waited on her.

"Good morning, Texada," said Malinda politely, although she still held a little contempt for this tomboyish girl who was almost the same age in years as she but whom she still considered to be much less mature in bearing, emotions, and morals.

"Top of the morning to you, Malinda," said Texada, her voice filled with the effervescence of a young woman in love. "Isn't it a beautiful day?"

Malinda looked behind her and through the window at a bank of dark clouds building up on the southern horizon, then, turning back to Texada, said, "If you like threatening skies, I suppose it is."

Texada wasn't about to let Malinda spoil her day. "We could be having twisters," she said, "and it would still be a beautiful day."

"Well, you're certainly in a good mood," said Malinda rather facetiously. "And what, pray tell, has caused this?" she asked, knowing how miserable Texada had been since Slater had left on the cattle drive and how distraught she had been at the funerals for Dent, Jess Tate, and Stan Grey.

Texada glanced around the store, then leaned over the counter toward Malinda. "I heard from Clete," she whispered.

Malinda was taken by surprise. "You did?" she said, suddenly as excited as Texada. "What did he say? Is he all right? Did he say when he's coming home? Did he sell the cattle for a good price?" She was as giddy as a schoolgirl, but she didn't care: it felt good.

"If you'll hush up, Malinda, I'll tell you."

"Yes, of course. Go ahead, and I won't say a word until you're done."

Texada looked around the store again to see if anyone else was within earshot. No one was visible. Then she poked her head through the drapes that covered the doorway to the back room to make certain her cousin Coll wasn't around. He wasn't. She turned back to Malinda.

"The truth is he's already home," she said in a whisper that had a bit of a giggle in it.

Malinda was stunned but not so much so that she couldn't gasp, "He's home?"

"*S-s-sh-h-h!* You want the whole county to know? Clete doesn't. He wants it kept secret because he's trying to catch the men who killed Dent and Jess Tate."

"I don't understand," whispered Malinda.

"Clete and the boys got back last night. They're holed up out to the Tate ranch. Clete said Jim Kindred and his bunch and the

Detchens tried to rustle the herd when they crossed into Louisiana.
He said he thinks the Detchens are the ones who killed Jess Tate,
and he knows for sure that they were in on the rustling because
he caught two of the rustlers and they told him so before they
were hung. Now Clete wants to keep it secret that they're back
until he's had a chance to catch Kindred and his cowboys and the
Detchens. I think he's planning on lynching them because he said
they haven't done anything in Texas that would make the law
hang them.''

Malinda's joy turned to worry with Texada's last remark. ''This
is terrible, Texada. Clete can't take the law into his own hands
like that. He'll get himself hung, too, if he does.''

''No, he won't,'' said Texada, pshawing Malinda for being
such a worry wart. ''There isn't a judge and jury in Texas that
would convict him for avenging the murders of his brother and
his best friend, especially when they see who was responsible for
killing them. In fact, they might even pin a medal on him for
doing away with the Detchens.''

Malinda couldn't argue with that kind of logic, but she still felt
it was wrong for Slater to take action outside the law, especially
since her fiancé would have to take the other side against him.
She gave this some thought, then said, ''Thank you for telling
me, Texada.'' She touched Texada's hand, then added, ''I'm glad
we'll be sisters one day.''

Completely caught off guard, Texada said weakly, ''Yes, so
am I, Malinda.''

Another customer entered the store, and they broke off saying
anything more about Slater.

48

Slater put guards around the Tate ranch to make sure no one came snooping and discovered that he and the Double Star drovers had returned. Then he spread the rest of the men throughout the county to look for signs of Kindred and his outlaws, while he scouted the Campbell Plantation.

After a near fruitless day of watching for members of Kindred's gang on the roads of Lavaca County, the Double Star hands regrouped at the Tate ranch after dark that Monday. Flewellyn reported seeing a Yankee officer riding toward Hallettsville, and Slater said he didn't see anything of the Detchens when he snooped around the Campbell Plantation. Bill Simons had better luck.

Slater had assigned Simons and his crew to watch the roads leading into Petersburg because most of the men who had been with Kindred and the Detchens were from that sleepy little town south of Hallettsville. Close to sundown, Simons and Bill Armstrong saw Tom Mather coming down the road from Hallettsville. When he was abreast of their hiding place alongside the road, Armstrong jumped out of the bushes and grabbed the reins from Mather's hand. The horse shied, throwing Mather to the ground. Leaping to his feet, he saw who was after him and started to run. Simons mounted up and rode after the fleeing outlaw. He took his lariat, lassoed Mather, then dragged him back to his horse, literally kicking and screaming. Simons asked Armstrong to shut Mather up, and Armstrong obliged by cracking Mather over the head with the barrel of his Colt's Navy. After tying up Mather, they waited until dark to take him to the Tate ranch.

"I want you to tell me where the Detchens are hiding out," said Slater when Mather was brought to him in the barn.

"I don't know what you're talking about, Slater," said Mather defiantly.

Slater could appreciate Mather's attitude, but he didn't like it. He grabbed the outlaw by the front of his shirt and jerked him to his feet. Through gritted teeth, he said, "I've already hung two of you murdering bastards, Tom Mather. Would you like to be the third?"

"You didn't hang no one," said Mather back at him. "You ain't the kind to do that to a man."

Slater thought for a second, then released Mather's shirt, smiled, and said, "You called my bluff, Tom. You're right. I didn't hang anyone. Jake here did it. Right, Jake?"

Flewellyn spit tobacco juice to one side, then said, "That's right, Clete. Hung both of them boys . . . real slow, too. Mather, you should have seen how Charley and Pete went. I tightened the loops around their necks myself and then we hoisted them up real slowlike. Both of them went to gagging and choking and their faces got redder and redder and then bluer and bluer and finally their tongues popped through their lips and their eyes bulged out of their sockets so far that I thought they were going to pop right out of their heads." He spit again. "It was about that time that they quit their kicking and become dead."

"So you see, Tom," said Slater, smiling, "you were right. I didn't hang anyone."

Mather suddenly realized how a mouse must feel when caught by a cat who isn't really hungry at the moment. He cleared his throat and said, "Did you really hang Pete and Charley?"

"By the neck until they was dead," said Jake.

"You see, Tom," said Slater, "they were uncooperative like you're being right now, and Jake doesn't cotton to anyone who isn't cooperative."

Flewellyn produced a rope with a hangman's noose on it. He gently slapped it on the palm of his left hand and said, "One size fits all."

Mather eyeballed the hemp loop and said anxiously, "All I know about the Detchens is they left us when we got near the Campbell Plantation. Honest, Slater. They rode off as soon as we crossed the Navidad. Both of them. I swear it."

"I believe you, Tom," said Slater, "but isn't it funny how you telling the truth now won't bring back my brother or Stan Grey or Jess Tate? You see, Tom, they're all dead." Slater's face became dark with hate and anger. "They're dead, you son of a bitch, because the gang you were riding with killed them. And I swore over my brother's body that I would see that every single one of you bastards got sent to Hell for killing them."

"Oh, no, Slater!" whined Mather. "Don't kill me! God, don't

kill me! I didn't shoot your brother! I didn't shoot anyone! I swear it!''

Slater doubled up his fist and slugged Mather squarely in the middle of his face, crushing the outlaw's nose and splattering blood on himself. Mather fell backward into a horse stall, his head landing in a pile of fresh dung. Crying, he rolled over and curled up in a fetal position as if that would protect him from further harm. ''Don't kill me,'' he bawled.

''Gag him, Jake,'' said Slater, ''and put him on a horse. We're going for a little ride.''

49

The next morning Colonel Markham awakened with the worst hangover of his life to that time. It's my own damn fault, he mocked himself as he rose from bed. If I'd just kept my mouth shut, there would have been no argument with Malinda and I would have had a pleasant visit with her. But he hadn't kept quiet, and now he was paying the piper, as the expression went.

The previous evening Markham had called on Malinda at Glengarry as had become his custom at the end of the day, and upon entering the house, he cautioned himself not to say a word to her about the warrant for Slater's arrest. Malinda presented her cheek to him, which he dutifully kissed in the presence of Josephine, then she gave him his customary glass of claret. He took a sip, then sat down in his usual chair after Malinda seated herself.

''Did you have a good day in town?'' asked Markham as he appraised his betrothed in her black gown. To his surprise, she had added a bit of color to it, a yellow ribbon tied in a bow at the center-front of the low-cut dress, which drew the viewer's attention to a hint of cleavage.

''Yes, I did,'' she said cautiously.

''Did you see Miss Ballard today?'' he asked.

''Why, yes, I did. Why do you ask?''

''I was merely wondering if she might have received word from

Clete.'' Having heard the rumor that Texada had spread about town, he already knew the answer to his implied question, but he didn't have any details, which he thought Texada would certainly have repeated to Malinda.

"Yes, she did say that she had received a letter from him," said Malinda, lying. "It came from New Orleans. He said he had some business to finish up there, and then he would be coming straight home after that."

"Did he say when he'd be back?"

"Not exactly, but Texada felt he would be returning near the end of the week."

Still trying to act the part of a casually interested bystander, Markham said, "It will be good to have him home again, especially now." But he couldn't stop his face from frowning in time to prevent Malinda from noticing it.

Malinda saw the downward turn of his mouth and knew immediately that he was insincere. Like her brother, she seldom hesitated to speak her mind. With a bit of harshness, she said, "You don't mean that, Lucas. I know you don't like Clete because he fought for the South, and I also know that now that Dent is gone you think of Clete as a threat to your place here."

"That isn't so, my dearest," said Markham defensively.

"Lucas, do not patronize me. I can read you like a book. You may not be so transparent to others, but to me . . ." She softened her tone, saying, "If I couldn't see what was inside you, Lucas, I wouldn't be marrying you."

Markham lowered his eyes and said, "Yes, my dearest. Please forgive me. I admit it. I do feel threatened now that Dent is no longer with us." He put down his wine glass on the end table, then went down on one knee before Malinda. "It's just that I love you so much, my dearest heart, that I fear losing you."

Almost regally, Malinda held out her hand to him and said, "You have nothing to fear in that vein, my darling. You will quit the Army, and we will be wed, and I will be yours until our days come to an end."

Markham took her hand, kissed the palm, then held it to his cheek. "Quit the Army, my dear?" The idea was totally foreign to him at the moment, although he had considered it more than once since Dent's funeral.

"Yes. Quit the Army. Glengarry is mine now, and when we marry, it will be yours, too. Exactly as we have discussed. But instead of waiting to resign your commission, you can do it now.

Then we can be married sooner.''

"But, my dearest heart, I have my duty to—''

Malinda cut him short, saying, "Your only duty is to me and Glengarry. You have to choose, Lucas. Either Glengarry or the Army.''

Markham stood and looked down at her, although she looked away from him, and he said, "You ask too much of me . . . at this moment, Malinda. I need time to think about it.''

"Then you may do your thinking elsewhere, Lucas Markham, and not in my house,'' she said angrily. She pointed to the doorway. "There is the way out, Lucas.''

So Markham left, rode back to Hallettsville, and got rip-roaring drunk at Lindenberg's Saloon. Sergeant Wickersham did his duty and put the colonel to bed at the end of the evening, and now Markham had the worst hangover of his life as he made his way from the hotel across the street to the courthouse.

Entering the square from another direction at this same time was Sophia Campbell, driving a freight wagon as fast as the four frantic mules pulling it could run. The conveyance careened around the corner of Second and LaGrange and bore down on Markham at full speed. Seeing the colonel before her, Sophia ceased whipping the team and reined them up as best as she could. Sergeant Wickersham, thinking the Campbell wagon was a runaway, threw himself into the path of the frightened beasts and helped bring them to a halt.

"Colonel Markham!'' shouted Sophia loud enough for the whole town to hear her and so loud that her voice echoed off the buildings to one side of the street. "I want to see you!''

No, not her, not today, thought Markham. But instead of saying what was on his mind, he straightened himself as much as he could, considering his condition, and approached the wagon.

Sophia stood up and said, "I want to talk to you right here and now, Colonel Markham!''

Markham smiled weakly and said, "Good morning to you, too, Mrs. Campbell.''

"Colonel, there's been a lynching!''

Markham's head suddenly cleared, then fogged again, but with new thoughts. "I beg your pardon, ma'am. Did you say there's been a lynching?''

"That's right, I did.'' She reached back and whipped a tarpaulin off the body of Tom Mather, the noose still around his neck. "When I went outside this morning at sun up, I found this man hanging in a pecan tree at the end of the drive. There's a note pinned on him that says every murdering rustler in Lavaca County can expect the same, especially my boys, Harlan and Farley.''

As Markham leaned over the side of the wagon for a better look at the corpse, a large crowd began buzzing around them.

"He's dead enough all right," said Sophia, "but I want to know what you're going to do about it, Colonel."

"Why do you come to me with this matter, Mrs. Campbell," asked Markham innocently. "This is the concern of the civilian authorities, not me."

"It's your duty to keep law and order around here, isn't it, Colonel?"

"Why, yes, it is, but—"

Sophia cut him off, angrily saying, "Then that's why I'm bringing this to you, Colonel."

Suddenly, Markham suspected that there was more to the lynching than Sophia wanted to say in front of half of the people in town that morning. He held out a hand and said, "Why don't we retire to my office, where I can get your statement properly, Mrs. Campbell?"

Taking his hand and her cue like a lady, Sophia said in syrupy tones, "Yes, of course, Colonel."

As soon as Sophia was standing on the ground, Markham turned to Wickersham and said, "Sergeant, send a man over to the jail and have Sheriff Foster come up to my office immediately." Then looking back at the wagon, he said, "And do something about this body." To Sophia, he added, "A crime like this is more under the sheriff's jurisdiction than mine, Mrs. Campbell, but I'll be glad to do what I can."

"Yes, of course," said Sophia as she allowed Markham to lead her toward the courthouse steps.

Once they were seated in Markham's office Sophia wasted no more time with amenities and gentle conversation as she came right to the point, saying, "Slater did it."

Markham was totally unprepared for this. Wrinkling his brow, he asked, "What makes you think Slater is responsible for that man's death?"

"That's Tom Mather out there. He was one of them that tried to rustle Slater's herd, that's why."

"How do you know this?" asked Markham.

"Harlan and Farley told me so. They came home last week scared out of their wits for fear that Slater was coming after them with a hangman's rope for each of them.''

Markham thought her statement to be rather curious, so he asked, ''Why would they be afraid of Slater?''

''He thinks they had something to do with the rustlers, that's why.'' Sophia eyed him like a crow that wasn't sure whether the carrion was dead yet and said, ''You don't know all the story, do you?''

''All of what story?'' asked Markham cautiously.

''About the rustling. Harlan and Farley told me all about it.''

''Why don't you tell me then?''

Sophia shook her head, scowled, and said, ''Colonel, the boys were made the camp cooks, which meant they had to ride ahead with the camp wagon instead of staying back with the herd. They were just about to pitch camp for the night when the rustlers jumped them. Instead of trying to shoot it out with more than thirty men, they hightailed it out of there and hid in the woods. Then the rustlers ambushed Slater's men, but they were beaten off. Harlan and Farley were coming back to camp when they heard one of the rustlers Slater had caught tell him that my boys were in on it.

''Now you know how Slater feels about my boys, Colonel. They could have come in and sworn on a whole stack of Bibles that they had nothing to do with it, and Slater wouldn't have believed them. So they stayed out and watched what happened next.'' She paused for dramatic effect, hoping to prompt Markham to ask her the right question.

He did. ''What happened next?''

''Slater hung them.''

Markham showed no surprise, nor was he horrified by her answer. He was quite matter-of-fact as he replied, ''I see, and then what happened?''

''They didn't stick around to find out. They rode as fast as they could to get home. They've been hiding out ever since, trying to figure out how to convince Slater that they didn't have anything to do with his brother's death.''

Markham's head was beginning to clear. He thought it odd that she should be the one to connect her sons with Dent's murder. Most likely, she was lying; Harlan and Farley were probably members of the outlaw gang and had taken part in the aborted robbery. If so, Slater was justified in wanting them dead, and they had every right to fear for their lives.

The pain in Markham's head became worse as he tried to concentrate on the matter at hand. Suddenly, he felt anger, and he realized instantly that the cause for all his problems, including his hangover, was Clete Slater. Ever since Slater came back to Texas, Markham had had no peace. Every problem he had could be traced directly back to Slater. Damn him! The sooner Slater returned to Hallettsville, the sooner he could be arrested and sent off to New Orleans to hang. Then Markham's problems would be over.

Or would they? No, of course not. If he arrested Slater and sent him to New Orleans, Malinda would never forgive him and their marriage would be canceled. That would never do. Malinda was everything to him. Without her, he had no future, no life.

But he had to rid himself of Slater. The man was in the way, his way, all the time. He had to be rid of him. But how?

A new thought struck Markham. A plan began taking shape in his brain. Yes, there was a way to get rid of Slater, but he needed help to do it. And sitting across from him was the very help he needed.

50

After figuring out that Slater and his drovers had returned from New Orleans and were hiding out at the Tate ranch because they wanted revenge on the rustlers, Markham ordered out his entire command and rode off to arrest his would-be brother-in-law.

A few months earlier the sight of a full company of Federal cavalry coming down the road would have terrified the entire countryside, but the Yankees had been around so long now that no one gave them much of a second thought when they rode past. Slater's men paid them no mind when they saw them coming toward the Tate ranch, and Slater wasn't even curious about their show of force until they rode up to the bunkhouse.

"Slater, are you in there?" called out Markham, still in the saddle.

"I wonder what he wants," said Flewellyn as he peeked out the window of the bunkhouse.

"There's only one way to find out," said Slater as he opened the door and stepped outside. On the porch, he said amicably, "Good morning, Colonel. Something I can do for you?"

Inside, Flewellyn and six other Double Star hands took up positions at the windows, each man with a loaded rifle or shotgun and a six-gun at his command.

"Slater, this isn't easy for me to do," said Markham, his words chosen with care and delivered with forethought, "but it's my duty. I hope you understand that."

Slater didn't like the sound of that. Eyeing Markham with suspicion, he asked, "What duty are you talking about, Colonel?"

"My duty as an officer in the Army of the Republic, Slater." He pulled the capias from inside his tunic, held it up for Slater to see, and said, "I have a military warrant for your arrest, Slater."

Without any order from Slater, Flewellyn and the other men thrust their weapons through the windows of the bunkhouse—closed or not—and took aim at Markham and his soldiers. "You ain't arresting no one!" shouted Flewellyn. "Least of all, Clete!!"

"Hold on, boys!" shouted Slater over his shoulder. "Let's hear the man out. There's probably nothing to this, but the man has got to do his job." Then to Markham, he said, "All right, Colonel, tell me why I'm being arrested."

"The charge is treason."

"Treason? I was pardoned for fighting for the Confederacy. I don't understand, Colonel. Did those politicians who started the war in the first place change the rules again?"

"It seems that some of your friends informed on you, Slater," said Markham. "In order to save their own necks, they told General Canby who led that raid on the supply train outside of Natchez."

"I don't know anything about a raid on a supply train outside of Natchez," said Slater. "Someone's been blowing smoke in General Canby's eyes if he thinks I had anything to do with it. I gave General Canby my word, Colonel."

Oddly, Markham believed Slater, but he wasn't about to let the truth interfere with his own plans. "Maybe so, Slater, but I have my duty to do, and that means you're under arrest."

"Hey, Colonel!" shouted Flewellyn. "We done told you already that you ain't taking Clete."

"Hold on, Jake!" shouted an angry Slater. "He's got eight to our one. You start shooting, and we'll all be dead in a few minutes."

"So will that Yankee colonel and a whole bunch of them Bluebellies,'' said Flewellyn with fatal determination.

"Dammit, Jake! The war is over! It's been over for a long time! Let it rest! This is just a misunderstanding, and I can clear it up if we don't do anything stupid like starting a fight right here and now. Do you hear me, Jake?''

There was quiet for a few seconds before Flewellyn reluctantly said, "Yeah, I hear you, Clete.''

Turning back to Markham, Slater said, "I'll get my horse, Colonel, and ride into town with you so we can get this cleared up right away.''

"We're not taking you into town, Slater,'' said Markham.

"Oh, no?''

"No. It seems there are several folks there who want you dead for the lynching of Tom Mather, and it's my guess that there are more who will try to do something foolish like your men here were thinking about doing. So to avoid any unnecessary trouble, we're taking you to Glengarry where we can guard you better from your enemies . . . as well as from your friends.''

That didn't have a true ring to it, but Slater felt certain that Markham would do nothing to harm him, if for no other reason than that the colonel was afraid of losing Malinda.

"Sounds like the wise thing to do, Colonel. I'll get my horse and be right with you.''

51

Malinda was sitting in the parlor when she heard the cavalry riding up the lane to Glengarry mansion. She went to the window to take a look, and when she saw her brother and her husband-to-be riding side by side, she was so delighted that she ran to greet them on the porch. The feeling didn't last.

"Clete, you're home,'' she said joyfully, trying to act as if she didn't know already that he had been back in Lavaca County for a few days.

"I don't know that I'm home yet, Malinda," said Slater wryly from atop his horse.

"Why, of course, you're home," said Malinda. "Isn't he, Lucas?" When Markham failed to reply immediately, she moved to the edge of the veranda and repeated the question. "Clete is home, isn't he, Lucas?"

Markham still didn't want to answer her. He climbed down from the saddle and tied his horse to the hitching post. "Take the prisoner down to the cellar, Sergeant Wickersham," he said. "There're some vegetable bins down there. Put him in one of them and put a guard on him."

Wickersham gave the order for the company to dismount, and the troopers alighted in unison.

"Lucas, what's going on here?" demanded Malinda. "Why is Clete your prisoner?"

Slater jumped off Nimbus, handed the reins to Wickersham, and said, "Would you see that he's taken good care of, Sergeant? He's been through a lot of campaigns with me, and he deserves the best."

"Yes, sir, Mr. Slater," said Wickersham, taking the reins.

Markham didn't like the way that his sergeant was behaving toward Slater. "Sergeant Wickersham, I believe I'm still in command here, or have you decided to throw in with traitors?"

Wickersham snapped to attention and said, "No, sir. I'll see that the prisoner is taken to the cellar immediately, sir."

"That's better," said Markham.

"Lucas, will you answer me?" demanded Malinda. "What's going on here? Tell me this minute or you can forget about setting foot in my house until you do."

Markham heaved a sigh but said nothing.

"Go on and tell her, Colonel," said Slater, a sly grin curling one corner of his mouth.

"Tell me what, Lucas?" asked Malinda.

Markham glared at Slater and shouted at Wickersham, "Get that man out of here, Sergeant!"

"Yes, sir," said Wickersham. "Riley, pick two men for guard duty and come with me." He tied Nimbus to the hitching post.

"Sergeant, you will not set one foot in my house until I know what's going on here," said Malinda.

"Malinda, please," said Markham. He took the first step up to the veranda.

"Please what, Lucas?" snapped Malinda, taking a step down

and effectively blocking his path. "This is my house, and until you tell me what's going here, you will not enter it."

Wickersham took Slater's arm and started to lead him away, but Slater refused to budge. "Go on and tell her, Colonel," he said. "Tell her what you told me."

Markham stared up at Malinda and said, "Your brother is under arrest for treason, and I intend to keep him here at Glengarry until his trial."

"Treason?" queried Malinda. "What are you talking about, Lucas?"

"Clete led a raid on an Army wagon train in Mississippi," said Markham, "and several good men were murdered. He's under arrest for that raid, and he will stand trial in Hallettsville before the week is out."

"I don't understand," said Malinda. "When did this raid happen? While they were on the cattle drive?"

"No," said Markham. "It was in early May, but it was after he was paroled, and that makes his crime treason."

Malinda looked at her brother and said, "Is this true, Clete? Did you lead this raid like Lucas said?"

Slater looked her straight in the eyes and shook his head.

"There!" said Malinda, pointing at her brother. "He said he didn't do it, so why is he your prisoner?"

"Malinda, please!" growled Markham. "Can't we talk about this in the house? I'll explain everything to you in there."

Slater laughed out loud and said, "Malinda, it's all right. I know I didn't lead any raid in Mississippi, and I can prove that I didn't do it. Colonel Markham is only doing his duty by arresting me. I'll get a trial, and I'll prove I'm innocent, and that will be the end of it. In the meantime, I'm under arrest, and Colonel Markham is being gracious by keeping me here instead of in the county jailhouse in Hallettsville."

"But he told Sergeant Wickersham to put you in the cellar," said Malinda. "That doesn't sound very gracious to me."

"What would you have me do with him, Malinda?" asked Markham. "Give him the run of the house?"

"Yes," said Malinda. "If you intend to make a prison of Glengarry, then Clete must have the run of the house."

"Very well then," said Markham with a sigh of exasperation. "You can have the run of the house, Slater, if you'll give me your word that won't try to escape."

"Only a guilty man needs to escape, Colonel," said Slater.

"You have my word that I won't go anywhere until we ride into Hallettsville for that trial."

"There," said Malinda. "That's settled now." She glanced at the sky, then added, "It's nearly time for supper. I'll have Josephine set a place for Clete." She turned and walked back into the house.

Markham looked at Slater in total disbelief, and all Slater could do was laugh. Damn you, Slater! thought the colonel. You may laugh now, but you won't be laughing for long. You can bet on that, my fine Rebel friend.

52

Word of Slater's arrest spread over Lavaca County faster than a March cyclone as the Double Star hands scattered in all directions, seeking help in case drastic measures should become necessary to save Slater from a Yankee noose. As always when events such as this one unfolded, rumors were rampant and farfetched, but none of them was as scary as the truth.

When he was informed that Slater had been captured, Major Stephens, under the powers of the provost marshal's office, ordered Markham to select four officers to serve on the court with Stephens. Markham was to serve as the prosecuting officer, and the most junior officer in Markham's command was to be assigned to serve as Slater's defense counsel. The trial was to take place in three days. They would make it quick, find Slater guilty, then hang him as soon as a gallows could be built in Hallettsville. The general said he wanted Slater hung in front of his own people so Texans would learn who the masters were now.

For his part, Markham kept this conversation from every man in his command and from Malinda.

Major Stephens was another matter entirely. Not unlike many military men, he was fond of strong drink, having a particular taste for Cuban rum, which he found to be abundant in Lindenberg's Saloon, and like many people who are staid, quiet, and soft-spoken when sober, he became quite loud and boisterous when imbibing spiritous liquids.

Two days after laying out his plans for Slater, Stephens repaired to Lindenberg's for an evening of relaxation. He was joined by the four officers who would serve on the court with him.

Some local citizens were standing in a knot at the bar drinking drafts of San Antonio Beer when the Yankees entered the saloon. After giving them the same look of curiosity that they would give any newcomer, the locals turned their faces away in disgust. Stephens found space at the far end of the rail, led the other officers up to it, and ordered a rum mumbo. Lindenberg said that he didn't know the drink, but Stephens told him not to worry and explained how to make the concoction out of rum, honey, sugar, and water. With a leery eye on his other customers, Lindenberg mixed the drink for Stephens, served it to him—and whiskey to the others— then watched the major down the first mug of his rum drink as if he had just come in from the hot summer sun and was drinking a glass of water. Stephens ordered another, and by the time it was placed in front of him, the first began to have an effect on his senses. By the end of the third mumbo, Stephens was spouting anything that came to mind, and the most prominent thoughts in his head centered around Slater.

"We're going to hang the Rebel bastard!" he muttered one moment, then shouted the next. "We're going to find him guilty, then hang him by the neck until he's good and dead. Just the way we should have done with all those Rebel bastards who fought against the Union. General Canby is going to promote me for hanging the bastard, too. Good for me."

His drinking companions merely laughed and went along with his outbursts, none of them wishing to do or say anything that might possibly upset this powerful superior. And so it went through much of the evening until Stephens had revealed everything that was in his plan for Slater.

Among the civilian patrons was Collatinus Ballard, who listened closely to every word Stephens said. Deciding that he'd heard enough, Ballard left the saloon at sundown and went straight home, where he repeated to his son Coll much of what Stephens had said that evening. The junior Ballard then ran all the way to his grandmother's house to tell his cousin Texada and Mrs. Hallet what Stephens had said at Lindenberg's Saloon.

"Sounds like liquor talking to me," said Mrs. Hallet.

"Liquor talk or not, Granny," said Texada, "I know those Yankees mean to hang Clete, and I'm not going to let them do it."

"What are you thinking about doing, girl?"

"Nothing that any woman who loves her man wouldn't do," said Texada. She disappeared into her room to change clothes.

"I wonder what she meant by that," said Coll.

"I know exactly what she meant," said Mrs. Hallet. "You go saddle up Pixie for her, Coll."

"Saddle up Pixie? What for?"

"Never mind what for!" snapped Mrs. Hallet. "You just go on and do what you're told, you hear?"

"Yes'm," said Coll, and he left.

Texada emerged from her room just as Coll was returning from the barn with Pixie. She was wearing her trousers, boots, shirt, and a man's hat. Her hair was braided in pigtails. She carried the same rifle that she had used to shoot at Markham on the night that Slater returned to Lavaca County.

"I sent Coll out to saddle up Pixie for you," said Mrs. Hallet. "I think he's coming with her now."

"Thank you, Granny," said Texada. She leaned over and kissed Mrs. Hallet on the cheek and said, "I have to try to save him, Granny. I just have to."

Mrs. Hallet caught Texada's hand and said, "You do what you must, girl, and may the good Lord be with you."

Coll came inside the house again. "Pixie's out front," he said. He stared at the rifle in Texada's hands. "What are you planning to do with that?"

"Never you mind," said Mrs. Hallet. "The less you know, the less you can tell."

"Tell what?" queried Coll.

"Nothing, Coll," said Texada. "Just promise me that you won't say anything to anyone."

"Especially your father," said Mrs. Hallet. "Lord knows he's a good man, but he's got a terrible bad habit of speaking out of turn, especially when there's a secret to be kept."

"I won't say nothing to him or anyone, Granny," said Coll. "I promise."

Texada kissed his cheek and said, "Clete's life might depend on you keeping that promise, Coll. Remember that, won't you?"

He nodded and said, "Sure, I'll remember."

With that, Texada ran out the door, leaped atop Pixie, then rode out to the Tate ranch to tell the Double Star hands what the Yankees intended to do to Slater.

53

On the day set for the trial, Slater was awakened before dawn by Sergeant Wickersham, who told him that Colonel Markham requested that they "leave quietly so as not to disturb Miss Slater's slumber." This sounded reasonable to Slater, so he complied without complaint or hesitation. He took care of his morning ablutions and sanitary needs, then ate breakfast with Wickersham and his men. The meal of cold mush covered with molasses and the camaraderie of soldiers reminded him of his days in the war. These Yankees are almost tolerable, he kidded himself as he ate. It was barely light out when he was taken to the blacksmith's forge where Markham was waiting for him.

"Good morning, Colonel," said Slater amicably.

Markham didn't return the greeting, saying instead, "Slater, it wouldn't do to let you ride into Hallettsville on your own horse, and it wouldn't look right if you were unfettered."

It took Slater a little more than a second to comprehend Markham's meaning, and once he did understand, his suspicions were aroused. He said, "There's no need for putting me in irons, Colonel. I gave you my word that I wouldn't try to escape."

"I know," said Markham, "but we must keep up appearances, Slater." He turned to the blacksmith and said, "Ankles and wrists, too." Then he walked away without looking at Slater again.

Slater thought of protesting this treatment but decided against it. Something tells me that he took a look in the mirror this morning and only saw that blue uniform he's wearing, he thought as he watched Markham walk away from him. As soon as his wrists and ankles were shackled, he was placed in a wagon and taken to the courthouse in Hallettsville for court-martial.

Only the direct participants—the court, the prosecutor, the defender, and the defendant—were permitted to attend Slater's so-called trial. Stephens called the court to order, then invited the prosecutor to state the government's charges.

Markham stood and accused Slater of violating the terms of his parole by continuing to make war on the United States of America. With all the feeling of a headsman wielding a broadax, the colonel reminded the court that the punishment for such treason was death by hanging. He sat down without looking at Slater.

Stephens asked Slater to stand and make his plea. The Texan eyed Markham with the growing suspicion that he'd been duped, and he continued to stare at the Yankee as he rose alone and denied the charge as calmly as any lawyer pleading a simple misdemeanor to a judge who was already in his pocket.

After Slater sat down, Markham stood up and called his first witness to the stand. Instead of Dick Barth, one of the men who had falsely placed the blame on Slater for their crime, Private Tinsley entered the courtroom carrying a piece of paper. He was sworn in as a witness, then Markham asked him to tell the court in his own words about the raid on the train of supply wagons that took place in May in Mississippi. Tinsley cleared his throat and read from the paper that he had brought with him. It was the statement that Barth had made to save his own neck from a Yankee noose. As Slater would learn as the trial progressed, it was only the first of the depositions that Stephens had brought with him from New Orleans.

As soon as Tinsley was finished reading the paper, Markham asked the court to have Barth's statement entered into the record as if it were testimony for the prosecution. After Stephens agreed to allow the statement as evidence, Markham said that he had no further questions of the witness.

When offered the opportunity to cross-examine, Slater's defense counsel, a young lieutenant, stood up and said that he had no questions for the witness. Stephens dismissed Tinsley, and the private left the room.

Slater glared at the lieutenant but said nothing to him. He had a hunch about what was happening here, but now was not the time to protest.

Markham called Marshall Quade as his next witness. Quade was another one of the men who had falsely blamed Slater for leading the raid in Mississippi. Corporal Riley entered the room carrying a paper exactly like the one Tinsley had been holding when he had come into the courtroom. Riley was sworn in just as Tinsley had been, and Markham asked him the same question that he had asked the private.

As Riley began reading the second deposition, Slater's suspicion that he was being given the mere pretense of a trial was confirmed. Worse yet, he knew there was nothing that he could do about it. Not now, anyway.

And so the farce went until Slater was convicted by the testimony of witnesses who weren't even present to be cross-examined by a defense counsel who was reluctant to do any defending. Without even adjourning to deliberate his innocence or guilt, the court found him guilty and sentenced him to be hanged three days hence. The only thing left was to take Slater to the jailhouse, where he could wait for his execution.

54

Knowing the outcome of the trial in advance, Texada and the Double Star hands had raced around the country throughout the night, paying every stockman—everyone except Sophia Campbell, that is—his share of the money that Slater had gotten for their cattle in New Orleans and telling them that the Yankees were planning to hang Slater on some trumped-up charges from Mississippi. Upon hearing this news, nearly every person in Lavaca County who had at least one good thought for Clete Slater wasted little time in rallying at the town square in support of their friend and neighbor.

Markham had worried that there might be a demonstration of some sort by the people of the county. With this expectation, he had posted his entire unit on the courthouse grounds during the trial. He was sure that this show of force would discourage the populace from making a fuss over Slater.

The colonel was mistaken. He was totally shocked to see over a thousand jeering men, women, and children upon his exit from the county building. He surveyed the situation and quickly realized that he and his troops were under siege; they had no way out except to fight, and this Markham was unprepared to do because of the women and children. Even when some youngsters threw rocks at his men, Markham refused to respond with force. He retreated through the courthouse doors to the foyer. Stephens and the other officers of the court stood to one side, while Slater and an armed escort stood to the other.

"What are you going to do?" demanded Stephens as a cold sweat broke out all over him.

"I don't know," said Markham honestly.

"You have to do something," said Stephens, his voice beginning to break with panic. "That's a mob out there."

"Major, I know who's out there," said Markham through gritted teeth. "There are hundreds of women and children out there as well as all of those armed men. What do you expect me to do, Major? Order them to disperse, then open fire on them when they don't?"

"Yes! That's exactly what I expect you to do! Those people are Rebels and—"

Markham cut him off, saying, "Major, the war is over! Those people are civilians. They are not the Confederate Army. Would you have me slaughter them just because they were once in rebellion against the Union? Would you have me start the war all over again right here in Hallettsville?"

"If it means saving our lives, yes, I would."

The damn fool means it, thought Slater. He had been listening to their conversation, and he figured that he'd heard about enough. "Markham!" he shouted to get the colonel's attention.

"Shut up, Slater!" snapped Markham.

"Let me talk to them, Colonel," said Slater.

"Do you think I'm crazy, Slater?" queried Markham. "Or do you think I'm just stupid? Let you talk to them." He shook his head with disbelief.

"Yes, let me talk to them," insisted Slater. "I don't want the war to start all over again any more than you do, Colonel. And I sure as hell don't want anybody killed for my sake. So let me talk to them and maybe I can get them to go home and leave you and your men alone."

Markham gave Slater's proposal some brief thought, then said, "All right, I'll let you talk to them."

"You are crazy, Markham," ranted Stephens. "He's their

leader. He's liable to incite them to riot, and then what will you do?''

Markham drew his pistol as he turned a cold eye on Slater and said, "If that mob riots, Slater will be the first man to die."

Slater shook his head, smiled, and said, "I don't know what my sister sees in you, Markham. Do you really think that stupid threat scares me? Hell, man! That dumb bastard there just got through sentencing me to hang."

"Who are you calling a bastard?" snarled Stephens, and then he slapped Slater's mouth with the back of his hand, splitting Slater's lip and rocking him backward on his heels.

Straightening up again, Slater said, "See what I mean, Markham?" Then he spit blood on Stephens.

Stephens was surprised for a second, but he soon recovered, screaming, "Why, you son of a bitch!" He raised his hand to strike Slater again, but Markham stopped him.

"Enough of that, Major!" growled Markham, grabbing Stephens by the arm and jerking him away from Slater.

"Let me go!" protested Stephens as he struggled weakly to free himself from Markham's grasp.

Markham fought back. "I said that will be enough! You will either obey my order this instant, or I'll put you under arrest and court-martial *you*."

Stephens backed off.

"That's better," said Markham. He released Stephens, then turning to his prisoner, he said, "Yes, Slater, I do see what you mean. All right, go out there and talk to those people."

Slater stepped outside, and the crowd gave him three cheers. When they quieted down, he addressed them. "I'm real touched that you folks think so much of me. For the life of me, I don't know why. I guess there's no accounting for taste, is there?"

"It was Texada who done it, Clete!" shouted Charlie Sheldon, one of the stockmen whose cattle had been driven to market by Slater and the Double Star drovers. Like his friends and neighbors and dozens of others that he didn't know, he held a shotgun in plain sight as a sign that he was ready to do battle to save Slater's life. "She rode all over telling everybody about this here trial of yours! We ain't gonna let 'em hang you, Clete! You can count on that! You hear that, you Yankee bastards?"

That started the crowd roaring again, and Slater didn't like the sound of it. "Quiet down!" he yelled. "Quiet down and listen to me!" He repeated the command until the crowd fell silent again.

"Like I said, I'm pleased to see all you folks, but this isn't good. These Yankees got real bullets in their guns, and I know for a fact that it won't take much aggravation to set them to shooting you folks."

"They wouldn't dare shoot us with our womenfolk and kids around us!" shouted Lou Whitehead, another cattleman who had trusted Slater with his stock.

Several other men voiced the same opinion, and that made Slater try a different tack. "That's not the point, Mr. Whitehead," he said. "The point is someone's going to get hurt if you folks don't go home and let this business work itself out."

"We ain't gonna let 'em hang you, Clete!" shouted Eldon Seals, yet another stockman.

"Who said anything about hanging?" asked Slater. "I didn't, I know that. Now look, folks. There won't be any hanging today. They're just going to take me over to the jailhouse now, and I'll be just fine there."

"Are they planning to hang you or not, Clete?" asked Seals.

Slater hesitated to lie to them, and once he did falter, they knew that the Yankees intended to hang him. Also, the sight of so many friends kept Slater from lying. "Yeah, I guess they are, Eldon," he said slowly. "But not for three days yet." His last sentence was lost in a roar of disapproval from the crowd.

"Quiet down, everybody!" shouted Texada. "Quiet down! Granny wants to say something!"

The throng ceased to complain and began to listen again.

Mrs. Hallet was sitting in her phaeton with Texada. Slowly, she rose to speak. "Like all of you," she said, "I refuse to stand by and watch these Yankees treat one of our finest young men this way. Last night, soon after I heard about this plot against Cletus, I sent Sheriff Foster to Austin to ask the governor to intervene and get Cletus a proper trial. Now I know Hamilton is a Black Republican, but I also know that Abner Foster is a fair man who will do his best to see that the right thing is done here . . . in spite of these Yankees. I expect Sheriff Foster to return here by late tomorrow with some sort of word that will keep Cletus from the hangman. Until then, I suggest we remain calm and continue to obey the law."

"That's right, folks," said Slater. "Just everybody step back and let things happen as they may. I'm certain that everything will work out for the best."

"I don't trust these Yankees," said Seals. "How are we to

know that they'll do right by you when they got you in that jailhouse?''

"They treated me fine when they held me out to Glengarry," said Slater. "I'm not worried."

"That was Glengarry," said Sheldon. "There's no gallows out back of Glengarry like there is at the county jailhouse."

"We wouldn't have to worry about that," said Whitehead, "if we burned the gallows."

That was an idea that appealed to just about everyone. A clamor arose for burning the gallows, and before too long, most folks were calling for the destruction of the jailhouse as well.

"What are we waiting for?" asked Seals. "Let's burn the damn thing to the ground."

A resounding cry of approval went up, and a majority of the mob rushed toward the county lockup on Front Street.

Slater stepped back into the courthouse to face Markham again. "Here's your chance, Colonel," he said. "My advice to you is to get the hell out of town before they decide to burn this place down, too . . . with you in it."

Markham wasn't stupid. He saw that Slater was right. There was no time like the present to get out of Hallettsville. As the good citizens of Lavaca County razed their own jailhouse, he had Slater put back in the wagon that had brought him to town that morning, then he led his entire command back to Glengarry.

55

It was one thing to hold Slater prisoner at Glengarry and give him the run of the house, but it was another thing completely to lock him up in the cellar. Markham knew that Malinda would be upset by it, but that was part of his plan. Not the part that he'd revealed to Sophia Campbell at the courthouse on the day Slater was arrested, because his relationship with Malinda was none of Sophia's business. Now it was time for him to clue Malinda into his scheming.

As soon as Markham and his cavalry arrived at Glengarry, he hurried into the house to explain to Malinda what had happened in town that day and to tell her about the strategy that he would say that he had devised on the trip home. "There was nothing I could do about the court, my dear," he said. "Stephens was in command, and he had his orders from General Canby. It was cut and dried, but not all is lost."

"How can you say that?" demanded Malinda. "Clete is to hang for a crime that he didn't commit."

"He won't hang, my dearest," said Markham. "I promise you that. There's a good chance that Sheriff Foster will return from Austin with some sort of reprieve."

"That's not likely to happen," said Malinda, "and you know it, Lucas."

"Yes, I do. That's why I plan to let him escape."

"Escape?" queried Malinda. "How?"

"I will have some men slip into the house after we have retired for the night," said Markham, "and they will go down to the cellar, overpower the guard, and help Clete escape. When the alarm is made, I will direct the search for him, and I will see to it that my men look in the wrong direction. It's all quite simple, my dearest heart."

"What men would you have help Clete to escape? Sergeant Wickersham and some of your other soldiers?"

"No, I'm afraid that would be too risky," said Markham. "I can't let anybody in the Army know what I'm doing. It wouldn't be good for my career."

"Then who would you get?"

He turned away from her and said, "I was thinking that I would ride over to the Campbell Plantation and enlist the aid of Mrs. Campbell's sons."

"Stewart and Tucker?" queried Malinda.

"Actually, I was thinking of the Detchen brothers," said Markham. He gave her a sideways glance. "Mrs. Campbell told me the other day that they were back and had been hiding out at her plantation because they were afraid of Clete and his men. It seems that they're afraid that Clete thinks that they had something to do with Dent's death."

"Maybe they did," said Malinda. "Would you let them kill my other brother as well?"

Markham faced her squarely and said, "Mrs. Campbell swore to me that her foster sons had nothing to do with Dent's death,

Malinda. Don't you think that I would do something about it if I had an inkling that they were responsible for Dent's death?''

"Yes, of course," said Malinda. "I know how you felt about Dent. I know you would want to see his killers brought to justice for his death.''

"Of course, I would. It's just that I think the Detchens can prove that they had nothing to do with Dent's death by helping Clete escape. Don't you agree?''

"I don't know what to think," said Malinda. "All I know is my brother is innocent and I don't want him to hang. If you think this plan will work, then try it. But I warn you, Lucas. If Clete is hung, I will never marry you.''

Markham moved closer to her, took her hands in his, and said, "I promise you that he will not hang, my dearest heart.''

Malinda looked into his eyes and tried to read his soul. Hoping that she was seeing the truth, she said, "I believe you, Lucas. As soon as I know for certain that he's safe, we'll set the date for our wedding. You keep your promise, and I'll keep mine.''

Markham kissed her cheek, then said, "You've made me the happiest man in all of Texas, my dearest heart.'' He kissed her cheek again, then backed away. "I'm off to see the Detchens and Mrs. Campbell.'' He left the mansion and rode off to the Campbell Plantation to set his scheme into motion.

56

Once he was back in the cellar, day soon turned into night for Slater. His mind was all awhirl with thoughts of the day.

Mrs. Hallet's disclosure that she had sent Sheriff Foster to Austin to plead with the governor to intervene for him completely caught him by surprise. The lady is amazing, he told himself. Yet he wondered how successful Foster would be, considering how his trial had been by the Army for a crime against the Army. Did Governor Hamilton have the power to interfere with a military court's decision? That was a perplexing problem, but one that he would think about later.

Slater was also incredulous over the show of support the good people of Lavaca County had given him that day. He was rather touched by it. I can't believe I have that many friends. Where did they all come from? I didn't know there were that many people living around here.

Malinda brought Slater his supper. She wanted to tell him that he shouldn't worry, that everything would be all right, that help would be coming before the night was over, but she held her tongue because the guard was too close and he might overhear. Instead, she asked, "Are they treating you all right, Clete?"

"As well as can be expected," he said. He smiled and added, "All things considered, I mean. How about you, Malinda? Are you all right?"

"What do you mean?" she asked.

"I mean, you and Markham. How is it with you two?"

Malinda held her head high and said, "Nothing is changed between us."

Slater studied her for a moment, then said, "I thought so." He burped a laugh and said, "For the life of me, Malinda, I don't see what you see in that Yankee. I mean, I always thought you were pretty, even for a sister. Was I wrong? Are you really so homely that you have to stoop to carrying on with a Yankee?"

Never flinching, Malinda continued to hold her head proudly erect as she said, "Four years ago I would have slapped you for making a remark like that."

"Four years ago you would have shot that Yankee bastard on sight, my dear sister."

"I can't expect you to understand, Clete. Not now, anyway. Maybe in the future you will be able to understand, but not now."

"Future?" he queried. "Haven't you heard, Malinda? Your Yankee colonel is going to hang me until I'm dead. Three days hence, as his puppet court put it."

"I've heard that Mrs. Hallet sent Sheriff Foster to Austin to speak with the governor in your behalf. Lucas believes that he'll be successful."

"Oh, he does, does he?" snickered Slater. "That's a good one, Malinda. You believe that, do you?"

"Yes, of course. Why shouldn't I?"

"I don't know. Why shouldn't yóu?"

"I'm sorry, Clete," she said, "I must go. I've had enough of your snideness for one evening." She turned and left without further words.

I never thought I'd live to see the day when my own family would turn on me, thought Slater.

He finished his supper, then settled down on his pallet of straw for the night. His head continued to be filled with thoughts of the day and hopes for tomorrow. *I hope Sheriff Foster can convince that Yankee-loving governor to do something to save my hide. God only knows what will happen if that son of a bitch hangs me. Texada will probably walk right up to him and shoot him dead and get herself killed doing it. Then what? More killings over me? What good is that? Absolutely none.*

Slater was almost asleep when a door creaking startled him into vigilance. His eyelids parted ever so slightly, but he didn't stir as he scanned what little there was for him to view from between the bin's walls. Nothing appeared to be out of the ordinary in the dim light. He listened closely for any other sounds and thought he heard the gentle footfalls of someone sneaking about the cellar. But before he determined whether he was hearing right or not, a dull thud reached his ears, followed by the thump of a body collapsing on dirt.

"Clete!"

Slater recognized that whisper. He sat up and whispered back, "Over here!"

In another second, Texada came into the bin, knelt down beside him, and immediately began hugging and kissing him.

Slater pushed her away and said, "Texada, what are you doing here?"

"I've come to get you out of here, Clete," she said between kisses.

"Get me out? How did you get in here?"

"Through the old escape tunnel."

"Old escape tunnel?" queried Slater before he remembered the tunnel his grandfather had dug from the cellar to the well house in back of the slave quarters as an escape route in case of an Indian attack or some other emergency. To the best of Slater's knowledge, the tunnel had only been used once for its original purpose, but that was long before he was born. As a boy, he had played in the tunnel with Dent and Malinda on several occasions, but as far as he could recall, they had never told anyone outside the family about the tunnel. "How do you know about it?" he asked Texada.

"Granny told me about it," said Texada.

"Your grandmother told you? How did she know about it?"

"That's too long a story to tell now, Clete darling. We've got to get you out of here before someone comes along and finds me here."

"I'm not going anywhere," said Slater.

"Of course, you are, darling."

"No, Texada, I'm not. Not until Sheriff Foster gets back from seeing the governor in Austin."

Texada heaved a sigh and said, "Oh, yeah, about that. He didn't go to Austin, Clete."

"Of course, he did," said Slater, not really believing it himself. "Your grandmother told the whole county that he did."

"She was making that up, Clete darling, so they would go on and leave things alone. It seems she figured you'd wind up out here instead of in town in the jailhouse . . . Did you know we burned it down this afternoon? The jailhouse, I mean. You should have seen it." She giggled. "Old Mr. Thornton was madder than an old wet hen. He cussed the whole crowd so much that folks got to laughing so hard that—"

Slater cut her off. "Texada, what about your grandmother's figuring?"

"Oh, yeah. Well, Granny figured you'd be brought back out here until the hanging, so she figured I could slip in here after dark and get you out and you'd be free again."

"She did, did she?"

Texada smiled and said, "She sure did."

Slater shook his head in disbelief and thought, I was right. The lady is amazing. Then he looked at the manacles on his wrists and the shackles around his ankles and said, "I'm not going very far in these." He held up his hands for emphasis.

"You can make it to the well house at least, can't you?"

"Yes, but I can't ride a horse with these on."

"I know that," said Texada. "Do you think I was born yesterday or something? Come on. We'll take those off after we get to the well house. I left some tools there that will do the job."

"Scuff your feet," said Slater as he stood up.

"What?"

"Scuff your feet," he repeated. "To hide your tracks."

"Oh, yeah."

They shuffled across the cellar to the cabinet that was actually the tunnel door. Texada opened it to let Slater pass through the doorway ahead of her.

"Wait a minute," he said in the darkness. "How do we see?"

Texada struck a match, found the candle that she had used to get to the cellar, then lit it. She handed it to Slater and said, "Does that answer your question?"

Slater's face twisted a little with embarrassment and perturbation, but he didn't reply. Texada closed the door behind them, and they headed down the tunnel toward the well house.

"Jake Flewellyn and the rest of the boys are waiting for us down the road a piece," said Texada as they walked. "Jake figures we can make it out of the county before sunup."

"Which *we* are you talking about?" asked Slater.

"Why, all of us, of course," said Texada. "Jake says the Yankees will think twice about coming after you if we all stick together."

"Jake is wrong. If we stay together, the Yankees will think we've started another war, and they'll be after us like a pack of hounds on a coon trail. None of the boys have done anything to break the law, so there's no need for them to start now. Besides, I'm not leaving the county until I finish what I started out to do."

"Do you mean the Detchens and Kindred?"

"That's exactly what I mean."

"Well, you can forget about Kindred and that bunch that rode with him," said Texada as they reached the ladder that led up to the well house. "Sheriff Foster figured out they were the ones who robbed Teddy Johnson's freight wagons, and he arrested them all. As soon as they posted bond to get out of jail, they rode off for Mexico because they were all afraid you and the boys would do to them what you did to Tom Mather."

"They feared right," said Slater as they climbed up the ladder. "And I still intend to do them the same as Mather."

In the well house, Texada produced the hammer and chisel she had brought along to remove Slater's shackles. He took the tools from her and with a few well-placed strokes broke the bolts that held the irons around his limbs.

A minute later they went outside, where Pixie and Nimbus were tied up.

"How did you get Nimbus here?" asked Slater.

"A woman has her ways," said Texada as coyly as she could.

Slater smiled, took her into his arms, and said, "I guess you do." Then he kissed her passionately and long.

It would have been longer, but Texada broke it off, breathlessly saying, "We don't have time for that now, Clete darling. As much as I want you now, I know we have to get shed of this place and find another one where we can be safe and private."

"Yes, you're right," said Slater. "I love you, Texada. I want you to know that."

"I always have," she said.

There was no more to be said. They mounted up and rode off to meet with Flewellyn and the rest of the Double Star hands.

57

Within minutes of the escape, the unconscious guard was found and all hell broke loose at Glengarry. Sergeant Wickersham alerted the duty officer, who in turn went to tell Markham. The colonel lay awake in his darkened room, giving the appearance of having retired. He knew Slater would be set free that night and was expecting the young lieutenant's urgent call. It was all part of his plot to rid himself of Slater, but it wasn't the plan that he had described to Malinda.

Immediately after being informed that Slater was no longer in his cell, Markham pulled on his trousers and boots and rushed to the cellar to investigate. He quickly, but incorrectly, deduced that someone had slipped onto the premises under cover of darkness, had gotten into the house through an unguarded window, had sneaked into the cellar, had knocked out the guard, then had retraced his steps with Slater in tow because of his chains. Of course, that wasn't how the escape had been made, but that was they way he had planned one to happen.

Even though the hour was almost midnight, Markham ordered every soldier to turn out to search for Slater in the moonlit night, and within the half hour, his men were assembled in front of Glengarry. He divided his force into six patrols, then sent them on their way. He would remain behind at the plantation.

Malinda awakened when the first report of the escape was made to Markham. She was excited that her brother had gotten away, but she didn't come out of her room until the troops had left to

search for him. She went downstairs to the parlor, where she found
Markham toasting himself with a glass of claret.

"My dearest," he said, raising his glass in salute, "your brother
has escaped just as I planned it."

Malinda went to him, put her arms around his neck, and kissed
him once in a fashion that was almost sisterly. Even so, Markham
was pleased with the reward.

"I'm certain he will be out of the county by daybreak," said
Markham, being quite full of himself, "but remember, my dear,
that from this moment on, Clete is on his own. I don't expect my
men to catch him. I'm certain he can elude them, but I can't say
the same for any other troops. And if he is caught, I can't promise
you he won't hang somewhere else."

"Yes, Lucas, I understand all that. At least, he has a chance
to live now and prove his innocence."

"Malinda, there was sworn testimony that he led the raid."

"Yes. The testimony of men trying to save their own lives by
pointing their fingers at my brother. Clete said he didn't do it,
and I believe him. If you had given him the opportunity to prove
his innocence in court, I'm sure you would believe him, too."

"I was only doing my duty," said Markham.

Malinda softened her tone a bit when she said, "Yes, dear, I
know. And now you've done the right thing by letting Clete escape. Thank you." She gave him another sisterly kiss.

58

While Slater was telling Flewellyn that he didn't want the Double
Star hands to get involved with his escape, Kent Reeves rode up
and reported that he and his brother had just seen the Detchens
sneaking around the pecan grove at Glengarry. They tried to get
close to the outlaws and possibly capture them, but just about
then, the plantation started buzzing with Bluebellies. They stayed
and watched for a while. The Yankees assembled, then most of
them rode off in all directions.

"What about the Detchens?" asked Slater.

"As soon as the Yankees left," said Kent, "they went to sneaking up to the house and climbed through a window in the back. That's the last we saw anything of them before I hightailed it back here. Clark is still keeping an eye on them."

"What would the Detchens be doing at Glengarry in the middle of the night?" said Slater, thinking out loud.

"I don't know," said Flewellyn, "but why don't we ride in there and ask them?"

"I told you already, Jake, that I don't want you boys mixed up in this."

"We just want to help, Clete," said Flewellyn.

"I know, but—" He stopped himself from arguing further because a new thought struck him. "Wait a minute! You can help, Jake. I'm thinking how bad I want to get Harlan and Farley, but I can't do that and have all those Yankees chasing me at the same time. I need you and the boys to—" He broke off again because Clark Reeves rode up just then.

"The Detchens left Glengarry, Clete," said Clark. "Looks like they're heading home."

Slater smiled and said, "That's better yet. Like I was saying, Jake, I need you and the boys to keep the Yankees busy while I deal with Harlan and Farley. I also need a gun and some ammunition."

"I sort of thought you might," said Flewellyn. He reached into a saddlebag, pulled out Slater's .44 and holster wrapped in a belt, and handed them to Slater. His hand went back into the bag and this time removed two cylinders for the Colt's. "Loaded these up for you, too." He handed the cylinders to Slater.

"Thanks, Jake," said Slater. Then he looked at Texada and said, "Before you do anything else, Jake, I want you to make sure Texada gets home safe."

"I'm not going home," she said with determination and belligerence. "I'm going with you."

"We've already talked about that, Texada. You're going home, and that's all there is to it."

"But, Clete darling—"

"I said my piece, Texada. I don't want to say it again."

Texada knew a man's final word when she heard it. She didn't like it, but she closed her mouth, biding her time until the right moment presented itself for her to do what she had wanted to do in the first place. She just sat still on Pixie and let

Slater finish with Flewellyn and the others.

"You create all the diversion you can, Jake," said Slater, "and I'll take care of Harlan and Farley once and for all. Just give me until sunup to get the job done."

"You got it, Clete," said Flewellyn. He turned to Texada and said, "Let's go, girl."

"Hold on a minute, Jake Flewellyn," said Texada. "I at least get to say good-bye, don't I?"

"Make it quick," said Flewellyn.

Texada moved Pixie beside Nimbus so she could be as close to Slater as possible without dismounting. "You'll come for me, won't you, Clete darling?"

"Texada, this isn't the time or place to talk about it," said Slater. He leaned over and kissed her lips hard for a few seconds, then broke away, saying, "I'll see you soon enough. Don't worry."

Sooner than you think, thought Texada.

Slater kicked Nimbus into action and rode off, cutting across the Campbell Plantation until he reached the two-track that formerly separated the original Campbell land from the acreage Sophia acquired on the deaths of her brothers. He was certain the Detchens would be taking this route home. He found a hiding place out of the bright moonlight and sat down to wait.

The minutes seemed to crawl by as Slater occupied himself with killing mosquitoes and listening to the creatures of the night stir nearby. At one point, he heard a rustling in the bushes across the road that worried him for a second, but when he saw the silhouette of a cow and a calf in the meadow beyond the hackberries at the edge of the lane, he realized he needn't worry, relaxed, and cautioned himself to remain calm. His patience was rewarded within the hour.

"I still say he didn't have no call to talk to us like that," Harlan was saying as the brothers approached Slater. They were still thirty to forty yards away from Slater's position. "It weren't our fault someone got to Slater before we did."

"Aw, don't pay him no mind," said Farley. "He ain't nothing except a goddamned Yankee. He don't make a hill of beans around here, Ma says. Leastwise, not as far as she's concerned. So don't pay him no mind."

"I still don't like the son of a bitch," whined Harlan.

"I don't like him either, but Ma says we got to be nice to him as long as he's useful to her. Now hush up about him."

"Don't hush up yet, Harlan," said Slater as he stepped out of the bushes into the lane. "I'd like to hear more about this Yankee you're talking about. His name wouldn't happen to be Markham, would it?"

The Detchens reined in their horses at the same time, and also simultaneously, they gasped, "Slater!" They were now only ten yards in front of him.

"That's right, boys," said Slater, raising his pistol, cocking it, and taking aim at Farley's chest. "Just hold tight to those reins, and we'll get this over real quick."

"The hell, you say!" shouted Farley as he spurred his horse and charged Slater.

Slater fired, but the bullet missed its target. Farley came on as Slater pulled back the hammer again and tried to sidestep the onrushing horse and rider. He was too late. *Oof!* Down he went, the wind knocked out of him, his gun discharging then flying from his hand and landing in the bushes. He rolled onto his side, dazed by the collision. He hardly heard Harlan cry out to his brother. "You got him, Farley! You got him!"

Farley reined in his horse and came back to where Slater lay on the ground. "I sure did, didn't I?" He jumped down from his mount and stood over Slater. "You ain't so big now, are you, Slater?" He reached into his boot and drew out his hunting knife. "Come on down here, Harlan, and let's see if he bleeds like Jess Tate did."

"Yeah, let's see if he does," chortled Harlan.

Just as Harlan's boots touched the ground, the clicking of a rifle hammer being thumbed into firing position sounded in the bushes across the lane from Slater's hiding place. Both Detchens heard it.

"I wouldn't do that if I were you, boys," said Texada as she stepped into the open with a big bore Sharps aimed at Farley.

Slater was still trying to get his breath back.

"Hell, it's only little Texada Ballard," said Farley. "Don't you know girls ain't supposed to play with guns, Texada?"

"I ain't playing, Farley. Now you move away from him and be quick about it or I'll blow your fool head off."

"Now don't do nothing stupid, Texada," said Farley as he began easing away from Slater, moving to one side of Texada as he did. "We was only funning about cutting up Clete here. Hell, girl, we was supposed to help him escape from Glengarry, so why would we want to hurt him?"

"You weren't there to help him escape," said Texada as she kept the rifle pointed at Farley and ignored Harlan. "You made a deal with that Yankee colonel, and you were supposed to get Clete out of there, then kill him. Ain't that right?"

"You sure are a smart one," said Farley. "Ain't she, Harlan?"

Texada's eyes shifted to Harlan. She turned to take aim at him, and as she did, Farley leaped at her. She swung the gun back at Farley and fired. The bullet missed him, but the flash caught the hand that was holding the knife. He screamed in pain and dropped the blade just as he crashed into Texada and knocked her to the ground under the same bushes where she had been hiding.

Slater got his wind back in time to thrust out an arm and trip Harlan as he went to assist his brother. Harlan fell headlong onto Farley and Texada. Slater scrambled to his feet, pulled Harlan upright, and smashed his face with a solid right.

Farley started to get up to help his brother, but Texada dragged him back down by his belt. He threw an elbow that caught her on the chin, knocking her out.

Harlan was down on his back, blood spewing from his nose. His upper front teeth were loose, and his lips were cut badly.

Slater started after Farley but stopped when the twin found the knife he had dropped seconds before. Grinning like a crazed ghoul, Detchen got up and began moving toward Slater, who backed up one careful step at a time.

"All right, Slater," said Farley, "the time has come for me to cut up your face like you did mine. Only I'm not going to stop with your face. I'm going to cut all of you up into little bitty pieces. And when I'm done with you, Harlan and me are going to have our way with that girl of yours. Maybe two or three times each. Then we'll cut her up, too."

Slater recalled an old trick. He fell backward, landing on his rump on the grassy run between the two sandy tracks of the road. Each hand grabbed dirt. Farley moved in for the kill. Slater threw the sand in his face. Farley screamed as the grit ground at his eyes. Maddened with pain, he began slashing the air with the knife, hoping to catch Slater with a swipe or two of the blade. Slater rolled away and got back on his feet. He caught Farley's knife-wielding hand in both of his, and the two of them went down in a heap.

"Harlan, help me!" cried Farley. "Help me, Harlan!"

The other twin was recovered enough to get back into the affray. With blood dripping from his chin, Harlan jumped on Slater's back and started punching him in the head. The blows hurt Harlan more than they did Slater, and they ceased as quickly as they began. Before Harlan could begin a different assault, Slater and Farley rolled over and Farley's knife stuck Harlan in the shoulder. Harlan screamed and pulled away from the two combatants.

Slater finally got the upper hand as he forced Farley to release the knife. He made a fist and slugged the twin on the jaw. He repeated the blow and wanted to make it three, but his hand was stayed by the appearance of one of Markham's patrols.

59

Markham was pacing in the parlor at Glengarry when the patrol brought Slater to the mansion. He heard the horses and only hoped it was his men with the prisoner. Sergeant Wickersham informed him that it was.

"Bring him in here immediately," said Markham.

"Yes, sir," said Wickersham. He left, but a minute later he was back, leading Slater into the room at the end of a rope that also had the Texan's hands tied together. "The prisoner, sir."

Slater didn't look good. When the soldiers caught him beating on Farley Detchen, they grabbed him none too gently and even allowed both Detchens to hit him and kick him a few times each, drawing the line when Harlan produced a knife and tried to cut Slater's throat. Slater's face showed multiple bruises and abrasions, and his clothes were torn and dirty. Even so, his spirit was still undaunted.

Markham stopped marching to and fro, looked up, and said, "That will be all, Wickersham."

The sergeant saluted and departed, closing the door to the foyer behind him.

Markham was more than distracted by Slater's reappearance; he was absolutely livid about it. "What am I to do with you, Slater?" he growled. "You have been a constant thorn in my side since the night you returned here from the war. Why couldn't you have been killed in some battle like all good Rebels? Why did you have to come back here?''

Slater looked back at him and calmly said, ''This is my home, Colonel. I belong here, which is more than I can say for you.''

''This will be my home soon enough, Slater.''

''You mean, it will be yours when you marry Malinda, don't you?''

''Yes, I do mean exactly that. Glengarry will be legally mine, but you needn't concern yourself about it. You won't be here. You'll be dead.''

''Are you going to hang me after all, Colonel?''

''Now that the Detchens have botched everything I suppose you'll have to be hung, but not by me, of course.''

''Of course, not by you. If you hang me, Malinda won't marry you, will she?''

Markham started to chuckle but was cut short when the door to the dining room opened.

''No, I won't marry him if he hangs you, Clete,'' said Malinda, entering the parlor from the dining room, ''and I won't marry him if anyone else hangs you.'' She was holding her right hand behind a fold in the skirt of her dressing gown.

''Malinda, my dearest heart,'' said Markham, his tone filled with surprise and pleading, ''I didn't know you were there.''

''Of course, you didn't, Lucas,'' said Malinda, ''or you wouldn't have mentioned the Detchens.''

''The Detchens?''

''Don't play me for a fool, Lucas. I heard you say that the Detchens botched the job. They were supposed to help Clete escape, remember?'' Before Markham could answer, she held up her left index finger and cautioned him, ''Think before you reply, Lucas. If you lie to me again, there will be no marriage between us.''

Markham stared deep into her eyes and saw that she meant every word of her warning. He heaved a sighed, then said, ''Yes, they were supposed to help him escape.''

''And were they supposed to murder Clete once they had gotten him away from Glengarry?''

''No, that wasn't part of the plan,'' said Markham defiantly.

''But you knew they might try to kill me after they got me out of here, didn't you?'' said Slater.

Markham hung his head in shame and said, ''Yes, I suppose so, but I told them not to harm you. Just get you out of the county for good. That's all I told them.''

"Just as I thought," said Malinda. "All right, Lucas. Now tell me how you plan to get Clete out of here this time.''

Markham was incredulous. "I can't let him go," he said.

"Yes, you can," said Malinda as she brought her right hand in view. She was holding a .36-caliber Colt's Navy revolver in it. Slowly, she raised it until the pistol was held at arm's length and aimed straight at Markham's chest.

"Malinda, my dearest, what are you doing?"

"I'm going to shoot you, Lucas, if you don't let him go.''

"You won't shoot me," he sneered.

Malinda cocked the hammer with both thumbs, then shifted her aim from his heart to his left arm and pulled the trigger. The bullet tore through the deltoid muscle, missing the joint, lodging in the wall behind him, and twisting him half around as he grabbed at the wound with his right hand.

The door to the foyer came open, but Slater slammed his body against it, knocking Sergeant Wickersham to the floor of the ante-room. "Stay out!" shouted Slater. "Stay out or I'll kill the colonel!"

Malinda peered at her brother curiously for a second, then realized what he was doing. She moved closer to Markham and said softly, "Tell them to stay out of here.''

A bit shocked, Markham looked wild-eyed at her, then at the smoking barrel of the Colt, and finally at the blood dripping over his fingers. "Do as he says!" he shouted. "Stay out of here!" Then to Malinda, he said softly, "How could you do this to me, my . . . my dearest?''

Looking him straight in the eye, she said, "You couldn't possibly understand now, Lucas. You haven't lived in Texas long enough yet.''

"But, my dearest heart, I love you.''

"Yes, I know, Lucas, and I am still willing to marry you, but only if you let Clete go.''

"He doesn't have to let me go," said Slater as he came closer to them. "And you don't have to marry him either way.''

Malinda glared at her brother and said, "Whether I marry Lucas or not is not your concern, Clete. Glengarry is mine, and I need a proper man to run it with me.''

Slater stared at his sister for a second, then said, "All right, have it your way, Malinda." He glanced at Markham, then looked back at Malinda. "You two deserve each other.''

"I'm glad you think so, Clete," she said.

"Fine," said Slater. "Now help me get this rope off my hands so I can get out of here." He took the gun from her.

"How will you get away, Clete?" she asked as she untied the binding line.

"Never mind that," said Slater. "Just go back upstairs and act like you weren't ever down."

"Go back upstairs?" she queried.

"Just do as I say, Malinda." He saw her eyes look warily toward Markham. "Don't worry about him. I may not like him, but as long as you want him for a husband, I'll be nice to him. I promise you I won't kill him." Then, to Markham, he said with a smile, "That is I won't kill him as long as he doesn't do anything stupid like tell anyone that you had a part in this."

"You needn't worry about that, Slater," said Markham. "I love Malinda, and as long as she'll have me, I want her for my bride."

"Nice and romantic, Colonel. No wonder she's willing to marry you." He turned to Malinda and said, "Now go upstairs and don't come down until he comes up after you."

"I still don't understand," said Malinda, "but I'll go if you say so."

"I say so, so get going."

Malinda started to leave, but she stopped at the dining room doorway, turned, and said, "Are you sure you can get out of here, Clete?"

"Yes, I'm sure," he said. When she turned away, he called her name again. When she looked back over her shoulder, he said, "Thanks for your help, little sister."

"We're Slaters," she said. "I had to do it. The family creed says so." And with that she left them.

"What did she mean by that?" asked Markham.

"If you don't know by now, Colonel," said Slater, "you'd better figure it before you marry her. It'll save you a lot of grief if you do." He waved the revolver at Markham. "But forget about that now. We've got other business to tend to here."

"You can't get away, Slater," said Markham. "My men are everywhere."

"That much you have right, Colonel. They are everywhere. Everywhere except where I'll be." He stuck the muzzle of the Colt's up to Markham's nose. "You called me a thorn in your side, Colonel. What have you been to me? I've tried to live here peaceably, and I've tried to help my friends and neighbors. But you've done your best to keep me from it whenever you could. You and those damn Detchens and their mother. I'd kill you, Colonel, but it would only hurt Malinda. And your superiors might send a replacement who's worse than you, and that would be bad for everybody in the county. So I'm going to let you live." He pointed at a chair and said, "Sit down so I can tie you up."

Markham did as he was told, still holding his wound. The bleeding had let up now. "You're a dead man, Slater," he said. "Every soldier in the Union will be looking for you."

"Every soldier, Colonel?" said Slater as he tied the rope around Markham. "Does that include you?"

"Me more than anyone, Slater. You are no longer just a point of contention between Malinda and me. Now you're a black mark on my military record. I have to hunt you and find you and make you die for what you did in Mississippi."

"That's just it, Colonel. I didn't do anything in Mississippi. I didn't lead that raid because I was riding across Louisiana when it happened. I told your so-called court-martial that, but you and that son of a bitch Stephens wouldn't let me prove it. Now I've got to do it the hard way."

"You're a traitor to the Union, Slater."

"Save your breath, Colonel. You can hunt me all you want, but you'll never catch me unless I want to be caught. Just remember that when you wake up."

"When I wake up?"

Slater didn't answer him with words, choosing to reply with a glancing blow from the butt of his revolver on the back of Markham's skull instead. "Sleep tight, Colonel," he said.

60

After making certain Markham was unconscious, Slater hurried through the dining room to the kitchen, where he opened the back door but didn't go outside. Instead, he went to the cellar, opened the door, stepped down to the first step, then closed the door behind him. The lantern in the makeshift prison was still glowing. He descended the stairs and made for the hidden passageway that led to the well house. Glancing to one side, he noticed an old brown felt hat that had belonged to Grandpa Dougald. He stopped, picked it up, touched its soft rounded crown, then remembered the old man who had worn it for so many years. He might have stayed there longer admiring the topper, but the sound of booted feet on the hardwood floor in the rooms above urged him to be on his way. He donned the hat, then went through the cabinet door.

Inside the tunnel as he neared the well house, he thought he saw light at the other end. Not daylight, he thought. It's too soon. Then he wondered if the Yankees had somehow discovered the tunnel's exit. Maybe they had made Texada tell them about it.

Texada! What had happened to her? Was she hurt? Or had she gotten away? She was fighting the Detchens with him one second, then was out of sight the next. In all the hubbub with the outlaws and the soldiers, he had forgotten her. But what of the Detchens? Had they forgotten her as well? Had they caught her after the soldiers took him away? Did they carry out their earlier threats to have their way with her? His mind raced as fast as sunlight as a myriad of confused thoughts exploded in his brain, all of them centering around a single image of Texada hurt and helpless.

Slater was so intent on thinking of Texada that he barely heard the footsteps coming toward him from the well house end of the tunnel. He crouched down and waited, all the time his thoughts going back and forth between his own present situation and whatever horrible circumstance Texada might be in, which he imagined to be anything from her being dead to being assaulted by the Detchens. The madness continued to build inside his head until he saw—

His heart found a new beat, one less frantic and filled with love and hope. Coming toward him was Texada. He jumped up and ran to her. She saw him and hurried her own footsteps. They came together, throwing their arms around each other and kissing each other madly and passionately.

"Thank God! You're all right!" said Slater breathlessly between kisses.

"Clete darling, you got away again," she said when her lips were free from his. "I'm so glad. I'm so glad."

"What happened to you?" asked Slater as he became reassured that she was real. "Were you hurt? Did they do anything to you? How did you get away?"

"The last thing I remember before I woke up was fighting with Farley," she said. "Then I woke up under some bushes just in time to see the soldiers make Harlan and Farley stop kicking you. I watched as they tied your hands together and threw you over some soldier's saddle. Then I heard the officer tell the Detchens that they'd better hightail it to Mexico with Jim Kindred and the rest of the outlaws because your boys would be after them as soon as they found out who helped the Yankees catch you. Harlan and Farley seemed to take his advice real serious because they got their horses and rode out for home like the bogie man was hot on their trail."

"They must have hit me good a few times," said Slater, "because I don't recall them riding off like that."

"Well, they did, then the Yankees took you away. I found Nimbus and brought him back to the well house with me thinking I might be able to sneak into the cellar and get you out again."

"I'd forgotten about Nimbus. I'm glad you remembered. I'll need a good horse if I'm going to catch up with Harlan and Farley again."

"No, Clete, you can't go after them now. You've got to get away from here. Markham will have more Yankees than ever looking for you now that you've escaped twice in one night."

"I've got to finish it with them, Texada. I owe it to Jess and Dent."

"You don't have to finish it tonight, Clete. They'll be looking over their shoulders for you and the boys all the time now, and Markham knows you're after them. He might be smart enough to use them as bait to catch you again."

Texada was right, and he knew it. There was no time for revenge now. The wise thing to do was save his own skin so he could fight another day when the odds would be more to his advantage. But Slater didn't always do the wise thing. He was determined to avenge his brother and his best friend, and that was that.

"Like I said, Texada, I owe it to Jess and Dent."

"What about me? Don't I count for anything? Are you so hell-bent on killing two worthless no-goods that you're willing to throw our love away?"

That was a kick in the heart that Slater didn't expect. He saw the tears welling up in her eyes and felt ashamed. "No, darling, I'm not. I do love you. I love you more than I thought I could ever love any woman."

"Then don't throw our love away, Clete darling. Leave the Detchens alone for now and save yourself. I love you, Clete, but I don't think I could live a single day if anything happened to you, and I know something bad will happen to you if we stay around here looking for a chance to get Harlan and Farley."

"Which *we* are you talking about this time?" asked Slater.

"You and me, of course. You already said your piece about including Jake and the boys, so naturally, I'm talking about you and me now."

"That's what I was afraid of." He heaved a sigh, then said what had to be said. "Texada, I can't take you with me. I'm a condemned man, and—"

"But you didn't do it."

"I know that, but the Yankees don't know it yet. Until I can prove I'm innocent, there's going to be a price on my head for sure. No one knows it was you who helped me escape, so the law won't be wanting you. If you run off with me, they'll know it was you, and then there will be a price on your head, too."

"I don't care. I only want to be with you, Clete darling. I love you."

"And I love you. That's why I have to go off alone. Texada, you don't know what it's like living on horseback. I do. I know you're a strong woman, but it would be selfish of me to take you with me. It wouldn't be fair to you."

"I don't care how hard it gets, Clete, as long as I'm with you."

"What about your grandmother? She's an old woman, Texada. She hasn't got a whole lot of time left here. How do you think she's going to get along if you run off with me?"

Slater had found the final argument. Texada had no response to his question as she faced the reality of their situation. "What will you do after you leave here?" she asked softly.

"Hide for a while, I guess," said Slater. "After that, I don't know. Go to Mexico after Kindred and his bunch, maybe. Or I might go looking for those polecats that said I led that raid in Mississippi. I don't know for sure, but I do know this much. Until I can clear my name and live up to my family's motto, I can't call myself Clete Slater. My granddaddy said that I should always be proud to be a Slater and that I should always do my best to uphold the Slater creed: 'Steadfast in honor and loyalty and justice.' That's exactly what I intend to do, but I'm not going to do it as Clete Slater. I'm going to do it as . . ." He shrugged and added, "I don't know. Maybe I'll just call myself that. Slater Creed . . . or maybe just Slate Creed, as a kind of constant reminder of what my life has to be."

Texada's tears cascaded over her cheeks as she said, "Will we ever be together again?"

"Yes, of course, we will, darling."

"When?" she asked hopefully.

Slater didn't have an answer for her. He heard a cock crow in the distance and realized that dawn would be coming soon. "I have to go, Texada," he said.

"When?" she cried.

"I . . ."

"When, Clete? When will we be together again?" she sobbed.

"I . . . I don't know the answer to that."

Texada wrenched herself away from Slater, turned her back to him, and moved away two short steps. "Then go! Go before it gets light out!" Slater moved toward her and put his hands on her shoulders, but she rejected his touch. "No, don't. Just go, Clete, and leave me be."

"Texada," he said softly.

"Go!" she screamed as all the anguish of love rendered her soul into spectral shreds.

With tears in his own eyes, Slater whispered, "I love you," then he turned and headed down the tunnel toward the well house.

Texada spun around to look at him one last time, but he was gone. "I love you, Clete darling," she said as if he were standing there with her. "I'll always love you, and I know we'll be together again. Someday."

WESTERNS!

at least a savings of $3.00 each month below the publishers price. Second, there is never any shipping, handling or other hidden charges—Free home delivery. What's more there is no minimum number of books you must buy, you may return any selection for full credit and you can cancel your subscription at any time. A TRUE VALUE!

Mail the coupon below

To start your subscription and receive 2 FREE WESTERNS, fill out the coupon below and mail it today. We'll send your first shipment which includes 2 FREE BOOKS as soon as we receive it.

Mail To:
True Value Home Subscription Services, Inc.   12562
P.O. Box 5235
120 Brighton Road
Clifton, New Jersey 07015-5235

YES! I want to start receiving the very best Westerns being published today. Send me my first shipment of 6 Westerns for me to preview FREE for 10 days. If I decide to keep them, I'll pay for just 4 of the books at the low subscriber price of $2.45 each; a total of $9.80 (a $17.70 value). Then each month I'll receive the 6 newest and best Westerns to preview Free for 10 days. If I'm not satisfied I may return them within 10 days and owe nothing. Otherwise I'll be billed at the special low subscriber rate of $2.45 each; a total of $14.70 (at least a $17.70 value) and save $3.00 off the publishers price. There are never any shipping, handling or other hidden charges. I understand I am under no obligation to purchase any number of books and I can cancel my subscription at any time, no questions asked. In any case the 2 FREE books are mine to keep.

Name _____

Address _____ Apt. # _____

City _____ State _____ Zip _____

Telephone # _____

Signature _____
(if under 18 parent or guardian must sign)
Terms and prices subject to change.
Orders subject to acceptance by True Value Home Subscription Services, Inc.